Sue Reidy, who lives in Auckland, New Zealand with her partner, attended a Catholic girls' school and studied Visual Communications at Wellington Polytechnic School of Design. Since 1990 she has had her own design practice. She has gained recognition as a graphic designer, illustrator and writer. In 1985 Sue Reidy won the BNZ Katherine Mansfield Short Story Award and in 1988 her short story collection, *Modettes*, was published by Penguin. *Four Ways to Be a Woman* is her second novel, her first, *The Visitation*, is also published by Black Swan and was shortlisted in the 1997 Montana NZ Book Awards. Sue Reidy has been awarded a prestigious Buddle Findlay Sargeson literary fellowship for 2000.

International acclaim for *The Visitation*:

'Catherine and Theresa Flynn are obsessed by the lives of the saints, and spend many hours recreating their bloody deaths in the back yard. But it's only when the Virgin Mary actually appears to them (with rosebuds between her toes and a message for the Pope about contraception) that the girls start to take their vocation as martyrs seriously. Religious kitsch and Kiwi provincialism hang in the air like the after-smell of Mrs Flynn's mutton chops'
The Independent, UK

'The Virgin's voice rings with visionary intent in *The Visitation*, Sue Reidy's dark, delicious comedy of sex, religion and growing up in 60s New Zealand . . . This gem of a first novel hits adolescence right on the rebellious tousled head' *She*, UK

'This excellent début is a wonderful portrayal of adolescence, sexuality and rebellion' *Womans' Journal*, UK

'This is a very funny book. Heart-rending too . . . Sue Reidy could be the female Michael Carson. *The Visitation* is highly readable. Great fun. Naughty and Catholic. Surely a winner'
Catholic Times, UK

'A wickedly funny, laugh-out-loud first novel from Reidy about two young sisters struggling against the strictures of Catholicism . . . An offbeat, surprisingly entertaining look at Catholic girlhood, by a writer with a predator's eye for comic detail'
Kirkus Reviews, US

'Reidy's *joie de vivre* and infectious sense of humour keep her portrait of Catholic childhood at once funny, affectionate and eminently entertaining' *Publishers Weekly*, US

'Set in New Zealand, [a] wonderfully offbeat, coming-of-age novel . . . Clever, witty, and funny, but also sad; a keen portrayal of female teenage angst and growing up Catholic' *Booklist*, US

'Funny and original' *Sydney Morning Herald*, Australia

'A jolly romp through the ghastlier side of Catholicism: martyrs, saints, masochism, hell and damnation set against the secure but stifling background of a New Zealand country town in the 1960s' *Newcastle Herald*, Australia

'Those who have had a Catholic upbringing will immediately recognise the world of *The Visitation*. Those who have not will have no trouble entering the realm of the novel as Reidy's unique voice and the truthful and touching view of humanity she presents entice you to keep reading' *The Dominion*, NZ

'The novel moves freely from comedy to the little tragedies of everyday life in an instant . . . This novel's mixture of wittily observed realism, vivid surrealism, and the glorious Virgin's apparitions may be initially disconcerting, but these elements work together to illustrate serious issues . . . This honest account of the struggle for selfhood should be liberating for all readers' *Evening Post*, NZ

'Reidy joins Christine Johnston, Anne Kennedy and Fiona Farrell in a growing line of Catholic women writers who employ magic or the supernatural to throw into ironic relief the basic pragmatism and lack of imagination of stalwart New Zealanders . . . *The Visitation* is a rich and witty novel' *New Zealand Books*

'What happens when Catholicism and adolescence collide? *The Visitation* by New Zealand writer Sue Reidy provides an amusing, readable answer . . . The girls rebel, discover sex, and chuck their faith out the window. Well, who wouldn't? *The Visitation* is a quirky insightful début' *More*, NZ

'In this disturbing book, Reidy seems determined to cast out her own demons and a lot of other people's besides. The grand guignol descriptions of the worst excesses of Catholic blind faith feel like a distilled compendium of a thousand disaffected Catholic women – sex and death and religion vomited up in a horrifying and fascinating torrent . . . In Britain, where *The Visitation* is published, the literati will be reassured about the melancholy strangeness of a New Zealand upbringing. It will probably be a hit' *The Listener*, NZ

Also by Sue Reidy

THE VISITATION
MODETTES AND OTHER STORIES

FOUR WAYS TO BE
A WOMAN

Sue Reidy

BLACK SWAN

FOUR WAYS TO BE A WOMAN
A BLACK SWAN BOOK : 0 552 99697 1

First publication in Great Britain

PRINTING HISTORY
Black Swan edition published 2000

1 3 5 7 9 10 8 6 4 2

Set in 11pt Melior by
County Typesetters, Margate, Kent.

Black Swan Books are published by Transworld Publishers,
61–63 Uxbridge Road, London W5 5SA,
a division of The Random House Group Ltd,
in Australia by Random House Australia (Pty) Ltd,
20 Alfred Street, Milsons Point, Sydney, NSW 2061, Australia,
in New Zealand by Random House New Zealand Ltd,
18 Poland Road, Glenfield, Auckland 10, New Zealand
and in South Africa by Random House (Pty) Ltd,
Endulini, 5a Jubilee Road, Parktown 2193, South Africa.

Printed and bound in Great Britain by
Cox & Wyman Ltd, Reading, Berkshire.

For Geoff

Acknowledgements

The following books have been particularly helpful in my research for this novel:

Your Breast Cancer Treatment Handbook: Your Guide to Understanding the Disease, Treatments, Emotions and Recovery from Breast Cancer, Judy C. Kneece, RN, OCN, Breast Cancer Specialist, EduCare Publishing, Columbia, South Carolina, 1996.

Living Beyond Breast Cancer: A Survivor's Guide for When Treatment Ends and the Rest of Your life Begins, Marisa C. Weiss, MD, and Ellen Weiss, Times Books, New York, 1997.

Spirited Women: Journeys with Breast Cancer, Petrea King, Random House, Sydney, 1995.

Grace and Grit: Spirituality and Healing in the Life and Death of Treya Killam Wilber, Ken Wilber, Shambala Publications, Massachusetts, 1991.

Battles with the Baby Gods, Infertility: Stories of Hope, Amanda Hampson, Doubleday, Sydney, 1997.

Motherhood Deferred: A Woman's Journey, Anne Taylor Fleming, Ballantine Books, New York, 1994.

Never To Be a Mother: A Guide for All Women Who Didn't – or Couldn't – Have Children, Linda Hunt Anton, HarperCollins, New York, 1992.

Pregnancy after Thirty, Mary Anderson, Faber & Faber, London, 1984.

Beating the Biological Clock: The Joys and Challenges of Late Motherhood, Pamela Armstrong, Headline, London, 1996.

Making Babies: A New Zealand Guide to Getting Pregnant, Fertility Associates, David Bateman, Auckland, 1998.

Special thanks to my partner Geoff Walker for his loving support, advice and encouragement. Thanks also to my London editor Averil Ashfield, to Diana Beaumont, Transworld UK, to Harriet Allen at Random House New Zealand, and Shona Martyn, formerly at Transworld Australia, for their suggestions and enthusiasm, to my agent Glenys Bean, to Jane Parkin for her valuable editorial feedback, to Belinda Robinson who read a later draft of the manuscript and offered advice.

It would have been impossible to write this novel without the people who so generously allowed me into their lives. Thanks to the priests both ex as well as those who are currently practising, who gave their time to be interviewed, to the women working in the public relations industry, especially Christine Dennis and Lauren Young, to photographer Becky Nunes, to the women who shared their experiences of infertility, to the brave and inspirational women who have fought breast cancer; my heartfelt thanks to Trish Nelson, to Francis Robinson, to the Auckland Breast Cancer Support Service, to the Auckland Cancer Society Library – a fantastic resource. Stephen Gilbert, plastic surgeon, kindly agreed to read the chapter relating to Bridget's plastic surgery. Jude Mannion gave me the original inspiration for the black tongue story and Adrienne Burn the story of destroying the strap.

I have used lavish amounts of artistic licence with all of the above material. Any errors of either a medical or a theological nature, or any other, are my own. My characters' opinions and stances do not represent those from any one individual, or book consulted, as part of my research for this novel.

I fully acknowledge the generous support of Creative New Zealand who awarded me a major grant to assist me in the completion of this novel.

Chapter One

Agnes

Agnes is in bed with a man nearly half her age, but she is not the slightest bit aroused. Her thoughts beat out a monotonous and repetitive refrain: *why am I doing this?* There is no love here, no possibility of joy. Instead, as an ever-present legacy from her past — vestiges of guilt. There, wouldn't Athena be surprised? Sex flavoured by guilt. For Agnes, guilt has often acted as a potent aphrodisiac.

Her eyes are wide open in the dark. His are closed. She barely moves. He seems undeterred by her lack of response to his efforts. They don't speak. She's been with some who like loose talk, dirty talk, like to be wound up. That's OK if they're experienced. With this one, he'll have dumped his load so fast, blink and it's over. You utter fool, Agnes. Tell no-one. In the morning you can deny it ever happened. You drank too much and you should have known better.

She traces the lines of his body. How can she possibly be expected to concentrate when her new lover is giving every indication that he is inept?

Light from a single candle flickers over their mismatched forms. Her lover, his Titian hair glinting in the light, is perched upon her like a dragonfly on a rock. Arms flailing, he utters little snuffling gasping sounds. You can never predict whether they'll be grunters, gropers, snorers or moaners. This one is a gasper all right. Listen to him go. He might be an amateurish groper (she can pick them, can't she?), but he nevertheless explores her every crevice with a tenacity and intensity approximating passion. *Hi-ho Silver.*

Agnes is again distracted. Images flash through her head like scenes from old movies constantly replayed. She needs a holiday from her own head. Someone to take her away, help her escape from what is, God forbid, mundane, ugly, difficult or painful.

Everything reminds her of something or someone else. A previous red-headed lover. A cock that felt the same. Although no cock looks the same as another, does it, Agnes? You should know that very well by now.

Meanwhile. Back at the ranch.

Oops.

A telltale warning flutter down below wakes her up. Not another premature ejaculator – dear God, no.

She stirs herself to take an interest (why not, it is her body after all), to attempt an appropriate response, thinking: at least I'm in my own bed. Not in some grotty flat. Better her pile of stale underwear than his. And at least she can rely on a decent coffee in the morning.

'Hey,' she cries, later than she meant to, but not yet too late. Stop, for God's sake. *Can't we talk about this?*

'I've changed my mind.' And she tries to wriggle out from beneath the sweaty body labouring clumsily above her. Idiot, *idiot,* she berates herself. All her own fault, she has definitely overdone it with the alcohol – not for the first time in recent weeks. Sections of the evening are mercifully blurred, already beyond accurate recall. Does she have anything to apologize for? This young man, for instance. He is young, even for her tastes.

'I don't want to continue.' She is no longer apologetic. She's pissed off with him.

A grunt is all the response she gets. *He is ploughing a field, the motor is hot.* A young man almost of an age to be her son. Except that she has never had a child, and never wanted one. She makes a half-hearted attempt to convince herself that this latest indiscretion doesn't count, but the woman within pursues her relentless dialogue.

Are you lonely? Desperate?

No.

Can't you do better than this?

What does it matter? But it does. The very emptiness of the doomed encounter ensures it resonates in the deepest recesses of her being.

His movements become more vigorous. She feels him straining to sustain the pace without coming. She is being gnawed by a shark in a feeding frenzy.

How did he end up on top? If she had been on top, she would be the one in the driver's seat, not this amateur blunderer.

'*Damn you.*' She squeezes his arm, pinches his ears. '*Don't you dare,*' she warns.

Too late, too late now by far.

He pumps furiously. Her body is pounded against the mattress. He will grind her to dust.

She simply wants it over with now. Hurry up, man, do the deed.

Pump, pump, pump.

Pound, pound, pound.

His breathing rasps, louder, faster as he loses himself to the urgent driving need. Until finally – oh the relief

– he gushes into the plastic sheath and throbs against her inhospitable womb.

All those millions of sperm – thwarted.

His face flushes. Eyes bulge, roll back in his head. The mouth slackens, torso shudders, before he collapses exhausted but satisfied alongside her.

He catches her eye finally. Grins.

The cheek.

He even dares to trace the outline of her lips with a forefinger. She can smell herself on him. He expects to be forgiven?

The penny drops.

He hasn't taken her protests seriously. For him it's spiced up their sex. Turned it into a game. A competition. The poor fool is labouring under the delusion he's won.

She throws a pillow at him. 'How *could* you?'

'But I was so close. It's not fair, not that close it isn't.' The bastard is still smiling too. Confidently he raises his hands behind his head and props himself up against two white featherdown pillows.

Fair?

Agnes can imagine what Clare would say. Something about not being under any obligation, ever. Having the right to choose. Athena, naturally, would never allow herself to be placed in a situation where it became an issue. She doesn't have sex. Doesn't even like sex – or so she says.

Should she ask him to leave now and get it over with?

'Want a back rub?' he offers, to her astonishment.

She agrees and within a few minutes is, even more astonishingly, asleep.

It is past nine when Agnes wakes up the following morning. She clambers out of bed dragging half the duvet with her. The room reeks of their sex. She opens a window. A big woman, she thinks ruefully as she catches sight of herself in the full-length mirror propped against the white wall. Not at all fat, but definitely big and raw-boned, conveying an impression of strength and determination. Someone to reckon with. A mane of uncombed hair. Maroon. At least it had been when it was first coloured. Since then it has faded and the regrowth is peeking through. She continues to observe herself in a detached fashion, seeing her body through his eyes, the long pale thighs, the vigorous growth of her black pubic hair extending almost to her navel and part way down her thighs. Wide hips, full creamy breasts. The chocolate-coloured aureoles fringed with long, delicate sea anemone hairs.

She becomes aware of the boy's attention. Marooned in the debris of stale sheets, he stares up at her through half-closed eyes. Narrow hipbones protrude to form the shallow bowl of his stomach. A skinny, hungry, freckled beanpole with spiky hair and rosy-tipped ears. He smells divine and who would have thought it?

Agnes continues to fossick in the clutter of lipsticks, crumpled tissues, a knotted used condom, white coffee cups, gutted candles, paper, magazines, a dictionary, until she fishes up a man's checked shirt, only to discard it when she notices the missing cuff button.

She has become a moderate version of what her mother has always predicted she would turn into – a slovenly trollop. Even now, there are bound to be unwashed knickers balled-up and forgotten under the bed, a pile of correspondence lying somewhere on a table long overdue for response, underneath a crumpled list of tasks not yet completed. If her mother were a fly on the wall of her life (a position she has often longed to occupy), she would have seen a multitude of tasks for herself in restoring order to chaos, sufficient to have kept her busy for at least a week or more. Agnes doesn't care. How can she feel creative in a pristine environment? Her mess inspires her. She wallows in it.

'You're a messy babe.'

'I'm nobody's babe,' she snaps. 'Least of all yours.'

Thank God. A six-foot, seventy-kilogram babe? Ridiculous.

'Have you ever been anyone's babe, then?'

'Might have.' She pulls on a pair of black lacy knickers and faded Levis.

'Tell me, go on, tell me,' he begs, rolling over onto his hip and leaning on an elbow, his freckled face bright with interest.

I'm not who you think I am.

No point in spelling it out.

'How old are you?' He hangs down over the bed and pulls out a crumpled pack of cigarettes from the pocket of his black leather jacket.

'Not in here,' she says quickly. 'No way.'

He jettisons the pack. Flops back on the mattress again. Sighs.

Her age isn't a problem for her, but maybe it is for him. Will he get teased by his mates? She tells him she is thirty-five. Well, it's near enough. She can comfortably pass for it. Her friend Clare has a theory that you can appear younger if you project yourself with loads of energy and enthusiasm.

'Do you always lose interest before you've finished sex?'

Only if there's a missing connection. 'No. Do you?'

He laughs at the idea. 'Guys don't.'

'You've never been impotent?'

'Never.' He pauses. 'S'pose they're often impotent, at your age. Ever go out with guys in their forties? Fifties?'

14

Not if she can help it. She finds a striped ribbed jersey and drags it over her head, pulling it down tightly over her boobs. May as well show them off. He gives her a sly look – as if he wants to grab them and stuff them into his mouth. Greedy boy. She cuffs him playfully over the head.

'Sometimes they can't get it up. I think I read somewhere that one man in ten has problems.'

He frowns. 'So what d'you do? Give 'em a hand job?'

'Occasionally.'

'Tell him to piss off, is that what you do?' He grins, flashes an incongruous gold-capped tooth.

'Sometimes, but not if it's a serious relationship. I'm not heartless, you know.'

'Could've fooled me.'

'Seems I fool a lot of people.'

He grins. She thaws a little. He is sweet after all. She remembers why she picked him.

'I'd top myself if I couldn't ever get it up. Shit, I would. No kidding.'

Why does she bother with young sprats? They know nothing. This one, Simon his name is, had amused her at first. They liked the same music. Both enjoyed dancing.

He had told her he fancied older women. Experienced women. Big women. Spun her a load of bullshit, she is now thinking. Trying it on. Seeing how far he could go.

She had wanted to believe him. 'You don't have to love someone to fuck them,' she imagines defending herself to Athena. Sometimes you get lonely in the middle of the night. You have an itch you want to satisfy and not just by your own efforts, for once. You don't want to hurt anyone, but you're not always ready to commit yourself either. Yet on a fundamental level,

15

nothing ever really changes. Men have one set of rules they play by, and women another.

She fantasizes being taken out of herself. Surprised. Receiving more than she gives. Being understood. Appreciated.

She wishes there were still men about who weren't either married or gay. She wishes there were young men who didn't expect a pretzel, a lookalike from an American sitcom in their beds. But why, wonders Agnes, would *anyone* desire an anorexic waif with insect legs, raisins for breasts, and nothing to say for herself?

'*You're* a challenge,' observes Simon.

A *challenge*. Where has he picked up that from? The knocks and hurts were ahead of young men his age, like tidal waves waiting to engulf. But then this is part of the attraction, she admits to herself. No baggage. A big harmless, know-nothing boy.

She is suddenly disgusted with herself. Tosses her young lover his T-shirt.

'Party's over,' she informs him. She throws over the cargo trousers as well.

Her repressed self, the dark self, the self she would rather remain in ignorance of, temporarily rears its head and is promptly squashed. Heaven forbid he should know her as she truly is. She recalls various ex-lovers, once intimate friends, men and women who have over the intervening years received gifts of her love and attention, some who have returned it with interest, while others, a few select others, whom she prefers to forget, have disappointed or betrayed her.

So where does Simon fit in? Will he be just another mistake, a cute diversion, another lover who hasn't worked out?

She prefers to have the expectations up front. No messy scenes on either side. Convenience. A good time. Civilized behaviour. Nothing too tricksy or weird. No bondage scenes, even in fun. No recriminations.

But Simon, it appears, has other ideas. He doesn't seem to realize their acquaintance has been throttled at its inception. He's babbling away to her while her mind has been elsewhere. What is the boy saying? She focuses on him again. He's talking about art. And he's drawing comparisons, favourable ones too, she is amused to learn, between her belly, thighs and breasts and those featured in Il Bronzino's gloriously erotic sixteenth-century Venus nudes. She is familiar with the painting to which he is referring – *Venus, Cupid and Jealousy*. Venus, full-bodied, sensual and voluptuous, with her softly curved belly and generous calves and thighs is the complete antithesis of the ideal body currently in vogue. Just as Agnes would be, if she were to compare herself to the more androgynous beauties whom, irony of ironies, she frequently photographs to earn her living.

Distracted by his chatter, for the young man is surprisingly articulate in the areas where he has a little knowledge, Agnes finds herself putting the coffee maker on the stove, heating milk in a saucepan, pulling white cups from the cupboard, placing them on the stainless steel bench top.

He is an art student, doing his master's year. A painter. But he's also keen on photography – her field. He asks if she would mind if he thumbed through some of her precious books. One entire wall of her lounge is devoted to books, half of them about photography and art.

She glances over at him, the thin white neck studiously bent over Joel-Peter Witkin's disturbing work, and feels a pang of absurd tenderness. Absurd in its inappropriateness, she reminds herself. A sore head reminds her again of the quantity of wine she must have consumed the previous night at the dance party.

Fortunately it's a Saturday. Agnes has no pressing plans other than shopping for groceries, cleaning her little apartment and maybe later on in the day (the arrangement had been casual) meeting Athena for coffee.

Simon raises the subject of their unsatisfactory first attempt at sex.

'Why didn't you like it?'

Agnes is impressed by his frankness.

She recalls a scene from a Joseph O'Connor novel. A priest advises a husband on how to interest his wife in sex. He tells his parishioner in the confessional that a man is like a light bulb, whereas a woman is like an iron, slow to heat up.

How should she phrase it so as not to make him feel inadequate? What if she causes him to lose confidence? How exhausting it is, how ingrained, the habit of protecting men.

'You can be honest with me, I don't mind,' he says.

Bullshit.

'I mean it.'

She gives him a shrewd look, but he returns her glance, meeting her eyes, apparently without guile. Maybe this is why she is with a young lover. Perhaps he can be trained. Delightful thought, perish it immediately, Agnes.

'Women take longer to become aroused,' she says. So basic.

He doesn't leap in to defend himself. He sits quietly, listening to her.

She tries to explain what it was like for her rather than accusing him of insensitivity.

He nods.

She elaborates.

He asks sensible questions. He doesn't interrupt when she's speaking.

Unexpected. Ten out of ten, Simon.

Even more surprising, he asks for another chance to prove himself to her. She stares at his amusing protruding ears, the tufts of red hair. At his eyes, sea green, full of intelligence. Pleading.

How can she refuse? She leads him by the hand. Love is where you find it, after all, she reminds herself. At least this is what she has always preached. What will her friends think? (They'll think you're nuts, Agnes, and you are. But apart from Bridget are any of them happy? No.)

Butt out, girls.

She rummages in a bedside drawer, produces a tube of lubricant and a new packet of condoms all the colours of the rainbow. They undress again and dive under the covers at the same time, breaking into uncontrollable giggles.

'Now, I want you to do exactly as I tell you,' she says mock sternly.

He grins. 'I love it when you're bossy. I hear madam and I will obey.'

Agnes's new young lover Simon works out more satisfactorily than she could have ever anticipated, given their unpromising beginning. He is amusing, sensitive – good company, in fact.

He sings in the shower. He hums when he cooks simple snacks for the two of them, whistles while he waits for the kettle to boil. He never thinks to clean up after himself in the kitchen. He leaves wet towels on the floor of the bathroom, which exasperates her (however, in all her years of searching she has not yet found the perfect man), but he does compensate for his failings in other ways.

He watches bemused as she sticks her head into every cupboard, looks under the bed, behind the doors, inside the wardrobe.

'What are you looking for?'

'I'm searching to see if there are any invisible servants in this apartment that I don't know about.'

He laughs. 'Chill out, Agnes.'

She tosses him a tea towel.

'Why are you so happy?'

'I don't know.' He sounds surprised, as if he never gives it a moment's thought. 'I just am.'

She looks down at his twenty-one years from the richness and depth of the experience of her own thirty-nine.

And she laughs out loud because in all those years, what might turn out to be half of her life on this earth, she has not yet discovered the secret of being happy. If she hangs around Simon long enough, perhaps she too might learn to take one day at a time – the way he does.

She has not yet displayed him in public. Early days yet. It may never be the right time. For the present he will remain her delicious little secret.

She has no intention of giving him up even if her friends do disapprove.

Agnes possesses a small tattoo on the side of her left buttock. A long-tailed mermaid, outlined in black and the pattern detail filled in with jade, aqua and red. When she was twenty, emblazoning this mythical creature on her body had seemed like an inspired idea. Now she finds mermaids vaguely New Age-ish and wishes she could erase it.

'Who did it?' asks Simon, idly tracing the outline with a long freckled finger.

'Oh, you know, one of those tattoo parlours you find in seedy backstreets. You could pick your design from their stock books, but instead I took along an old engraving I discovered in a library book that appealed to me. I think the tattooist made a pretty faithful imitation of it.'

'It's well executed.'

'Yes, I was lucky. I could have ended up with something absolutely hideous.'

She remembered how important it had seemed at the time, to make a statement. Whom had she wanted to impress?

Naturally her mother had been horrified. The predictable wail of dismay echoed accusingly down the phone line: 'Agnes, how *could* you? Why did you do it? You can't ever change your mind if you want to erase it. You're stuck with it. *For ever.*'

Agnes had listened with growing impatience. There was no denying it, she did goad her mother and if she had still been a member of the One True Faith she would no doubt have had to go to weekly Confession and repent. But she wasn't and she didn't.

Little has changed over the years in the dynamics between Agnes and her mother. In the interim Agnes has resigned herself to the knowledge that nothing she does will ever completely satisfy her mother. When Agnes stops to think about their relationship, she feels genuine guilt – she is a convent-bred girl after all. But she insists that her mother's distress is not *her* problem. Not her responsibility.

Her mother's complaints and criticism have festered into a wound that Agnes cannot staunch, for to do so would be to change herself completely and this she is not prepared to do.

There are no babies. No happy family home. No husband or partner in sight.

'Agnes, Agnes, Agnes.'

21

How her mother's voice can easily soar to a heartfelt wail of anguish over the phone.

The latest crime? Her mother just happened to be driving through Agnes's neighbourhood 'doing one or two essential little messages'.

Like hell, thinks Agnes.

'In the course of driving around, minding my own business, I was astonished to come across you, Agnes, and to observe you engaged in an animated conversation with a very, very young man. The two of you were drinking coffee at one of those outdoor cafés where you seem to spend most of your time. Lord only knows when you get any work done, but that's by the by. You were so besotted, you and that boy, you failed to notice your own mother had parked across the road and was busily waving at you. Imagine how I felt, Agnes.'

There was a brief pause.

'Why, why, why can't you find someone of your own age, for goodness' sake? What's *wrong* with you? All I've ever wanted is for you to be happy. Is it so much to ask. *Is it?*'

Agnes is furious.

She hears a stifled sob on the other end of the line.

'How long were you spying on me, Mum?'

'I wasn't spying,' comes the indignant reply. 'I was just—'

Agnes holds the phone away from her ear.

Agnes recalls her mother at forty. Agnes at the time was twenty, recently graduated . . . and hyper-critical.

Let's face facts here, Agnes Mary Lucy O'Neill – you were a prize bitch.

She was convinced her mother had been born middle-aged, conservative, old-fashioned and knowing nothing of any real significance. Innocent, ignorant

22

and puritanical. That was her mother then, and still is today.

Her mother: anxious eyes that always darted this way and that. Comparing, evaluating, inevitably coming up with wrong answers. Hands that were likewise always on the move, straightening, aligning objects, tidying – endlessly tidying, sorting and putting away. Examining her clothes for loose threads, stray hairs, stains. Patting, stroking, knotting, untangling, mending, picking up, picking holes in things, in people – mostly Agnes.

She had made Agnes want to scream.

Agnes had seen no option other than rebellion.

But that was then, this is now.

Agnes now feels more compassionate towards her mother. She sees the obsessive cleaning, the sacrificing, the bad cooking, for what they were. Duty. Love and devotion.

No longer can a Hail Mary put wrongs to right. Agnes's mother is fully justified in imagining the worst. Agnes has committed a mountain of sins, both mortal and venial, far too many to be easily obliterated by the recitation of a quick Our Father or Glory Be as a penance. But within Agnes, as she senses the brick wall of her fortieth birthday looming ahead of her like someone else's unbelievable nightmare, something is stirring; evaluation is taking place. Agnes is doing her own stock-taking and the conclusions she reaches alarm her. She struggles to recall any achievements and develops instant amnesia. Has anyone, apart from her mother, ever truly loved her? Has any other human being truly known her, accepted her, warts and all? Agnes is afraid to hear the answer come reverberating back at her.

Chapter Two

Clare

Monday. Clare starts her day at the gym, as she does four days out of every seven. At seven-thirty a.m. she is in her T-shirt and leggings ready to begin her work-out. The women who have just emerged pink-faced from the six-thirty classes are already queuing at the showers. The changing room is crowded and chaotic – Lycra city. Dozens of naked or partially clothed bodies, arms and legs flailing, shoes being put on or removed. Blow-driers roar, dozens of metal locker doors are wrenched open and banged shut. A row of women rub moisturizers onto their legs and arms. A middle-aged woman with a defiant roll of flesh protruding over her knickers stands bare-breasted at one of the communal mirrors flossing her teeth. Focused on the task at hand, she seems cheerfully oblivious to the contrast she presents in the midst of taut young bodies flanking her.

Clare wrinkles her nose at the familiar pungent odour of perspiration, perfume, hair spray, depilatory creams, deodorant, talcum powder, moisturizers, shampoos and gels. A young woman in black lace bra and G-string with a Walkman headset clamped to her ears bops to the beat as she irons her work blouse.

24

Clare eyes with amusement the tattooed snake emerging from the crack in her buttocks.

She reluctantly trudges upstairs and climbs on a cycle to warm up. She scans the room to see if there is anyone she knows and greets Maud, a history professor in her fifties, already going hell for leather on the new cross-trainer machine.

Alongside her on the bikes her neighbour is engrossed in a magazine story about a woman whose partner has confessed, Clare notes by reading over her shoulder, to enjoying a secret life as a sex pervert. The woman's legs slow on the cycle as she becomes gripped by the story.

Yawn.

She dreads the week ahead. Already her mind is racing with all the tasks that lie ahead of her as a public relations consultant that day and the next and the day after. Her appointment book is crowded with wall-to-wall meetings and social engagements that fall into the category of schmoozing. For Clare nothing is ever purely social. Everyone is a potential client, or else a contact who knows something or someone who knows someone else (the goods, darling) who can arrange an introduction, a deal, a sponsorship. She has three stories to knock out before the end of the day, a TV channel to bring on board with a new pet project, a bad debt to chase up, a staff member to chastise, a prospective new client to charm and cajole into her orbit.

How many times in her career has she been at this stage with a new client? Coaxing them like a sick puppy to a feed bowl. Hand-holding to get them on side until they trust her, realize she really can deliver what she promises. For she always promises – the sun, the moon, the stars coming out to play. She jealously guards a goldmine of an address book whose pages bear witness to years of carefully nurtured contacts.

Back at the office Clare checks her e-mail. A note from Harmony Heaven requesting a change of meeting time. Two lines from Agnes regarding their lunch date. A paragraph from a cousin in England. She e-mails a paragraph in response, even though she doesn't really have time, plus a yes to Agnes, and suggests a new meeting slot for Harmony.

She checks her watch. Just enough time for a quick bagel and a long black. While she's eating she'll have another read through the background notes on the prospect who is due at her office in half an hour.

They size each other up. Clare dislikes him on sight. The temperature in the boardroom drops a couple of degrees. Dermott Maloney. He heads one of the larger and more prestigious Auckland law firms. She doesn't relish the idea of working with this arrogant bastard. They already have more blue chip clients on board than they can comfortably service without taking on more staff, but her partner Fran is convinced that his company will flesh out their profile, give them clout in a new area. The arrival of Maloney and Monroe on the scene has highlighted an area of potential conflict between Clare and Fran. Her partner is keen to expand but Clare is reluctant to do so, especially if it means their longtime clients may lose some of their valued and legendary personal service.

Maloney's body is bulky beneath the expensive navy wool suit. She catches a whiff of a spicy male fragrance. The hands are incongruously small and beautifully manicured. Self-satisfied, self-important – a face like a block of granite. Mr Bulldozer. Brain like a cold blade moving slowly but relentlessly on his target. Not someone she could ever give a fuck about

– him or his business. There would be no relationship of trust here, merely a smooth, clearly understood service rendered and then paid for, on the nail. Or will he be one of those slippery types who drags the chain on payment, vaporizing when Fran moves in to apply the pressure to collect the debt? Surprisingly it's often the bigger companies who are the more un-reliable.

Although this is not a formal pitch, as a matter of policy Clare presents her company's credentials. Her PA has done her homework effectively, which means she is also able to anticipate and address potential areas of concern. At the appropriate moment she wheels in Fran to do the girls' equivalent of rah-rah back-slapping – the hail-fellow-well-met number. Fran is brilliant in this role. Built like a tank herself, she matches bulk with bulk. Bulldozer gives her the once-over and is reassured – as they all are, thinks Clare. Both partners are multi-skilled. Fran is the finance whiz and media guru, while Clare supplies the marketing and strategic input as well as the creative flair.

They take turns fronting the company to new prospects. It is critical to select the right partner to lead in the first presentations. They make an effort to match client to consultant. Both partners are able to relate comfortably at boardroom level. They tread a delicate line between convincing the potential client they're the right people and at the same time not giving away all their ideas for nothing. They've now been in the field long enough to ensure that most new business comes to them directly from personal referrals.

In order for Clare to accept a new client she has to be able to see the possibility of a successful outcome. There has to be something in it for both parties. Not only that, but there has to be some redeeming feature in the client's product or service. Her integrity is her currency, after all.

'With PR you're taking out an insurance policy,' she tells Bulldozer. 'Building brownie points with the public. Your service is worth a lot of dollars. To invest in communications at the front end, rather than only when the shit hits the fan, is a basic precaution. It's actually very simple.'

He nods.

Bingo. Clare knows she has hit pay dirt.

'And we don't do cheap,' she continues, deadpan.

The prospective client's eyes flicker as this statement makes its impact.

Doesn't do cheap. He'll pass that on to the lads, have a laugh over a drink. *Who does she think she is?*

The best. He knows it. Very professional. Discreet.

Clare waits for him to walk out of the door.

'Hit me with it,' he says. He's grinning at her with a new respect. It changes his face completely. The granite splinters. Somewhere, deeply buried, there lurks a sense of humour.

There's inevitably a jockeying for ascendancy in the relationship with new male clients. Boring, but predictable. These days Clare wouldn't kowtow if her client was God Herself. Clare prides herself on the accuracy of her first impression character assessments. Only rarely does she get it wrong.

'I don't commit myself to prices on the spot,' she says. 'I'll think about it and get back to you with a proposal within a couple of days.'

'Sounds fair enough to me.'

Clare has already decided she'll steer him away from the retainer option he has proposed – too easy to come unstuck. They'll accept him on a straight fees basis.

She's desperate for a pee, tries not to be too abrupt in ushering him out to reception and into the lift.

Does she give a toss whether he responds to her proposal or not? Increasingly there's a sameness about her commercial transactions. Money is no longer one of the driving forces. It takes a lot more to excite her. Too readily now she drifts into automatic pilot. Ironically, the more arrogant and off-hand she is in her approach and responses the more the guys seem to go for it. Makes her wonder why she kissed arse for so long. When had she first realized she could stop being deferential and get on with it? If people didn't like it – too bad.

Last week, for example, she had facilitated a meeting between one of her trainee consultants and Pedro, an impetuous man in his early thirties who was bringing an internationally successful tenor to New Zealand to tour the three main centres. Clare had already sussed Pedro as a cowboy, and she and Fran had made the decision to flick him on as soon as the job was done. They'd only taken him on as a one-off project, for Rose, their junior, to cut her teeth on. Already Rose was struggling to deal with a media crisis – one of the bigger radio stations had broken media embargo. Not only that, a proposed full page profile in a national daily promised the following Saturday had been bumped off due to a massive four-page story on the Clinton-Lewinsky scandal.

'You're quite clever, for a girl,' he quipped on hearing Rose's strategy for containing the crisis.

'I suppose you think that's funny,' said Clare.

'Side-splitting. No sense of humour – that's your problem.'

'Actually,' Clare reminded him, '*you're* the one who lost his rag with the *Herald* features editor. We're here to offer sensible professional advice, remember? And your attitude is getting right up my nose, buddy.'

He backed off. 'Jesus, open my mouth and get my

fucking head blown fucking off. Sorry for existing.'

'Let's get down to business, shall we?' said Clare. She had pulled back then to allow Rose to take over the reins.

'Why do we have to deal with arseholes like him?' Rose cried, once he had departed.

'Don't worry, honey. We plan to ditch him, *when* we've completed this job *and* been paid for it. We don't put up with shit. Personally, I won't take crap from anyone. Particularly an up-himself wanker like our friend Pedro. Some people won't be told.'

'Can't you work with more women clients?'

'Women are sometimes more devious in the way they go about stabbing you in the back. At least with these guys they're upfront about what they are.'

'Don't you trust anyone?'

'I trust myself.'

All she has to do is not want anything too much. Make it obvious she can walk away. The old icing on the cake number. Of course she now has the confidence that was lacking in her late twenties – a well-honed gut instinct. There is something to be said for age and the experience that goes with it. What she hadn't counted on was that when she finally got it right, she might lose the motivation.

She can see already the epitaph on her tombstone: Clare O'Leary: Legendary for her ability to leverage contacts.

Or, perhaps: Here lies Clare 'Don't fuck with me' O'Leary. No shit hit her fan.

Or: Clare O'Leary. She served her time: fifty-five hours per week for forty-five years.

Another thirty years of the same – the thought of it is enough to fill her with despair. How do men do it? What quality of stickability is lacking in her? She has never been a defeatist. On the other hand she has never had to struggle to find reasons to keep going before. Working and winning have been as natural as breathing. So what has changed? Her biological clock? Ticking away the months until she turns forty?

The nuns had come down hard on the bold girls.

'Clare!'

'Yes, Sister?'

'Come here, girl.'

'Yes, Sister.'

'WHO DO YOU THINK YOU ARE?'

'No-one, Sister.'

Sister Ambrose, red-faced, spittle on her lips, hellfire in her eyes, stood over her.

'Remember this. Pride comes before a fall, Clare O'Leary. You've got too big for your boots, that's your trouble. Too high and mighty. For your own good we'll have to cut you down to size, won't we?'

Crack went the wooden ruler on the scratched desktop.

Only a warning this time. She could breathe again.

A tiny paper dart landed on her desk a few moments later. Clare unfolded it in her lap.

Mad crow Ambrose, she read in Agnes's loose open handwriting. *Mad old bitch. Mad old cow. I hope God cuts* her *down to size.*

Ambrose called her up to the front of the class.

She held out her hand. 'GIVE . . . IT . . . TO . . . ME. And perhaps you'd like to share your wit with the whole class.' She glared at Clare.

'I don't know what you mean, Sister.' Clare's face assumed an innocent expression. Agnes's note was safely in her pocket.

'Don't play games with *me*, Clare O'Leary. You know very well what happens to girls who lie.'

31

'N-n-no, Sister.'

'I'll *tell* you what happens to naughty girls who lie to their teachers.'

The nun picked up the strap.

'Their tongues turn black. *Black as the ace of spades.* That's what happens to disobedient, lying, insolent girls, Clare O'Leary.'

Clare refused to cry out. But at morning break when Sister was away in the staff room, no doubt boasting of how she had successfully drummed some sense into that show-off too-big-for-her-boots O'Leary girl, Clare stole the hated leather strap. She and Agnes cut it up into hundreds of tiny pieces with Agnes's pocket knife. Afterwards they flushed the pieces down six different toilet bowls.

This act of rebellion, neither the first nor the last in their chequered history at the convent, became for them imbued with a deep religious significance. The relating of the tale, much exaggerated over the years, was eventually transformed into a victory of epic proportions.

Destroying the strap had not been their only misdemeanour. As the last wedge of leather disappeared from sight down the bowl, Clare and Agnes each solemnly made a small nick in their own tongues. When the outraged nun discovered the strap was missing, suspicion naturally fell on Clare and her shadow Agnes O'Neill. She advanced on them, a black-robed avenging angel holding her righteous wrath high before her in a beacon of triumph. She wanted their shame and humility, their abject apologies. She wanted dry mouths, tears, and quaking kneecaps.

They would have none of it. Refusing to cower with fear, they stood straight and tall before her. On being questioned both girls opened their mouths still swimming with the accumulated blood of their self-inflicted wounds. Their tongues were not black as Ambrose had predicted, but red and slippery with sin.

They could not restrain their pride and delight at their cleverness.

'*You insubordinate brazen little madams*,' she hissed. Her face was swollen and dangerous with pent-up anger. Her robe smelled of chalk dust, lavender water and mothballs.

Awed by their own defiance Clare and Agnes waited to be struck. No-one had ever usurped Ambrose's authority before. There wasn't a sound from the girls behind them.

'Then . . .' Clare always paused here for dramatic effect. The audience at this point, eyes shining, smiles already curved on mouths primed to split wide open, urged her on to the punch line, collaborating with her to crucify Ambrose the mad bitch.

'The old bat completely *lost it*. You should have seen her. Flipped her lid. Picture it – a turkey gobbling wattle neck, gibbering platitudes. Screaming her tits off. Hell flames were just around the corner. Agnes and I were destined for the fiery furnace – beyond redemption.'

They were sent home in disgrace. Agnes was caned by her father on both hands and the backs of her legs. Clare was sent to bed without any dinner.

'Both sets of parents then greased and smarmed their way back into the nuns' good books, of course.'

After a couple of days of punishment and deprivations the girls were allowed back to school with a warning – one more incident and they would be expelled.

'We got away with it.'

Clare and Agnes had been in agreement. It had been worth every bit of pain from their split tongues, the welts on Agnes's legs, and Clare's hungry tummy, just

33

to see the expression of outraged disbelief on Ambrose's face when they had opened their mouths to display their wounds.

Clare analyses her current success. Somewhere along the way she has gradually and imperceptibly changed into a person she no longer recognizes. A woman with whom a man called Adrian cuddles up in bed at night, his arm curved proprietorially around her waist. In the twilight between wakefulness and the onset of deep sleep she has begun to feel as if they are chained together by Adrian's hairless pale arm – like two divers plunging soundlessly into the depths of a big black hole. Drowning without realizing it.

She has paid a high price for her success, a price that her male colleagues haven't had to pay. To put in the hours and succeed, it has been impossible to have a child. She could have had a nanny but, as Adrian keeps reminding her, nannies have to go home sometime. She and Adrian rarely finish before seven. What would happen to her consultancy if she was unable to put in the hours, if she found herself after the birth unable to focus on maintaining the clients she had – let alone plan any new business initiatives? She has worked tirelessly to build her company. It has eaten up the past ten years of her life. It is now eight years since she took on Fran who had bought a 45 per cent share of her business. Would she be letting Fran down if she took a year out to attend to the demands of a new baby?

The phone goes non-stop. Even when Clare's calls are screened, her staff are besieging her with queries. The pressure of administration is unending. She knows the stress of deadlines is killing her millimetre by millimetre. But what is the alternative? Sometimes when she is very tired she hears a little voice inside asking her why she is working so hard. When is she going to stop and take a break? She inevitably becomes angry with herself when she hears the little voice because she has no answer for it.

'Why do you drive yourself so hard?' asks Agnes, beside her on the cycles when they are next at the gym together.

Clare slows down. There is real anguish in the face she presents to Agnes.

'I don't know.' She shakes her head. 'There's got to be more to life. Aspects of my lifestyle that made perfect sense to me ten years ago seem plain crazy to me now. If I continue the way I'm going will I believe in my fifties that such a single-minded focus on my career has been a mistake?'

'Of course you will. If you're questioning your work style now, by fifty you're bound to be doing something completely different. If you're not, I'll be disappointed in you.'

It's not as if they need all the money they make. She and Adrian are both doing well. His architectural practice is growing. He's taken on more staff. There's a building boom on again. The property market has gone berserk. Adrian and his staff can't design apartments fast enough to satisfy the demand. He and Clare have finally been able to put some money and assets aside for the future. They have leveraged their house to finance two little apartments and recruited tenants to pay the mortgage.

'Money for jam,' says Adrian. 'Keep this up and we can give up our day jobs.'

As a result of recent conclusions she has come to about her lifestyle, Clare has begun to train herself to take a regular lunch hour, something she hasn't done for years. What does she do in her lunch hour? If she's not lunching in cafés with friends, clients or potential clients, she's out spending. Designer garments, exquisite objects, luxury items for the house. She justifies it to herself. If she's working so bloody hard, if she's sacrificed so much for her work, then there ought to be some sort of reward.

It's time now, she believes, to have a baby. She cherishes a secret fantasy about joining the other mothers – being accepted as part of a tribe, no different from anyone else, piling the kids in the family wagon and heading off to the beach for the morning. Having a legitimate excuse for not showing her face at the office for a few years. For the first time in her life she views domesticity and child rearing as a prospect to embrace instead of one to flee from.

Not that she would dream of letting her mother in on her dilemma.

Clare's father greets her with a whiff of peppermint-flavoured breath and the customary quick peck on one cheek. She is not accompanied by Adrian on this her regular fortnightly visit because he has, as usual, found something better to do. His continued absence, while tactfully not remarked on by her father, does not, however, go unnoticed.

'So what's new?'

She follows him into the house. What has happened to her over the past fortnight that she needn't censor? Work is considered by both parties to be a safe topic, although of greater interest to her father than to her mother, for whom Clare's job remains an unfathomable mystery.

'I've been so *hectic* at work.'

'That's not news,' complains her mother, scratching the back of her head. 'Damned fleas. Dan, did you put that powder down, as I asked you?'

Her father rightly interprets his wife's enquiry as an implied criticism and pretends not to hear her.

Little in the house changes from visit to visit. Healthy-looking pot plants crowd every available surface. Photos of their many grandchildren line the mantelpiece and on one wall dozens of small framed black and white photos of the family at the farm, each of the children in their graduation gowns, school photos, her parents' parents. A gallery of O'Learys and Featherstones. Library books (thrillers mainly) are stacked on a side table.

Clare studies her father's bald head bent over the fireplace as he rearranges the logs with the poker. She worries about him. He's often short of breath these days, becoming easily exhausted, fuelling her mother's frustration.

Clare's mother is an insomniac. She endures her life in a permanent state of exasperation, nailed to the cross of Clare's father's ineptitude. She should have been the man, the breadwinner. She frequently reminds everyone how much better a job she would have done had she been given half a chance. Clare's mother might be dissatisfied with her life, but she hangs in there, grimly determined to make everyone else's life a misery too. She is indefatigable.

'I've almost finished my novel,' she announces brightly, tapping her fingers on the armrest.

Clare wonders if she has heard correctly. What novel? Her mother can't write. She has never given any indication that she possesses an imagination, let alone any particular aptitude for writing.

'As I was *saying* . . .' repeats her mother.

'Your mother has been a veritable powerhouse,' interrupts Clare's father. 'At her PC every day churning out the words. I'm no judge, but I'd have to say—'

Her father's literary opinion is destined, as are so many of his views, to remain unexpressed, as his wife cuts in with an imperious wave of the hand.

'I'm in a writing group.'

'Mum, you've really surprised me. Fantastic. How long have you been meeting? Why haven't you ever told me?'

'Oh, you have your own life,' replies her mother dismissively. 'Always *so hectic*. So wrapped up in *yourself*.'

'That's not *fair*. Every time I visit I ask you what you've been up to. But you've obviously decided, for reasons I can only guess at, that your writing must be kept a deep dark secret.'

Her mother, like her daughter, has an answer for everything.

'I simply wanted to see if I could finish it. As a matter of fact, I've recently passed it around my writing group.'

'What's it about? Have they given you any feedback yet?' To think she had believed that nothing her mother did could surprise her.

'I find out this week at our next meeting.'

Clare suspects the worst without even sighting the manuscript. What could her mother possibly have to write about?

'Can I read it?'

'When it's published, and not before.'

Clare struggles with an irreverent and almost uncontrollable desire to laugh.

In the background Clare's father's cup rattles an anxious staccato on the saucer. His wife deliberately ignores the warning signal. She leaps to her feet and finds an urgent matter to see to in the kitchen.

Clare doesn't follow her. She is eight years old again and her mother has just commanded her to unpick, because apparently it isn't of a high enough standard, most of the handstitching on the traycloth she is making in the school sewing class under the tutelage of Sister Dorothy.

A liver-spotted hand reaches over to pat her arm in commiseration.

'If it's any consolation,' whispers her father, 'I haven't been allowed to read it either.'

Her mother returns to the room. Soon she launches energetically into one of her pet topics – the inadequacies of their local parish priest. A hopeless manager of parish affairs, it would seem. No sensitivity. Head in the clouds.

'Organize? Pah! He couldn't organize his way out of a paper bag.' His list of failings, at least in her mother's eyes (there is little opportunity for her father to express his own views), is legion. An inept communicator. Stale. He should be put out to pasture. She's a good mind to write to the bishop, although – 'fat waste of time that would be, he's not much better.

'What they *desperately* need,' says her mother, chomping on a stalk of celery, finally remembering to offer the plate of carrot and celery sticks to her daughter, 'is some fresh blood. Trouble is, they aren't getting the numbers these days. No new recruits. It's a crying shame, it is.'

'That's right,' agrees Clare. 'Somehow celibacy doesn't seem to hold the same appeal for men in the new millennium.'

Her mother shoots her a sharp look. 'In my opinion,' she grabs a carrot stick, 'the nuns ought to have a lot more power and say in how things are run.'

Clare can see her mother is working herself up into a right little lather. Time to make her excuses. She gets to her feet.

'What, off already? But your mother has cooked

dinner specially for you.' Her father looks upset.

Clare flops back into her seat. Only two more hours to go.

Her mother has tried a new recipe. Filo Surprises. Clare dutifully chews her way through the dried-out tuna stuffing. Her father helpfully pats her on the back when a few flakes of burnt pastry become stuck in her throat.

'I'm fine,' says Clare, eyes streaming, coughing and spluttering.

Her father gives her another whack on the back and a half-chewed pellet of food shoots out of her mouth and onto the table.

She leaves her parents' house in a state of agitation. As usual she has revealed little of real importance to them. For instance, how she is dreading the coming weekend with Adrian's two teenage kids. Mike is sixteen and Tiffany is fifteen going on twenty-one. It is only in the past two years that Adrian has been granted more open access to his children. Although he doesn't put pressure on Clare to run around after them or to cook, she is expected to be present for most meals.

Clare is still adjusting.

They aren't so bad, but they make it painfully obvious that they wish they could have their father to themselves. Even after five years Clare still hasn't got used to the fact that while they are around what she thinks, feels and needs simply doesn't count. Adrian indulges them shamelessly.

She recalls their previous visit. Tiffany wanted to go out to a party and be allowed to come home whenever she felt like it. Clare had waited for Adrian to set a realistic curfew. Midnight was reasonable, she had thought. Adrian had delegated responsibility to her to set the limit, which meant she was inevitably blamed for the conflict that ensued.

'You're not my mother,' shouted Tiffany. 'It's none of *your* fucking business what I do.'

'While you're in this house you'll do as we say,' retorted Clare.

And here lies the crux of the problem. She is not backed up by Adrian, whose over-indulgence of his children is, as she has told him a hundred times, inevitably coloured by a residue of guilt, the legacy of his messy divorce – and they are all disadvantaged because of it. Naturally he denies that he is over-compensating, or that there should be any limits to the unconditional love he expresses to them – now that he finally has the opportunity to make up for lost time.

'I could spit,' Clare tells Agnes at the gym. 'I feel as if I no longer have rights and authority in my own home. I am not consulted, not heard.'

'Really? That's not very fair, is it?'

He forms an unholy alliance with his children that leaves her dangling at the apex of her triangle, frustrated at seeing no clear role for herself.

'He avoids confrontation, so it never gets resolved.'

'What can you do about it?'

'I leave them to their own devices as often as possible and lead my own independent life. It reduces the conflict between Tiffany, Mike and me but it seems to increase the distance between Adrian and me.'

'It sounds an impossibly difficult situation.'

'One thing's for sure. I'm *never* going to marry Adrian.'

'Oh? You've discussed the possibility with him, have you?'

'Well, not exactly.'

Agnes grins. 'I get the picture.'

'Why should I mother Adrian's children when he

refuses to consider the possibility of us having a baby?' Clare's voice rises.

There is a long silence.

Agnes slows her pedalling.

'I didn't know you were hanging out to have kids,' says Agnes in a very quiet voice.

Clare feels diffident about even raising the matter with Agnes, whose views on the subject are well known to all her friends. As for the men, well, it doesn't take them long to work it out. Agnes and babies? No way.

But Clare and babies?

Hello.

Chapter Three

Athena

In a corner of her bedroom on a low table draped with a white lace cloth Athena Wildblood, who in a previous life was known to friends and family as Elizabeth Casey, has set up a shrine to her namesake, the Greek goddess Athena. She sits cross-legged on faded Turkish cushions wearing a Kashmiri woollen shawl over her mauve T-shirt and tracksuit bottoms. On her feet are a pair of green-striped rugby socks. She gazes at the twenty-centimetre plaster statue of the virgin warrior and begins to recite an incantation she has recently composed. The little goddess with her helmet and shield who personifies wisdom and restraint never fails to give her solace.

She lights the two fat white candles arranged on saucers on either side of the altar and rings the Tibetan brass bell alongside her. Her crinkly hennaed hair is in danger of catching fire as she bends to light the incense sticks projecting from an aluminium stand. The atmosphere is soon pervaded by the sweet, woody scent of patchouli and the aroma of candlewax.

The door is closed. She is safe, she hopes, from the prying eyes of her daughter Jewel. Her knees ache. She has never fully mastered the half-lotus position.

Perhaps what she is experiencing is an early-warning twinge of arthritis in her knees. Something else for her to worry about.

'Oh, daughter of Zeus,' murmurs Athena to her protectress. 'You who can persuade an olive tree to grow from a rock.'

She strokes the amethyst she is holding in her hands to access its healing powers, focusing her attention on the crystal until she begins to feel herself fusing with the energy residing inside it. Breathing in love, breathing out negativity.

She gets off to a promising start, repeating her mantra for at least sixty seconds before the first stray thoughts emerge, like sea creatures from the depths, with myriad beckoning arms, to tempt her. A replay of a conversation with Agnes about her new young lover. Agnes had admitted (under duress) that her latest lover is a mere student. Why doesn't she find someone nice of her own age? Why does she always have to have a lover anyway? Athena returns reluctantly to her mantra. An itch under her right arm distracts her. A dull ache in her lower back. Then she's too hot. Her shawl is discarded.

The thoughts of Agnes and her torrid love life continue, maddeningly, to exert a powerful grip on her imagination. How is it that Agnes finds it so easy to attract lovers, while she appears to be fated to remain forever alone and yearning?

'But aren't you terrified of AIDS?' Athena has often asked her friend.

'I don't take risks, it's not worth it. But at the same time I'm not going to live like a bloody nun just because I don't happen to be in a serious relationship.'

It's been ten years since Athena allowed a man anywhere near her. She had shuddered. 'I just don't understand. What do you get out of it?'

'A good fuck,' Agnes had laughed. 'Plus, if I'm lucky, a great hugger, or someone who can entertain me with his wit.'

Athena achieves another half-dozen repetitions of her mantra before her mind is once again seduced by trivia. Her eyes open and are mesmerized by a dustball beneath her shrine. And another under her bed. A spider's web taunts her from the corner of her ceiling. The paint on the skirting boards is chipped. Her whole room is in need of an urgent spring clean. When will she ever get on top of the tasks in her life? Be able to relax because everything is under control? Managed. Sorted. Painted. Repaired.

The nuns taught them to examine their consciences daily. From habit Athena has maintained the practice of vacuuming hers last thing every evening.

The mantra!

Athena closes her eyes again and makes another attempt to harness her unruly thoughts, to breathe slowly, deeply, and with awareness. But just when she has settled into a steady rhythm, her reverie is interrupted by her daughter pounding on the bedroom door.

'Mum!'

Athena struggles to her feet and hurries to the door, closing it behind her. 'What do you want?'

'I want the car.'

'You can't have it. I might want to go out later.'

Goddess forgive her for telling a white lie. Well, she might have to go to the shop for a litre of milk. Anyway, why should Jewel automatically assume she can commandeer her mother's car any time she wants?

Her daughter is out of control. She hates everybody, everything. Opposition to her demands flips Jewel into a tantrum. On the slightest pretext she will berate her mother for her failure to provide the right environment, latest gear, the kind of food Jewel craves. The

45

list of Athena's shortcomings is endless.

'Why wasn't I born into a *normal* family?' shouts Jewel. Her face contorts into an expression calculated to inflict maximum pain on her mother. She ticks off her litany of complaints on her fingers.

'My mother's a New Age fruitcake. My father left because he couldn't stand you. No brothers and sisters. You never have any bloody money. We live in a shit heap. Eat rabbit food. You dress like a hippie in your ridiculous dolphin leggings and mauve T-shirts. You do it deliberately to humiliate me in front of my friends. No-one else has a mother like you.'

Athena gapes at her.

With a shout, Jewel sweeps two of Athena's prized crystals from the mantelpiece. They fall to the floor with a resounding crash. Athena gasps and runs over to pick them up and inspect for damage. This only rouses Jewel to new heights of abuse.

Stupid bitch. Crystal crone. Pathetic excuse for a mother. Shit for brains. Space cadet. You care more about those fucking rocks than you do about me.

Athena cringes, her face a picture of bewilderment. 'I don't understand why you are always so angry.'

'You don't get it, do you, *mother goddess*,' taunts Jewel. 'You're a fucking *embarrassment*. A *cunt*.'

Jewel storms from the house. Athena suspects she is off to see a boyfriend. She can only speculate; naturally she is never kept informed.

Distraught, Athena spies through the window as Jewel climbs into Athena's car and speeds off into the distance. At this moment she doesn't care if she never sees her again, although she would like her car to be returned in one piece. She briefly considers changing the locks and kicking her daughter out, leaving her to fend for herself. It would serve her right.

Athena is fed up with the bickering. If only she had

listened when she was a girl to the voices in her head pleading with her to enter the convent. If only Jewel's soul had seen fit to rebirth itself in some other mother's belly.

Clare's, for instance. Except that Clare has always been paranoid about contraception. No man was allowed near her without a bullet-proof condom, even if Clare was already on the pill.

'You can't be too careful,' Clare always said. And: 'There's no such thing as an accident.'

These sorts of comments have always been badly received by Athena, who has waited and watched for more than twenty years for Clare to slip up and prove she is human like everybody else.

Athena puts on the kettle to make herself a cup of Red Zinger. Drained of emotion, she slumps into a cane easy chair with her steaming mug while she waits for her bath to run. Just as well it's Saturday. She won't have to put a brave face on for her massage clients.

'I must,' she murmurs to herself, 'I must . . .'

Must what? She must pull herself together, that's what. She should set clearly defined boundaries. Tell her daughter that she simply will not be spoken to in such a way. But will it make any difference?

Athena soaks in her fragrant rose-scented bath staring up at the walls and ceiling of her pink bathroom. *Mum, do you realize you have absolutely no taste?* She observes for the umpteenth time that the room is in need of a paint.

Tears prick her eyes. Why is it so difficult being a mother? Why didn't someone warn her? If this is simply a phase she and Jewel are going through, please Goddess, let it end soon before one of them kills or maims the other.

Athena remembers Jewel as a four-year-old. A head-turner with shiny curls and blue eyes. A little girl who thrived on routine and the security of meals at set times, hair brushing at seven, story at seven-fifteen, bed at seven-thirty. A child who was wary of surprises or secrets.

Now she has spiky bleached hair and her black clothes and heavy black boots are a daily affront to the pastel-clad Athena.

But when did she last have any semblance of control over Jewel's behaviour and thoughts? It's patently obvious Jewel now cares only about herself. Athena has almost given up. She may as well talk to the wall. At least the wall doesn't answer back.

'Cunt.'

Imagine. She would never have dreamed of addressing her own mother in such a fashion. Athena's tears slide down her cheeks and onto her neck. Why does her daughter hate her? More important, why isn't she standing up to Jewel?

When Athena was sixteen she had felt vulnerable and confused, and terrified of men. At seventeen, by this time at university, it was inevitable that she fall easy prey to the sybaritic Sebastian. She remembers being dazzled by his wit, in awe of his knowledge of fine food and wine, and impressed by his apparently effortless A grades. She never saw him study. Nobody did. Later when she knew him better she saw through his pettiness and his cruelty. She discovered the real Sebastian, a young man deeply insecure and full of self-loathing. She realized that his supposedly easy path through university had been the result of determined and systematically applied effort. He worked while others were sleeping and slept while they breakfasted and set about their morning. No-one ever saw him before lunch. He generally awoke in a foul mood and shaved ferociously, glaring at himself in the mirror and inevitably inflicting a small cut. This little foible in someone who was normally so fastidious had always surprised Athena. Sebastian cultivated his image assiduously – a long fur coat and corresponding fur hat in winter – this was before animal rights were an issue. In summer he wore immaculate cream trousers, matching cream silk shirt and a crisp panama hat.

'Not a poof, is he, Lizzie?' Athena's father had asked her discreetly, on first meeting his daughter's boyfriend.

Sebastian had been her first lover. Why had he chosen someone as inexperienced as her – someone so naive and lacking in confidence? Not long after she met Sebastian and they became lovers, she lost her nerve. There was a distinct moment in the relationship when she knew she was poised on the brink of a precipice, unwilling to retreat, yet uncertain about committing herself further.

She had stopped attending Mass on a regular basis and the guilt associated with this lapse, as well as the pressure she was under from her parents with their narrow-minded judgements (she was 'living in sin'), caused her much distress.

In desperation she arranged to meet her old mentor, Father Pat Flannery. He had taken them for religious instruction in the seventh form. Agnes and Clare had from the beginning challenged him remorselessly. She and Bridget had become fond of him despite the fact that they often disagreed with his opinions. Their questions and doubts never seemed to affect his easy good-humoured response to them. Of the four she was the only one who had maintained the contact. She saw him as an avuncular figure, more approachable than her own father.

They met at his suggestion in a small luncheon bar where the coffee was weak and bitter and the food execrable. Triangular white bread sandwiches curling at the edges, dried-out sausage rolls, Scotch eggs, limp lettuce, spaghetti already baked hard on stale white hamburger buns in the warmer. Leaky custard squares, huge calorie-laden cream sponges. Everything in the café interior was a shade of brown, beige or mustard. Patterns and surfaces clashed. Athena's lip curled at the nasty pottery cups and plates. Strongly influenced by Sebastian, she had become a snob. She was still at this stage Elizabeth Casey. 'Lizzie' had not yet transformed herself into Athena Wildblood, healer and masseuse.

'It's on me, Lizzie,' Father Pat insisted.

She protested politely but was relieved when he overrode her.

'Come on, eat up. I'll bet you don't get enough to eat in that flat of yours.'

He didn't know Sebastian, who had standards, and always lived way beyond his means. He gave the impression of being so knowledgeable about finances that Athena had already learned to defer to him. If he required loans to tide him over rather more frequently than she would have liked he more than made up for it in other ways. She dined well thanks to Sebastian. Probably better than Father Pat, whose housekeeper, he informed her, was an uninspired cook. Lizzie was irritated by his assumption that priests (unlike nuns) shouldn't be required to sully their precious hands with cooking or cleaning.

She decided on a cheese scone as being the safest choice, and a pot of tea. They found a table by the window facing the street. She sipped her tea and marvelled. This was grown-up stuff. Here she was in the company of a priest. Not in a confessional, nor in the presence of her teachers or parents, but on her own.

She studied him covertly, both repelled and fascinated by the sight of his ageing body, at the hairs sprouting from his nostrils, his ears and eyebrows, in such abundance, at the bobbing turkey gizzard of an Adam's apple. She recalled with a certain amount of smugness the smooth, hairless, lean shape of her lover's body. How could this fuddy-duddy old priest possibly understand or remember what it was like to skip lectures and tutorials for days on end while you fucked as if there was no tomorrow?

'What's on your mind, Lizzie? You haven't brought me here to pass the time of day, have you, girl?'

His kindly red face with its receding hairline and prominent nose was as safe and familiar to her as those of her own family. The grey eyes under the roof of his errant black eyebrows regarded his pusillanimous former pupil with wry amusement.

She suspected that she would always be perceived by Father Pat as just a girl. How old did she have to be before she was taken seriously and treated as an adult?

He waited patiently for her to speak. They must learn that from sitting cramped in the confessional hour after tedious hour listening to endless litanies of petty sins and misdemeanours, she supposed. What husbands they would make.

Sebastian, unfortunately, had proved not to be a listener. She had believed, naively as it turned out, that it was possible to change him. Their love would transform him into a better person. It hadn't taken her long to realize that he considered himself to be perfect just the way he was.

'Are we here to discuss the nature of sin, Lizzie? Is this what you've dragged me here for?'

She took courage from his sympathetic expression. 'I suppose so,' she admitted.

The idea of discussing sin with all its myriad associations, in this overtly secular environment, seemed both bizarre and incongruous to her. Sin, hell and punishment belonged more properly at her parents' home, her old school classroom and parish church. How could it have the remotest connection with the dingy little lunch bar with its fake Austrian decor?

Athena stared dully at the pattern on the table-cloth, as if she might find there the answers she sought.

Above her the windows were festooned with drooping bunches of gingham frills. Grimy net café curtains screened the diners from the curious gazes of passers-by. A large doll in traditional Austrian folk costume stood astride an old beer barrel.

A squat, bosomy, middle-aged waitress, wearing a frilled gingham apron and white puffed-sleeved blouse, heaved her broad-hipped body between the little tables. She dumped Father Pat's goulash soup on the checked tablecloth.

He gulped a mouthful and grimaced.

'As bad as that, is it?'

''Fraid so. Tomato purée and mixed veg, straight out of their cans. Unadulterated.'

He poured generous amounts of pepper and salt over the soup.

'I've wrecked it now, but what the hell,' he said with a frown after a second sip. He solemnly chewed on a piece of dry toast.

'Go on then, surprise me,' he said. He looked at her quizzically.

Athena's mind immediately drained of words, as if he had pulled the plug on a basin full of water. *Why are we born? Should I be with Sebastian? Will I be punished?*

'I don't know where to start,' she had bleated, knowing she was being utterly pathetic.

He sat back in his chair, arms folded, the last crust of toast demolished between his discoloured crooked teeth. He had reminded her of a tired old spaniel. Would he judge her? Embarrass her?

He propped his elbows on the table, rested his chin in his hands, let out a deep sigh before launching himself into the discussion.

'Let me guess. You've met a man. You fancy yourself madly in love with him. He's the one you've been waiting for. The stuff of dreams. You've been at it like jack rabbits ever since. Only now you're consumed by guilt. *What have I done?*' Father Pat's eyebrows shot up in mock dismay. 'And now you want me to absolve you. To tell you it doesn't matter a damn, you haven't committed any sins and all will be forgiven and forgotten. Isn't that right, Lizzie?'

'I—'

'Yes or no?' he said brusquely.

'Yes.'

'All right then. Do you believe you are sinning, Lizzie?'

Athena had taken her time to reply. 'No,' she said honestly.

'To commit a sin, you must have the awareness of sin. You tell me now you don't have this knowledge or belief.'

'It doesn't *feel* like a sin, Father.'

'So why the guilt afterwards, then?'

'I can't help it.' Oh God, she was being pathetic again.

He leaned forward over the table, inadvertently spilling the remains of his soup. 'I don't *want* your guilt,' he said fiercely, dabbing the wet tablecloth with his serviette. 'And God doesn't either.'

She blinked. Tears sprang into her eyes. She couldn't bear him being angry with her. She felt crushed and stupid.

'It's not that I want to think of myself as a sinner, Father,' she said.

He brushed his hand wearily over his forehead as if burdened to an unbearable degree by the mountain of sins to which he had been compelled to listen over the past two decades.

'Call me, Pat,' he said. 'You're a grown woman now.'

But was she? Even at nineteen Athena didn't consider herself a grown woman. She wasn't ready for the responsibility. Part of her still hung back from fully embracing adult life. She was uncomfortable with the familiarity of 'Pat'. Priests were meant to keep their distance, while still being available. To be all-knowing without being all-seeing.

'I'm afraid of the consequences of my actions.' She was crying by then, having abandoned any pretence at appearing adult and sophisticated.

'No-one can predict the consequences of changes in your life. But you have to start somewhere, one step at a time. Do your best, that's all anyone can do.' He passed her a clean white handkerchief.

She wiped her face and blew her nose. 'What if my best isn't good enough?'

'It has to be. Thanks to your parents and the good nuns you have what we call an *informed* conscience.'

Where had it got her?

'From those to whom much is given, much is expected,' he muttered.

'What was that?'

'Nothing. Claptrap I should have thrown out years ago.'

He patted her hand in a clumsy yet well-intentioned

attempt to reassure her. She had flinched at the contact.

You didn't touch priests.

They didn't touch you.

No hugging. Even when obliged to present her face for a peck on the cheek she held the lower part of her body away from him as if the merest contact might constitute a sin.

It didn't take much to sin.

When he left she had felt oddly comforted. He had been perfectly accurate in his assessment. All she had wanted was someone to tell her what to do, what was right.

Whenever Athena recalls this confused and troubling period of her life, she wonders why it took her so long to reach the point where she was able to accept responsibility for herself and trust her own responses.

Afterwards she had admitted to Sebastian that she had made contact with her old confessor.

He had laughed in disbelief. 'My God. They have brainwashed you, haven't they? It's all crap, Lizzie, can't you see?'

But she hadn't been ready to relinquish the old comforting beliefs, the familiar phrases that promised forgiveness and redemption.

He shook his head. 'I'll never understand you.'

True. He didn't ever come close to understanding her or meeting her needs.

She never saw Father Pat again. He became one of the people she mislaid in her twenties. Along with the duller of her old school friends and relatives, he was consigned to the scrap heap. When she realized, too late, that she had lost more than she had gained in this inevitable process of discarding people, she had by then lost contact, her address book was outdated.

Fragments of her past could no longer be reassembled.

Many years later Athena was interested to learn that Father Pat had, like them, bailed out, traded in his soutane for a wife and kids. She had even heard, although she found it hard to credit, that his wife was a former nun from their old convent. He had seemed an old man to her at the time. Now she realized he couldn't have been more than forty-five when they had last met.

'Bet he'd been having it off for years and got away with it. What a hypocrite,' said Clare.

'Good on him, I say,' approved Agnes.

'Absolutely,' Bridget had agreed. 'It was a courageous thing to do. Obviously he must have felt he was living a lie, why else would he have left?'

'He was good to me.' Athena felt obliged to defend him. 'You could talk to him. He listened. He didn't always judge.'

'You must have caught him at a good moment. That wasn't my experience of him,' remembered Clare.

'Naturally. You were always so tough on him. I'm amazed you weren't expelled, Clare.'

'Priests *should* be open to challenge. The Church has a lot to answer for.'

At the beginning, neither Athena nor Sebastian had any intention of settling down permanently. Why should they? Marriage was for 'straights' who wanted to rot away in the suburbs. But with Jewel soon on the way, Athena's father had laid down the law.

If he hadn't, reflects Athena seventeen years later, as she soaks in her sanity-restoring bath, Sebastian might have pissed off and she might have had an abortion. Which might not have been a bad thing, considering how Jewel has turned out. Tough love, that's what's required now – if it's not too late.

Thank the Goddess she only has the one child. Not that she hadn't been tempted when she was first with Roger. Imagine two Jewels – or, perish the thought, three. Clare and Bridget have no idea how difficult and unpredictable motherhood can be. It's not only the sacrifice of time and career, money and opportunities, it's also the realization that in the end your best efforts have been wasted. And forget about gratitude. Jewel has no memories of the love her mother has unstintingly bestowed on her throughout her childhood. It is small consolation to Athena that she can recall little of the experience of her own mother's love and devotion in *her* early childhood. Let alone establish the connection between the cheerful woman in her early sixties with bright dyed hair and the unhappily married, frustrated, dutiful Catholic mum who had trotted off to Mass every Sunday dragging her complaining children behind her.

Athena is delighted that her mother has broken free. She began by leaving her husband as soon as the last child left home, got herself a job at the local plant nursery and studied horticulture by correspondence. Fifteen years later she has her own herb shop, selling not only plants and herbal remedies but also crystals and essential oils. She even has a lover ten years her junior.

'Follow your dreams, darling,' she urges Athena. But how is Athena expected to do this when her house is completely permeated with Jewel's negative energy? At least her bedroom is untainted – thanks to her crystals – one placed strategically in each of the four corners of her room. Negative energy has a tendency to hang out in the corners of rooms.

Athena has a theory: she has encountered Jewel before in a previous life. There are ancient issues she and Jewel have to work out in the present. She doesn't yet know what they are but she is confident that at the right time all will be revealed.

It's bad karma, brought into this life.

Naturally she does not discuss this particular theory with Clare, who would, predictably, respond with scorn and derision.

But how else to explain Athena's tormented relationship with Jewel?

'It's not my bloody fault!' shouts Athena into the empty room. Who cares if the neighbours hear?

Her phone rings and there is the sound of her recorded message as the answerphone switches on. She listens. A client wanting to book in for a massage. She decides that she'll return the call in the morning when she's feeling more energized.

Athena has been told, although she cannot recall the precise identity of her informant, that most people experience a low period at least seven times every day. It is disheartening for her to conclude that in the end she is as much at the mercy of her fluctuating moods as the next person – and just as mystified by the feelings of fear, grief, anger, or anxiety that seem to float into her consciousness without warning, and often without obvious reason or meaning, at every hour of the day.

How can this be after the vast quantities of affirmations and visualizations she does, the soothing qualities of essential oils she burns on a daily basis, her struggles to meditate and gain enlightenment, to adopt a vegetarian diet, to maintain a healthy lifestyle, to get plenty of sleep and regular exercise?

With Jewel out until all hours with God knows who, Athena is again poignantly reminded of her aloneness. She longs for a soulmate. Someone who will understand and believe she has been a good mother. She has tried. Ask Clare, Agnes or Bridget. They have witnessed and advised, sharing the anguish of Athena being abandoned by Sebastian the Sadist, and subsequently by Roger the Rat. The latter had, she discovered after the break-up, already propositioned her friends and been turned down by all of them — so they said. Athena speculates about Agnes. The degree to which she likes men and claims to enjoy sex puzzles Athena. But Roger?

If only she had someone to listen to her problems and give her support. She has recently tried to visualize her ideal. But the identity, even the sex, of the soulmate continues to elude her. Perhaps it is a woman. A survivor like herself. Someone who can identify with her situation and help her to improve it. A gentle man might be OK. But the trouble is, even a gentle man who has done some personal growth is bound, sooner or later, to expect sex to be on offer. She has read the books, knows what she should have felt while in bed with Sebastian the Stud.

She's never been with a woman. It can only be an improvement on her experiences with the men who have strayed into her life.

As she lies in the bath, every now and then letting a bit out and topping up with hot water, she begins to imagine a woman soulmate.

A toe reaches up to turn a tap. She doesn't know many lesbians. If she becomes a lesbian does it mean she'll have to throw out her make-up? She likes lipstick.

And where will she meet her soulmate? She'd be too nervous to wander by herself into one of those clubs.

Whatever she does she'll have to keep it a secret from Jewel.

Athena continues to linger in her bath. She studies the body that she imagines sharing with a soulmate.

She's let herself go.

If she struggles to muster enthusiasm for her body, how can she expect someone else to love it with a forgiving and uncritical eye? Even in her twenties she was 'cuddly'. When she was a teenager, her family tactfully referred to it as puppy fat. What had Sebastian or Roger seen in her? She can't believe that either man had been smitten solely by her personality.

What does the merciless Jewel see? A wimpy mother who is attempting to believe in herself by working at her affirmations.

'I can read you like a book, mother goddess.'

Athena has an unpleasant recollection of Jewel's rasp-like voice sawing away in her ear.

'I can tell from the slightest wiggle of your eyebrow what you're thinking.'

Athena cries and cries. And of course Jewel will notice the state of her face and respond without a pang of conscience, let alone a drop of sympathy. For Jewel never cries. She has a chip of flint inside her chest instead of a heart.

When will the pain stop? The problem of Jewel looms as large and formidable as an iceberg on Athena's horizon.

Jewel on the phone recently to a friend: 'Mum is spazzing out again. Going ballistic. I have to go now — she wants the line to commune with one of her crystal crones.' This was followed by a shrill outburst of mocking laughter.

Daydreaming, Athena dries herself slowly. Until she catches sight of herself again, this time in the mirror.

You'd be all right, Lizzie, if it weren't for those hips.

Sebastian. A change of name has not succeeded in silencing the anxieties and humiliations of the old Lizzie with her almost craven desire to please. The name, those voices, they still have a claim on her.

She allows the towel to fall, revealing her breasts.

Nice breasts.

Pity about the thick ankles.

Athena places a hand beneath each dewy melon, cups them together creating a magnificent cleavage. What must it be like to suck, nibble, bite, lick such treasures? How lucky men are to have access to women. Who is out there waiting to take an interest in her? Will she be touched again in this lifetime?

Athena has never known what it is like to be nurtured by a devoted man. All her life she has received her emotional support from women. How did she survive the endless compromising demanded of her in the relationships with Sebastian and Roger? Suffering Sebastian's inexplicable rages, enduring Roger's unpredictable moods, feeling both confused and battered by the inescapable torrents of abuse launched at her on a daily basis.

Eventually Sebastian, and later Roger, had moved on to graze in greener pastures.

Good riddance, decides Athena.

She saw Sebastian only the other week, after a gap of almost a year.

Naturally he had ignored her, unless, thought Athena, he was becoming short-sighted in his middle age. Patently still searching for eternal youth, and, according to Jewel, working out with weights obsessively at the gym. Dating younger and younger women.

There he was for all to see – a spectacle swaggering down Ponsonby Road in his Gaultier dress and bleached hair (yes, it was true, he was wearing a dress), across from where Athena, Clare and Agnes sat outside a café at a pavement table enjoying their Sunday coffee. From their vantage point they were able to

61

observe the peevish expression now permanently etched on his face.

'Pitiful,' said Clare, her eyes bright with malice. 'Bet he's got a small dick – you can tell from the walk. Am I right, Athena?'

Chapter Four

Bridget

Bridget has spent most of the morning on a thigh and one nipple.

Getting flesh to look right is always a trial, not helped this time by the fact that she has miscalculated and mixed an insufficient amount of her base colour. She scrapes the dregs of acrylic off her plastic palette in an old sink already encrusted with several skins of paint and begins to mix a fresh batch, testing it at intervals by daubing a smear onto a piece of watercolour paper and buzzing it with a blow-drier. She places each test swatch alongside the section on the painting she is trying to match until she gets it right.

Although Bridget mutters and grumbles to herself, she actually doesn't mind being this painstaking. It's part of the craft. The beauty of acrylics is that she can't really mess it up. It's a forgiving medium; her style has adapted to accommodate its particular idiosyncrasies. Quick drying, you can't scrub or overwork. Once she has her idea, her subject, and the composition sorted, she paints by instinct, applying the paint in swift energetic strokes, leaving confident gestural marks to create the effect she wants.

Nothing much on the radio this morning. Kim Hill interviewing yet another politician. She continues to daub away at the woman's leg with dwindling enthusiasm. A tear drops onto her overalls, followed by another until she is weeping at her easel. Perhaps she has PMT. At the reminder of yet another period on its way she breaks into a more intense fit of crying. Kim and the politician in the background are a Greek chorus apportioning blame, analysing past mistakes, gazing bleakly into the future. Who is responsible? Who will pay?

'Ratepayers will cough up, that's who, you great dork.' If she is having a bad day Bridget frequently berates Kim's interviewees.

Her shoulders heave. She is having a dark morning of the soul. Eat your heart out Thomas Aquinas . . . or was it John of the Cross? Who cares? One of those male mystics. She was always near the bottom of the class in religious studies, whereas Clare was invariably top, not because she was particularly interested in Catholic dogma but because she couldn't stand to be beaten at anything – especially by a boy.

Coffee time. Bridget shuts the door on her gloom and despair and steps out into the sunshine and her Grey Lynn subtropical garden. Twenty-six degrees and high humidity. Perspiration trickles between her breasts. An army of cicadas have set up an orchestra to cheer her. Nikau palms and tall stands of rampant scarlet cannas surround the converted shed at the bottom of the garden. Fleshy banana palms and taro leaves big as shields flap in the breeze. She trudges down the mosaic path she constructed from broken crockery and ceramic tiles, past brightly coloured bromeliads, clivias, strelitzia and the brugmansias with their opulent white trumpet flowers, past a stone fountain and birdbath, until she reaches the house. She's still

64

clutching her lifeline in the form of a little transistor radio. Her eyes and ears are blind and deaf to the stridulating of the cicadas and fecundity of the garden she has created with Matthew. Each unfurling frond and budding flower is a poignant reminder of her own infertility.

She puts on the kettle and goes into the bathroom. She glares at her face in the mirror – what good has it done her to be so beautiful? Men are generally intimidated by her appearance. At first meeting, women seem to expect her to be stuck up. Only Matthew understands. She knows that the two of them often give the impression of the ideal handsome happy couple and yet both are currently feeling as if someone has taken an ice cream scoop and carved out their insides.

Bridget looks around at her house, like Clare's, so perfect, so undisturbed and there wells up in her such an intense longing for a pair of sticky little fingerprints on the glazed French doors that she buckles at the knees.

She hasn't prayed for years. Not until this past year. Now she's making deals with God, impossible reckless deals where she would sell her soul if it would make a jot of difference.

She knows precisely when she ovulates. Once she wasn't aware of such a phenomenon. Her body released eggs or bled. Various parts of her anatomy ached or swelled up, depending on the time of month. She had always taken it all for granted. Not any more. She takes her temperature, has read all the books. She uses a diaphragm after sex to retain as much sperm as possible. If she has time she also remains in bed after morning sex, pelvis raised on a pillow to hang on to Matthew's precious cargo.

For the past three years a considerable proportion of

her waking hours and energy has been directed towards the idea of producing a baby. Even her paintings have begun to feature predominantly mother-child themes. Glorified madonnas.

In her twenties she put off the decision, focusing instead on establishing herself as a painter. She had not been interested back then in teaching, even though she was qualified. Before she had become known and her work sought after, she had subsidized her meagre income by casual waitressing and gardening – jobs that wouldn't absorb all the valuable energy she preferred to channel into her art.

Matthew had gone along with her wishes, even though the initial impetus to make a decision about a baby had come from him. He had always fancied himself as a father.

'It should have been you who was born the woman and I the man,' Bridget had lamented in her twenties when there seemed to be all the time in the world and they would remain young, talented, and beautiful for ever. She had experienced Matthew's wistful mention of babies as pressure. For it was indeed pressure, albeit lovingly but determinedly applied over the years. She would come across his pictures of appealing babies magnetized onto the fridge, the flush tank in the toilet, the full-length mirror in the bathroom. Once they had joked about it.

When had she begun to claim Matthew's fantasy as her own? Three years ago? Five?

Bridget has been with him since she was eighteen. She cannot conceive of a life that does not contain the comfort and security of Matthew as its centrepiece. It bothers her sometimes that they might be too close. She has, except for one small lapse in her early thirties, been faithful. She believes Matthew has too.

'You lead a charmed life, you and Matthew,' Agnes

has observed on more than one occasion.

It is perfectly true, she does. They're comfortable financially, thanks mainly to Matthew, she has to admit. It takes her two years to prepare for each exhibition, so he's supporting her.

Bridget has fantasies of teaching her child to draw. Naturally, any child of hers would be artistic. All her longings focused around the idea of a daughter. But these days she couldn't care less about the sex of her child. She will be undyingly grateful if it is healthy. If it has the right number of fingers and toes.

Bridget and Matthew have run through almost all their savings on attempts at in vitro fertilization, and they may as well, she thinks, have dug a big hole in the ground and buried their money in it for all the good it's done. Don't feel bitter, Matthew says. But why shouldn't she feel resentful? Sooner or later she knows she is going to have to face facts. A time will come when they will have to turn their backs on the fantasy of having a family and simply get on with their lives. But how do they make the transition? Switch direction, forget their longings and start afresh? And the worst aspect of their circumstances is that no-one seems to understand how painful an ordeal it has been.

'Nothing else matters,' she sobs to Matthew. 'I just want to be pregnant. I want it so very badly. Is it so much to ask for?'

She is eighteen again. Meeting Matthew for the first time. She has been observing him all evening at a student party. They have been shyly circling each other trying to gauge the extent of the other's interest. He has long glossy dark hair and a happy friendly face. There is no trace of the suave young lawyer he will eventually become. Her antennae, finely tuned, are reassured. Nothing about Matthew appears to be threatening. Nevertheless, from habit she proceeds with caution. She recalls being very stoned. Did they dance together? Yes, of course they did. Matthew was an innovative dancer. She wore a loose ankle-length cheesecloth dress that floated sensually about her slim body. She was barefoot.

Matthew? Patched jeans, boots, a filmy white Indian embroidered shirt through which she glimpsed a delectably smooth tanned chest.

He disarmed her with his gentleness.

She drifted into his arms and later that evening into his bed without a backward glance. She felt as if she had always known him and sensed instinctively that he would protect her from the glare of the world, from the unwelcome advances of men she mistrusted and feared.

He would become her rock, her shield.

She was perfectly content. Matthew likewise was perfectly content. He was adored, respected and given a clearly defined role to play and he responded with enthusiasm. He was not reluctant to commit. Nor was she. She had no doubt they would last for ever and ever.

Together they considered and evaluated her talent. Her painting must come first. Children could wait.

Why oh why had they waited, agonizes Bridget twenty years later. She is swept up in an unbearable wave of grief and regret.

Isolated in her pain, Bridget wonders who she can confide in. Agnes has never shown the slightest interest in having a child. Athena's experience of mothering has caused her nothing but heartache over the past five years. This leaves Clare.

'I'll have the seafood chowder. What about you?'
'Same.'

The café is crowded with office workers, men and women in expensive stylish suits. A Miles Davis track weaves its way through the intermittent roar of the espresso machine, the whirr of the coffee grinder, the clatter of white cups being stacked and the competing buzz of a dozen animated conversations.

'So . . . how are you?' asks Clare, determined to catch the eye of the waiter.

'Frustrated. Obsessed.'

Clare scarcely dares ask the obvious. 'Do you know why you can't have a baby?'

Bridget gives a hollow laugh. 'You mean, which of us is to blame? Matthew or me? At first the doctor thought it was Matthew, his sperm count was too low. He was sent to a urologist. Then they thought we might have incompatible mucus. Basically, they don't know, they can't explain. We've done the rounds, the gynae-cologists, the IVF specialists. We're the unfortunate statistic – the one couple in ten who can't manage it.'

She sips her chilled water. The past few years have been a nightmarish round of blood tests, urine samples, thermometers, temperature charts and, when she was on the treatment programme, the hormone injections to stimulate ovulation, the agonizing over releasing eggs, wondering if they would fertilize. And on and on. A roller coaster and still no end in sight.

Clare pats her hand awkwardly. 'How far are you prepared to go?'

'All the way,' says Bridget adamantly.

Clare nods. 'You know, when Adrian and I got together he was very relieved I didn't want to have children, because he certainly didn't want any more. Now he accuses me of changing the rules on him.'

'What do you mean?'

'I've decided I do want a baby, after all. He's most put out.'

'Surprise, surprise.'

'The latest – he's now threatening to have a vasectomy.'

'Is he serious?' Bridget moves her water glass to make space for the chowders.

'Very. I think he's scared I might put one across him – pretend I'm on the pill when I'm not.'

'You aren't?'

'Of course I am. You know me. Besides, I have no desire whatsoever to become a solo parent. It's too difficult.'

'How much does he see of the two kids he already has?'

'Plenty. We have them every second weekend, two weeknights and most holidays.'

A Samoan waiter with the kind of biceps that bear witness to a punishing gym routine edges past their table. Clare orders another mineral water.

'Another flat white,' says Bridget. 'Think Adrian will change his mind?'

'I'm working on it.'

Bridget finds unexpected respite from her own pain in sharing Clare's dilemma.

'What's the bottom line? How much do you want a baby? Enough to leave Adrian if he won't agree to play Daddy with you?'

'I don't know. It's not that simple. If I leave him I mightn't find anyone else I can love who is also prepared to have a baby.'

'True,' agrees Bridget. 'It's a risk you'd have to be prepared to take.'

'And I'm no chicken, you know.'

Bridget knows all the odds. It's been her major preoccupation for three years. 'By the time you're thirty-nine,' she says, 'it can take you up to fifteen months to fall pregnant.'

'You're joking, of course.'

'And that's in optimum conditions.'

'They write books about people like us,' says Clare. 'You know, the women who graduated in the mid to late seventies. We had the pill, we had been socialized against having a family, career was everything. We deferred motherhood. Look at us now.'

'Yeah, but we had some good times, didn't we?'

'Would you do it any other way if we could start again?' asks Clare, deep in thought.

'D'you know, I can't answer that. I wanted so badly to become a good painter. The way I feel right now I couldn't care less about my achievements. They mean nothing to me. I've always assumed that when I was good and ready I would just pop out a baby. No problem. It was only a matter of *when*, not *if*. Now I feel as if I may have to completely rewrite the script of what my future is to be.'

Bridget gulps. Tears glimmer in her eyes. Little crystals of hopelessness and defeat. She can't bring herself to admit to Clare that once she had howled for nearly three weeks. Grieving day after day in her studio until she couldn't enter it any more. But one day she had simply stopped, and recommenced her painting. 'I have no more tears inside me,' she had announced to Matthew. But of course she had been mistaken. There was an avalanche of emotion still inside her waiting to be released.

They split their bill and walk together to the car park.

She begins to cry again.

'You won't always feel this way,' Clare reassures her, putting an arm round her. 'This time next year you might feel completely different, you'll see.'

Bridget pulls away abruptly. '*Don't* tell me how I should think.'

71

Clare is taken aback. 'I didn't mean—'

'I *won't* feel better. I can't bloody have kids and I don't believe I'm *ever* going to feel better,' she says fiercely. 'I'm a failure.'

Passers-by give them odd looks. Clare ignores them. She shepherds Bridget away.

'It's not something you get *over!*' yells Bridget. 'It's something you *endure*. Something so fucking *fundamental*.'

There's a long silence. The lift reaches the floor where Clare keeps her car.

'Shit. I'm *sorry*. Didn't mean to crack up on you like this.'

'I wish I had some answers,' says Clare. She too is weeping.

They walk to the car. Clare unlocks the door for Bridget and goes round to the driver's side.

'Why are *you* crying?' asks Bridget in a cold little voice when Clare has settled herself in her seat and clicked her belt into place.

'Feelings can be contagious,' answers Clare.

'You have *nothing* to cry about. How can you possibly have the faintest idea what we've been through with IVF? The hopes dashed. The time wasted, the indignities, the shame. The recriminations when Matthew and I have taken out our disappointment and frustration on each other. No-one in the world but Matthew can truly appreciate what I've been through, and even he doesn't know the half of it. I cry at the silliest things. Hopeless. Why can't I just get *on* with my life? Why can't I stop experiencing terrible yearnings for what I *can't* have?'

'It must be just awful for you.' Clare delays starting up the car and twists her body to face Bridget.

Bridget puts her head in her hands, her body quivering with pent-up emotion. She gropes for Clare's hand.

72

'I do understand,' admits Clare. 'I keep myself so busy I don't allow myself time to feel much, but if I stop and think about it I feel sad and hurt that Adrian couldn't give a damn about having a child with me.'

Bridget stops crying and raises her head. She looks across at Clare, meeting her eyes.

'How can Adrian refuse you? It's so unfair. If he really loved you he would give you a child.'

'You may find this difficult to believe, but I can see Adrian's point of view. He already has children and can you blame him if his divorce has tarnished the idea of happy families?'

'*Yes,*' says Bridget adamantly. 'If I were you I would refuse to give up.'

Chapter Five

Agnes

Agnes arrives at the advertising agency at nine for a briefing meeting. She is kept waiting in reception for twenty minutes. Par for the course. This particular agency is notorious for being disorganized and for treating its freelancers in a cavalier fashion. It still pisses her off no end.

The ubiquitous pretty young receptionist, a Cameron Diaz clone with a put-on breathy Marilyn Monroe voice, brings her coffee. It's obvious the poor woman makes the most of every opportunity to emerge from behind her steel reception façade. In the interval between coming over to inform herself as to how Agnes prefers her coffee and disappearing to procure it, Agnes and the other visitor, a male sales rep, are treated to a performance of appealing little baby pouts, giggles, simpers, knowing conspiratorial looks, pretend scowls, raised eyebrows (milk *and* sugar?), seductive glances tossed over the shoulder to titillate the rep. She variously saunters, swaggers, minces, then finally, climactically, bends to lower the coffee tray allowing them a calculated but fleeting eyeful of pert little breasts.

Agnes struggles to contain herself. She doesn't dare catch the eye of the rep. The young woman is in the throes of an identity crisis. Geisha? Hooker? Glamour queen? Girl next door? Waif?

She is shown into a large square room decorated in the style of an old pub-cum-church. It too is having an identity crisis, she notes. Heavy stripped worm-eaten beams create the illusion of supporting a ceiling. The floor is roughly painted concrete. Crudely carved wooden folk statues of saints and madonnas in gaudy colours are ensconced in carved wall niches. Candles stand on a wooden slab at mantelpiece height. Beneath is a video monitor and recorder. Black-garbed staff are huddled on wooden pews around a scrubbed kauri table.

No-one at the agency boardroom table is over twenty-five. Agnes knows this because they asked each other after they saw the Polaroids she had brought in. No-one thought to ask Agnes her age, and naturally she didn't volunteer it. She's not about to slit her own throat. Not when she is working in such a youth-driven market. This agency is no exception, having sourced the requisite creative playpen crammed with boys with attitude who have become the new taste gurus – the 'cool spotters'. The gospel according to the word out on the street. When they're not out snowboarding, or at raves, they're feeling the pulse of 'Gen-X' by osmosis, discovering, using, thrashing and, ultimately, trashing, the minute a style has become mainstream. They're recycling culture at breakneck speed, turning traditional marketing approaches upside down. Seeking or inventing the next new trend to flog it, attaching it to either a new 'smart' drink, or to the plethora of fast-moving consumer goods – soap to cereals, catfood to nappies.

Agnes's mind is full of useless pieces of information. She knows, for example, that catfood is one of the four biggest-selling fast-moving consumer goods in the New Zealand market. She knows where the art director has purchased his shirt, the brand of fragrance he is wearing, the market share of the particular brand of biscuits on the plate in front of her. Yet . . . she also suspects that she is no longer in the driver's seat. Change is occurring faster than she can process it. The art director and copywriter form a cosy clique which excludes her. She has no desire to form anything other than a professional association with them. She is bored by the dance parties. She would rather be crawling into her bed at midnight than beginning to apply her lipstick having just slipped into a sexy little black number ready to dance the night away.

'How old is she?' The art director frowns at the test shots.

'A well-preserved thirty-six.'

'She *could* pass for thirty,' says the stylist. 'With the right lighting.'

Agnes observes them coolly. Their contempt. Their judgements. The complete absence of the subversive or the radical. Confined by their own 'cool quotient'.

By the end of the meeting, although everybody had originally agreed to use an older model, the age will be lowered as usual to around eighteen or nineteen. And Agnes will be briefed to produce yet another shot of another half-starved-looking waif without tits or thighs.

'She looks very lived-in.' The art director tosses a Polaroid back onto the pile of rejects. He opens a canister of Beroccas. There is a fizzing sound as the tablet dissolves in his glass of water.

'Heavy night,' he says.

Agnes sighs. Is she going off the boil? She simply

cannot take this work seriously. No-one other than her gives a damn that this particular fashion chain is actually selling most of its garments to women over thirty. She picks up one of the rejected model tear sheets. It wouldn't matter who the woman was. There would always be something that wasn't quite perfect.

Also, it wouldn't matter what the product was, she thinks, because the idea would be to eroticize it. Not that anyone came right out and said: 'OK, now eroticize it.' But it was understood all the same. Just about anything or anyone could be remade sexy. Sexier. If you threw enough money and technology at the problem. There is always a point at which these meetings come to seem very surreal to Agnes. She is about to surrender one more time to a make-believe world where appearance is the only valid currency. She suspects that the 'cool spotters' are on to the impostor in their midst.

She begins to anticipate the thought bubbles emerging from speakers' heads, insubstantial as clouds.

Yahdiyahdiyah.

'Yeah. Cool. Let's do it.'

'You've gotta be aspirational,' reminds the copywriter, when Agnes dares to question the wisdom of using a schoolgirl to appeal to an older target market.

'What would I know?' murmurs Agnes. 'I'm only the photographer. I just happen to believe in creating imagery coded to reach its target audience. Silly me.'

She knows she has a reputation in the industry for being odd, difficult and headstrong but at the same time for being a reliable and inventive photographer.

The style gurus pore over model portfolios. As Agnes has predicted, they finally select an eighteen-year-old 'babe' sans breasts, waist or hips.

'D'you think her hair is too boring?'

The subject of wigs is introduced.

'We could dye it for the shoot. Something she could rinse out a few days later. What about red?'

'I imagine something with a lot of texture,' contributes the stylist, whose own hair is as sleek as a seal's skin.

'The make-up?'

The stylist purses her lips and fiddles with the enormous crucifix dominating her flat chest. 'Let's keep the face very pale and emphasize the mouth – a slash of red red red.'

'What about the backdrop?' asks Agnes.

'I like the idea of lime,' gushes the art director. 'You know that *fab-u-lous* clean lime?'

'You can't have lime,' says Agnes. 'It'll make her look too bilious.'

'Oh all *right*.' A petulant finger stabs a colour swatch book. '*Yellow* then.'

'Bright.'

'Bright, but her skin has to look good.'

'Sort of . . .'

'Smooth. Silky.'

'Sexy.'

'I see dark and moody. I see shiny skin. An oily slithery creature.' The copywriter pauses, overcome with his own lyricism.

He receives zero acknowledgement. Agnes is amused to observe his little moue. Spurned. Pearls before swine.

'The model's gotta have attitude,' insists the art director.

'A sort of *fuck-you* attitude,' agrees the copywriter.

What would this arrogant jerk know about attitude, thinks Agnes.

They have been discussing the shoot for an hour. Agnes is no closer to understanding what the agency actually wants.

She watches them flick through the pile of Italian, French and British fashion magazines searching for ideas to plunder.

She hears Clare's derisive snort and voice in her ear. 'They wouldn't know if their bums were on fire.' Agnes suppresses a smile.

'We've done a visual,' the account executive informs her.

Agnes is surprised no-one has thought to produce it before now.

She studies the magazine photo that has been glued onto a laser print of some sparse lines of scratchy-looking type under which sits the tiniest logo they can get away with. A wasted-looking stick insect glares out at her from the page.

'That's just to keep the client happy. It's not really how it's gonna be.'

The copywriter: 'A hint of perversion?'

Silence. Agnes can hear cogs slowly turning.

The Suit fixes the copywriter with a Look.

He holds up his open palms in a gesture of surrender. 'OK, OK. Nothing weird. Just kidding.'

'Maybe the girl's giving the finger,' suggests the art director. He beams around the table.

Little Jack Horner, thinks Agnes.

The copywriter is instantly enthusiastic. 'Why fucking not?'

Agnes continues to drink her coffee calmly and waits for the inevitable.

The Suit clears her throat. 'Call me old-fashioned, but our client is *not*, I repeat *not*, looking for shock value. This is the *Bernice* account, not Lacroix, or even Gaultier. We have a single-minded proposition, will you keep it in mind?'

The art director expels an impatient sigh. '*O-K*. No finger then. But you know what I mean. We're not

79

talking bland and fucking understated either.'

'No way, man.' The copywriter joins the fray. 'We're not into mumsy and boring in this agency. Do it with Bernice, man. On Bernice. To Bernice.' He waves his arms.

'*Under* Bernice.'

Heaven help these boys if they ever get allocated a baby food account, thinks Agnes. Tampons. Underwear. She shudders.

'Fuck you. Right? I want it to be one of those "in your face" shots. OK, Agnes?' The art director looks to her for confirmation.

'Absolutely. No question.' Agnes snaps to and remembers her lines. A gal has gotta eat. After all. 'We're looking for young and spunky,' she agrees.

'But our market is not young and hip,' the Suit reminds the would-be style spin doctors.

'Trust me. It's going to look fucking great,' crows the art director. With his hands in the air he sketches the curves of a woman's body. 'So. This is how I see it. She's in this slutty black dress with fuck-me black leather boots that go right up to her' – he catches the Suit's eye – 'her knees,' he finishes lamely. 'But her *body* language says "fuck you" and she has funky red lips and this dyed sort of reddish-coppery hair.'

Everyone except the Suit, and Agnes, who has immediately drifted off into a daydream about her new young lover Simon, agree the result is going to look 'fucking great'.

'This is not a slutty range.' A deep cleft appears on the Suit's brow.

'It will be when we've finished with it,' promises the copywriter.

'You'd better give us a quote,' reminds the Suit, as Agnes gets up to leave. 'But there is *some* flexibility in the budget, you realize.'

Agnes mentally doubles the figure she had in mind.

She tucks her notes into her briefcase. 'How likely is it that you'll get approval for this job?'

The art director measures a minuscule gap between his thumb and index finger. 'We're this close.'

'We're too radical for them,' confides the copywriter as he and the art director walk Agnes to the lift. 'They're scared of it. They've never done anything quite like this before. They don't know what they're approving. Suckers.'

'Let's keep it that way. What the client and the Suit need,' screeches the art director, 'is to do one of those fucking New Age fucking counselling courses and sort themselves fucking out. Agreed?'

Agnes wishes she could despatch the whole god-damned agency off on a counselling course – preferably to another galaxy. Her nerves are jangled. Her mind is full of doubts: why is she doing this kind of work, associating with these jerks? Anger: towards the copywriter and art director with their egregious philosophies and attitudes.

One week later, the art director calls Agnes on her cell-phone. He is livid.

'No go,' he says. 'We have to fucking use someone over fucking thirty. Can you fucking believe it?'

'No,' replies Agnes. 'I'm stunned.'

'Oh well,' he says, resigned. 'We'll get around it somehow. Once we've scanned the tranny we'll touch her up in Photoshop. Lengthen her legs, give her a better shape. A fuller mouth. Get rid of every wrinkle, any imperfections. You won't recognize her when we've finished. They should thank us on their bended knees for what we're doing for fucking Bernice. Because, the truth is, Bernice are basically a bunch of tasteless wankers and their clothes are total shit.'

Agnes decides it's wisest not to make any response. She wonders if the Bernice client has any idea how much she is despised by the agency creative staff.

Agnes is finding that the photos she slaves to produce are increasingly being manipulated in the designer's computer so that in the end the result bears little relation to the image she has captured. How, she wonders, can this constant sanitizing and undermining of women's body images promote anything other than a world-weary cynicism? Still, she reminds herself, she is only doing it for the money. She doesn't have to *care* about the project. She doesn't have to *love* the people she works with.

So why not do the job, take the money and run? As she has done for years?

Out on the street she passes a Saab with an opened driver's door. Inside an Asian man is clipping his fingernails. He flicks a bored glance at her before returning to his nails. Nearby a young woman hugs the wall of a shop coiled over her cellphone.

Agnes stops in at a café, narrow as a corridor, with cowhide on the seats and rusting sections of farm machinery bracketed to the walls. It's late afternoon and most of the tables are full. A woman at the next table wearing a shiny brocade waistcoat and chandelier earrings is holding court. Agnes takes a seat near the window overlooking the street.

She spies Simon strolling down the opposite side of the street. He is accompanied by a pretty young woman. There is something in the proprietorial way she takes Simon's arm to point something out in a shop window that signals immediately to Agnes that they are lovers. She can scarcely bear to watch, but at the same time she cannot tear her eyes away. She sees their hands join together, fingers curling, hips bumping as a cluster of other pedestrians approaching from the opposite direction force the pair even closer together.

Has she been sharing Simon all along? The woman can scarcely be more than twenty. A fellow student? A third year possibly. Does it matter? Surprisingly, Agnes finds it does. The young woman couldn't be more of a contrast to Agnes. And her arms. They're obscenely thin. How can any adult possess arms that thin?

For the next six hours Agnes is obsessed with the image of the girl-woman.

But she knew what she was getting into.

Didn't she? Good fun. A joyous interlude. A fling. No expectations on either side.

She has deluded herself again. Telling herself fairy stories to transform galling reality into a palatable truth.

'The work I do to earn my living is crap, crap, crap,' Agnes tells Clare in a great sweep of emotion on the phone after work. She is determined not to mention Simon. She needs time to sort out her responses.

'No matter how it's packaged, or how I've justified my assignments in the past, the fact remains – it's crap. Half of my life is used up and what do I have to show for it? Am I any more sorted out now at thirty-nine than I was at twenty? Or thirty?'

'Of course you are.'

'I feel a strong sense of urgency to make changes.'

'You're not the only one.'

Depression hovers like a huge ball of shit right over Agnes's head. Anxiety niggles her.

'Meditation has been on my "to do" list for years, so why have I never got round to it? Likewise, why have I never practised yoga, or learned another language? Three of the many skills I've always intended to investigate, but, typically, I haven't got round to pursuing.

Will meditation follow the way of the rest of my good intentions? Can I commit myself to do this one task every day for the rest of my life?' She sighs deeply.

'Hey, don't get so worked up, Agnes.'

'The thought of having to summon up the energy required to make even a *tiny* change in my routine utterly daunts me. Can I, will I, *should* I, squeeze in one more activity and commitment into my hectic life? . . . How did I become this busy, anyway? . . . Are you busier than you were five years ago?'

'Definitely.'

'Ten years ago?' Agnes kicks off her shoes.

'*Ten years ago?* My God, we were practically in a coma back then. I can't believe how much I get done in a day now.'

'Everyone seems to be working harder, longer hours. But what for? Who benefits?'

'I do,' answers Clare. 'I run my own company. I benefit. My partner benefits.'

'I've got this split-level brain, you see. I'm forever holding several balls in the air. Thinking of three things at once. Never giving anything a full one hundred per cent. I live with financial insecurity. I never actually go broke, but there's always the possibility. I ask myself if I'm getting enough creative satisfaction from my work, if I've still got anything relevant to say. I worry endlessly about everything. I'm scared of becoming a professional worrier – like my mother,' says Agnes.

'My theory is that once we hit forty we will become more and more like our mothers.'

There is a pause while they contemplate this prospect.

'There are only so many hours in a day. I don't want to be still working this hard in ten years' time.' Agnes takes the cordless phone through into her bedroom, flops onto her unmade bed and lies naked under the overhead fan trying to cool down. Clare's authoritative voice resounds in her ear, carrying with it no hint of uncertainty, or of living a life skating over thin ice. If she were with Clare in person she would be able to feel the energy emanating from her. How does the woman ever turn her mind off enough to sleep at night?

'You might be achieving even more than you are now.'

'Oh yeah? How?'

'I'm not talking about more *effort*.' Clare is lying on her couch three kilometres away clutching her own cordless phone. 'It's all about working *smarter*.'

Agnes feels exhausted just thinking about it. Clare the Superwoman. Good on her. And she wants to have a baby? She's nuts. She'll kill the kid. There will be timetables for everything. The nanny's schedule will be on the computer. Child behaviour experts will be consulted around the globe via the Internet.

Saturday. Agnes is having a bad morning. The cat has sicked up on her sofa. She has a spot on her chin and Simon is, of course, out of the picture now. A couple of days after she first saw him with his new girlfriend she had called him and arranged to meet in order to officially terminate their involvement and to return the small number of possessions and books belonging to him that remained in her apartment. He had not handled the meeting well. Considering his age and relative inexperience it was scarcely surprising, she thought, that he had appeared out of his depth and not in control of himself. He was by turns apologetic, remorseful, belligerent, defensive and finally quiet and sad. She had remained dry-eyed throughout the proceedings. He had accused her of being hard-hearted. She had laughed in response and gently reminded him that it was he who had found himself a new lover, not her, that she was the rejected one, not him.

'I'm sorry for hurting you,' he said finally and gave her a clumsy hug, plastering a kiss on her cheek, missing his intended target – her lips – as she had turned her head slightly at the wrong moment.

'We can still be friends,' he offered, noticeably on the verge of tears.

'Of course,' she had lied. Considering the circumstances, it was better to make a clean break, she had decided.

'I learnt a lot from you,' he said, instantly shattering the poignant moment.

Time to call a halt to the proceedings, she thought, before he said things they both regretted afterwards.

Agnes had managed to remain fairly detached at the time, determined to salvage her dignity. Over the previous twenty-four hours it had become even more obvious to her that they should never have become involved in the first place. If she hadn't had so much to drink at the party and if she hadn't impulsively brought him back to her apartment . . . Pointless now to go over and over the same territory. Now it was finished, which was right and appropriate and from now on she would be more sensible.

Afterwards she had shed a few tears over him, but she had succeeded in restraining herself from destroying the many pictures she had taken of him.

That mad red hair. Those sea-green eyes. His bad singing when he was in the shower. His refreshing enthusiasm. Agnes blew her nose hard and returned the photos to the file box.

So here she is, on her own again and not quite knowing where to put herself. For a brief moment she considers calling Bridget and then dismisses the idea. She is sick to death of Bridget's baby obsession – a crashing bore, to be honest, being forced to listen to the same heartrending story every meeting.

'Can't you at least *act* as though you're sympathetic,' Bridget had lashed out at her when they last got together for coffee.

'I feel powerless to help.'

Bridget had retorted that she didn't want any bloody help, thank you very much, and was it so unreasonable to expect a friend to be willing to listen when she was going through a difficult time? *Was it?*

Even if the difficult time dragged on for three years? thought Agnes. In the face of Bridget's hurt and anger she had been reduced to silence. Since then she has made more effort to listen and to appear sympathetic. Yet, privately, she continues to remind herself about all the advantages of being child-free that no-one is ever honest enough to admit.

She pours herself a glass of chilled white wine even though it's only eleven a.m. and plonks her naked body on the end of the sofa not yet trashed by her cat. She dolefully contemplates the damp patch resulting from her failed attempt to rid the sofa of both stain and odour. She frowns at the phone, willing it to ring. The day is rapidly sliding into a potential trough of despair and self-pity, especially when Agnes turns her attention to the lamentable sight of snail tracks of cellulite crawling up the sides of her thighs, and then to her belly (that like so much else in her life seems fated to elude any attempts at discipline and control).

Finally the phone does ring and it's Clare.

The sad detritus of Agnes's Saturday morning pours into the phone.

Clare finds it hilarious. She shrieks down the line. 'Has puddy cat done a vommie?'

Clare would *never* permit her cat to sleep inside

overnight. No cat doors for her. No problem with her large house and garden. Apartment dweller Agnes has no choice but to keep her cat indoors.

'Seeing your Simon over the weekend?'

'He's not *my* Simon any more. I think he's found someone his own age.'

There is a pause as Clare absorbs the news.

'Are you really really upset?'

'A little bit,' lies Agnes. 'But not as much as I thought I would be. It was always on the cards. Of course I became fond of him. He was a breath of fresh air. But it couldn't ever have been anything other than a very pleasant interlude. We didn't delude each other on that score.'

'Oh, sure,' says Clare, sounding unconvinced. 'Shall I come over?'

'Yeah, that'd be great,' mutters Agnes, because she doesn't feel like being alone right now. She has fucked up again on the man front and no doubt she will have to endure Clare telling her in the head girl-ish voice she reserves for these occasions: 'I told you so.'

Small comfort.

Instead, Clare manages to convey in a few words that she does indeed understand the impulse that drove Agnes to fling herself into such an inappropriate and ultimately doomed relationship.

'Sometimes I *long* to go to bed with someone other than Adrian, to experience that giddy intoxicating stuff once more before I die. Yet I don't, because the resulting mess and hurt simply don't justify a momentary whim. But that's not to say that I might not lose my head and heart one day, before I'm too old and decrepit to inspire lust in anyone other than a geriatric.'

'Of course a *man* wouldn't start by changing his hair,' says Clare in her emphatic manner. No-one can give

Clare advice. She knows it all, or else has heard something, read something, bound to have been on some course or other.

'No?' says Agnes. The four friends are enjoying a late Saturday afternoon coffee on Agnes's tiny balcony.

'Definitely not. A man about to embark on a new life would start with his next career move.'

'My bad hair is getting in the *way* of my career.'

Bridget snorts.

'Visualize your goal and do affirmations every day,' advises Athena. 'That way you'll end up creating whatever reality you choose.'

Athena's ideas are so wishy-washy, thinks Clare. There's no intellectual substance to back up her pronouncements and she's as bad as Agnes with her time management. Unlike Clare, who has recently attended a seminar on goal setting and prioritizing time and is keen to share her new knowledge – especially when these skills appear to be sadly lacking in her friends.

'Nothing is going to happen unless you decide on an action plan. I'm serious. Do you ever ask yourself where you want to be in ten years' time, Agnes?' challenges Clare, sweeping her long blond mane off her shoulders with an impatient gesture. She doesn't realize that she does this constantly whenever she is addressing a group, and that while men are charmed by the gesture, her friends are not. Bridget places her hand on Clare's to restrain it.

'Ten years? I'm trying to get through the next *week* and already I feel overwhelmed,' groans Agnes, clutching her head.

'Is this simply a phase you're going through?' ventures Bridget in her quiet voice.

Agnes is struck for about the billionth time by Bridget's kindness, the way she can be relied upon to dispense sensible advice. Because she has known

Bridget for longer than she can remember she has stopped noticing that her friend is drop-dead gorgeous. She takes in Bridget as a blurred impression without really seeing her the way others must experience her. If good design is a question of millimetres (as the art directors she works with constantly impress upon her), then whoever assembled all the parts to create Bridget was a genius. The scattering of freckles combined with the huge brown eyes, the generous mouth and long thick wavy auburn hair. The kind of hair most women would envy. She is tall and slim – everything is the right shape and distance apart and in perfect proportion – except for her fingers which are long, thin and white and her neck which seems to be at least twice as long as that of most other human beings. Lucky Bridget, on whom time has scarcely made an impact, thinks Agnes. Her brow is still smooth and clear, and she has a well-defined jaw – unlike Agnes and Athena whose jawlines have begun to show signs of an impending heaviness that will no doubt increase as they progress through their forties.

Bridget now looks at Agnes with an equally intense gaze reminding her in an instant that she recalls every phase of the past twenty-six years. Agnes cutting her hair very short when everyone else in the class was trying to grow hers long enough to sit on. She was the first to dye her hair in the sixth form, bringing the wrath of the Reverend Mother down on her. Agnes was the first of the group to have sex, the first to have an abortion, to travel overseas, to start her own business, to begin therapy. She had briefly dipped into the New Age movement and as quickly rejected it. Now Bridget can see that Agnes's world is about to be turned upside down again. Agnes's life has grown too small for her, like a favourite garment that has shrunk in the wash and no longer fits.

Agnes wishes her friends didn't know her so well. It is impossible to hide from them, to pretend everything is fine when it isn't.

'*You* are going to meditate?' says Athena. 'I *don't* believe it.'

'You Doubting Thomas.'

Agnes had once used the phrase to Simon. 'Thomas who?' he had asked, face blank.

Twenty people are already seated in a circle in a room at the meditation centre by the time Agnes arrives ten minutes late to her first class. Most of the class is comprised of women. There are three men, two of whom are the trainers. Everyone except Agnes is wearing name tags.

A trainer asks each of them to talk about why they have come to the course.

'I've come here so that I can introduce some calm and control into my life,' contributes Agnes when it's her turn.

The trainers give approving smiles. Responses vary among the members of the group. There are not only the merely curious, but also businesswomen who want a quick easy technique for managing stress, as well as the genuine seekers who hope in some unspecified way to change their lives. A common theme emerges: the desire to improve their lives, to find the 'something missing', to become more focused.

The first session is devoted to awareness of the breath as it enters and leaves the body. Agnes is surprised to discover she will not be expected to make her mind blank or even to enter into a trance.

A few simple preliminary steps are explained and then they all sit upright with their feet flat on the floor, backs straight, chins level and eyes closed for their first practice.

In the vacuum created by the absence of music, speech or movement, Agnes becomes conscious of the tiny sounds usually filtered out. She hears rustling and adjusting of clothing, snorts and snufflings resulting from blocked nasal passages, intermittent sighs, muffled coughs, sniffing, swallowing, scrapings of feet on a wooden floor. Outside noises intrude – traffic, horns tooting, snatches of conversation of passers-by. In the distance, faint music, a plane overhead. Every sound is magnified as she listens for a few moments with that rare quality – her undivided attention. In those few brief moments she forgets the breath she is supposed to be observing. She is oblivious of her work pressures and anything other than extraneous sounds and the dull ache in her lower back.

At the tea break Agnes notices the only man who is not an instructor sitting shyly by himself. The women seem to have formed little groups that exclude him. He has an attractive face with clear light blue eyes and straight black eyebrows. He wears a loose maroon jersey and faded black Levis. With the exception of the course leaders she and this man appear to be the oldest in the room. She glances at the sticker on his chest.

'How are you finding it so far, Daniel?' she asks politely.

'It's well organized isn't it? I'm impressed. However, I'm not sure if I know what I'm getting myself into.'

'Wait till we actually try to meditate.'

'That's the test,' grins Daniel.

'Why did you decide to take up meditation?' asks Agnes. He had responded only briefly in class to the question.

He hesitates and smiles uncertainly, as if coming to a decision to trust her.

'You don't have to answer that.'

'I have anxiety attacks sometimes,' he admits frankly.

'You do?' Agnes is disarmed and intrigued by his honesty. He is not trying to impress her. It's obviously a mere statement of fact, not even a precious jewel of information entrusted to her for safekeeping. She wants to press him for further details. Volunteering a little information about herself might encourage him.

'I'm here because I have difficulty making commitments to myself and sticking to them. Not professionally, you understand, but personally. I tend to take on too much, my energy dissipates and then I have difficulty focusing or prioritizing.'

'I have the opposite problem. I'm too focused. Too disciplined in every aspect of my life. I need to loosen up.'

Agnes unobtrusively checks his left hand. No ring. Doesn't prove he is unattached, however.

'Have you come along on your own initiative, or has someone encouraged you to sign up for the course?'

He smiles.

Is she this transparent?

'I'm on my own,' he says. 'No-one makes any decisions for me.'

Agnes likes the sound of his voice. She likes the way he towers over her. He has an amazing body, very tall and lean. His skin is very pale in contrast to the black hair.

He is a social worker.

'And you?'

'I'm a photographer.'

The following week she finds herself looking out for him. She seeks him at the tea break. He seems pleased to see her. She has meditated only three times over the past week. He, however, has succeeded in meditating on six of the previous seven days.

Agnes reminds herself it is not a competition.

'It's just as difficult as I imagined it would be, finding the time,' she says ruefully. 'The spirit is willing, but the flesh . . . I don't know — it's pathetic, isn't it? I've never been a morning person. I'm too fond of my evenings.'

'I've done something a little bit similar before.'

'Oh? What?' She cocks an eyebrow.

He pauses.

Agnes inclines her body towards him ever so slightly. She beams encouragement at him.

Daniel clears his throat noisily.

'Actually, I used to be a Catholic priest.'

Chapter Six

Athena

'I think most human beings are looking for something,' says Athena.

'Mmmmm . . .' Clare responds cautiously.

'But you have to look inside first, don't you think?' Athena persists. 'Whatever it is we're looking for, we all have it inside us. We just need to get it out. And that's what Agnes needs to do — connect with her higher self and open up her heart chakra.'

Spare me, says the expression on Clare's face. Athena has just committed the unpardonable sin. No-one drops in on Clare and Adrian, not without phoning first. Athena believes you shouldn't have to do that sort of thing. Certainly not with old friends.

Clare goes out to the kitchen to put on the kettle.

Athena tips out the contents of her woven flax bag to find a sachet of camomile tea. She knows that Clare would not, among her collection of Japanese green teas and various brands of coffee, possess such an item.

'What Agnes actually needs is more work and some decent money. Have you ever considered, Athena, that if more people had more money then there wouldn't be half the problems in the world? Psychotherapists would have empty appointment books.'

'Yes, but . . .'

'But *what*?' Clare becomes exasperated.

'Everyone is doing the best they know how, I realize that.'

'Are they?' Clare stares hard at her friend until she is obliged to avert her gaze.

'You're so negative,' complains Athena, raising hurt eyes, her wispy red hair flying about her face like so many raw nerves.

'No, I'm a pragmatist. I know what I can change and what I can't. Agnes is going to make some changes because she's ready to. That's all.'

'Whatever you love, that's what is going to work for you. Following your passion.'

'The problem with Agnes is that she channels her creative energy into men who aren't worth a pinch of shit and she calls it being free, living an independent life.'

Athena starts to pack her possessions into her bag. Herbal teabags, a small brown jar of vitamin C tablets, a tortoiseshell comb, a paua-framed mirror, two small crystals, a notebook. A signal to Clare that the visit is over.

Clare stands. Athena remains seated. She stares fixedly at the grey-painted timber floor.

Clare is astonished to observe a tear trickle down Athena's face. Followed by another and another until she is openly weeping. She begins to talk in a strained voice.

Clare pays close attention, but even so the explanation is disjointed and confusing. Something about broken crystals, about being called a cunt and a space cadet.

Clare sits beside Athena on the black leather sofa and puts her arm around her.

'Tell me,' she says. 'Tell me everything. Leave nothing out.'

The problem of Jewel continues to prey on Athena's mind. Had Clare, Bridget, Agnes and herself been more impressionable as young girls? They had been good girls, at least in primary school. At Jewel's age? They might have raised questions, of course, and occasionally been disobedient, but they weren't openly scornful, or dismissive of all figures of authority. Unlike Jewel, who never sought her mother's approval for anything. What would have happened, ponders Athena, if they had refused to attend Mass or had laughed at the very idea of Confession or at the blessings that came from receiving the Sacraments? Or if they had ridiculed the notion of living in a state of grace?

Athena can see the comfort and appeal of living in a state of grace, to be blessed by a god or goddess.

As a teenager Athena developed a crush on a home-sick Irish priest. She positioned herself as close to the front row as she could persuade her family to sit. Sunday after Sunday she ate her heart out. Had he noticed her? Making bets with herself – would he look in her direction? Would he smile his divinely attractive smile especially for her? After Mass he might seek a moment alone with her. He might bend over her, whisper in her ear and miraculously everyone else in the parish would have gone home early, her parents nowhere to be seen. What would he say to her? She fantasized about the fascinating conversations they would have, how she would dazzle him with her knowledge of theology. Her imagination stopped short of kissing him. She didn't know what men and women did together.

They did Nothing At All, stressed her mother, unless

. . . they were married in the sight of God in the Sacrament of Holy Matrimony. So how could Athena imagine what she hadn't experienced, let alone understood?

He had been graceful at the altar, all eyes upon him. Handsome and good, gentle and kind, he had been an object of gossip and speculation in the parish, as she discovered many years later. She pictures him now, his right hand cutting a swathe in the air, then returning to the centre and up again before slowly falling. His hands coming together and closing like a fan on the congregation.

May the peace of Christ be with you always.

In her former life as Elizabeth Angela Casey, as a child in the sixties, Athena Wildblood had often wondered if the priest sincerely believed he could grant peace to a random assortment of people whose primary connection to each other was a common faith. As if peace could be conferred by the good will of a mere gesture, blind faith, and a few mumbled words of Latin, which few parishioners understood.

The child Elizabeth loved the mysterious Latin words to flow over her, and after a while, to her surprise, she began to comprehend some of them. She loved it at the *Kyrie* when the priest (in those days with his back to the congregation) raised his arms like a conductor, as if beckoning God down onto the altar while at the same time begging for mercy. The *Kyrie* swiftly followed by the *Gloria*, the ancient hymn of praise, until finally the priest turned to face them, his arms extended.

Dominus vobiscum. The Lord be with you.

At the end of the first reading: *Deo gratias.*

Munda cor, whispered the child Elizabeth. Cleanse my heart. Wash away my sins. When it came the time to receive Holy Communion she prepared herself by picturing a cosy set of miniature lounge furniture installed inside her heart. This was for the moment when she finally swallowed Jesus and he slipped down inside her until he found the door to her heart, entered it and made himself comfortable. She ate the host slowly and carefully, playing with it on her tongue, moving it around her mouth, careful not to touch it with her teeth.

Transubstantiation really occurred on the altar.

Miracles were possible. She would be gifted with the ability to speak in tongues and to fly. Her doll would come alive just like the one in her comic book.

Wrapped only in a towel Athena pads down the hallway past Jewel's bedroom. Pauses. I shouldn't, she tells herself sternly.

Yet after the way she has been treated why should she respect Jewel's privacy? She enters the room in a defiant mood. She sits on Jewel's bed, and then guiltily jumps up, smoothing the duvet.

Athena scans the room. She sniffs the air like a cat.

What did she expect? The white room is pristine as usual. Perhaps Jewel has set her room up this way deliberately, so that if Athena ever interferes with anything she will know immediately. Not an object is out of place. Black duvet and matching linen. Black Anglepoise lamp arched over a small black table, books arranged alphabetically on shelves. A box of index cards used as a study aid is placed at an exact right angle to the corner of the desk. Two freshly sharpened red pencils. Two shiny black pens. A black vinyl container full of alphabetically filed CDs rests on top of the bookshelf. A poster of an exhibition at the Gallery of New South Wales, given to her two years previously by Sebastian, is still in pride of place above the bed. Athena melts at this rare evidence of her daughter's vulnerability. The original arrangement had been that Sebastian take his daughter at weekends, but as the years passed these weekends have become less and less frequent. As for child support – forget it. Her daughter takes nothing about him for granted. Recently she has taken it upon herself to initiate contact. She has a hundred excuses for his continued neglect.

Poor Jewel.

Remaining alert for Jewel's return, she stands in the centre of the room, her eyes raking every surface to check she has missed nothing. She opens a couple of drawers. Tidy piles of black socks and pantyhose. Nothing suspicious there. One black lace bra. Where did she get the money? Several pairs of black under-pants, one black cotton singlet, two black jerseys. Jewel takes a malicious delight in destroying any pastel-coloured offerings given to her at birthdays and Christmases by well-intentioned grandparents and relatives.

Under one of the drawer liners Athena discovers something both unexpected and incongruous – a frilly virginal white nightie. Fascinating, but she hasn't time to dwell on the implications of this delicious find just yet. She quickly moves on, aware that Jewel could return at any moment.

Athena moves purposefully towards the wardrobe, her heart pounding. Memorizing the exact position of each black garment, scarf, shoe or boot, she checks the wardrobe and locates what she didn't realize she was searching for.

A new laptop. Sleek, black, sexy. Expensive.

In the distance a door slams.

This time she will confront Jewel. She will be strong. Forthright.

My daughter, the thief.

Footsteps clomp down the hallway.

'MUM! How dare you come snooping in my bedroom. It's outrageous. YOU BITCH! PISS OFF! NOW!' Jewel gives her mother a shove. 'YOU HEARD ME, YOU DOPEY COW.'

Athena loses her balance. 'Ahhhhh!'

She sprawls in an ungainly heap at the foot of Jewel's bed. Her towel tumbles from her breasts. Half-naked, feeling at a distinct disadvantage, she stares up with a shocked face at her nemesis.

'You *disgust* me,' hisses Jewel.

Athena's old fears come flooding back. She forgets she is an adult. She reverts to her childhood, when her father's wrath caused her to shake like a jelly. The legacy of fear and anxiety is so powerful that her overwhelming desire is to do anything to make it go away. She is momentarily paralysed, a rabbit caught in the powerful headlights of her daughter's gaze.

'You had no right to come into my room without my permission.' Jewel's face is ugly with contempt.

Something finally clicks in Athena's brain. 'Is that so?'

No longer cowed, she rearranges her towel and clambers to her feet. Her heart is hammering away at such a rate she fears she may have a heart attack. 'I was concerned about you and I was right to be.'

She points to the laptop. '*Where* did you get the money for this?'

'That's *my* business,' retorts Jewel. She presses the play button on her ghetto blaster. The room is immediately filled with a wall of discordant sound punctuated by male voices rapping obscenities.

Athena reaches over and switches it off again.

'I *don't* like your defiant behaviour. I *don't* like your treatment of me. I won't put up with it. If you and I are going to continue living together in this house then I insist you have to make some changes.' She takes a

101

deep breath. Anger has made her bold and reckless. 'Or you're out on your ear. You can leave school, get a job and go flatting.'

'Fuck off,' taunts Jewel. 'I'll go and live with Dad.'

'All right. Off you go then.'

For the first time a flicker of uncertainty crosses Jewel's face. She knows as well as Athena that her father doesn't want her around cramping his style with the latest bimbette.

'If you snoop in my room one more time, I'll go. I mean it.'

'If you raise your voice to me one more time, you're out of here.'

'You've got one more chance.'

'Likewise.'

'I mean it.'

'So do I.'

'I don't believe you.'

'Try me.'

Chapter Seven

Clare

Clare is hiding at home having a mental health day.

She is at home because she is fat. She is also ugly, worthless, unloved, unlovable. And unappreciated.

She has PMT, but try getting her to admit it – especially not to Adrian, who has no idea, not a clue, never has and never will. He can't read her mind and he should be able to by now, if he knows what's good for him. It's not as if she is asking for much. A few kind words tossed her way, a morsel of affection (to be ignored when it suits her). Not to be challenged on anything if it is none of Adrian's business.

Her answer service is on. She doesn't want to speak to another human being for the rest of the day. Particularly to Adrian, who before he left for work told her that he hoped she would be in a better mood when he arrived home that night, because right now he was finding it difficult to like her, let alone to love her.

She had responded as if he had kicked her in the stomach. Normally she would have challenged him and they would probably have had an argument. It would have affected her work all day, and his not at all. This morning it is all she can do to keep breathing and justify to herself why she should continue to do so. She deserves nothing. Indeed, why should Adrian love her? Why should anyone?

Adrian had behaved as if he didn't care if he never saw her again. They will probably separate. Her fault, of course. How could any man put up with her?

Clare 1: 'Do you have any friends?'

Clare 2: 'No.'

Clare 1: 'Have you ever achieved anything of note in your life?'

Clare 2: 'Are you kidding?'

Clare 1: 'Can you think of one valid reason why Adrian should continue to live with you?'

Clare 2: Silence.

Clare 1: 'Are you unlovable, ugly, useless and a piece of shit?'

Clare 2: Silence.

She feels more fat and worthless than ever and sobs into the sofa for an hour after Adrian has departed.

Will he return in the evening or, because he can't like her let alone love her, will he go out with their friends, deliberately excluding her (to punish her, of course) and have an enjoyable time?

She pictures him surrounded by a circle of understanding faces as he complains about her. The men would be thankful that it wasn't them who had to put up with her. The women would try to take her side but would have to conclude, in the end, that he was right: she's dreadful.

This dark fantasy is enough to set her off again and she bursts into a renewed fit of weeping.

'You poor bastard,' the men would say in holier-than-thou voices, dripping with sympathy. They would press his hand meaningfully.

'If there's anything we can do, buddy . . .' And:

'If you ever want to have a serious talk . . .'

Perhaps she should kill herself now and be done with it.

No. Too much effort.

How unfair life is. It is unlikely that anything will ever improve.

Everything is fucked. Why not admit it? She is powerless. She can do nothing to lessen the world's suffering or to prevent the planet's inevitable decline.

Clare weighs fifty-six kilos, but she drags herself heavily about the house as if she were a ten-tonne truck. She stubs her toe, bruising her knee against a table leg, banging her head on a high shelf.

She has only herself to blame. It was the right decision not to go into the office and inflict her clumsy, fat, worthless body on her colleagues and employees. She has spared them this insight into the person she really is when her guard is down. They would despise her, never want to have anything to do with her ever again.

The weather is foul, in keeping with her mood. Naturally. She is irritated by the sound of the sash windows of her Epsom mansion rattling in the wind. The elegant house closes in on her. The pared-down environment she and Adrian have created is almost devoid of colour. They abhor clutter. Even the paintings are rendered in off-whites, blacks or greys. She paces distractedly, straightening chairs and table legs, realigning the coffee table books and magazines, freshening and tweaking the flower arrangements. But no matter what she does, the house remains bleak and empty, in contrast to cosy evenings when the curtains are drawn, a comforting warm glow emanates from the gas heater, and mouth-watering smells waft from the kitchen where Adrian the gourmet cook is preparing a delicious dinner.

Will she ever experience this simple happiness again?

Would she feel better if she left the house? But where could she go? The library? Relatively safe. She's hardly likely to come into contact with either clients or colleagues there. And there's always shopping in one of those suburban malls where she'll see no-one she is likely to know. However, in her current frame of mind she could end up spending an excessive amount of money on clothes that she will afterwards hate and therefore never wear. Adrian will enquire if her impaired judgement was the result of a brain spasm.

If she does go out it means she will have to drive. For someone who is experiencing difficulty simply negotiating her way around the furniture without mishap how likely is it that she'll make it safely to the library without an accident? It could result at the very least in a lamp-post being wrapped around her neck.

No. She should be adult and sensible. Except that she doesn't feel sensible. She feels crazy and reckless. How will she endure the next eight hours without killing the cat? Herself? Or someone else – possibly Adrian.

Maybe one of her friends is also having a mental health day? She debates with herself. Should she ring one of them to check?

A coffee, a whinge and some sympathy, that's what she needs.

First she retrieves her messages from both her cellphone and from her telephone at the office. No emergencies. Nothing that can't wait for a few hours. Fran, suggesting a change of date for their directors' meeting, and insisting she take the whole day off. Bulldozer, wanting to talk to her about his media training schedule. She and Fran are grooming him so that he becomes *the* spokesperson on any matters

106

concerning reforms of the criminal justice system. There is also a message from Harmony Heaven, who are yet again changing a meeting time.

At the beginning running her company had been fun. A challenge. She has proved she could do it and has Harmony Heaven to thank for providing the foundation upon which everything else has flowed to her. She is a self-made person, but she has also enjoyed a few lucky breaks.

Clare met Rhonda and Sally, the directors of Harmony Heaven, when she first began her consultancy in her late twenties. She could see the potential in their products – health and beauty preparations aimed at women – but it was obvious they were being handicapped by atrocious packaging, lack of a branding strategy and weak advertising.

'Branding is critical, and design is *everything* with beauty products,' she had told them. 'You're selling a promise. Radiant skin. Sex. Eternal youth. Much more than just a pot of cream or a few pills. Your positioning has to be spot on.'

Because she had only just begun her company, Clare agreed to a monthly retainer which would exclude major projects and anything 'extraordinary'. She was fairly safe. There would be a consistent amount of work, standard releases each month. Fortunately, her contacts were good in women's magazines.

They had all been impatient to get started.

Clare had asked for as much background information on their major lines as they could source. She needed a week to come up to speed and then they would have another meeting.

It was already clear to her that one of the products would benefit by being associated with an endorser. Her mind was already busy working out how to create different selling points for the different markets. She had recognized an opportunity when she saw one.

Deciding to attend to most of her messages later, she next calls Athena. Of course she is out. Why are friends always out when you're having a crisis? She lets the phone keep ringing in case Athena is in her garden. Often between clients she will go outside and hang out a load of washing or pull out a few weeds.

No reply. Why isn't Athena's answerphone working? Usually if she is busy with a client her recorded message for Athena's Bodyworks will switch on.

No doubt she is out at some bloody silly crystal gathering.

What a bitch she is. She stomps into her Italian kitchen. White aluminium gleams back at her. She flings open the fridge door, cunningly concealed behind its aluminium façade. Adrian has recently been to the supermarket and the fridge is well stocked with treats. She pulls out several items at random — acidophilus yoghurt, ice cream, cheeses, Indian pickles, plump Greek olives, leftover chicken vindaloo — and arranges them on the benchtop.

It's only a couple of hours since she ate breakfast, but what the hell, she's so fat already what difference will a couple of extra kilos make?

She glumly spoons white chocolate ice cream onto a plate and tips half a canful of peaches swimming in syrup on top of it. Over this she pours a generous dollop of gooey chocolate sauce.

Afterwards she is consumed with guilt and self-loathing. She calls her personal gym trainer, who by a stroke of good fortune has just had a cancellation and is prepared to give her a session as soon as Clare can 'get her butt over and onto the exercycle'.

Clare drives very carefully to the gym.

'C'mon, girl, work those abs . . . quads . . . pecs.'

Clare smiles. Exquisite and deserved punishment.

Clare sits out on her deck with a book taking advantage of the last of the warm weather before winter sets in. The long afternoon stretches before her, an afternoon for once not punctuated by the tyranny of hourly meetings and obligatory phone calls. She puts her book down for a moment and studies a couple of sparrows pecking at the dry crusts, all that remains of the stale bread she tossed onto the lawn that morning. With an effort of will she resists the powerful urge to leap into her car and speed to her office — where she would once more regain her sense of purpose. She pictures herself besieged by staff plying her with questions, while on her desk a steadily growing pile of urgent phone messages waits. In her computer a queue of e-mail messages, on her cellphone (which she has temporarily switched off) another bundle of queries. All these communications requiring immediate answers and decisions that only she can possibly provide, proving beyond a doubt to herself and everyone around her that she is completely indispensable.

Her blood quickens at the realization. Adrian is perfectly right, she wouldn't last five minutes as a mother with a new baby without a nanny in permanent attendance. She would become impatient at having to pace herself to an infant's schedule instead of being free to impose her own task-oriented, results-driven frenetic agenda onto the shape of her life.

This thought is swiftly followed by another image — a fantasy where she is returning home from the office after a punishing day where she hasn't succeeded in salvaging even a nanosecond to feel a drop of emotion, so focused has she been on working her way through the daunting pile of tasks demanding her full attention. Her company has begun to seem like an insatiable beast with jaws open ready to devour every last breath and shred of energy and creativity lodged in her weary body.

She approaches the front door. Her heart lifts. She can already hear a stampede of tiny footsteps racing to meet her. A tattoo of welcoming enthusiasm. She gathers to her every delicious scented mouthful of it, pressing it to her own body as if she would devour it, loving it to bits, and the tyranny of her workday is sloughed off like a dead layer of skin.

Mummy, Mummy, Mummy.

Chapter Eight

Bridget

'Do you want to talk about it, darling?' asks Bridget's mother. She calls her twice a week.

'No,' says Bridget. If she talks about it with her mother of all people then she'll be a complete mess and she can't *stand* to cry in front of her.

'But *why*, Bridget?' asks Clare, when Bridget calls her.

'It goes way back. Something about proving that I've got my life under my control, only it's patently obvious that in *this* area, the one closest to my mother's heart, I definitely haven't.'

'Does it matter?'

'Yes,' says Bridget gruffly. 'It does. I can actually hear the disappointment in her voice.' When she gets off the phone she has another cry – her second bout this morning. Then she feels guilty for having been abrupt with both her mother and Clare.

Matthew phones. He hears heart-rending sobs at the other end of the phone. Bridget is incapable of uttering a word. 'I'm sorry,' she cries eventually and hiccoughs.

'What for?'

'For being such a cot case.'

'Don't worry about it. Do you want me to come home at lunchtime?'

'Would you?'

Matthew comes home and hugs her for several minutes.

'What would you like?'

She thinks about it. 'I don't know. Something.'

'Food?'

'Not yet. Soon.'

'Do you want to go to bed?'

'Maybe.'

'Shall we try it? See if it makes you feel better.'

'I know I'm being pathetic. Cheer me up. I can't bear to be in this depressing frame of mind another minute . . . Do you love me?'

'Course I do, silly.'

They climb into their king-sized bed.

He holds her close and when he feels her body relax against him he bends over her, lightly teasing her nipples with his tongue and teeth until they become taut and aching. He strokes her gently. She lies on her back with her eyes closed, too exhausted by her emotions to respond with anything other than complete surrender. Gradually her anxious thoughts drift away and she is able to focus on all the delicious sensations enveloping her body as Matthew restores her to life.

'Has anyone ever told you what gorgeous tits you have?' he says with tenderness.

'Only you. About a million times.'

'Do you ever get bored with being complimented on your tits?'

'Never.' Tears spring unbidden to her eyes.

They slip into a routine developed from practice and

long familiarity with each other's preferences and responses.

Afterwards when they're lying draped over each other, almost asleep, it occurs to Bridget that perhaps they possess a greater degree of intimacy in their childless state than they might otherwise have enjoyed.

Matthew strokes her hair, runs a hand idly over her left breast.

Does he realize how much this simple gesture calms her?

'I'm lucky,' she says with a solemn face.

'How so?' His hand is still playing with a breast, lingering now on one small section.

'I have you, don't I?'

Why isn't it enough? But nothing is ever enough.

'What's this?' he asks quietly.

'What?'

Bridget feels her breast. A small hard lump. A definite lump. One that wasn't there when she last examined her breasts. When was that? A few months ago?

'Better get it checked out,' advises Matthew and he climbs out of bed to put his clothes back on. 'Don't worry,' he smiles, observing the panic on her face. 'I'm sure it's nothing important, but let's make sure, eh?'

Bridget's mind is already leaping ahead, anticipating her breast being chopped off, picturing herself in the house in five minutes' time experiencing the anxious lonely sensation that will overwhelm her when Matthew has gone. This stolen lunch hour is a rare luxury for them. She envies him every morning as he leaves for his work punctually at seven-forty-five a.m. as a partner in a small but thriving law practice: another day spent in the company of others – stimulating company, every moment filled to capacity, no time to think of his own problems. And ten and a half

113

long, often lonely hours, before she sights him again at the end of the day.

She is suddenly angry with him. Does he really give a damn any more whether they have a child?

'You're not committed to this.'

'Yes, I am.'

He doesn't fool her.

'Prove it then.'

He gives her a long steady look. It chills her blood. She knows that despite his protestations he has given up. He's already moved on and left her behind. Her stomach plummets.

How long has she been feeling this anxious? She can no longer remember how she used to be. Yet is she asking for so much? Only a baby. Even the stupidest woman can give birth. Here is she, Bridget Cecilia O'Connor, unable to conceive. If there were any justice in the world, she thinks, it would be a couple like her and Matthew who became parents, bright, talented, with so much to offer a child, so much thwarted aching love just waiting to be given away, and not some woman who already has more kids than she can support or care for. When she reads in the papers that incidents of child abuse have increased she feels nothing but rage. Matthew always begs her to calm down or she really will have a heart attack. I don't bloody care, she retorts.

'It's time to move on. The doctors don't fucking *know* why we can't have kids.'

'I'm not blaming you,' gulps Bridget. 'I'm sorry, I'm sorry.'

'Let it go,' says Matthew in tones of quiet desperation. 'We have to put it aside and get on with our lives. Why can't you accept it? We can't have a baby. It's just not possible.'

'No. I can't accept it. I will never accept it.'

114

Matthew sighs. He touches her shoulder and when she doesn't respond he consults his watch.

'I have to go,' he says. 'I've got so much on at the moment. Wall-to-wall appointments. I can't wallow in misery all day.'

'Like me, you mean.' She raises a tearstained face to him.

'I haven't got time for an argument,' he says.

'It's not an argument. We're having a discussion.'

'Whatever. I don't have time now. Later. OK?'

'It's all right for you. It's not *your* life that's on hold.'

'Can't you relax? If only you were more relaxed . . .'

'RELAXED?' screams Bridget. 'How can I relax? Tell me.'

'Don't get so worked up,' he pleads.

Bridget picks up a plate and hurls it across the room.

'*Fuck* the experts! The bloody gynies and specialists. They know nothing. Sweet *fuck all* is what they know.'

They watch the plate shatter into a dozen pieces against the yellow wall and smash onto the floor into several dozen more. Even Bridget is astonished at the intensity of her rage. Bloody doctors, she could murder the lot of them.

The mood she's in she could easily go on the rampage and smash the entire contents of their house.

Not that she would . . . but she could.

Fifteen or so minutes would do it. Scary but true. Does Matthew realize he is living not only with a cot case, but with someone who is rapidly degenerating into a complete nutter?

'Now just calm down,' pleads Matthew, placing his hands on her shoulders in an attempt to restrain her.

She flings his hands off.

'CALM DOWN?' she shrieks. Another plate hits the wall. She picks up a vase and throws it onto the floor. She hears a high-pitched sound like a siren in her head. Blood rushes to her face and her heart pounds. An untamable beast is trapped inside her, ready to emerge, talons flailing.

'Hey!' Matthew sounds alarmed.

She couldn't care less. Her demon is on the loose.

'Look,' he says, his face serious and concerned. 'I really, really want a baby – just as much as you do. But we can't. Fact.'

'It's all right for you. You've got the bloody fucking office. Your work is more important than I am.'

Wisely Matthew doesn't even attempt to comment. He edges with caution towards the door.

She immediately pulls him back.

'Where do you think *you're* going?'

'Bridget . . . please.'

Bridget feels like running out into the yard and pulling her hair out in tufts. She knows she has lost control, but a part of her also knows that she has to take this issue to the limits and beyond, before she will be in any state to confront the truth.

Her eyes dart frantically about the room. Matthew follows her eyes, trying to pre-empt her. He makes a quick lunge towards the coffee table just as she reaches out to grab a potted plant.

She is too quick for him. She picks up the plant and heaves it out the back door (fortunately it is open) and onto the deck, scattering dirt over a wide area of wooden planks.

He runs out and drags her back inside.

'DON'T TOUCH ME,' she warns. She is breathing heavily. Her eyes are wild. Damp strands of hair cling to her forehead.

'Bridget . . .'

The ringing in her ears finally ceases. She collapses onto the floor. Her body shudders as she breaks into loud unrestrained sobs.

He squats down alongside her and wraps an arm round her shoulders. He cries but without making a sound.

How they suffer. They sit like this for half an hour before Bridget's wailing diminishes to a few sniffs and hiccoughs. He hands her a box of tissues.

Matthew rings his secretary to move his next appointment. He makes Bridget a cup of sweet strong tea.

'Shall I ring Agnes or Clare?'

She shakes her head. All the fight has gone out of her.

With a quick glance at his watch Matthew picks up his briefcase.

'I'll ring between clients to see how you are,' he calls over his shoulder.

She stares bleakly at his retreating back and wishes she were dead.

She ought to get out of the house more. Working from home – that's part of the problem. Sapped of emotion, she is in no mood to work in her studio. Not this afternoon anyway. But if she can no longer muster enthusiasm to paint, what is she to do? How will she occupy her time? She needs people. Distraction. To stop being so preoccupied with her own problems and become involved in others' lives again. But where to begin?

She turns her mind to the women lawyers in Matthew's office. Well groomed and sharply focused. Women for whom babies are not yet an issue. Dynamic, attractive women who might be already providing a welcome respite for Matthew from Bridget and her angst and grief. She shivers at this thought and then berates herself: *Pull yourself together, Bridget. Get a life.*

117

Bridget goes to her studio and pulls out a carton from a cupboard. Beneath foamy layers of white tissue are a dozen lacy-knit bootees, a tiny blue jacket threaded with delicate satin ribbons, several woollen baby singlets, a gauze wrap. She caresses each item, smoothing out the jacket before carefully wrapping each garment in tissue again. She carries the carton over to her car and opens the boot.

She pulls over to the side of the road after only a few blocks and debates turning back. The beast has retreated to his cave. She feels numb, as if a giant steamroller has crushed her into the ground and she is nothing more than a speck of paper, thin and blank, no more substantial than a breath of wind.

She sits for fifteen minutes staring out the window, seeing nothing.

Stay.

Go.

No one course of action seems more important than another. She could drive the car into a tree. Would anyone care? She could run naked through the street scattering baby clothes in the air and shouting at the top of her voice.

And what would that solve?

She turns the key in the ignition and drives to the City Mission where she hands over the box to a harassed-looking older woman who, after a quick smile and acknowledgement, takes the box from her.

Bridget waits to see if she will open it and exclaim over the contents.

'Was there anything else?'

'No . . . yes.'

Bridget snatches back her box from the counter and retreats out the door.

Chapter Nine

Agnes

Under her name on Sudha's business card is her job description. Not a hair designer, or even a hair consultant, but a hair artist.

Sudha plucks a hank of hair from each side of Agnes's head and holds them out stiffly like antennae. She grins impishly at Agnes. 'No last minute change of mind?' she enquires.

'Do what you like,' replies Agnes. She knows she harbours unrealistically high expectations. Her bad hair day had extended into a period of several weeks, leading her to wonder if her slackness was perhaps a precursor to letting herself go completely — sliding down the long slippery slope towards fatness, blandness, becoming jobless in the process. One step closer to becoming a bag lady in her old age. No pension, no savings, no looks, no children to look after her. One day, no doubt, she will actually give up, topple headlong kicking and screaming into a disgraceful old age. Stop dyeing her hair (never!), struggling to lose weight (possibly), sticking to a low fat diet, scrambling to get more exercise, to have the right attitude, to network for more clients. The whole goddamn exhausting routine.

Who needs it? Her struggles to simply remain afloat, sane, fed, employed and moderately attractive are enough to make her want to crawl into bed for a week. She is *always* tired. How can this be normal?

. . . Unless she has a fatal disease, and her doctor (she has never trusted doctors) has, with criminal negligence, failed to read the vital signs when she last reported in sick.

Sudha interrupts her paranoid thoughts. 'We'll update your look.'

As if, Agnes thinks, she is an old model toaster or jug being serviced.

'You could do with some colour, too. A copper on the base with dark golden highlights. What do you think?'

'Sounds OK to me.'

'Cool,' replies Sudha.

Unlike most members of her trade Sudha does not do a big line in small talk. Her vocab, decides Agnes, is tragically restricted. It's cool that Agnes runs her own business. Cool that Agnes wants to make a radical change in her appearance.

Bitch, Agnes berates herself. Does she need an Einstein to style her hair? Anyway, what a relief to have someone else prepared to take responsibility for her appearance.

Sudha gathers Agnes's hair together in a bunch and secures it with a rubber band.

'OK, close your eyes.'

She hacks off the ponytail as if it were a piece of old rope (afterwards she gives it to Agnes as a keepsake).

Agnes gazes into a tall mirror shaped like a vagina while the colourist, a young woman in black satin hipsters and a see-through black Spandex top, begins to apply the colour in layered sections separated by plastic strips. Agnes breathes in a strong whiff of ammonia.

When the colourist has finished, Agnes is left to sit for a long time flicking through magazines. She seizes the opportunity to catch up on mindless fads and addictive gossip about the stars.

She scans a story on liposuction, another on plastic surgery. An article warns of the dangers for women of eliminating all fats from their diets. Aerobics are out, spinning is in.

One article advocates eating more carrots along with other red or orange fruits and vegetables. The humble potato is revived. Consumption of other foodstuffs is alternately reviled or cautiously encouraged. Can any of these so-called experts be relied upon? Agnes thinks not. In a year's time carrots will no doubt be vilified while women, utterly confused by the barrage of conflicting advice dished out by the magazines, will be persuaded to return to a Mediterranean diet rich in olive oil.

Agnes reads on. Should she be grilling her chicken or steaming it? Should she be eating it at all? Aren't chickens stuffed full of noxious hormones? Stressed to the max from being expected to breed and lay eggs under intolerably cramped conditions?

Sudha comes over to check the progress of the colour and Agnes wrenches her mind back to the present. A salon junior shampoos and massages her head. She kneads Agnes's scalp with her small strong fingers. The experience is so pleasurable that Agnes wishes she could prolong it to an hour instead of a mere few minutes. She could easily fall asleep.

Through an open window facing the street she can hear a car alarm go off. A man swears angrily. A car impatiently toots. A smell of petrol or oil, something stale, drifts up from the pavement, mingling with the cloying sweet odour of mousse, spray, shampoo, hair wax and fudge.

She had walked into the salon in low spirits. Nothing in her life has turned out the way she intended. Had she started off with a plan in her twenties? It seems so long ago that she can now scarcely remember.

When she is feeling down she inevitably compares herself to Clare – usually unfavourably. How is it that Clare has five-year plans, flow charts, spread sheets and God knows what else – software for everything? Naturally she was the first to get connected to the Internet, to send and receive e-mail, to join a cyber-space chat group. To buy her jeans and CDs on the Net, to subscribe to the *Guardian* and *New York Times* and download the articles she wanted. She was also the first of her friends to buy a laptop. This was immediately followed by a sleek little cellphone. She had a Filofax, but soon swapped it for an electronic diary. And so forth and so on. She has a to-do list, and items are ticked off the list at the end of the day and prioritized ready for the following one.

In contrast, Agnes has only a 'get-through-the-day' list. Whether she intends it or not, Clare generally succeeds in making everyone else around her feel grossly inadequate.

'It's not *what* you do that counts, but *how* you do it. Even the *action* of doing, of living in the present, matters,' Athena has often claimed.

It's one of the few points on which Agnes and Athena agree.

'Who wants Clare's insane life?' asks Athena.

'Even if Clare has a two-hundred-dollar designer pepper grinder? Even if her next holiday is going to be in New York? If every stitch of her underwear is silk? Even if she does have a facial, or else a body massage, at least every other week?'

'Put like that . . .'

The junior briskly towels Agnes's hair dry.

Agnes scrolls back through other half-remembered conversations.

Athena: but is Clare *happy*?

Agnes's view: Clare is a pretty good actress.

Athena: Clare is out of touch with her feelings.

Bridget's opinion: both Agnes and Athena are envious of Clare.

'So?'

However, Agnes really does love Clare despite everything. When she thinks of Clare's Alessi kettle, her Dualit toaster, the La Pavoni coffee maker, not forgetting the Philippe Starck chairs, she recalls their mutual origins with a pang of mixed shame and nostalgia — their mothers' home-knitted jerseys. The nuns' much-darned stockings. The brown paper, onion-string bags, hessian sacks, fruit boxes and white parcel string their mothers stored and reused until they finally disintegrated. There was a bin of plastic bags plastered with faded logos they were forced to regularly wash and recycle. Postage stamps which as schoolchildren they collected to raise funds for the missions, along with the foil milk bottle tops (where did they end up?). Jelly packet coupons and tea coupons were likewise hoarded for the purpose of obtaining discounts or free gifts, or to be eligible to go into the draw for some item or other the nuns needed. Agnes remembers the crooked peggy squares that they (even Clare) struggled to knit over twenty-five years ago, later sewing the squares together in garish combinations to construct rugs for Vietnamese orphans. Did the orphans ever receive the rugs and soft toys they laboured over? Agnes will never know. No-one will. The debris from her past accumulates: messy, unfinished, unprocessed.

*   *   *

Agnes studies the stylists, slogging away on their Saturday, her day off. Why would anyone imagine that being young equated with happiness or freedom? It never did with her. Being young and inexperienced was seen to be a disadvantage. Now she is almost old enough to be the mother of some of the stylists. Does Sudha see her as middle-aged? Yet how can she be viewed as anything else in this room full of obsessively image-conscious hairdressers?

Sudha is dressed in layers of coarsely textured fabrics in browns, black and bone; pieces tie and overlap, a skirt over trousers. She wears high-heeled black lace-up boots and has extremely short jet black hair with jagged ends, giving the impression of having been shorn haphazardly with a pair of blunt scissors. The overall effect, obviously carefully calculated, lends her a gamine Audrey Hepburn appearance (if Hepburn had been Asian). The other stylists are also of mixed ethnic origins, Chinese, Samoan, Korean and Maori. A couple could be refugees from the seventies; others are wearing underwear on the outside of their clothes.

Agnes has worn mini-skirts four times already in her life, knee-length or 'midi' skirts and dresses twice before, has done the sixties revival look three times and recycled the seventies hippy style twice. Isn't it time finally to step off the treadmill and please herself?

Agnes's hair is beginning to resemble Sudha's even though her face is a completely different shape – round where Sudha's is elfin. Are all of Sudha's clients dished out the same style, regardless of what suits them? Agnes's hair is gelled, tweaked, twisted, twirled, blow-dried and sculpted with a moulding mud to create the necessary volume. Sudha holds up a mirror to the back of Agnes's head. 'Like it?'

Agnes doesn't recognize herself, this tall, elegant

woman uncoiling from the chair like a crumpled butterfly emerging from a grey cocoon. Her hair is no longer a tangled mess, now there's a defined sleek shape. Not a helmet. She looks younger by at least five years.

She can't wait to show it off to Clare.

Agnes decides to tell Clare about Daniel, the former priest whom she has met at the meditation class.

'I hear alarm bells, Agnes.'

'It's not what you think.' Agnes bursts out laughing at the very idea. 'No way. Although he is a lovely man. But . . . an ex-priest? No, I don't need that kind of complication in my life.'

'Sure, and I believe you too,' smiles Clare.

Agnes invites Daniel to her apartment for dinner. It's not often she cooks for someone else. It's easier, given her odd working hours and frequently empty fridge, to arrange to meet friends and colleagues in a local café, or a cheap Asian. When she does make the effort to cook for herself, she produces enough to last for at least two meals, if not more.

She has acquired the survival habits of one who has, by circumstance rather than from choice, found herself living alone. She has learned to enjoy her own company by providing distractions that prevent her from falling into the trough of doubt and anxiety that too much opportunity for introspection can lead her into. She plans her social calendar well in advance, leapfrogging from one event to another two or three evenings later. Empty Friday or Saturday evenings are not permitted to creep up on her unawares. Her social buddies are several years younger than she is, usually single and or gay.

Daniel is not the type she has been attracted to in the

past. She senses his vulnerability, his air of being an outsider, someone not easily catalogued. He may well be that rare breed – a good man.

He would probably run a mile if she were to zero in on him and apply a little heat. He *should* run a mile, she thinks.

He arrives on time at seven-thirty, awkwardly clasping a bottle of Chardonnay.

Her first impression: I hate his clothes.

So what if her response is superficial? It's a fact. He has no dress sense.

His face is pale. She can tell he's nervous by the tightness of his mouth. The way his eyes flicker, not properly looking at her, is a dead giveaway. He's even hyperventilating, every few minutes taking in a big swallow of air, chest heaving. Laughable, the idea of a man being terrified of her.

If it wasn't so tragic.

He's just a lonely vulnerable human being – isn't he, Agnes? Except that his manner is having an effect, making her jumpy too.

Go on, Agnes, put him at ease, why don't you.

'Take a seat. You can give me the bottle. Thanks.'

Divested of his shield he passively allows himself to be led over to a black sofa where he perches like a heron on a pole. He stares across at Agnes as if waiting for her to tell him what to do next.

Bloody hell, Agnes.

He makes a gesture indicating her hair. 'It's very different, suits you. I like it very much.'

She pats it, still getting used to the change in her appearance, expecting to feel the familiar heavy weight of long hair.

Now what's he doing? He's placed a cushion on his lap and his hands criss-cross it in a series of jerky little movements.

'A drink. Let me pour you a drink. The Chardonnay? A beer?'

'D'you have any whisky?'

'Whisky? Of course. Single malt?'

The glass is empty within a few minutes.

'Another?'

'A small one. Yeah, that'd be great.'

He sits on this one a while longer.

'Do you have a drinking problem?' she asks, without stopping to think. As if she has any right to adopt a moral high ground in this area.

'Two whiskies don't make a man an alcoholic. At least, not in my book.'

'I'm sorry, I didn't mean—'

He waves a hand dismissively. 'Don't give it a thought.'

Flustered, Agnes puts the finishing touches to her dinner preparations. She's stuck to something she knows she can achieve with a minimum of fuss and stress. Lemon chicken, mushroom risotto and a salad of rocket lettuce and fresh herbs, followed by Greek yoghurt and fresh fruit.

So far so good.

The whisky relaxes him. He gains confidence while she's preoccupied with the food and begins to prowl around the small apartment, studying the framed prints which cover almost every wall surface. His attention is immediately drawn to an old photo of Agnes in her mid-twenties with a shaved head.

'My punk phase,' laughs Agnes.

He wanders down the parade of her life. Agnes's first communion, her confirmation picture. A photo of her large family.

'There's a mob of you, isn't there?'

'You can thank the rhythm method of birth out-of-control.'

He moves on to Agnes, Lizzie and Clare in mini-dresses at fourteen, the four of them in midi-skirts at fifteen, Bridget and Agnes in home-made maxi-dresses at seventeen. 'That one was taken a year before my friend Bridgie and I escaped to art school.'

At art school their rake-thin bodies teeter on platform-heeled clogs; they are achingly aware of their sex appeal in their flared jeans and skin-tight tie-dyed T-shirts. 'Our hippy phase. We thought we were very cool.'

He pauses before Agnes in sixties revival mode at age twenty-five, in seventies revival at thirty-eight. Clare and Agnes power-dressing in heavily padded jackets in the mid-eighties, champagne in hand. 'Clare had just scored a new client that day. We were celebrating.'

Finally he turns his attention to the larger prints. 'Your own work, I presume.'

'Some of it. There's a couple of my friend Bridget's paintings.' She points them out. 'The rest are prints by local photographers whose work I admire.'

She doesn't ask him for his opinion because she's not ready to trust his ability to evaluate anything on her walls.

'Your work is very powerful. Dare I say – passionate?'

'Self-portraits, actually.'

You're on trial, mister. She's put on a few pounds since those nudes were taken.

He wisely chooses not to make any comment.

She takes the chicken out of the oven and dishes it out onto a serving plate, her face hot, and not just from standing at the stove.

The salad is quickly tossed and the rice spooned into a bowl.

'Can I help?'

'You can put these plates on the table.'

There are no candles, although she had debated putting some on the table when she was planning the dinner, only to reject the idea as being too lacking in subtlety. After all, she wasn't planning a seduction.

She wore a simple black lace fitted shirt over her trademark black bootlegs. No jewellery, minimal make-up.

She invites him to help himself.

He is looking at the chicken with a concerned expression.

'Sorry, I forgot to tell you – I don't eat meat,' he apologizes, selecting only the rice and salad and piling it onto his plate.

Shit.

He *is* getting to her. She gets up from the table and fossicks about in the fridge. Fortunately she has recently been to the supermarket and deli. There are a couple of exquisite slices of smoked salmon she had been saving for Sunday lunch. Perfect.

'Do you eat seafood?'

'Yeah, I do.'

There are so many questions she wants to ask him, but where does she begin without scaring him off? She's discovered that he is a social worker.

'Your background didn't create any difficulties?'

'You'd be amazed,' he says. 'The social services would collapse without all the Catholics and ex-Catholics running them. The biggest thing was, I had to upskill. Get the right qualifications, to be totally accepted. I've squeezed in a number of university courses over the past few years, as well as tackling demanding full-time work.'

'What do you usually get up to on a Saturday night?'

'Not a lot. There's always study. Sometimes I go to a

129

movie by myself. It's not so easy if you're a single older man from an unusual background. I'm still getting to know people. I was transferred a fair bit when I was a priest. It's a couples' world out there, I've discovered.'

'It sure is. Tell me, do you have any close men friends?'

'Two or three. Unfortunately, they don't live in Auckland.'

The hands are still now. A promising sign.

'So. How do you meet new people then?'

'I meet lots of people through my work. I get on OK with them. But it doesn't follow that I want to spend my free time with them.'

A lost soul? She senses a neediness in him and it makes her wary.

'How old are you, Daniel?'

'At last count? Forty-five.'

She had thought him older. Must be the way he dresses. He doesn't look after himself, probably has a lousy diet. He'll be visually illiterate, know nothing about art, let alone photography.

Agnes can't prevent herself feeling critical. A last ditch attempt to convince herself that he doesn't, couldn't possibly ever, matter to her.

'Can I question you now, if you've finished with *me*?' he asks with an amused glint in his eye.

She laughs, spluttering on her mouthful of chicken.

What does he dream about? What is he like in the sack?

Stop it, Agnes. Answer the man's question now.

'Go ahead.'

'Have you ever been married?'

'Not as far as I know.'

I wonder if he snores.

130

'Children?'

'No.'

'Can I be very personal?' he asks tentatively.

'It depends. Give it a shot.'

'Did you ever think about having kids?'

Hey, nice one, Daniel. You want to move past first base and you haven't been here an hour.

'Occasionally, I've thought about having kids. I've been pretty busy all through my thirties. Building my photographic business, paying off this apartment. You know – *life*. There always seemed to be other more inviting things to focus on at any given moment. My own private work, for instance. Reading about it, thinking about it. Doing it.

'What else? I suppose I never happened to be with the right man when the thought of a family crossed my mind. I've been on my own a lot. It's not something I ever planned would happen. So it's fortunate that I enjoy my own company, isn't it?'

'You're unusual. A complex sort of woman.'

'Not really. There are actually quite a number of women like me. What's so great about the classic nuclear family anyway? It hasn't worked. Look at the number of sole parent families.'

He raises his hands, open palms. 'Hey, steady on, no need to be defensive. It's none of my business. I'm sorry. I've obviously triggered a raw spot there.'

Agnes looks slightly mollified. 'I know it's not the done thing. *Everyone* has kids. It's mother nature kicking in. With me, it simply didn't happen. But it doesn't mean I'm cold, or selfish, or uncaring, you know. I'm the eldest of five. I helped bring up my younger siblings so I'm no stranger to childcare. Believe me, I'm not missing out on any earth-shattering experience there.' She sticks her chin out at a defiant angle as if daring him to disagree.

'I hope you don't think I was implying that you were some sort of freak. I think of myself as a pretty straightforward sort of person in comparison.'

Agnes leans forward, a forkful poised in mid-air. '*Bullshit*. You're either being disingenuous or lying. No-one is straightforward. Everyone has their story. Their motivations, or lack of them. Agendas, whatever you call them, fears and phobias, joys and hopes. Not everyone gets what they want out of life.'

Agnes realizes she is becoming very intense. How many wines has she had?

'You don't *know* me,' she bursts out. 'You can't make any *assumptions* about anything. Don't even try,' she warns him.

For a long moment they stare at each other. He takes her measure. She takes his.

Is this what she wants? What if, when he has become intimate with her, and she is as vulnerable as a turtle without its shell, he decides she is not, after all, what he was seeking? Then what, Agnes?

You don't gain anything of substance, she reminds herself, without risking all.

No?

Go on.

What if . . . ?

Do *it*.

She takes a deep breath.

'Coffee?'

'Not at this hour.'

'Tea? I have jasmine, green, hibiscus, regular, or Earl Grey.'

'Regular, thanks.'

She stacks the dishes mechanically. He watches her. She turns down his offer of assistance. The last thing she wants is them colliding in the tiny kitchen.

She opens the tea canister. Warms the pot. Pulls the

strainer out of a drawer. Arranges chocolate biscuits into a fan shape on a plate.

They move away from the dining table towards the sofas. Agnes puts Borodin's string quartet on the CD player.

'So you like that one too,' he grins.

He leans back, closes his eyes and allows the music to wash over him.

Agnes wonders how such an attractive man lasted as long as he did in the priesthood without a woman parishioner racing him off his feet.

The tea grows cold in the pot. She forgets to pour.

Without opening his eyes and with a beautiful smile on his face he says softly, 'Are you awake there, Agnes? What does a man have to do to get a cup of tea? Shall I do the pouring?'

'What? Oh, sorry, I forgot.'

What sort of body does he have?

They sip their tea. They lock eyes again. Damned if she is going to open up to him just yet. Maybe never.

She looks away first. She feels very tense. Fiddles with a silver earring. Removes both earrings. Places them on the table. Picks one up again. Puts it down.

In films sexual encounters happen so naturally, she thinks. There is an inevitability in the slow dance of attraction played out by two perfectly matched human beings. Beautiful – it goes without saying. Young, naturally. The woman a size ten. The man works out, a walking symphony of lean muscle. His hand is steady. He knows what to do, recognizes precisely when the moment is ripe for the plucking.

In your dreams, Agnes. An image of Simon flashes across her mind – their half-hearted liaison, along with the spectres of other short-lived affairs – all doomed to failure.

'Tell me about your work, Agnes.'

'It's late, don't you think?'

'Not too late.'

Midnight actually. He's keen.

'OK. My private work – as distinct from what I do to earn money. I've been working on a series of images for about two years now. I want to make a statement about women and ageing – subversive images, the antithesis of what I do to earn a crust. It's partly about me coming to terms with turning forty, and also a comment about the fucked attitude in the area I work in – an endless round of advertising campaigns, underwear catalogues and fashion shoots.'

'If you hate your job, then for God's sake, why are you doing it?'

'That's just what I've been asking myself. I have to earn my living, pay the mortgage, the studio rent. I could bear it all if I occasionally had a show. So that's what I'm aiming for. I'm excited about it. There's a group show coming up and I'm going to be part of it. It's about time I initiated more of my own projects.'

She suddenly realizes how exhausted she is and picks up the cups and saucers from the coffee table.

'I've enjoyed our dinner, but I'm tired now. I need to sleep.' She already knows he's not the type to exert any pressure on her to go to bed with him.

He stands up and retrieves his jacket from the arm of a chair. Good. He's got the message then.

What kind of impression has she made on him?

'I'd like to see more of you.'

'Maybe.'

God, why did she say that? *Of course* she wants to see him again.

'That doesn't sound very enthusiastic.'

'I do want to see you, but I'll be honest – recent experience has made me cautious.'

His face registers disappointment. He's not good at dissembling – neither was Simon. Yet why pretend something she doesn't feel? Her instincts have so often led her astray in the past. She can't afford to keep committing such errors in judgement.

Anyway, what is the hurry?

Chapter Ten

Athena

Where did Jewel get her laptop? Until now she has refused to divulge any information other than to swear she didn't steal it.

Uncharacteristically, Athena is persistent.

'For fuck's sake,' shouts Jewel. 'I was given it. *There. Satisfied?*'

She is wearing a transparent black lace dress. The back is cut so low her black bra is clearly visible. Her daughter's pale body is heartbreakingly thin beneath the lace, observes Athena with a pang. She hasn't been well endowed in the boob department either.

Poor kid.

'Who gave it to you?'

Surprisingly Jewel gives her a straight answer.

'Wing.'

'Who?'

'Just Wing,' she answers sullenly.

'An Asian boy?'

'Yeah, Chinese. Gotta problem?'

'I don't give a damn what race he is. I just want to know what kind of person he is. Tell me. Don't play games. What have you done for him that has encouraged him to spend so much money on you?'

A sly expression steals over Jewel's face.

'My business. Back off.'

Athena has no success in gathering any further information.

So Jewel has a boyfriend. How very astonishing. She cannot imagine Jewel loving anyone except herself. Athena is ablaze with curiosity and concern. She can't resist searching Jewel's room again as soon as she leaves the house. She doesn't know exactly what it is she hopes to find, but a thorough search turns up nothing out of the ordinary.

Once, Athena can't remember exactly how long ago, the love she bore her daughter sustained her. She had hoped that Jewel would eventually grow out of the ghastly phase she has been going through for the past two years. But what if she doesn't? If she persists in mocking every aspect of her mother's actions and attitudes?

Athena can't think why Wing would lavish such attention on Jewel, unless she undergoes a complete personality transformation when she is alone with him.

It pains her to admit it but Jewel is not a likeable person. Athena cannot understand how she can have produced such a creature, one so lacking in compassion or respect for others. Her daughter has an acutely honed awareness and intolerance of others' physical imperfections and character defects. Athena feels sorry for Jewel's teachers – especially the males, who are no doubt oblivious of the fact that the mere presence of their overweight bodies with repulsive hairs bristling unrestrained from ears, nostrils and eyebrows, their bad haircuts and tasteless clothes cause serious offence to their star pupil.

'They could at least wear deodorant,' she complains.

Jewel will not tolerate any male over the age of thirty occupying her physical space inside a distance of one metre.

'Don't you think you're being a tad excessive?'

'They're disgusting. Gross. Clueless.'

Jewel had once told her mother that what the world needed was a big clean-up to eliminate all the ugly people. She wished she could do a giant make-over on all her teachers. She loved the before and after pictures in magazines – cringing girls with bad hair and poor complexions and no colour or dress sense who were transformed by experts into clones of the stars from *Melrose Place* or *Friends*.

Jewel is obsessive about cleanliness and her own personal hygiene. She showers three times a day and tidies her room daily before barricading herself in with the cordless phone to call Wing.

She could be an alien, thinks Athena.

Sebastian's genes, of course.

Sunday. Athena's mother arrives for a visit, full of her customary good humour and enthusiasm. She never arrives empty-handed. Today it's a prettily wrapped bunch of flowers from her own garden and a new tape for Athena to listen to. While Athena is convinced she is increasingly resembling an ancient shipwreck, marooned on the shores of her unsatisfactory life, her mother succeeds in appearing a good ten years younger than her actual age of sixty-one. The smiling bespectacled face, framed with shiny chestnut curls, immediately lifts Athena's spirits. She hugs her mother's plump body and sniffs the distinctive scent of one of her Body Shop perfumes. Today she wears a loose-fitting silk dress patterned with a bold floral print and over the dress, a mohair cardigan. Silver bell earrings swing from her ears.

'I'm hanging out for a cuppa.' Without waiting for a reply her mother marches into the kitchen as if she owns it, fills the jug and pulls two favourite mugs out of the cupboard. She also notices a load of washing waiting to be hung out and automatically picks it up and carries it outside to the line.

'I've had the most *fabulous* sex lately,' she announces to a bemused Athena as she breezes in the back door with the empty basket.

Athena pours the lemon and ginger tea. The kitchen seems suddenly to have shrunk. There is less air to breathe.

'Jock's the best lover I've ever had. An improvement on your father, that's for damn sure.'

Athena still visits her father at least once a month. She finds very little to say to him and receives the strong impression that she is a disappointment to him. He has steadfastly refused to learn to cook. She is expected to stock his freezer with meals to last several weeks. Athena might refuse to be the good Irish daughter and cook for him but that doesn't stop her feeling guilty. She supposes that he is getting by on toast, canned soup and takeaways.

'He can rot for all I care. He's not my responsibility any longer.'

'Mum!'

Jock, on the other hand, is a well-off divorced carpenter in his early fifties, who is keen on both astrology and boating. He knows his wines and is able to cook a passable Spanish omelette. Her fortunate mother gets to sail round the islands in the Hauraki Gulf on her days off.

Athena drains her cup with resignation. In her opinion there are subjects, and sex is definitely one of them, where it is preferable not to share the intimate details with one's mother. But it seems there is

139

virtually no aspect of her mother's newly discovered sexuality that is not considered open for discussion with her daughter. Stopping her mother once she has got started is about as likely as restraining Niagara Falls.

'Every night without fail.'

'You'll wear him out.'

Her mother gives her a lascivious grin. 'Fat chance. He knows when he's on to a good thing.'

She laughs until her eyes water. She is still laughing when she leaves the room to seek out her granddaughter.

Athena tiptoes to the door of Jewel's room to eavesdrop.

She hears shared laughter, but how can that be possible?

She hears a few muttered comments, more conspiratorial whispering and giggling and then Jewel's voice: 'My funkster grandmother. Way to go, Gran.'

The funkster grandmother emerges flushed and beaming from the bedroom.

Athena frowns. How does her mother do it?

'Why do you insist on blaming yourself for Jewel's atrocious behaviour?' Clare wants to know when she arrives for her next massage. She pokes and prods in the amorphous morass of Athena's emotions like a surgeon with a blunt knife.

Athena's hands stop stroking Clare's back. Her stomach clenches. Clare and her probing questions and forthright opinions.

'I must have done something. Said something . . . I don't know what.' Her voice trails off. She has examined her conscience. She *has* been a good mother.

Beneath her, Clare's body tenses. Can't she ever relax?

'Athena, your daughter is behaving like a complete bitch and I don't know why you stand for it. *I* certainly wouldn't.'

Athena bites her lip. What would Clare know? She's never been a mother. But what's the point in alienating Clare? Old friends should stick together. Athena does a lot of gritting of teeth and turning the other cheek. The nuns would be proud of her.

She was in her twenties before she came to terms with the fact that she was never going to be rewarded for being a nice person. She wears her kindness like a second skin and is hurt and bewildered when she is treated with indifference or disrespect. Athena's disingenuous optimism, gullibility and good intentions are inevitably misconstrued, perceived by men, and certainly by her daughter, as weakness.

She is too nice for her own good. Miss Perfect, the girls had taunted her at the convent. Miss Goody-goody-two-shoes – Miss Prude. Athena didn't even need to try to become the classic good Catholic girl. The behaviour trait was etched into her DNA, said Clare.

'You are too good, you've sacrificed too much for Jewel,' says Clare firmly, feeling perfectly entitled to be this blunt. Rights conferred on the basis of a twenty-six-year friendship. Clare had been the first girl to approach skinny Lizzie when they all started college and say hello.

'But you *want* the best for your kids. It's only natural.' Athena rotates her knuckles on Clare's shoulders a fraction harder than is actually necessary, but Clare is so preoccupied with her thoughts she doesn't even notice.

'What's natural about being abused?' comes the crisp reply.

Athena questions if there had been a critical moment

141

in her interactions with a prepubescent Jewel, when, if she had only responded differently—

'Stop whipping yourself,' says Clare, picking up on her thoughts. 'Do you really believe motherhood and guilt go together? Can't have one without the other in tow. You did your best. But don't forget, she's a teenager. They're all vile. Hate their parents. Can't wait to separate from them. It's normal. Don't you remember?'

'We weren't as bad.' Athena criss-crosses Clare's back in a series of figures of eight.

'*You* mightn't have been. You were a good girl, or have you forgotten that too? Everyone was stunned when you broke out and ran off with someone as dishy as Sebastian. No-one realized at the time what a jerk he would turn out to be.'

'I always had poor taste in men. How did Bridget strike it so lucky? Was she better prepared than the rest of us?'

'She attracted her share of bastards, but she was unnaturally good at seeing through them.' Clare hasn't finished with Jewel. 'Leaving is important. Leaving home, separating from the parent.'

Athena kneads Clare's left thigh. 'But it has to be done the right way, don't you think?'

'Jewel will take off one day like a cork exploding from a bottle of champagne. *Bang!* A grand gesture, that's our Jewel.'

Clare, Agnes and Bridget have all taken turns to babysit Jewel in her childhood and fancied themselves as aunts in loco parentis. Yet, of the three, Clare is probably the most favourably disposed towards Jewel. She has a grudging respect for Jewel's uncompromising stances. It doesn't mean she is prepared to tolerate Jewel's shabby, contemptuous treatment of Athena, but she is convinced there must be an element in Jewel's rebarbative personality which is salvageable.

'Now she wants to change her name.'

Clare's body quivers with barely suppressed laughter. Athena pauses in the act of stroking the sole of the right foot until Clare's body stops shaking.

'To *what*, for God's sake?'

'*Sarah.*'

'Let her. You changed your own name. Remember? Your mother swore she would never forgive you.'

'But—' Athena begins to protest.

Clare cuts her off. 'Let her go, Athena. You can't prevent her. Could anyone stop you? How many people warned you about Sebastian? You refused to listen. Convinced you knew best.'

'Did I? Was I that stupid? Anyway, what makes *you* such an expert?'

'The advantage of distance. I'm not involved. Set limits over the really important stuff, Athena, and forget about the trivia.'

'I'm the wrong mother for Jewel,' says Athena as she replaces the towels on the table. 'You would have been more effective. Tougher.'

'Tough love, that's what's required now,' agrees Clare, stepping into her lace stretch knickers.

Athena owes a great deal to Clare. It was she who had volunteered to lend Athena the money ten years previously so she could learn to massage, to purchase a good table and to equip herself with a basic kit of essential oils. After she had completed three short courses her friends urged her to wean herself off the Domestic Purposes Benefit by starting her own business.

Many of Clare's, Agnes's and Bridget's friends and colleagues came to Athena for solace from the pressures of their hectic lives. She became privy to all

143

manner of confidences and quickly realized that if she wanted to keep her business, especially with Clare's friends, it was advisable to forget most of what she heard on the table. She has since repaid Clare and, in addition, given her a year's worth of free massages. When the year was up Clare still continued to come on a fortnightly basis.

Athena may owe Clare a debt of gratitude, but they remain planets apart in their philosophies. A waste of breath explaining chakras and energy fields to Clare. New Age mumbo-jumbo she calls it. Why can't Clare make an effort to understand and respect her real work? Doesn't she realize Athena is not just a masseuse and aromatherapist?

She is a healer.

Yet why is it that no matter how many positive affirmations she repeats, she never succeeds in feeling herself to be Clare's equal?

I'm jealous of her, Athena realizes. As a young convent girl she would have felt under a strong obligation to admit to entertaining uncharitable thoughts, to expressing malice, being ungrateful, or committing sins of pride and laziness. They all resulted in her receiving a penance of three Hail Marys and an Our Father to appease Him Up There.

Bless me Father, for I have sinned. I have been greedy, disobedient, told lies—

How many times have you told lies?

I can't remember, Father. So many times.

Daily. Every hour?

Try to do better next time. The Lord so loves a trier, did you know that?

Yes, Father.

Now then, make a good act of contrition, tell God how sorry you are.

Only she wasn't sorry. Not a bit.

144

For your penance . . .

God, it made her so flaming mad now. The weight of those paltry sins.

She had been determined that her daughter wouldn't be forced to bear the same burden, have Catholicism rammed down her throat the way it had been for her and her friends. Has she gone too far the other way? Jewel couldn't care less about the consequences of her words and actions. Is it because she hasn't had the fear of God and hellfire drummed into her? The words atonement and reparation don't exist in her vocabulary. The concepts of mercy and punishment are just as foreign to her. She is afraid of nothing. She will conquer any world she chooses to dwell in.

If you can't find it in your heart to repent now, there is an eternity waiting ahead of you.

Athena pictures Jewel's scorn and derision should she insist on a visit to the confessional. Do they still have confessionals? Recently Clare had related to Athena with much amusement her experiences at a Catholic wedding, which included a nuptial mass. She had observed people hugging each other halfway through the service. 'Peace be with you,' they had said with conviction. Clare recalled that she had found something slightly distasteful in the outbreak of hugging.

'Imagine if despite everything there's no escape – the priests, our parents, they get you in the end, we've just been fooling ourselves,' she had told Athena.

'Or worse, that it's all true and we really do rot in hell.'

Clare leaned forward. 'Promise me something,' she said. 'If I ever insist on returning and repenting, I want you to talk me out of it. If I contract a life-threatening disease and I'm away with the fairies on morphine, promise you'll protect me. Don't let my parents bring

145

in the bloody priest and create some sham of a deathbed repentance. Promise?'

Athena howls with laughter at the very idea. This is why she has remained friends with Clare — for her irreverence towards their common history, her sense of humour, their in-jokes.

'The nuns taught us nothing that really mattered.'

'True. It's a crime they sent girls as ignorant and innocent as we were out into the real world. And not just the nuns either. Priests. Parents. Everyone.'

'Yeah. But we've survived. God only knows how.'

'By the way,' says Clare at the front door. A gleam in her eye. 'Some goss for you. Agnes has a new man. You'll never guess. An ex-priest.'

'Wait,' pleads Athena, 'tell me more.' But Clare is already off down the shell pathway.

'Can't, sorry.' She tosses the words over her shoulder. 'In a hurry, talk to you later.'

Athena watches Clare striding to her car, keys jiggling in her hand, leather briefcase slapping against one leg.

An unexpected lump blocks her throat.

Clare.

Always running to deadline. Enslaved to diary. Subject to budget. Speeding through her life as if there were no tomorrow. The only time she stops is when she is on Athena's table.

Athena wishes Clare would allow her to get stuck in and open those blocked chakras.

What Clare really needs, reflects Athena, is a karmic vacuum.

Athena knows just the person.

If she could only persuade Clare.

But she knows already what Clare's response would be.

Chapter Eleven

Agnes

He was persistent. The Sunday morning after the dinner her phone beeped at ten a.m. Agnes was still in bed absorbed in a Margaret Atwood novel, a steaming mug of coffee alongside her on the bedside table.

'Hello.'

'It's *me*.'

God she hated it when men did this.

She sighed with resignation. 'Hello, *me*.'

He invited her to dinner at his flat. Caught unprepared, suffering from a temporary loss of nerve, she almost turned him down. If he had applied pressure, she would have. As if he sensed this he had waited patiently for her to make up her mind.

His flat is an old wooden bungalow located four kilometres from the centre of the city. He has created a comfortable yet unpretentious environment for himself. Not at all what she had expected.

There's no bad art for starters. A framed print of a Piero della Francesca madonna. A richly patterned hand-woven Indian rug is thrown over a shabby old green sofa. A red Madras cotton cushion provides another vivid splash of colour. In a corner of the large lounge is a stripped kauri dining table. In the centre of the table a hand-painted ceramic bowl is piled high with oranges and lemons.

'I've enjoyed creating a home,' he says simply.

Agnes blinks hard.

Unsurprisingly, there is ample evidence of his reading life in the industrial shelving that runs the length of the hallway. She scans the spines for clues: Brian Moore, Don DeLillo, Paul Auster, Julian Barnes, Doris Lessing, Iris Murdoch, Flann O'Brien. A few Irish histories, some T. S. Eliot. Ken Wilber, Meister Eckhart, Viktor Frankl and Matthew Fox stand out in the row of theology, psychology and philosophy texts. There's a shelf containing books about meditation.

She's curious about his bedroom. She imagines a priest's cell. Again he confounds her stereotypes. A cheerful patterned duvet cover. Photos of his brothers' and sisters' children are grouped on one wall. On the bedside table is a crudely painted carved wooden statue of a madonna. He tells her it is from Guatemala. A priest friend had given it to him.

'So. You still have a few friends who are priests?'

He looks surprised at the question. 'Of course.'

'You weren't given a hard time then?'

'My friends know me. I've been true to myself. Who could object to that, Agnes?'

He takes her through to his little kitchen and makes her a cup of weak instant coffee.

'Daniel, this coffee is shit, I can't drink it.'

'Sorry.'

'My mother says I drink so much coffee, if I don't watch it, I'll turn into a bean.'

He laughs, his blue eyes crinkling with amusement.

Nice eyes, she thinks.

'Can I ask you about the time when you were a priest?'

'You mean, can we get it out of the way?'

Agnes grins and settles herself in more comfortably on the couch.

He picks up his coffee, takes a sip.

'Where do I start? What do you want to know?' He sits, legs astride in his long baggy shorts, chin resting in his hands, elbows planted on his knees.

Bony slightly crooked knees. Sweet knees.

'I'd like to know more about you.'

Sweet knees?

'What's the hurry? Can't my history emerge gradually as we get to know each other?'

'I need to know now.'

He gives her a penetrating glance. 'Why now? Will it make a difference to whether or not you want to see me again? If I give you the wrong answers will you be turned off me?'

'How can I say? What I do know is, I can't even begin to know you until we talk openly about the fact that you spent twenty years of your life as a priest. It's a very long time to spend only to then chuck it in, don't you think?'

'Are you judging me?' he asks quietly. 'I hate to be judged. I'm not sure what my crime is.'

'I really am interested.'

He runs his hands through his thick black hair. Grey wing-like streaks slope down to each temple.

There's a long pause.

She takes in the dishevelled hair, the frayed collar. She can't read him. He bothers her in ways she can't even begin to explain to herself.

They both start to speak at the same time.

'You make me nervous.'

'I'm sorry. I didn't mean to. Look, if you don't want to talk . . .'

'I never said I wouldn't.'

'OK then. Why did you leave the priesthood?'

'Politics.'

'Not sex?'

'That's a myth. What the tabloids would have you believe. Actually, it was the politics. Many of the priests in my generation bailed out. A generation simply disappeared.'

'Fairly predictable, I would have thought.'

'Of course, some left because of the celibacy issue, but not everybody. My generation were very idealistic. They genuinely wanted to make people's lives better. The Church, however, is run like any army or multi-national company. It's pretty easy to buy off the Church, to get them on side.'

'They were, after all, perfectly happy to be chaplains to Hitler and Mussolini.'

'Exactly. I left because it began to seem to me as if the Church was irrelevant. After John XXIII, the opening up of priestly mission was discussed. But the institution of the Church was still into management expansion theory – empire building rather than the redemption of the world.'

'But that's nothing new. Think of Gregory and the Crusades. The notion of holy wars and wiping out the infidel.' She is fascinated. 'So what was your gripe?'

'There are many things I treasure about Catholicism, but I began to believe that I had outgrown it. I was deeply frustrated with the Church's refusal to ordain women, the continuing imposition of celibacy, the lack of inclusiveness – of acceptance of gay men and lesbians, of people whose marriages failed. Then there was the inflexibility regarding the contraception issue. The attitudes of the bishops and of the incumbent pope. Need I go on? The "Roman" part of the institution is living on another planet.'

'Do you think radical changes will happen?'

'Not in my lifetime.'

'So you don't like the pope?'

'He's a disaster in many ways. He's no fool, mind you. Very talented. Multilingual. But the fact remains that he has been shaped by his own Polish culture. The Italian popes were more flexible.' Daniel puts down his cup and leans back on the couch.

'Have your beliefs changed?'

'What has changed most is my concept of God.'

'Oh?'

'I've never been into the Judaic Old Testament view of God—'

'Very anthropomorphic.'

'Yeah. But I've also never been able to get my head around the idea of "personality" in relation to God either.'

'No? Isn't that because the notion of personality involves some finite limited creature in which personality resides?'

'Exactly.'

'I haven't thought about God in years and have no intention of beginning now. What about you? Your feelings? Your fears and personal doubts? Give me the guts.'

'I don't know you well enough yet to go spilling my guts on the floor.'

'OK, sorry. I've been too pushy, but I'm just so interested. Well, can you at least tell me then – are there still people out there who think of you as a priest?'

'The less I acted as a priest, the less people saw me as a priest.'

'Did it take you a number of years to arrive at your decision to leave?'

151

'It was a gradual process, yes. I'm not a person who makes instant decisions.'

'Apart from the politics, was there a critical moment? A personal crisis? Was it a question of faith? Did you have your own "dark night of the soul"?'

'I did.' But he doesn't offer to elaborate.

'Were you lonely?' she asks gently.

'Of course. But that's not a condition peculiar to priests as far as I'm aware. I've seen married couples lonelier, believe me.'

'True.'

'Being a priest was a simple way of living. But I wouldn't describe it as grinding poverty.' Deftly he swings the conversation back to her. 'Do *you* ever feel lonely?'

Agnes has to think for a moment. She keeps herself too busy to feel lonely.

Daniel pats her knee. 'You were miles away.'

'Mmmm.' A habit she has developed from years of living on her own, being in business on her own, of wandering off, becoming lost in the maze of competing thoughts and ideas.

What Agnes really wants to know, of course, is whether Daniel has had much experience with women.

'How old were you when you entered the priesthood?'

'Eighteen, when I entered the seminary.'

Agnes shakes her head. 'So young. How can anyone make such decisions when they know nothing, have experienced so little?'

He shrugs. 'It's what you did. I believed I had a calling. I've never worked out why – we're not talking telegram from God stuff. I wanted to be of use, to give of myself. The Brothers encouraged me. My mother was keen. My family was devotedly Catholic, but not

152

fanatical, you understand. I was brought up to be tolerant. Everything conspired to make it seem like a good proposition. I went along with it. Becoming a priest was the way I expressed myself in the world. Some people paint pictures. I offered Mass.

'You seem fixated by this aspect of me. It's in the past now. I've moved on.'

He tells her about his current work with poor families, dysfunctional families, the logistics of placing at-risk kids with new foster families. The follow-up stuff. The joys and frustrations. His dedication to his work comes through with every sentence he utters.

She listens and it is as if she has just received a bruising by colliding with a fast-moving object. She feels lightheaded. Who cares if his clothes are hopelessly out of date and his hair appears to have been hacked at by blunt gardening shears?

This time it is she who asks if they can meet again outside class.

They may well become close friends. That's enough. She could do with another reliable male companion, a purely platonic male friendship in her life.

And that's as far as it goes. So, as he poses no threat to her and he doesn't turn her on, where is the harm in seeing him again?

Agnes hums as she drives back to her apartment.

Chapter Twelve

Clare

Clare is driving from her downtown office to her therapist's feeling weary and stressed as she struggles to switch gears from corporate to personal mode.

She mulls over a possible endorser for a new Harmony Heaven product. That afternoon she had facilitated a meeting in which they had brainstormed potential recruits. A growing list of names had been tossed backwards and forwards.

One would be scrapped, another would be added to the shortlist. The name of a reputable older broadcaster was mentioned by Rhonda.

'She doesn't endorse.' Clare had sucked on her pen. 'Leave it with me. I'll give it some more thought. Ask around. See what I can come up with.'

She is drained of energy. She has come to expect that a knot will develop and settle itself in the base of her stomach a few hours before she is due to see Fiona her therapist. She is struck by a poignant image of herself attempting to keep it all under control at the meeting, yet feeling at the same time as if she is falling apart inside.

Her morning had begun as usual with a punishing

routine at the gym. She had just been given a new pro-gramme. Driving to the gym still half asleep, Clare was aware of the winter sun as a blinding orb suspended low on the horizon, framed by skeletal branches of bare trees. Inside the changing room she had marched past taut trim bodies and heavy-hipped Bessies. The lovely and the unlovely. On into the women's gym where she confronted a veritable scaffolding of white-painted steel, black vinyl and grey rubber. Her heart sank. At that moment every aspect of her life seemed leached of colour. Several of the windows were partially open. A cold blast of July air slugged her in the chest as she wearily climbed on the bike to warm up.

Stalled at a set of traffic lights, she dictates a few ad-ditional names for endorsers into a tiny tape recorder she keeps in her briefcase. Everyone around her also seems to be using their car as an extension of their office. Two men and a woman are talking into cell-phones. A woman is absorbed in reading a magazine propped up against the steering wheel.

Seeking distraction from fretting about work, or else her stalemate with Adrian, Clare switches on the radio and becomes absorbed in a story about the sea turtle. It's supposed to be protected, but of course there are always people who ignore conservation restrictions.

God it makes her mad.

On the domestic front, house prices have slumped. The apartments she and Adrian invested in with such confidence have slipped in value. Now there is a glut of rental accommodation on the market. Adrian is stewing over his failure to extract payment from a recalcitrant developer who has temporarily skipped the country, owing a fortune to a trail of enraged debtors. In the meantime, Clare is paying the bills until he is paid what he is owed.

155

And now those poor sea turtles, some selfish bastards are set to destroy them as well. Everything is being slowly contaminated. Athena is right. The earth is in pain and crying out to be healed. You can't count on anything any more. People being decent to each other. Not being raped or maimed or robbed before you died.

Clare abruptly slams on her brakes with an unpleasant screech, narrowly escaping ploughing into the Mazda in front of her.

Concentrate, Clare.

The traffic stalls again. She groans with frustration, even though she knows perfectly well that what she puts up with is nothing compared with London, or even New York. But this is why she lives here, isn't it, so she can avoid all that, experience instead this small-scale version of a traffic jam so she can enjoy a better quality of life.

Huh? Just who is she kidding here?

Adrian and she haven't been able to get away for a weekend for several months, due to either his deadlines or hers. Both of them often resenting each other's work and the price they pay to keep the show on the road. And what's it all for, she is increasingly asking herself. An ulcer and an early grave? Is this what women fought for? But if she does succeed in her ambition to have a baby whose work would take second place, hers or his?

'Yours, of course,' Adrian always insisted. '*You're* the one who's so keen to have a kid, not me. I've done my bit.'

She had snorted derisively. '*Your* bit? You've dipped out, I'd say.'

And away they went. Hammer and tongs. Swords and knives.

How expert they had become, fighting without leaving any visible scars.

They were trapped on an endless conveyor belt — destination unknown. They generally sped past his family, turned a corner, rolled down onto hers, collided, lost momentum for a bit, picked up speed and then tumbled down onto the baby issue, dipped down into his work, and round another bend to her work, her sacrifices.

Her *extravagances*, claimed Adrian.

'If you don't stop shopping,' he had threatened, 'I'll leave you.'

'Oh, phooey,' retorted Clare. 'Besides, it's *my* money I'm spending, not yours. Or have you forgotten? It's me who is paying the bills right now.'

The issue of babies could be relied upon to draw blood.

'I never promised you a child,' Adrian reminded her.

'Why are you being so negative?' complained Clare.

'Not negative. Realistic. One of us has to be realistic. Your head is full of romantic sentimental notions of motherhood. God knows where you get them from. Not from your own family, that's for sure.'

'I've always assumed we would share the responsibility for the child.'

'Why should you assume that? It's nothing to do with me. Certainly not what I want for the rest of my life. No way.'

'Where does this leave me?' In the past she has always staunchly maintained she would never have a child unless her partner assumed responsibility for half of the caregiving, became a househusband or, at the very least, shared the cost of a nanny. The irony implicit in the current situation is not lost on her.

'You'll give in. You'll agree to it eventually.'

She will work on him, wear him down.

'I'm entitled to make my own decision about whether or not I have a baby.'

157

'Not in this particular relationship you don't.'

'You're telling me I can't have a baby, is that it?' Clare had shouted.

'I'm telling you that you can't have a baby with *me*. Read my lips. *No, no, no.*'

'Do you think that's fair?' she demanded.

'It's got nothing to do with fair, and everything to do with us being two individuals at different stages, with *completely different* agendas.'

'Don't believe you,' she had taunted.

'You'd better. Try me. I'd walk out first.' Arms folded, jaw set, Adrian had stared at Clare with a grim expression on his face. No amount of beautiful possessions and exquisite dinners could compensate her for the set expression on his face.

'You weren't this stubborn when we first got together.'

'You weren't interested in getting pregnant when we first got together. Remember?'

'I'm allowed to change my mind.' A fist of panic had thwacked her in the stomach. 'YOU!' She had flung a cushion at him and marched out of the room in disgust.

'I wasn't put on this earth just to meet your unreasonable demands,' he called after her.

Unreasonable?

Hot tears had stung her eyes.

After their arguments they each sulked in lonely misery at opposite ends of the house. Clare's eye make-up streaked in snail's tracks down her cheeks. Adrian tight-lipped and stiff-backed. How she hated him then, hated him more than she had ever hated anyone in her life before.

Yet, mysteriously, an hour or two later they could well be in bed together, frantically making love as if their lives depended upon it and swearing to never leave each other.

But before this happy outcome was achieved, dinner was cooked in silence. Two gins quickly downed. Well, two for Clare. She counted three, sometimes four for Adrian. That got her talking again. *His* drinking problem, she carped.

She should talk, retorted Adrian childishly.

She not only hated Adrian then, she had also hated herself for the person she had become in the five years they had been together.

They had fallen into a pattern. Each unable to admit they were wrong, unwilling to make the compromises necessary for two fiercely strong individuals to coexist peacefully.

Plagued by memories of the previous night's fight, Clare continues her interminable journey to the house in Grey Lynn where Fiona waits in her immaculate lilac office on her blue velvet armchair.

Clare hasn't confided to Bridget, or indeed to any of her friends, that she has been seeing a therapist for the past three months.

'You cannot both win,' Fiona gently reminds her. 'On the baby issue, one of you will be making a sacrifice in order for the other to have what he or she wants.'

'But why *me*?' wails Clare, her face crumpled and damp. Her friends would not have recognized her.

'I should leave Adrian,' she sniffs tearfully. 'It's the only option.'

'Is it? Why do you want a baby so badly?'

'I just *do*. I don't have to justify it, do I?'

'You can do better than that,' insists her counsellor, in full pursuit. 'You're an intelligent woman. You insist that for the past twenty years you have had no

159

desire to have a baby. Why now? What has changed for you?'

'Previously I felt as if I had options. I could change my mind at any time. Now I feel as if it is Adrian who has decided my fate.'

'Really? You've only been with him for five years. Did you ever consider having a baby with any of your previous partners?'

'No. As I said, I always imagined I had oodles of time. I put it off until later.'

'I'm simply trying to show you that your own choices in the past have also led you to this point. You can't just shove all the blame onto Adrian.'

'Listen to me.' Clare feels as if she has to point out the obvious. 'I haven't got much time left. I'm about to turn forty. I *have* to resolve this. I feel quite desperate about it.'

'How desperate? Enough to seriously consider giving up a relationship which you claim, on the whole, gives you what you need?'

'Our relationship actually worked. Until Adrian and I started arguing about babies. It's crazy, I know it is. I mean, I don't even get on with his children.'

Another issue altogether. She will save that for next time.

'Tell me, why *can't* I have it all? A partner who wants to have a child with me. Career and mother-hood. Motherhood without feeling obliged to be "supermum". Career and nanny without feeling guilty.

'You know, Fiona, I'm just so tired and burnt out. Exhausted to my very bones from toughing it out in what has turned out to be a mean old world. I'm ready, I think, for a change of pace.'

Fiona gives her a sympathetic nod but makes no comment until she sees Clare has finished.

'Haven't you proved beyond a doubt to everybody,

particularly to yourself, if not to your mother finally, that you are as good as, if not better than most men?'

Clare shrugs. 'I no longer feel as if I have to prove myself. That's not the issue. If I were to have a baby now, my child would be ten when I am fifty, twenty by the time I reach sixty. A teenager who would be requiring university fees subsidized just as I am approaching retirement.'

Clare clasps and unclasps her hands. 'Is it too late for me? . . . But other women have managed it. Forty-year-old mothers, second-time fathers in their fifties. It's not so uncommon now, after all. Although Adrian has made it only too clear what he wants for his future. *His* future, mind you, not my future, or *our* future.'

'But what do *you* want for the rest of your life? If it is not to be a future that includes Adrian, then what do you want instead?'

'Maybe I should leave Adrian as soon as possible, while I am still of an age to meet someone else to have babies with?'

'Perhaps we can explore this together at our next appointment.' Fiona smiles and indicates that their hour together has come to an end for today.

Clare thanks her, writes out her cheque, makes a new appointment and blunders out of the office.

Why should it be she who takes on the role of the sacrificial offering? Clare mulls over her options as she drives away from Grey Lynn and onto the southern motorway towards Epsom.

She recalls an old expression in vogue around the time she was a student. *Gold digger.* It was used to refer to those canny female students who haunted medical, law, or dental school in the hopes of catching a handsome young professional middle-class white male. These very same women are now sensibly ensconced in wealthy suburbs. Early in the proceedings they had produced the requisite two children. Now they are no doubt supervising the uprooting of their English cottage gardens, and the installing of replacement Italian gardens complete with lavender bushes, yew hedges, shell paths and miniature citrus trees in terracotta urns. Children now conveniently off their hands, leaving plenty of time for tennis, a dabble in the odd charity, regular trips abroad, lots of lovely clothes, no obligation or pressure whatsoever to get out and earn their living – because they are kept women.

She and Agnes have always regarded such women with contempt. Yet maybe the gold diggers weren't so stupid after all. She and Agnes have been working their butts off for twenty years, with another twenty-five years of hard slog ahead of them. No sign of a respite on the horizon. A life sentence, and no legitimate excuse to escape it.

'No rest for the wicked,' her mother is fond of quoting. Her mother's more banal pronouncements have inevitably been the ones that have stuck in Clare's mind.

Clare mentally lists all the women she knows who are searching for a man to father children. Why? Because her male peers, now on their second or third marriages, are mating with women ten years younger. Their opportunities to reproduce, unlike Clare's, are not limited by any biological clock.

Two of her own previous partners, Henry and Mark, both now in their early forties, are in fact currently with 'babes' (Mark's word) in their late twenties and very early thirties respectively. Her former partners, in a last ditch attempt to reclaim their lost youth and prove their virility, are now impatient to reproduce.

She has retained sporadic contact with both men. Mark has been frank with her.

'Sure, I deliberately went for a woman in her early thirties,' he confessed. 'It makes good sense. If I had chosen someone my own age whose biological clock was near midnight, the pressure would have been on the relationship from day one to have a kid. I wanted to give the relationship a chance first. The relationship, not the kid, has to be the priority.

'And what about you, Clare?' he had asked, leaning forward to catch her answer. Friendly, but detached with the ex. Doesn't want the old dear to miss out. He hopes someone (Adrian?) will do the decent thing by her.

Clare is well practised at presenting herself as an old pro. 'Oh, I'm pretty committed,' she had answered in an 'I couldn't give a damn' manner, accompanied by a bright convincing smile. 'The company is my baby.'

She waited for him to tell her to 'cut the crap, Clare'.

But their separated selves are far more polite and willing to turn a blind eye to half truths than they ever were as a twosome. Instead of challenging her, Mark had looked at her with respect.

'You always were a goer, Clare.'

The old dear, old pro, the goer, had paid for the coffee, given her former lover a quick peck on the cheek and gone home to bawl her eyes out.

Clare has a nagging sense of being left behind. For the past five years, the length of time she has cohabited with Adrian, she has believed, mistakenly, she now realizes, that it was she who has left *them* behind. For it to be otherwise is unthinkable.

'I'm not the kind of person who cries easily,' Clare admits to Fiona at their next session. 'But in the past year I have cried more than in the previous fifteen. What does this mean? Am I losing my grip — and not just when I have PMT either — although even those

163

symptoms seem to have worsened over recent months.'

'I've known some women's periods to get worse as they become peri-menopausal.'

'Menopausal?' shrieks Clare. 'Banish that awful word. I haven't even had a bloody baby yet. How did I come to be in this ludicrous situation? Somehow, I've selected a mate who is serious in his refusal to do his duty and father my child. And it appears I can blame no-one but my own stupid self.'

'Well, I don't think it's terribly constructive to go down the road of blaming people—'

'Why not? As you've demonstrated, I've made a series of choices in my life that have led me to this point. My biggest fear has always been that I would make a poor decision, take a wrong turning and wreck my life. Find myself ultimately alone and frequently lonely, as are my friends Athena and Agnes, scavenging like flies for leftovers in the rubbish tip of others' failed relationships.'

'Is that how they view it?'

'Agnes swears that she likes living alone – but I don't believe her.'

'It sounds to me as if you have never been without a partner. Never known failure or rejection.'

'I guess that's true. But has my luck run out now? Were Henry and Mark really so unsuitable, so undeserving, so dull? The reasons why both relationships disintegrated are long forgotten and buried in a haze of recriminations and regrets. If only we had been more skilled, or had taken ourselves off to decent counselling. Would the separations from my previous partners still have come to seem so inevitable, so right? Have I simply been running away from myself all along without realizing it?'

Fiona doesn't immediately venture an opinion.

Typical. Instead she asks Clare what *she* thinks.

'I think I did make the right decisions at the time.'

Although Adrian has his faults, until she had begun to stir up the issue of babies, she had been far more content with him than she had been with either Henry or Mark. Despite having to contend with Mike and Tiffany. She had got on extremely well with both children before they had entered their teens – a fact she often forgets.

Adrian has on occasion accused her of keeping a score card in her head and stated that no man alive could ever measure up to her ideals and expectations.

'Is this true?' asks Fiona.

'Well, Mark was great in bed, better than Adrian actually, but he was impractical, wouldn't have known one end of a hammer from another, and he was a lousy cook. But on the plus side, he also made me laugh and was very easy-going. We rarely fought – I simply got terminally bored.

'Henry was average in bed, but he made up for that by being a terrific cook – almost as good as Adrian. He was forever building or repairing something or other in our house. On the debit side he had no sense of humour, a terrible temper and was hopeless with money. Adrian, on the other hand, can cook as well as fix things, he is witty and stimulating – although rather selfish. His performance in bed ranges from abysmal to extraordinary – depending on his current levels of stress.'

Fiona nods.

'If on the eve of turning forty I'm questioning the wisdom of previous relationship breakdowns, will I at fifty be regretting that I left Adrian? Or will I be relieved that I stayed and made a success of the relationship? . . . Even if it means abandoning the notion of having a child?'

'Life is a risk. A gamble. There are no guarantees — you know that, Clare.'

Clare hurtles on, words tumbling over each other. 'Yes, but what if I make the wrong choices?'

'You don't have to rush into any decisions. Keep thinking about your options. In the meantime try to keep the dialogue open with Adrian.'

'This is my last chance to have a baby. It's now or never.'

It was all very well for the nuns to recommend developing an informed conscience, or to leave it to almighty God in his infinite wisdom, et cetera. Or for Athena to rabbit on about trusting your passion, your own instinctive responses and following them – wherever they might lead. It doesn't help right now. Nothing helps.

Recently Clare has been disconcerted to find herself simply unable to keep her life compartmentalized. Fragments of the past have an unnerving habit of infiltrating the present. Only the other night while making love with Adrian (yes, they still do it), they had both been appalled to hear Clare murmur *'Mark'* when Adrian entered her. He had lost his way for a moment there.

'Sorry,' she had whispered.

Last week she had yelled *'God, Henry!'* when Adrian had thrown the coloureds and the whites together into the washing machine. (As if she hadn't told him a million times.)

Oops.

Another life. Another Clare. Somehow these lives must be kept separate and not blur, one life drifting out of control into another. Otherwise chaos will reign and she will be – as her father would have put it – up shit creek without a paddle.

Chapter Thirteen

Bridget

'Do you think we're the last literate generation?' Agnes asks Bridget as they stroll down Takapuna beach on a late Sunday afternoon. 'Will our friends' kids be reading books in ten years' time, or will they have a computer strapped to their wrists instead?'

'Forget ten years' time,' replies Bridget, who has taken up art teaching again. 'Right *now*, they aren't reading. Instead they're skimming magazines, watching videos, playing computer games, surfing the Net. You know, I was talking to a pupil the other day and she told me she had just read *Little Women* – the abbreviated version based on the film, as distinct from the original novel. She hadn't even realized there was an original. I despair.'

'I used to love that book. I loved it *so much*. Now you've depressed *me*.'

In the distance a windsurfer streaks past. The last swimmers of the day are bodysurfing towards them. Closer into shore a man in his forties, pot belly into the wind, clutching a doll by its legs, water swirling around his ankles, waits for his daughter to stream in on her floatboard.

Bridget turns to face Agnes. '*You're* depressed? Try teaching art to kids who see it as a free period, an excuse to slack off. Kids who can't see any relevance in anything artistic or creative. I have to prove art is important. Imagine. They test me, to see how far they can push me before I'll explode. They like knowing they've succeeded in getting under my skin. I dared to reprimand a boy the other day and he aimed a staple gun at me.'

'What did you do?'

Bridget watches the man lead his daughter out of the water.

'I ducked out of the way.'

'Did he get suspended?'

'No, but he's been given a warning.' Bridget concentrates on the sound of her boots crunching over the crushed segments of tuatua shells and fragments of black volcanic rock.

'I heard they're suspending six-year-olds now. I saw an article.'

'Kids can be wicked, even at six.'

'Do you know many people who have good parenting skills?'

'No.'

'Yet despite everything you still want to have a child, Bridget.'

'I don't want to talk about it,' answers Bridget in a clipped voice.

'Why would anyone want to bring a child into this fucked-up world?' persists Agnes, rubbing salt into the wound. She wishes she could retract her thoughtless words the second she has uttered them.

'I'm not having a bloody baby, Agnes,' yells Bridget, suddenly losing patience.

'You've given up then?'

'Yes. We have. I'm getting on with my life.' She stomps on ahead.

'God, Bridgie.' Agnes hurries to catch up.

They head back up the beach arm in arm, in silence. Past the cold water tap where children are cleaning their feet, past a wooden picnic table where a bloated man with very white skin has a rash like a series of handprints scattered over his back. His Asian wife/lover/companion stands looking out to sea with a blank expression on her face. Bridget wonders if the man has been bitten by sea lice, if the woman is one of the huge influx of recent Asian migrants, if they are married, how they met.

She thinks too about how much she loathes teaching, how exhausting it is. Why had she ever believed it might provide a ready-made answer?

She no longer wakes up every morning thinking about babies. Instead she frets about breast lumps and what they might turn into. She really must go to the doctor – she's procrastinated long enough.

'It feels like a piece of gravel.'

Bridget watches Maryanne's face for clues as to her response.

'Well, it's very hard,' agrees Maryanne. 'And it doesn't move around.'

She completes her examination of Bridget's breast and underarms. Her hands are cold.

She asks Bridget about her family history on her mother's side.

'My mother had a mastectomy at forty-four. But she's had no recurrence of the cancer since.'

'Hmmm. Do you know if she was peri-menopausal?'

'I think so. I'll find out.'

'OK.'

OK, what? A wave of panic builds in Bridget's chest.

'Because the lump is so hard and because it doesn't move, we won't take any risks. I think we should get it looked at as soon as possible – just to be absolutely certain.'

'Because of my mother's history?'

'People can make too much of family history. It doesn't *necessarily* follow, you know. Plenty of women get breast cancer who have no family history of it,' Maryanne says gently and gives her a smile that is meant to be reassuring.

Although the doctor seems both competent and compassionate, Bridget is not reassured. She feels frightened, vulnerable and apprehensive.

'So. What happens next?'

'Do you have private insurance?'

'Yes.' Thank goodness Matthew had insisted.

'That's good. These days in private you can have the tests, the biopsy and get the results all in the same day. Whereas in public, it might take a week.'

Bridget grips the sides of her seat. She knows the doctor has just told her some important information and she has not properly heard it. Her mind was too preoccupied with imagining worst case scenarios. Apologizing, she asks Maryanne to repeat what she has just said.

'I'll refer you to a specialist. You'll have mammography and ultrasound. Then you'll have a needle biopsy under local anaesthetic so they can take a tissue sample. Only a biopsy can tell you for sure. Mammography on its own is not enough. You can have normal mammography results and still have breast cancer.'

Bridget drives home in a daze. She still hasn't taken it in.

'What if the lump is malignant?' Matthew demands to know, his face creased with anxiety.

Bridget can't remember what the doctor said. The consultation is a blurred memory.

Matthew becomes annoyed. 'You must have asked her?'

'I . . .'

'Call her in the morning. Get the facts, for Christ's sake. And take notes.'

'Don't boss me,' says Bridget with a stubborn set to her face. 'It's my bloody lump.'

If the lump turns out to be malignant, Maryanne tells her, then they'll want to know if the cancer has spread into the lymph glands. 'The aim will be to remove the area of malignancy.'

'Surgery.'

'That's right.'

'And if it's spread to the lymph glands?'

It doesn't bear considering.

Over the next few days while she waits to have her biopsy Bridget spends a great deal of time on the phone to Agnes, Clare and Athena. Clare had discovered a lump once, but it gradually disappeared. Agnes has fibrocystic breasts and is always discovering lumps. She never knows which lumps she should worry about and which ones are OK. Spurred on by Bridget she rushes off to her doctor for a physical examination and a referral for a mammogram, seeing she is about to turn forty. Athena usually examines her own breasts with massage oils at least once a month. She decides that from now on she will do it once a week. Not that she's being paranoid. But you never know.

'You never know,' they all agree. Once taken for granted, it now seems that breasts are a potential liability.

* * *

The results from the biopsy reveal that the lump is malignant. Bridget sits very still in the specialist's surgery clutching Matthew's hand. This is not happening to her. She'll wake up in a minute and find she's only been dreaming. But the specialist's voice drones on. He could be speaking Spanish. She can't concentrate. Doesn't want to, is about to lose it and burst into tears . . .

Get a grip, Bridget.

How can he be so calm and professional when it's her body they're discussing? An operation. Pain. Suffering. Disfiguration.

She forces herself to ask the questions she is most afraid to ask. She won't lose her whole breast, only a part of it.

That's bad enough. It's no consolation that her situation could be worse. A whole lot worse.

'Don't go there,' says Matthew.

The hardest part is breaking the news to her parents. Her father just sits there, slumped in his chair without saying a word, his face the colour of putty, poor old bugger. She suspects that he is reliving the time when her mother went through the same scenario. Her mother's instant and emotional response helps to unpeel the outer skin of her numbness. She automatically reassures her mother, who is anguished at the thought that she may have passed on the cancer cells to her daughter.

Dozens of questions fill Bridget's mind, questions she now wonders why she hadn't asked her mother at the time of her mastectomy. But that was when Bridget was in her early twenties and living away from home. Death was light years away. The full impact of her mother's surgery hadn't fully registered because she had been so determined to keep her fears surrounding the possible death of her mother at arm's length. Yet her mother has been fortunate. Contrary to expectations she has not experienced a recurrence of the cancer. Maybe Bridget will follow the same pattern.

She realizes that most of her mother's information is now hopelessly out of date. Survival rates are higher now. There's more information available. Her mother had shut the experience away, there had been little outside support or counselling. Bridget's news has reopened the wound. Bridget hopes she will not become overly protective, freighting her daughter with her own long-buried fears.

Bridget is overwhelmed by the amount of information about her condition that she has to absorb quickly. She reads everything she can lay her hands on. She has fits of depression as the news filters through her awareness. But underlying everything is a sense of disbelief. It can't be happening to her.

Bridget wonders if she will die. What if they don't grab all the bad cancer cells and they leave some behind, and these rogue cells develop into something even worse, and eventually they devour, not just an area of her breast, but her entire body?

She drives out to the western suburbs, stopping twice en route to consult a map. The house is an ugly weatherboard box painted an acid lemon with bottle green trims, a mirror of poverty and neglect. The lawn hasn't been mown for several weeks. The section is bare save for a single stunted lemon tree in the centre of it and a sprawling clump of red hot pokers at the front. A lean-to carport is tacked onto the left of the house. Parked inside it is a rusting old Vauxhall. Bridget moves a doll's pram to one side of the concrete porch so she can knock on the door.

173

She hears a dog bark loudly inside the house in response. Through the bubble glass panel she sees a dark shape advancing towards her. The door is finally opened by an overweight man in black lint-covered track pants and a grey marl sweatshirt, carrying a two-year-old on his shoulders. A labrador salivates in the doorway. It pushes abruptly past the man with the child, brushing against his legs and depositing a residue of silver hairs in its wake. It continues to bark in a hostile manner. The child drums her heels against the man's chest.

'Stop that, Danielle,' he snaps, clamping her legs firmly against his chest to prevent further assaults.

'Giddy-up, horsie,' demands the child, undeterred, yanking at the man's thinning hair.

He slaps her.

A deafening wail of protest splits the air.

Bridget considers turning on her heel and returning to her car.

'Woof, woof, woof,' barks the dog, sniffing Bridget's legs and licking her hands. She retreats a few steps, raising her hands protectively to her chest.

'He won't hurt you,' laughs the man. He lights up a cigarette.

Bridget doesn't believe him. Why is it that doggy people simply refuse to acknowledge that not everybody likes animals? She hates dogs.

The dog thrusts its head into her crotch. 'Get away,' growls Bridget. 'Is this Martina's house?' she asks, resisting the urge to kick the dog out of the way.

'Yeah, c'mon in. She's expectin' ya.' He takes another deep drag on his cigarette.

Feeling apprehensive, she follows him into the hallway. The house stinks of dog. She lifts her feet to negotiate the toys scattered over the stained mustard carpet. The dog bounds ahead of them. Loose strips of a tacky patterned wallpaper flap against the walls in the draught as they pass by.

Martina is a plump exhausted-looking woman in her mid-thirties, a dishwater blonde in a cheap peach-coloured tracksuit spiked with dog hair, and suede fur-lined ankle boots. She smiles at Bridget, revealing a mouth that includes several missing teeth.

'Hi. Are you Bridget? Come with me.'

Bridget notices another child playing with Lego on a beige vinyl sofa. A baby rocks the side of a playpen, creating a monotonous squeaking sound. A television drones in the background. Bright cartoon creatures scamper across the screen.

Bridget trails behind Martina.

'In here.' The woman shows Bridget into what is obviously a child's bedroom. In one corner is a cot splattered with dents and scratches. Suspended above it, a mobile of fabric clowns. A purple plastic bin full of toys is stacked alongside. On the floor is a single mattress covered with a floral-patterned flannelette sheet.

Bridget stares, her fears confirmed. 'Don't you have a massage table?'

'Not yet, but I'm saving for one.'

'So . . .'

'If you'd like to take your clothes off, we'll get started. I've turned the heater on. The room will warm up soon.'

'I'm not sure about this.' Bridget hesitates. If only she had been sensible and gone to see Athena. She had thought it would be easier with a stranger. The anonymity of the encounter would provide a relaxing ambience that was impossible on Athena's table where she would be fussed over and assiduously plied with loving queries and truckloads of advice she wasn't in the mood to listen to. She had wanted someone who wouldn't demand anything of her – conversation, acknowledgement, listening – only payment after an hour of complete silence and relaxation. But exactly who had recommended Martina? She has absolutely no idea. Just goes to show how stressed and apprehensive she has been feeling about the partial mastectomy looming ahead of her. It's affected her brain – obviously. She had looked under the health/healing/massage section at the back of her diary and Martina's name had been third on the list with an asterisk beside it. The first two women on the list had not been able to give her a booking until at least three weeks' time. She realizes now that she hadn't asked the right questions on the phone when she had booked her appointment. She had made the completely erroneous assumption that Martina was some sort of body healer. She had pictured a peaceful sanctuary, a tastefully appointed room with tinkling bells, crystals, scented oil burners and soothing music. She had pictured a raised table – purpose-built. Someone with experience and training. Someone with a list of existing clients.

Instead she has landed the masseuse from amateursville.

'You're not planning to do a runner on me, are you?' asks the woman shrewdly. She frowns at Bridget.

Bridget is momentarily distracted by a glimpse of the woman's roots showing through the bleach.

'I'm not happy about being massaged on the floor.'

'No-one else has complained.'

Bullshit, thinks Bridget. Absolute crap.

'Give me a chance to prove to you what I can do.' A pleading note enters Martina's voice. 'My bloke was laid off a few months ago and he's still out of work. I'm only trying to get a business off the ground.'

'All right then,' agrees Bridget, resigned. A business? How could the woman possibly be referring to this amateurish set-up as a business? The idea is ludicrous.

The woman rolls up her sleeves in a business-like manner. 'Did you bring cash with you, like I asked?'

'Yes. Of course I did.' Bridget's doubts about the woman persist. 'Have you had much experience? Attended courses?'

Martina stops rummaging in her basket of oils for a moment and looks offended by the question.

'I've been trained,' she says brusquely.

A couple of weekend workshops would be the sum of it. Bridget has no confidence in the woman. Next she'll be trying to pass herself off as a counsellor as well.

What is she doing here? She must be mad. If she has any sense left she should put her clothes back on and march out of the house. She owes this woman nothing.

But she remains standing in the room, unable to flee, yet reluctant to undress. She realizes she is exhausted, eager to lie down.

Martina covers her body with thin pink towels.

'Lie on your stomach,' she instructs. 'I'll start with your back.'

What does it matter? It's only an hour she has to endure.

'I'm cold,' grumbles Bridget.

Martina pulls out a baby blanket from the cot and drapes it over her legs.

'That's better.'

Martina warms her hands by the heater. 'My hands are very cold today,' she warns.

Bridget shivers in anticipation. She hears Martina pour oil onto her hands and the slippery sound as she slides one hand against the other. Martina lowers the towel from Bridget's shoulders but leaves her legs covered.

Bridget braces herself.

The woman's hands are at first surprisingly gentle. She runs her thumb and index finger up and down the length of Bridget's spine, then sweeps each of her open palms in opposite directions up and down Bridget's back. This is pleasant. What follows isn't.

There is a scratching sound as the labrador demands entry to the little bedroom.

Bridget hears Martina's knees creak as she gets to her feet and opens the door a crack.

'Rocky!' she hisses. 'Go away! Shoo!'

The dog whines plaintively and rubs itself insinuatingly against the door.

Bridget wishes she had a gun.

'No . . . NO! GO AWAY!' yells Martina. She struggles to push the dog away with her foot and shuts the door firmly in its face.

Bridget clenches her teeth. In one hour she will be out of here and she will never return. *Why oh why* hadn't she gone to Athena? She can't even recall the reason why she had felt that it would be easier with a stranger.

The dog's paws clatter on the strip of lino outside the door. It continues to whine as Martina kneels down alongside Bridget and resumes the massage.

There is a brief pause and then a thudding sound as the Labrador launches its body against the door.

'Give me *patience*,' mutters the masseuse. Her thumbs delve into the knots of tension in Bridget's upper back. The room reverberates with the sound of the dog flinging itself against the door, which rattles ominously on its hinges.

If that bloody dog does that once more, Bridget promises herself, I'm going home. Dying would be a merciful release compared with this torture.

Martina staggers to her feet again and pokes her head round the door, successfully blocking Rocky's entry by jamming a tree trunk thigh into the narrow opening.

'BARRY!' she bellows. 'Put that bloody dog *outside*!'

'I'm *busy*!' yells Barry in response. He sounds desperate. As if to corroborate this there is a chorus of childish wails in the background.

Martina returns to Bridget.

'Ignore the dog,' she advises. 'He'll soon get bored and go off and annoy someone else.'

But Rocky has by now whipped himself into a frenzy behind the door. Bridget pictures the wood veneer being shredded by the dog's insistent claws as he alternately whines, howls, scratches and assaults the door.

Bridget's heart races.

'We need some music,' announces Martina brightly. She fiddles with a small ghetto blaster and loads a tape. Dolphin music, is what Clare would call it. Random electronic tinkles, interspersed with a little flute here and there. Amorphous bland crap, thinks Bridget, her tolerance wearing thin.

'Do you have any classical?' she asks hopefully.

'I don't do classical. What I do have is ambient music, or else country. Take your pick.'

'Ambient it is then.'

Martina crawls about the floor changing her angle on Bridget's back.

'How're ya doin' down theah?'

'You're hurting me,' protests Bridget.

'You've sure gotta tonna tension here. Ya body is like concrete. Did ya know that?'

Bridget doesn't care. I won't cry, she tells herself repeatedly. I won't. *I won't.*

'Could you give my back a rest, move on to a different part,' she suggests.

It seems, however, there is no section of Bridget's body that is without pain. Her thighs, her upper arms,

179

her calves. She utters a yelp when Martina works on her thighs. This has been a huge error, all she wants now is to escape the masseuse from hell and her monster dog.

'Stop,' she begs. 'I've had enough.'

The dog utters out a low moan from his sentry post behind the door.

'Rocky's a real softie, y'know,' confides Martina as if Bridget hasn't spoken. 'He's only like this because he can't bear to be a minute outta my sight. He even follows me to the toilet and waits outside the door. Isn't that *so* touching?'

About as touching as a gorilla crawling up your bum, thinks Bridget.

Martina is right. Her body does feel like a slab of concrete – obdurate, unyielding. She has to grit her teeth to prevent herself from crying out to this stranger.

'I can't move,' she murmurs, mouth muffled by mattress.

Martina waits impatiently for Bridget to get up.

Bridget continues to lie there passively. She lifts an arm experimentally before letting it flop like a dead fish with a thud on the mattress.

'Get up when you're ready,' prompts Martina.

Bridget experiences a moment of nostalgia for Athena's solicitous ministerings. She realizes now she has been foolish, possibly even selfish in depriving Athena of an opportunity to care for her by using her skills. With Athena she would have been safe. She would have been understood. Explanations would have been superfluous.

She hears the by now familiar creaking of joints as the masseuse stands up and makes her way to the door with a heavy tread. There is a joyful yelp as Rocky is reunited with his mistress. Following the click of the door shutting there is, mercifully, a silence so deep

Bridget fears drowning in it and being unable to ever rise to the surface again.

Soothed by the warmth of the oil-fired heater and the comfort of the towels covering her nakedness, she dozes.

She is wakened abruptly twenty minutes later (although it feels like only two) by the clamorous entrance of Martina and Rocky.

A wet tongue the texture of sandpaper rasps against her face.

'Get that *bloody* dog off me!' screams Bridget in a shrill voice.

'Would you *please* get up,' Martina insists. 'I'm expectin' anotha client soon.'

'I'm not moving while that damn beast is loose in the room.'

Martina grips the Labrador by the collar and hauls it unceremoniously out of the room. The door slams shut behind them.

Bridget struggles to her feet and reaches for her clothes.

Martina is waiting for her in the lounge, a baby in her lap.

'How was that?' she asks, conciliatory now that Bridget is dressed and payment is imminent.

Bridget, torn between admitting the truth and producing a harmless white lie which will allow her to gracefully make an exit, prevaricates, and finally, unable to decide, makes no reply. If this offends Martina – too bad.

Bridget fishes in her wallet for the fifty-dollar note and places it on the table. Martina makes no attempt to retrieve it.

'Well, goodbye then,' she says in a chilly voice.

'Goodbye,' mutters Bridget. She blunders out of the lounge into the narrow hallway, almost running towards her car in her desire to escape from the house.

'*Wait.*'

Bridget swivels her head. Barry is lumbering up the path after her, the dreaded Rocky at his heels. A clutch of fear grips her chest. But it is only her scarf, waving like a banner from Barry's hand.

'You left this behind.'

'Thanks,' says Bridget gruffly. She raises wet eyes to him.

'Hey. Y'all right?'

His forehead wrinkles at her in the first demonstration of concern she has experienced since entering the property. Barry is visibly startled when his wife's client collapses onto his shoulder, her body heaving with racking sobs.

Barry pats her shoulder awkwardly and leads her back to the house.

'What the—?' Martina is irritated until she catches a glimpse of her client's tear-streaked face.

'I knew somethin' wasn't right.' She jiggles the baby on her hip. 'I just knew it. Shit a brick. What'll we do? You poor lamb, you shudda told me. Howwiz I to know?' Her voice enters the shrill register.

'Martina, no-one is blamin' *you*,' says Barry, taking the baby from her. 'Put the kettle on, will ya.'

'Right. Yeah. Cuppa tea then.'

Their eyes signal alarm to each other over Bridget's head.

'D'ya wanna phone someone?'

'No,' replies Bridget in a pathetic voice. Her surgery is scheduled for two days' time. She leaks tears, mucus. Frightening emotions are escaping like effluent from an overflowing drain. Life is impossible, unpredictable, mortifying. Her dignity unsalvageable.

She shares a cup of strong sweet tea with her hosts. Rocky is at her feet, no longer plaguing her with his

182

attentions. As long as he is silent and still Bridget can tolerate him.

'You're sick, aren'cha,' asks Martina, suddenly alert, covering her mouth, narrowing her eyes at Bridget.

'I have cancer.' There, she said the C word.

Five days after her needle biopsy results Bridget finds herself in hospital having a partial mastectomy.

Chapter Fourteen

Agnes

Early one Sunday morning Agnes drives Daniel to the beach at Whatipu on Auckland's west coast. They stride out into the open expanse of black sand. Apart from a couple of solitary anglers they have the beach to themselves. They are feeling invigorated and optimistic. Finally something is beginning to spit and fizzle between them, but it's taken Agnes time to recognize the signs, because previously love has always begun with an immediate crackle of attraction swiftly followed by an abundance of fiery sex. This delicate preamble, this careful dance they both know is a prelude to sweet intimacy, has caught her unawares. They aren't at the hand-holding stage yet so they walk separately and purposefully along the sand enjoying the salty air and the big surf crashing in their ears.

Agnes is thinking about her approaching group exhibition, which marks a turning point for her – an entry level acceptance into a world wider than that of purely commercial photography. She is pleased with the four portraits she will be showing. One each of Athena, Clare and Bridget. But it is her own self-portrait that she is most proud of. She has succeeded in capturing a mysterious and elusive aspect of herself that she wants to explore further, one that she can scarcely explain to herself, let alone to Daniel. It doesn't bother her unduly, she supposes that there will always be parts of herself that are impossible to completely understand, or to share with others. The Agnes revealed by the camera's lens is not exactly a stranger, but she may as well be. She does look forty – even the photos taken at her modest little birthday party had confirmed that for her. But along with the evidence of ageing there is a new serious, questioning, almost anxious expression in her eyes. New little crow's feet and the beginnings of lines around the mouth. This is not the 'forever young party animal', the 'hip' photographer, the consummate professional, the brittle and independent 'don't fuck with me' Agnes, the untidy, unresolved thorn in her mother's flesh, the fiercely loyal woman friend, or any one of a number of personae Agnes adopts automatically as she closes the door on her apartment each morning to drive to her studio. And here is Daniel, she thinks, exposing to the light of day yet another aspect of herself to become acquainted with.

As if he can read her thoughts Daniel asks her about the impending show and confirms that he will definitely be at the opening. Agnes is pleased but at the same time she wonders how Daniel will fit into her world. What will her friends and colleagues make of him?

'Daniel, does it bother you that we operate in such different worlds?'

'No. I think it's great. Why, do you have a problem?'

'No,' lies Agnes, wishing she were a more generous person.

She asks Daniel about his work because she is both fascinated and horrified by his accounts of the many dysfunctional families and complicated webs of relationships, the degree of suffering that he and his colleagues are exposed to on a daily basis. Poverty. Neglect. Self-mutilation. Truancy. Breakdowns in communication between children and their parents. Broken, incompetent, often violent people who live in the same city as she does and whom, unlike Daniel, she will most likely never meet. This past week has been particularly agonizing for him. One of his families has been blown apart, mother and children separated from a father who has been abusing his two little girls, as well as the daughter of a family friend.

'Does your well of sympathy ever just dry up?'

'It never dries up, but I do have to take care to remain reasonably detached so that I can be of most use to my clients. In some ways the work isn't so different from what I was called on to do as a priest. Be there to listen to families who were having problems.'

Agnes struggles to hear Daniel above the sound of the wind that bites into their cheeks. Wet strands of hair are flung about her face.

'You know, I've always thought it a bit rich – priests counselling families. What would they know? Are they trained for it?'

He braces his body against the wind. There is a sharp note to his voice.

'If you take that line, what would you know either? You haven't had a family.'

'I've had intimate relationships, which is more than priests do.'

'I've had strong friendships with men and women, both married and unmarried.'

He averts his face from her, strides on ahead. She pursues him, skipping sideways to avoid an advancing wave.

The waves have left a wide ribbon of residual foam

that wobbles in the wind before being broken up into clusters of bubbles that are tossed willy-nilly down the beach in a dozen different directions.

'Were you ever attracted to a parishioner, a woman?'

'Yes, from time to time. But I didn't act on it.'

'It seems hard to believe. I have to say, Daniel, I'm wary of you. Your background doesn't exactly teach you how to conduct a relationship with a woman. Enforced celibacy promotes distortions in relationships. There's that whole power and control aspect too. Priests are only *men*, for Christ's sake.'

'I'm not an emotional retard, if that's what you're implying,' he flashes back at her. 'As you've seen, I do know how to behave with a woman.'

Who is the defensive one now, thinks Agnes, wrapping her woollen scarf more tightly around her neck.

'If you wanted to become a priest you had to be single,' says Daniel. 'That was the deal. However, I do think the Catholic Church is the poorer for not having both married and single priests.'

'I couldn't agree more. I think the fact that there are fewer guys opting to become priests these days speaks for itself.'

'There's none so blind . . .'

'Do you have any regrets?'

Will he tell her the truth? Is he, ludicrous though it might seem, a forty-five-year-old virgin?

'I've paid a high price for not having a wife and kids,' he admits, mashing his beanie over his ears to ward off the cold.

'Yes . . .' Agnes urges him on. *Let's flush this one out.*

'I had wondered . . . if I might have left my run too late.'

He turns to her.

She sees a wide grin on an ageing face reckless with hope.

Oh no. No. No. No way Jose.

They stop for a rest. Agnes pulls out a thermos of coffee from her backpack. They find shelter behind a sand dune covered in pingao grass. Seated on their parkas they chew on wedges of her mother's fruitcake.

Despite his revelations Agnes continues to have the sense that he is holding himself back. She longs to expose the real Daniel.

It is not until they have embarked on their return journey that he finally begins to speak more freely.

'I haven't had what you'd call normal relationships.'

'I'm no guinea pig.'

Get me out of here.

The first splatters of rain plop onto the black sand. They quickly unfold their parkas from their bags and put them on before continuing.

'I'm not expressing myself clearly,' he adds. 'Normal, as in relationships that contained a sexual aspect to them. I had a lot of growing up to do. I went off the rails for a while after I left. Most guys get the chance to go through an experimental stage in their late teens and then move on. I missed out on that crucial stage.

'Previously, I had had a sense of community, of belonging. Suddenly I was out on a limb. I looked for a crutch to numb the fear and doubts. I was an outsider, an alien. I belonged nowhere. I didn't know where I was going.

'As a priest I had made a personal rule never to drink if I was alone. It's too easy to slip from having one drink to three or four. Before you know it, you're hitting it hard every night. So. I had to stick to my resolve. No drinking alone.

'But when I left, everything changed. I mean *everything*. For a few weeks I didn't know what day it was. I could scarcely have told you my name. I wasn't

"Father" any more. How could I advise others when I couldn't even help myself?

'I asked myself who or what had I been saving myself for? What was the point of all the sacrifices I'd made? Did God exist? Had I simply been deluded for all those years? Had my life as a priest made a scrap of difference to anyone?

'It started with a few drinks every night to relax. I felt very tense a lot of the time, you know.'

'I can imagine,' says Agnes, not without sympathy.

Her response to Daniel has swung full circle again. They stop where they are in the middle of the bleak, inhospitable beach. His forehead is plastered with matted wet hair. His eyes are red-rimmed from exposure to wind and rain, and he's blinking against the onslaught of tiny grains of sand. A tear rolls down his face.

Poor bastard, she thinks. Her instincts tell her to grab him and hug him hard, but something continues to hold her back. A niggling inner voice asks her why the legacy of his background should become *her* problem. And, does she realize what she is getting herself into?

Also, there is Clare's voice: *I hear alarm bells, Agnes.*

They pause long enough to watch a flock of terns take off into the air one at a time before the beach is once again cleared. They could be the only ones on earth. Around them a seemingly endless stretch of sea, sand and sky. To their left are the dark blurred outlines of the Waitakere Ranges.

'So. You haven't been in a long-term intimate relationship then?'

'Not really, no.'

She had been right all along. Alarm bells? Sirens, more like. Going off the rails — had he meant sexually, or just with the booze? She suspects she's pushed him hard enough for the moment.

189

'Agnes, you're so transparent. I may not have been in a long-term relationship, but I'm no longer a sexual novice, you know.'

'So, you're not a virgin.' She cannot disguise the relief in her voice.

He laughs. 'Until recently, I hadn't met a woman who I felt sufficiently strongly about to even consider the possibility of setting up house together. I also didn't feel ready. But I knew I would know when I was.'

'Personally, I'm in no hurry to dive into another relationship.'

'Why not?' He sounds surprised.

'I want to be really sure next time. I've made mistakes before. I don't plan to jump into bed with anyone from now on without getting to know him properly first.'

He stares at her full in the face without flinching. 'That's fine by me.'

'Good.' She grins at him. Holds out her hand.

He takes it. His hand is cool – as you'd expect in such weather. Her fingers curl around his. He gives her hand a squeeze.

It feels nice.

Cautiously he unclasps her fingers and places his arm round her. That feels good too. She grins at him and regains the feeling of optimism that accompanied her arrival at the beach. A little hum of contentment whirrs away in her chest.

Daniel can cook. Another surprise. In fact, he prides himself on his cooking, even collects and studies recipe books. He cooks her an Italian cheese and potato casserole. She reciprocates with spinach ravioli.

They still haven't had sex. There's no pressure on her. None on him.

They can now sit in the same room without feeling obliged to talk the entire time. She values his quiet measured responses. His thoughtfulness.

'I don't have to impress you,' says Agnes, thinking aloud.

'Actually, I've been meaning to speak to you about that,' says Daniel in a mock-stern voice, waggling his finger at her.

She still hasn't mentioned her fling with Simon. Fun while it lasted but ultimately superficial and therefore unsatisfactory on so many levels. She is now embarrassed. How can she possibly make Daniel understand the frame of mind she was in at the time?

How quickly we judge, she thinks. How often we get it wrong. She wants very badly to do the right thing, to achieve a clarity of vision, a surety of knowledge and intention. To be able to say with conviction – this is the path. Or – this is the person. Not to be muddling along any longer, deluding herself that what she has is the best she can realistically aim for.

She now has a sense, in the comfortable silences that fall between them, of homecoming. She looks up and reads the compassion in his eyes.

Why should anyone feel sorry for *her*?

'*I'm* OK,' she says defensively.

Daniel chuckles and ruffles her hair with affection. 'Hello, Ms Independent,' he hums.

'Don't look at me like that.'

Daniel grins.

'How?'

'As if you want to eat me.'

'Maybe I do.'

Chapter Fifteen

Athena

The miracle seekers are a drab and motley bunch. Athena Wildblood cranes her neck and looks around her. The hall is packed to capacity, the audience being heavily biased in favour of older women – but you'd expect that, she thinks – it's always more of a problem to get men to do work on themselves. A sprinkling of sleek black Asian heads is dotted among the crop of grey. The stage is framed by the curved fronds of fake palm trees, legacy from a recent school production. The buzz of chatter in the background almost drowns out the soothing tones of recorded pan flutes. Headlines and claims in the promotional flier grab Athena's attention: 'Eliminate your old conditioned patterns', and 'Achieve lasting happiness'.

She passes the flier to her mother who has accompanied her, jolly in her new purple polar fleece jacket and trouser suit.

'Oh, I *am* looking forward to this.' Her mother also scans the hall to see if there is anyone she knows. She waves in a very flamboyant manner to several acquaintances whom she recognizes, mouthing gleeful hellos, and adopting agitated hand signals in response to their acknowledgements, until Athena, mortified by the attention they are attracting, begs her to stop making a show of herself and to sit quietly until the celebrity speaker arrives.

A burst of loud applause greets New Age guru Ruby Adelaide Starr as she strides out to the front of the stage with her husband. Her thin body is draped in a layered black dress with batwing sleeves. She flashes a dazzling set of teeth at the five hundred people staring up at her. After greeting the audience effusively, emphasizing how pleased she is to be in 'Nooo Zealand', she launches into her colourful life history. The music and lights fade, leaving her under the spotlight.

Athena and her mother lean forward in their orange plastic seats, determined not to miss a word.

'My life was one unending struggle. The only thing I knew was *survival*.' The Californian accent belts through the microphone. 'And I survived the only way I knew how. By working my butt off. I had a daytime office job and at the same time I was bringing up four children *completely alone*. I didn't even know where my previous husband lived. He had sent no money to support our children. Everything was up to me. My oldest son had gotten himself into crack. My youngest son had become completely withdrawn. I despaired of ever finding my way out of the black pit of poverty and powerlessness that I'd crawled into with my family.'

Athena's enthralled mother tuts and murmurs in sympathy.

Athena pokes her in the ribs.

'I never had any fun. I was at war with everyone I met – so full of anger. I could understand how you could pick up a gun and blow anyone standing in front of you off the face of the earth. I'd gotten pretty close to it. I often wished I were dead. Like, the pain was *that* bad. That's how insane and miserable I was before I met Quentin Starr,' she admits frankly. 'He changed my life for ever and I will be eternally grateful to him. We were meant to meet, and to recognize each other as *soulmates*.'

Taped music surges.

'But this is not the first lifetime we've been together.'

Ruby Adelaide Starr beams as she turns to the slender attractive man who has become her third husband. She pats her bleached permed wad of hair. Big hair, like on the soaps. He even smiles adoringly at her.

True love, soulmates – the whole caboodle, thinks Athena with envy.

Why is it that some women manage to have it all? Both financial and emotional security together. Being adored by a younger man. Ruby Starr has got to be at least fifty. And he can't be more than thirty-five.

Athena sighs. The man or the woman on a white charger who will sweep her away from Jewel and the cottage in such desperate need of maintenance and renovation is still nowhere to be seen.

How many times has Ruby Starr told her story? Making money by the truckload from her own pain. Will these visiting Americans have an answer for her? She knows the kind of pain Ruby Starr refers to; it is the pain inflicted on her by Jewel every minute of the time they spend in each other's company. Selfish Jewel with the cruel tongue and the Chinese boyfriend Wing, who foolishly lavishes gifts on her. He's in for a shock when he discovers what she's really like. What sort of favours does Jewel do for him? People don't just *give* you things for nothing, not without expecting something in return, she has warned Jewel.

'*Mum!*' snapped Jewel, and the way she said it

transformed her mother's name into a form of abuse. *Mum*. Something the cat dragged in. A nuisance, something trashy and smelly.

'We weren't put on this earth to become robots. That's why we're here to encourage you to release your true potential. Access the miracle within. It's that simple — your choice to remain stuck, or to heal yourself, and move *forward*. Tune in to the truth. If you have a belief in yourself, then your potential is unlimited. That's what I'm telling you. *Unlimited*. Do what you were *born* to do. If it feels right — *do it now!*'

Ruby hits the audience with the sales pitch for her workshops, finishing by adding: 'If you're serious about transforming your reality, then invest in *yourself*.'

If only it were that easy to tune in to the pleasure of her own body, to let go of her painful memories, thinks Athena. If Ruby Starr had to live full time with a girl like Jewel, or to endure the pain of dealing with a best friend suffering from cancer, she wouldn't be proselytizing about manifesting dreams.

Athena's mind frequently turns to Bridget. She has rearranged her work to spend more time with her friend, cooking meals to pop into her freezer, buying flowers, scented candles and fragrant oils she can ill afford. She's even recorded a tape of affirmations for Bridget to play to herself while she rests. She has encouraged Bridget to visualize her cancer cells being destroyed by the good cells, to train her mind until it is like a kind of female Lone Ranger stalking high in the hills and into the furthest nooks and crannies of her body with her new weapons of visualized white light and positivity. So far, amazingly, Bridget has gone along with all of Athena's ideas.

Ruby descends into the audience. Her dangly silver

spiral earrings catch the light. Her dress shimmers. Close up Athena can see the pancake make-up and smell a strong perfume.

She is an obvious target in the front row.

'Tune in to yourself on a *soul* level,' Ruby Starr commands Athena, as if she can actually see deep inside her head.

'How?' asks Athena, pink with embarrassment. She concentrates on the woman's glittery silver shoes, anything but look Ruby directly in the eye, lest the contact unleash a tirade. She can sense her mother wriggling in the adjacent seat, disgruntled at being ignored.

'Concentrate on seeing *good* pictures in your head as opposed to *bad* ones. Reinforce the good pictures. Do this every day and soon it will become a habit.'

Athena's mother opens her mouth to comment. But to Athena's immense relief Ruby floats away from her with a tinkly laugh and turns her attention instead to a woman sitting further down the row.

'Do what you *love*,' she commands the woman. 'Stop blocking yourself. I can see you're a blocker.' She waggles an index finger from side to side. 'Your block doesn't have to be there, you know.'

From the patronizing tone in her voice she could be talking to a child, thinks Athena, wondering why she suddenly feels in such a bad mood – this kind of talk usually acts as fuel to feed her life. Instead, this woman is getting on her wick. Maybe it's not so much the content of her lecture, which she basically agrees with, but the way she's delivering her message.

The 'blocker' woman looks anxiously up at Ruby who, without missing a beat, moves on to more receptive members of the audience, grazing among the front rows, bestowing little gems of advice and wisdom in her wake.

'What do you need to know to understand *your* situation?' she gaily enquires of an elderly woman whose twisted body is confined in a wheelchair. The woman stares at her hopefully.

Athena swivels her head.

'What did you come to learn?' chirps Ruby to a sallow-faced teenage girl. 'How do *you* tune in?'

'I don't know,' she answers in a soft voice, blushing under Ruby's scrutiny.

'Garbage,' snarls the woman along from Athena. 'Absolute crap. I'm bloody outta here.' She collects her shoulder bag and jacket and stands up to leave.

Quentin Starr follows her out.

The woman who had been sitting on the other side of Athena leans towards her. 'She'll cop it,' she says, twisting her head to indicate the direction in which Ruby's husband has proceeded.

'It's overwhelming, isn't it, the idea of having to make such big changes in the way you live your life,' says Athena, heaving another sigh. 'I mean, where do you start?'

The woman gives her a shrewd look. 'Depends on what you're aiming for,' she replies.

She is a tall, slightly built woman in her mid-thirties, dressed in a figure-hugging white T-shirt, worn brown leather jacket, jeans and Cuban-heeled boots. Her red hair is cropped very short with a ragged fringe. The intelligent freckled face is long and pale with a strongly defined jaw line.

'The trouble with this kind of talk,' muses Athena, 'is that it leaves you with more questions than answers. What, for example, is the third dimension she made reference to?'

'Want to talk about it over a coffee?'

Athena hesitates and glances over at her mother.

'Don't worry about me. I've got plenty of friends

here. I'll get a lift with one of them, no problem. Enjoy yourself. Off you go,' she urges.

'Oh, and I'm Rita, by the way.'

'I'm Athena.'

Rita gives her the directions to a nearby café. 'See you there.'

On their way out they pass a queue of women lining up to put their names down for the exorbitantly priced weekend workshop.

The café is hopping when Athena arrives, packed with twenty-somethings having a good time. The music is cranked up and they have to shout to be heard.

'How did you hear about Ruby Starr?' bellows Rita.

Athena tries to recall. 'A flier in my local health shop.'

'I went along for a laugh.'

'You did?'

'My editor sent me along. We're doing a feature on New Age gurus – flushing out the fraudsters. It's not difficult, they damn themselves with their own words. Let the discerning reader decide for herself. The Starrs were a hoot. Don't you agree?'

'No.'

'You're not serious about all that New Age garbage, are you?' Rita stirs her coffee.

'Some of it. So I'm part of your research, am I?'

'You can be if you want. I'm interested in your opinion of the Starrs.'

'They seem very sincere.'

'It's not enough. I don't think it is. All this naive positivism – it gets on my nerves, to be honest.'

'Is it so bad for someone to spread a few rays of optimism in a world that's so full of sadness and crime and negativity?' asks Athena, scooping up a melted marshmallow from her hot chocolate.

'Oh sure, let's all go running around manifesting soulmates and wealth and the universe will shower them upon us, hallelujah.'

Athena laughs. 'You can't expect changes to happen overnight.'

Rita raises her eyebrows. 'No? Maybe I misheard. I thought all I had to do was to get rid of my blocks and soulmates would be beating a path to my door. A few glib phrases and suddenly we're all giving warm fuzzies? I don't think so. Life is more complex, more unpredictable. There's so much that is out of our control.'

'That's why I think it's important to have a path that you're following, otherwise you're just drifting, completely at the mercy of your own fears and demons.'

'Ah, but what if you don't believe that there is a "perfect answer" or a "right way"? I try to live spontaneously and simply get on with my life. Besides, paths only look like paths in retrospect.'

Athena thinks about this. 'That's very insightful.'

Rita shrugs. 'Yeah, well.'

'What did you expect from the Starrs anyway?'

'What we got. Nothing more, nothing less. An audience of gullible suckers. And these American New Agers, they're larger than life, aren't they? So colourful. So energetic. They're definitely in it for the money. See the prices of those workshops? I ask you.

'Honestly, Athena, it's all a bit too touchy-feely for me. I like hard cold facts. You couldn't debate with those people. Their brains are like cotton wool. They'd vaporize if you challenged them on their claims.'

'Did you try?' asks Athena, thinking how much she dislikes this woman. She must have been mad agreeing to have a drink with her.

'I've made a time to see them tomorrow.'

'Your life must be interesting on the magazine. I suppose you meet a wide range of people,' she says politely.

'Mega stress, it feels like. I need a holiday.' Rita stretches and yawns.

Athena is intimidated by Rita and only too aware that she is not presenting herself to best advantage.

'I guess what I'm saying is, people who are attracted to people like Ruby and Quentin Starr are often lost, vulnerable people,' says Rita. 'They're looking for a quick easy fix-up, an answer to all their problems. Why do so many people hand over the responsibility for their lives to these fakes, that's what I want to know? Any ideas on the subject?'

'So the Starrs' work is not valid simply because they attract needy people?'

'I didn't say that. But you must agree, there are a lot of charlatans about.'

'I don't deny it. But I'm not one of them, I assure you. I try to work with integrity.'

'Now that's a phrase I frequently hear when I come into contact with New Agers. Athena, the impression I have is that *many* of these New Age practitioners and so-called healers are patently charlatans and I plan to expose some of them. Honestly, I'll be doing the world's vulnerable suckers a big favour. Because how on earth is the average punter supposed to seek and find the genuine article among the frauds?'

Rita has a penetrating way of staring that makes Athena feel distinctly uncomfortable. Another Clare?

'What's your line of work, Athena?'

'I'm a healer. I do massage, aromatherapy.'

'I see.'

'I don't mean to be defensive, but I truly am not in the business of duping anybody. I offer a professional, quality service to my clients.'

'Maybe I should book a massage then. Yeah, I'll do that.'

'Not too touchy-feely for you, is it, Rita?'

Rita laughs. 'You have a sense of humour, after all.' She has a big contagious laugh.

Athena can't help but grin back. She fishes in her bag for a business card. Rita appraises it, expressing admiration for the loose line drawing of a pink flower, the wobbly green hand-lettering.

'Very professional.'

'Thanks.'

Rita picks up the little photo of Jewel which had fallen out of Athena's wallet onto the table along with the business card.

'Your daughter?'

'Jewel is her name. Only now she insists on calling herself Sarah.'

'I don't have any children.'

'You're lucky. Jewel is not easy. A will of iron and a heart of stone, that's my Jewel.'

Rita pulls a face. 'I hope I don't bump into her.'

Not a chance, thinks Athena.

'Well, see you around then,' says Rita brightly when they part.

Athena smiles in return without committing herself. She knows she'll never set eyes on the woman again. Rita won't book a massage. They have nothing in common.

Out of the blue Rita calls her to book a massage.

She has a great body. The kind of body Athena wishes she had. Narrow hips, breasts that aren't too big. Lovely skin.

Rita books for a second session. A third.

'Want a coffee sometime?' Rita asks casually after the third session as she writes out a cheque.

'OK.'

'So . . . where?'

'You choose.'

Rita rents an apartment and shares it with a woman systems analyst.

'I spend all my money on travel,' she says. 'I'll worry about the future later.'

'Lucky you.'

'You don't travel?'

Athena gives a derisive laugh. 'Oh, yeah, sure I do. I'm off to Portugal for Christmas. Last year – Vietnam,' she says in a sarcastic voice, because she has a secret fear of ending up a bag lady in her old age. She certainly won't be able to count on Jewel to spare her a thought.

'Your daughter . . .'

'She's been the battle of my life. And I've done it alone.'

'You expect me to feel sorry for you, is that it?'

'No.' Athena feels unaccountably flustered.

'If you go about things the same way you've always done, then you'll get what you've always got. And if you keep telling yourself that life is a struggle, you can guarantee it will be. You don't have to be a New Ager to know that. Rock the boat, Athena.'

Rita's words are far too challenging. Athena leaves the café with a frown on her face. She will never see Rita again.

'Hey, sad sack, are you on for a movie?'

Athena is momentarily speechless with surprise and pleasure.

Rita collects her and drives her to the cinema. Athena observes her new friend, trying not to be too obvious about it. She likes the way Rita walks. Nice easy stride. Loose arm movement. Terrific posture. How did she learn that? And so confident. Not dissimilar to Clare. Rita would like Clare.

Athena asks herself: but why *me*?

Clare's advice: fake the confidence, Athena. After a while it's no longer an act. It's for real.

Athena doesn't believe her. A five-year-old child could penetrate her flimsy defences.

She wants Rita to see where she lives, but only if she can guarantee Jewel/Sarah won't arrive back unexpectedly and make a fuss.

Rita agrees to visit on Saturday afternoon.

They're sitting on Athena's back veranda chatting, feet up on the wooden railings, companionably sprawled out on the sagging old sofa, when Jewel arrives home from a night on the town. She's been clubbing until four or five, becoming very drunk, or else having taken Ecstasy – all funded, no doubt, by the smitten Wing.

Jewel stomps through the kitchen. She yanks out a couple of drawers, slams them shut. Bangs the bathroom door. Bellows an incomprehensible stream of words at her mother from the opposite end of the house and appears a few moments later to demand in a shrill voice: 'Where are my jeans, you mole?'

Athena's stomach begins its familiar churning. The shame of having a witness.

'Where were you last night? You didn't come home.' She can't help herself, having been awake since two in the morning indulging in the worst of parental fantasies concerning the fate of missing daughters.

'None of your bloody business.'

Jewel's words jab home. Athena knows she will never become inured to the pain.

But what is this? A movement behind her.

'Don't you DARE speak to your mother in that tone of voice.' Rita, feisty and determined, confronts Jewel the Ungrateful Daughter, Jewel the Taunter, the Selfish, to protect Athena the Wronged.

Jewel is momentarily nonplussed, then: *'Who the fuck are you?'*

'This is Rita,' murmurs Athena, waiting for Rita's hair to combust and for Jewel to launch into her usual aggressive onslaught.

Silence, loaded silence. Shallow breathing, high up in the chest, fast and light, fast and light. Hearts pounding, *boom, boom.*

Jewel folds her arms across her chest. Rita folds hers. Athena wants to relieve her bladder very badly.

'None of your business,' says Jewel. She prods Rita in the chest. 'Butt out. Butt out both of you. Cows. Moles. Trolls. Crystal crones.'

Rita laughs scornfully. 'You're full of hot air, girl.'

Jewel turns on her heel and strides down the hall. In the distance they hear a door slam.

Athena turns to Rita with a wry grin. 'Welcome to my life.'

Chapter Sixteen

Clare

Clare had not anticipated the frustrations and headaches resulting from her dealings with Bulldozer's company. He hates to be told, to be corrected, proved wrong. Plans for his company to sponsor an exhibition at the Auckland City Art Gallery are proceeding well, but the media training has not begun auspiciously.

He had postured and preened, maintained a non-stop barrage of comments and rebuttals. Accustomed to occupying centre stage in any conversation, believing himself to be the life and soul of any party with his anecdotes about high profile cases he had won, his predictions regarding the political scene, his enthusiasm for both opera and rugby, he had gesticulated too extravagantly. Clare had preached restraint. He must stop stroking his jaw, scratching his nose, fiddling with his ears, waving his hands about – his characteristic mannerisms and poses were far too distracting. He reacted to each suggestion or instruction she made as if it were a personal attack. He was a poor listener. Yet just as Clare was about to give up on him, suddenly things clicked into place. He began to follow her advice. It was as if the initial battles had been a kind of test and now he was prepared to settle down and trust her.

'You'll be master of the fifteen-second sound bite by the time we've finished.'

He gave her a pleased smile. He had told her that if there was one thing he dreaded and hated more than anything it was to be made to appear an idiot. He abhorred journalists. Didn't trust a single sodding one of them, he said. Nevertheless, the notion of being groomed as a spokesperson on any issues concerning reform of the judicial system obviously appealed to his vanity.

Over the weeks he had grown to rely on Clare's shrewd insights and 'no bullshit' approach.

She had despatched his survey results, his facts and figures, to the appropriate people in the media. Often his information was picked up and used as the basis for journalists' stories. But not in every instance.

In vain did Clare remind him, when he gave her a roasting about it, that there were no guarantees. Public relations was not advertising, she reminded him. One could suggest, recommend, call in favours, grease the wheels, but in the end one had no real control.

'What the hell am I paying you for then?'

Of course he understood the score perfectly well, he simply liked to throw his weight around. Clare recognized that a woman like her, not easily intimidated, was a challenge to him.

But Clare is fed up with pugnacious men finding her a threat and pushing her to the limits of her tolerance just to see if they can crack her.

Or else fuck her.

He has proved to be a very complex character. As Clare and Bulldozer have become better acquainted the velvet gloves have been well and truly ripped off.

To Clare's surprise they share the same Catholic

background. He has spent three years studying for the priesthood before opting out and switching to law and becoming a barrister. More surprising to her, considering the murderers and rapists he chooses to defend, he has remained a Catholic. But it doesn't alter the fact that he is still an arrogant bastard and a bully.

Even more surprising, he admits to a love of poetry: Auden, Spender, Whitman, Eliot. Clare has observed that, predictably, he only ever makes reference to the male poets. His conversation is peppered with a lively mix of aphorisms, poetry and expletives.

One day, without making a big fuss about it, she had dropped a treasured slim volume of Sharon Old's poetry on his desk – *The Dead and the Living*.

Afterwards she had regretted her gesture. What had she been thinking of, risking sharing a collection that included poems like 'Sex without love', and 'Miscarriage', with one of the most unlikeable men she had ever met?

The previous night Clare dreamed of Bulldozer. His heavy jaw and short nose were mashed into her face, his fleshy lips sought hers, and down below, unspeakable atrocities occurred: an erect penis, long as a parsnip, prodded its way with fierce determination deep inside her.

She had woken in the darkness drenched in perspiration, heart pumping, head pounding . . . and very aroused.

Clare may find Bulldozer a difficult man, but she is unable to simply shrug him off. Over the weeks and months she has thrived on their vigorous interchanges, on his ready wit and shrewd advice. His flashes of humour and the immense charm that he can turn on and off at will. She has come to believe that somehow he has succeeded in penetrating her defences. He has seen through her veneer of sophistication to the little girl who, many years ago, struggled to adapt, to measure up and to learn city ways.

Other than her old school friends few are aware that inside the successful Clare resides the little farm girl from the Kaipara. She's buried deeper with every passing year, with her string of qualifications, every new designer garment or object purchased, every book read, every satisfied client, her climbing bank balance, her beautifully renovated house located in a good area, her joint property investments. All these things are solid proof to her, to her family, that she has made it, climbed out of the mud. Fled from the harsh caw caw of the big grey herons, the hooting of the paradise shelducks, the quarrelsome tones of the magpies. And in the evenings, tucked up in bed in the room she shared with her sisters, listening to the mournful notes of the morepork in the distance and the sounds of fish jumping in the still waters of the tidal inlet.

It was a miracle that they survived on a run-down hopeless farm, her father never quite managing to make a proper go of it, her mother tongue-lashing him, goading him into action, questioning his every decision – until finally he couldn't take any more, sold up, moved them to town, to Auckland, a year before Clare was due to start college.

The farm had resembled a huge graveyard of half-finished tasks and lost hope. Broken fences, the surviving posts straddling the fields like gaping teeth in an empty jaw. Fallen macrocarpas, collapsed sheds, rusting corrugated iron roofing, truck tyres half submerged in the mud, possum traps everywhere, sheet tin wrapped around the telegraph poles to foil those insatiable animals, abandoned rowboats, forgotten machinery lying in the fields left just where it had

208

broken down. The fields were littered with misshapen fallen trunks bleached white after years of exposure to the elements. Rusting petrol cans, stoves, dirty concrete cylinders — the remnants of old drains — were strewn about the fields. Patches of watercress flourished in the ditches. In the long wet winters the cattle churned up the fields of mud and slush and in the summer the tracks from their hooves dried into deep holes and ridges that scarred the ground and made it hazardous to cross on foot.

Clare often dreams of the land while nestled up to Adrian in her soft bed with its fine Irish linen sheets, in stark contrast to the patched sheets of her childhood and the hateful hand-me-downs. The galling sight of her mother's embarrassing baggy flesh-coloured bloomers flapping on the line, alongside the row of pink brushed-cotton nighties. She smells again the damp wool of her father's bush shirt, passes the mud-crusted upended gumboots drying on top of a cluster of sticks at the back door, a sack for a doormat. In early spring the rare splash of colour from her mother's daffodils lined the white gravel driveway.

Enough, dreams Clare, still digging her escape tunnel as if she were a girl again.

As they struggled to adjust to the change in that first year in town, both her parents rose at five-thirty from habit. Her mother, getting the porridge started, as she had at the farm, then frying up thick rashers, the pink strips with rinds of pure fat curling and spitting in the black cast-iron pan, with sometimes a few slices of black pudding thrown in as well. (These days they're on an enforced low fat diet, her father with one heart attack behind him and her mother with a disturbingly high cholesterol count.)

Happy memories of the farm: the walk-in pantry with row upon row of gleaming preserves in the big

Agee jars. Shelves from floor to ceiling: peaches, apricots, beans, tomatoes, plums, pears, apples, relishes, chutneys, sauces, jams, jellies.

In autumn the family had always scavenged in the hills and surrounding paddocks for the saucer-shaped mushrooms which her mother dished up swimming in black juice and melted butter accompanied by stewed tomatoes and crisp golden doorsteps of fried white bread.

Torchlight flickered across the water when they went floundering. And she loved to accompany her father and brothers as they went out in the boat to collect a feed of scallops in the summer.

September and October were the best time for eating the fat rock oysters they scraped from the rocks around the strip of coast bordering the farm, the children chipping the frilly shells off the rocks then flinging them over their shoulders into a tin bucket. The mussels likewise were there for the taking, carried home and steamed in a big aluminium pot, dipped in malt vinegar, tangy, tender, delicious. Clare licks her lips at the memory.

'Free tucker,' rejoiced her father. 'The Lord provides. My, isn't it good to be alive.'

But during the preparations for a recent dinner party, she had recalled with particular distaste the memory of slabs of greasy mutton, legs of hogget and lamb, slabs of cold corned beef, when Adrian had, in his inimitable style, done something terribly clever with peeled lambs' tongues.

The year hurtles on. How far she has come from her days as a stubborn and resentful little farm girl. Soon it will be Easter. Only a week and she will be forty.

She can hear the crackly sound of the transistor; like another body appendage it accompanies Adrian from bedroom to bathroom to kitchen and back to the bedroom on his round of morning ablutions and dressing rituals.

It's Good Friday. On retiring to bed Clare had expressed the desire to sleep in. Fat chance. Adrian is a creature of habit – he cannot lie in and waste half the day. He's a lark. Clare is an owl.

Clare feigns sleep. She overhears Adrian addressing the cat in terms of endearment, not unlike the pet phrases one might lavish on a toddler. Adopting a more adult tone he calls out to her from the hallway.

'The pope is looking exhausted,' he announces, half dressed, his head appearing briefly in the doorway.

'*Good,*' replies Clare with feeling. '*Bastard*. He can drop dead for all I care.'

'Tsk, tsk,' admonishes Adrian with a cheeky grin. He has missed a blob of shaving cream on his left ear lobe. This morning Clare has time to notice such details and find them endearing. This morning she decides she loves Adrian after all.

He is carrying a cup of tea and a magazine for her, the transistor dangling from a black cord on his wrist.

Clare props herself up with an extra pillow and wriggles her toes with pleasure at knowing there is nothing to prevent her from lying in bed reading for as long as she chooses.

'The Italian feminists are protesting outside St Peter's about the Good Friday service. They want the pope to wash the feet not only of the priests but of the nuns. What are they on about? What is this arcane ritual? Explain.'

'An old tradition. You know, Jesus supposedly washed and anointed the feet of Mary Magdalene the whore, and afterwards dried them with her long hair. Something like that.'

211

'Sounds erotic. Like too much fun for the Catholic Church.'

'That's right. Since then the pope has symbolically washed the feet of a few priests at the Good Friday service.' Clare drains her mug. 'Anyway, I don't want to talk about Catholics. The subject depresses me. Especially today.'

'Why today?'

'Good Friday has such dismal associations from childhood. We weren't allowed to go anywhere. Just moped around home, fasting and repenting. We spent most of the afternoon in church. I hated it. I was so bored. You see, you shouldn't have got me talking about it. Now I'm feeling grumpy.'

'Can't think why.'

'You!' Clare flings a pillow at him.

Adrian laughs and ducks his head. 'I can see I'll have to cheer you up then.'

He tosses a large exquisitely wrapped chocolate egg onto the duvet. 'Happy Easter. But you're not allowed to eat it until Sunday, OK?'

This is Adrian at his best. Cheerful, mocking, witty. Their relationship succeeds, it seems to Clare, when the focus of discussion is something outside each other, or their relationship and their expectations of it.

Adrian strolls to the local dairy to buy a carton of milk and a tin of catfood. Clare remains in bed reading. Soon she lays down her Kate O'Riordan novel and thinks about Bridget. She imagines the worst. She checks her own breasts every other day. If it can happen to Bridget with her blameless life, her talent, and her healthy diet and fit body, it can happen to anyone.

One in twelve women.

Clare swings from being optimistic about Bridget's future to believing the worst – how can they know for sure Bridget is in the clear, that the cancer won't recur? Bridget's surgery has caused Clare to assess her own life. The combination of worrying about Bridget and being, as they all are, on the cusp of forty has, it often seems to Clare, led to a failure of nerve. Her path, once clear and relatively obstacle-free, now appears to be full of U-bends. She experiences sporadic attacks of fear and panic. It is comforting to realize that Agnes is in a similar state of mind.

Although on the surface it might appear that their goals are very different, Clare clings to the idea that Agnes is a kindred spirit, a companion on the same stage of the journey.

At least, this is what she has until recently always believed and taken for granted. But now Agnes seems to be changing. She is a great deal calmer now that she is meditating most mornings. In this regard, the change in Clare's friend is extraordinary. Also, there is now this unlikely and peculiar relationship with the ex-priest. Clare doesn't know what to make of it. For once Agnes seems to be proceeding with caution and not losing her head to a passing fancy. Clare has met the man, whom she regards as decent, thoughtful and caring. But he is too conservative and serious for Agnes. She cannot imagine Agnes settling down in marital bliss, being prepared to compromise on her home environment, let alone being comfortable with setting up a joint bank account. But then maybe she doesn't know Agnes as well as she thought she did.

'Why oh why can't people, friends in particular, remain the same?' she has lamented to Fiona. 'Why must they – and everything for that matter – keep changing?'

'Because that's how it is. The fact that our lives, ourselves, our friends and our families are constantly changing and evolving, that nothing and no-one lasts for ever, is a profound truth of our existence on this

213

earth. We suffer when we resist that reality, rather than simply accepting it.'

'How I wish that life wasn't like that.'

Clare continues to feel that she is living behind a sheet of smeared glass because so much has become murky and confused. It's not like her to feel this uncertain. She longs with all her being to return to her safe and familiar life, to the convictions and beliefs she has previously clung to so tenaciously, for they had satisfied most of her requirements.

Clare spends a small fortune on her birthday party. What with caterers, wine, the two waiters and the cleaner she is unlikely to see much change from two thousand dollars. Naturally, she and Adrian split the cost between them.

Clare is satisfied. Her birthday has been well and truly celebrated. Adrian has been devoted and attentive – in public. She has received many expensive and tasteful gifts. Even Bridget had attended, although she had departed early, before the candles on the cake had been lit.

Everyone had complimented Clare on how fabulous she looked – *'darling'*.

Gorgeous for her age, she understood them to mean.

Slim. Fit. Attractive.

But definitely forty.

Still, it had been a stunning party. Everyone had enjoyed themselves. They all said so.

And yet . . . and yet . . . Inside Clare the little worm of discontent continues to twist and turn.

Increasingly she feels as if there is a distance slowly growing between Adrian and herself. It's as if they are operating on automatic pilot. As for the sex – she can take it or leave it. Recently, they have been tending to leave it.

Chapter Seventeen

Agnes

Friday night. Agnes, one glass of wine already under her belt, and now on to her second, is singing and dancing to Garbage in the lounge. The door buzzes and she admits Daniel, who is carrying pizzas. The apartment instantly reeks of grilled mozzarella.

She observes that he looks very Friday night-ish. He's had a hellish week, and he's obviously not yet unwound. In this mood he is likely to pick an argument.

Agnes stops dancing, stranded in the centre of her tiny lounge, sensing the storm building, only she can't figure out why.

'Too thrashy for you?'

'Too everything for me. I CAN'T STAND IT!'

'You can't stand *me*, is that what you mean?'

'I didn't say that,' he replies in a weary voice. He slaps the pizza boxes on the table and flops down on the sofa.

She is annoyed with him. How dare he arrive and spoil her good mood with his negativity? She wishes he would just piss off. Who needs an ex-priest with a bad haircut and daggy clothes anyway? She still hasn't ventured an opinion on his appearance, mainly because she hasn't wanted to hurt his feelings, but also because she suspects he would regard such an opinion as shallow. He has no idea he was about to become her biggest make-over project. Not that he would thank her for interfering.

She gives herself a mental shake. It's only too easy to think of reasons for dumping him.

'The plates are in the cupboard to the left of the stove,' she reminds him in a frosty voice.

'Right.' But he doesn't stir himself.

She contemplates him. This is the real thing. The everyday tarnish on romance. Will he put the loo seat down after him? Wipe the basin after shaving? Do the dishes as a matter of course?

Lost in her thoughts she is surprised to hear him make a reference to Simon. How on *earth*? But it goes some way to explain the tension in the room.

'He was just a *boy*.'

'He was twenty-one. And I didn't exactly *drag* him to bed.'

He winces.

'Don't adopt the moral high ground with me,' she says in a sharp voice. 'It doesn't behove an ex-priest.'

'That was below the belt.'

'Lay off me then. OK? What I did was my business. It was before you, anyway — so what does it matter now?'

Daniel gives her a thoughtful look. 'It does matter. It changes everything. Can't you see that?'

Agnes feels a flutter of panic in her solar plexus. 'Don't be *ridiculous*.'

They continue in this vein for several minutes, with both of them making increasingly damaging and reckless statements.

She watches helpless as Daniel strides out her door,

leaving her feeling shocked and furious at the home truths he has lobbed at her. She carries the two boxes of cold pizzas to the fridge – she has lost her appetite now – and grabs the bottle of Sauvignon blanc. She turns up the music again and pours herself a drink. After ransacking the usual hiding places for dope she at last produces a roach. Better than nothing, she thinks. She spears it with a safety pin and lights up.

She replaces Garbage with Tori Amos and soon loses herself in the familiar voice winding itself sinuously around her insides like a lament.

Deceit, lies, betrayal. Was there anything he hadn't accused her of?

In the morning she wakes with a headache. Every accusation flung at her by Daniel continues to hover in the air like a bad odour.

Afraid of commitment – you got that one right, Daniel.

Thirty-nine going on nineteen.

Huh?

Obsessed with superficial appearances. For Christ's sake, Daniel, that's her job.

She has never disliked someone so much in all her life.

It goes without saying that she couldn't care less if she never sees him again.

How much space does a man need?

'A week,' he says, after she finally swallows her pride and makes the first call. 'I need at least a week to sort out my responses. I'm having a rethink.'

Not another control freak, she thinks. *Please.*

'You don't think it would be more productive to talk about it?'

'No,' he replies stiffly. 'I need a clear head first.'

He won't budge from this stance. Agnes puts down the phone.

Daniel visits her in the evening exactly one week later. They are both excessively polite with each other. Agnes slots a Mozart violin concerto into the CD player.

'Don't change your music just because of me,' he insists.

'But I *adore* Mozart. I'm very eclectic in my tastes, as you'll discover.' She smiles at him.

'It's not that I don't love you,' he says awkwardly.

She pricks up her ears. *Love?* Who mentioned love? Hope flickers into life only to be dashed seconds later.

'You're not the person I thought you were,' he complains.

But then . . . nor was he now the man who had first stumbled into her lounge in his unflattering clothes, she realizes. She was right to be wary of commitment.

Daniel puts his head in his hands. 'I'm at a loss,' he admits.

This is all the encouragement Agnes needs. Instinctively she goes to him. Places her arms round his shoulders. He sinks his head in her chest.

She trembles.

He looks up at her. 'Are you cold?'

'No. Yes.'

'Your teeth are chattering.'

'Yes.'

She strokes his forehead, his hair, his neck.

He is unaccustomed to touch.

She longs for once in her life to feel cherished.

When he swings round to face her again she feels naked. Her breathing quickens.

Lust gathers like a whirlpool in the centre of Agnes's being, lending shape to her pent-up emotions.

Swirling, gathering energy, power. Does he realize? He's not blind, is he? Or is she mistaken?

Show me your face.

One glance then.

He turns. He has seen. He knows.

Agnes. Agnes. Agnes.

I know.

He pulls her towards him. She lurches forward and plants a kiss on his mouth. His grip around her tightens.

Agnes's hips connect with his.

Slam.

He has one hand on her waist, the other on her upper back. Every molecule of her body tingles. Her breath is coming fast.

So is his.

They pause on the brink. Should they? Shouldn't they?

Suddenly, without a word being uttered – it's all on.

A flame of excitement shoots from her chest to her groin – or is it the other way round? It leaves in its residue a sweet ache in her cunt. She can feel his erection through his jeans, pressing against her pelvis.

He fumbles at her bra. When she has helped him to unclasp it she flings it impatiently over her shoulder where it lands on top of the television. They stagger to her bedroom where they pull and tug at each other's clothes, breathing quickly, exchanging no endearments, only terse instructions.

Off come her panties.

She unbuttons his shirt.

Down come his jeans.

She grabs his balls.

He moans quietly.

Her face is flushed. Her lips parted. Eyes half closed.

'Condom,' mutters Agnes. She fumbles in her drawer

219

and pulls out the raspberry-coloured and flavoured prophylactics she had purchased in a shared moment of hilarity with Simon.

She catches his expression at the moment of realization.

He immediately loses his erection.

He doesn't know whether to be embarrassed or angry.

Agnes shrugs her shoulders and gives him a wry grin.

'Don't worry about it. There's no rush.'

He gives her a relieved glance.

Agnes hugs him. Is there anyone out there, she wonders, for whom sex is uncomplicated?

They decide to sleep in the same bed.

But that's all, they tell each other.

'No pressure, OK?'

'OK.'

Naturally, sleep is impossible. Instead they lie awake in the darkness for the greater part of the night, each offering to the other, tentatively at first and then with increasing confidence, glimpses of their real selves. Dreams and achievements are shared, interspersed with admissions of doubts, frailties and disappointments, petty humiliations and embarrassing mistakes. Leitmotifs of paths followed, or not followed.

At four in the morning, drained of words and feeling hopeful, Daniel reaches for Agnes. She rolls over towards him and this time there is no hesitation.

Chapter Eighteen

Bridget

The phone rings and rings. Half the female population of Auckland seems to have heard via the women's grapevine that Bridget has had a recurrence of her breast cancer and will most likely have a double mastectomy. The callers and visitors often have well-meaning but misguided advice, accompanied by chilling anecdotes which they insist on describing down to the last detail. She feels increasingly burdened by the weight of her friends' experiences of cancer and death. They all know someone who knows someone who — horror stories. Lumps not detected in time, or cancer misdiagnosed. Phone call after phone call laments that the national breast screening programme for the over-fifties has been delayed for the fourth time. Scandalous, agrees Bridget.

The results from her latest three-monthly check-up are even more devastating to Bridget than her very first diagnosis because she had allowed herself to believe she had it licked.

'I want you in for a chat.' That's all the specialist said, and she had known instantly.

'It is most unfortunate,' he says, 'but we do have a plan of action.'

He has discussed her case with both the oncologist and the mammographer and is able to set out her options for her. His voice, considering the nature of the information he is imparting, is extraordinarily calm. It's the same troublesome breast, apparently. A partial mastectomy has not got rid of all the bad cells after all. He now recommends a double mastectomy. She does have a choice, she could have just the one offending breast removed, but there is a very strong chance that before too long the other breast will be affected as well. She is welcome to get other opinions, of course.

No breasts at all? Bridget simply cannot absorb the news. Matthew swears loudly, clears his throat and blows his nose.

'Meantime . . .' the specialist tells them, he has also talked to a plastic surgeon who has microsurgery skills and discussed the possibilities for reconstruction.

After Matthew and her mother it has been Athena whom Bridget most needs to confide in.

Athena has plonked herself down, unsuspecting, at Bridget's kitchen table.

Bridget takes a deep breath.

Athena stares at her in disbelief. 'A recurrence? But you've been looking so well. Oh, those lovely breasts. That dear, dear body,' she mutters. 'Bridget, I'm stunned. What's the prognosis?'

'You know the stats. Breast cancer is the biggest killer of women under fifty in this country. But I'm trying very hard not to be pessimistic. My doctor says that seventy per cent of women who get treatment will survive. Survival rates are much higher these days, you know. But I'm still scared shitless.'

'Of course you'll survive,' replies Athena. 'So what can I do?'

'Just be there. I'm going to need my friends.'

Bridget doesn't attempt to disguise her bouts of depression, her fears and anxieties, her sadness. She oscillates between being determined to adopt a positive attitude and feeling pessimistic and panicked.

'So young,' mourns an aunt.

'It's not a death sentence,' snaps Bridget, and decides she will leave her answer service on for a couple of days.

She seeks second and third opinions from specialists to help her with her decision. The consensus seems to be that the risks associated with not having both breasts removed seem too great.

'I don't want to live with the uncertainty,' says Bridget. 'I'll get them both lopped off.'

The following day she is just as likely to have reversed her decision, to be plagued with doubts. 'What if I have the other breast off for nothing? How do I decide? And then there's the decision about reconstruction if I go ahead. Do I have it now or later?'

As her moods continue to seesaw, Matthew puts his own needs aside. All the focus is on Bridget. She has a desperate need for reassurance. He holds her while she cries, while she screams. He listens even when she abuses him, God, the hospital, her doctor, the specialist, when she shouts that life is *so fucking unfair.*

Why me?

She asks this over and over in those first few days as the news sinks in. Why must *she* keep suffering while other people, her friends for example, get to lead their charmed lives? They think *they* have worries? she cries. They know nothing.

Matthew has no answers. Of course it is horrendously unfair. He too questions why Bridget has drawn the shortest straw in the suffering stakes.

'What am I supposed to learn from this?' she asks, when her tears have dried. 'Will it make me a better person? Cure my faults? Give me good karma? There's got to be a goddamn point somewhere, otherwise I may as well slash my wrists now and be done with it.'

She wishes she could apportion blame, but there is no-one to blame, not even herself.

'I didn't cause my disease.'

'No-one said you did.'

'If only I hadn't got so stressed about having a baby.'

'No,' insists Matthew, hugging her to him. 'It is not your fault. Stop torturing yourself. There is no reason, no sense, no meaning. It just *is* – goddammit!'

Bridget cannot yet see what good can come out of her situation.

'And after this big one, can I have a break from having to accept unendurable problems?' she begs, crumpling once again in his embrace.

Matthew rubs her shoulders. 'If I had any say in what goes on in this world,' he says, 'I'd make sure you never had another thing to worry about in your entire life.'

'It's just as well you haven't had children,' says her mother.

Bridget goes very still and quiet. She knows her mother's tactlessness is not intentional. But still.

'Don't let cancer stop you living,' says her mother quickly, realizing she has made a blunder. 'Look at me,' she chirps.

Eileen still wears a prosthesis, but she urges her daughter to go for reconstruction. Bridget feels under pressure. How can she be expected to make a decision about reconstruction when she's still trying to come to terms with the prospect of losing both breasts? One of the breast clinics from whom Bridget seeks advice encourages her to have reconstruction done at the same time as her mastectomy.

'That way,' explains the specialist, 'you'll wake up still feeling like a woman.'

'I don't rely on my tits to feel like a woman,' snaps Bridget.

Does she?

'It won't make any difference to me,' says Matthew. 'You'll still be you.'

Bridget doesn't believe him. He's always told her he's a breasts man, forever complimented her on her gorgeous breasts.

How will it affect their sex life?

'If you decide to go for the reconstruction, do it for yourself and not for my benefit. I'll support you whichever decision you make.'

Matthew advises her to make a decision about reconstructive surgery further down the track, after the mastectomy, when she has had enough time to think.

But Bridget doesn't want any additional operations after the mastectomy if she can possibly help it. If she uses a prosthesis it means every time she changes her clothes she will be reminded of what's missing. Why not have a reconstruction at the same time? Why should she accept anything less than she already has? There are several factors in her favour for the type of reconstruction she has in mind. She isn't too thin, she can afford to lose a little excess belly fat, she doesn't have a history of diabetes, and she doesn't smoke (which would probably make her ineligible for the operation).

The TRAM flap operation looks to be her best option for reconstruction. Abdominal tissue is reasonably similiar to that of a breast to the touch. The surgeon will take tissue from her lower abdomen, divide it in half and slide the sections up beneath the skin to matching openings in her chest, and form them into two new breasts. The double mastectomy and reconstruction will involve an eight-hour operation. She will end up with a smiley-faced scar from hip to hip just above her pubic hair. OK, she can live with that. They'll form a new tummy button. In her case the plastic surgeon can retain her nipples and tuck them back into position during the operation.

'Can you really bear to go through with this?' asks Matthew.

'Yes,' she decides, certain now. 'I want it over and done with in one hit.'

'I'll be frank, the surgery is traumatic,' says the plastic surgeon.

She swallows nervously. 'I am worried about the pain. I'm not good with pain.'

'Everyone responds differently to the pain. Some women have a very strong pain threshold and others have no tolerance whatsoever. You'll have a morphine pump in the hospital and afterwards we'll send you home with plenty of painkillers, don't worry. And I need to inform you that as with all surgery there is a small amount of risk. For example, tissue breakdown, hernias.' He goes on to explain to her what this means.

'You need to have realistic expectations, Bridget. Do you realize that you might not have any sensation in your new breasts?'

'I've been trying not to dwell on that too much.'

'Moving tissue around results in nerves being cut, I'm afraid. However, in your case, because we should be able to retain your nipples, you may get some sensation back through the skin – but I can't guarantee it.'

The momentous nature of the operation she is about to undergo strikes her anew. For a minute or two she is unable to speak.

'You do know, don't you, that the convalescence will be much longer because you're having the reconstruction at the same time as a double mastectomy. Are you prepared for this?'

If this is the price she has to pay. She can live with this too.

'However, you could wear a bikini if you wanted by the time we finish with you,' he promises. 'You'll have a much flatter stomach. *Most* women are pleased.'

She doesn't want to seem ungrateful but she would rather have a rounded belly if it meant she could keep her old breasts.

She asks the surgeon to show her photos of the chests of other women who have opted for a TRAM flap reconstruction and steels herself to look at them. The results are much better than she had anticipated.

Other women have coped. It's not as if she is a pioneer, after all.

'I can't wait to be well again. To look and feel normal.'

'I want you to keep me informed,' says Bridget firmly to her specialist, because she can see already that those who don't ask don't get. 'I want to stay in control of what's happening.' Even as she makes her request she realizes the futility of it. Control? Who is she kidding? She's on a roller coaster, logged into the system. She fills out forms, does her research, sorts out how much of her expenses the medical insurance will cover, makes copious notes, writes letters, replies to well-wishers' cards. She also sees a specialist breast cancer nurse for advice and information and through the Breast Cancer Support Service makes contact with

227

other women who have undergone the same surgery procedures.

Beneath it all Bridget is very, very frightened.

'I've never felt so freaked out in my entire life,' she tells Athena.

She is afraid of the pain that is to come. Uncertain as to how she will cope afterwards, she wonders if she will ever be able to paint again, ever regain the full use of movement in her arms.

Hope. The darting shadow of hope often eludes her. One minute she has it firmly by the tail, the next it has slipped out of her grasp and she is left staring into an unfathomable pool, its clouded surface reflecting back nothing but her own dark anxious thoughts. Fears beat against her temples like the wings of bats in a cave. Her world has tilted on its axis.

Where does she acquire her strength and courage from? She has found herself in an unknown and unfamiliar landscape, looking for signs in a desert. But she is never going to discover the answer to why it was she who was chosen to suffer, so she may as well get on with it, she decides.

This is what it comes down to: she has no choice but to push on, wherever this illness leads her. To experience, endure, heal and, finally, to conjure up from she can't imagine where some sort of faith in her own recovery.

Bridget goes to a private hospital for a straightforward preparatory procedure several days before the main surgery. She is in and out of the hospital on the same day. While she is under the anaesthetic the surgeon makes a small incision and ties off and alters the position of some blood vessels. This will increase the blood supply from the abdominal muscles to the potential flap.

Her torso is now a map of the surgeon's art.

'This is what we'll do.'

He traces paths across her body showing the lines and angles of the cuts that will be made. He presses heavily with his red, black and blue markers. His hand is sure and steady. She particularly notices this.

'Don't wash it off,' he tells her.

She has complete faith in him.

It may be six months after the operation before she feels completely recovered. There is so much to be done in the meantime. She is on her feet all day, finishing a painting promised for a group show, racing out to do her messages, purchasing nighties, toiletries, borrowing a stack of books from the library, setting up the house ready for an invalid's return from hospital. There are a hundred and one tasks crying out for her attention and of course she overdoes it.

On the day before her surgery she wakes in the morning feeling wetness against her skin. She opens her eyes and gasps, in shock, as she realizes that she is lying in a pool of her own blood.

She is rushed into hospital. The ligature has come off one of the blood vessels that was tied off in her one-day surgery the previous week. She is prescribed complete bed rest in hospital while they attempt to stabilize her condition.

The following morning Matthew arrives very early at the hospital. He is allowed to accompany her only as far as the theatre door. His face is paper white. Even his lips are white. His lips move but no sound emerges. His eyes are glazed. There is nothing she can think of to say to him that will make things better.

The plastic surgeon touches up the lines on her body with markers. The last thing she remembers is the delicious sensation of floating into darkness as the anaesthetic kicks in.

Chapter Nineteen

Athena

Athena is giving Rita the works. Extra dollops of the extravagant oil of rose mixed with a little frankincense and geranium. Heavenly. She is deliberately going over time, not that Rita is in any state to concern herself about time, her deadlines or anything other than focusing on Athena's magic hands soothing away aches and pains. Her fingers linger rather longer than usual over the tops of Rita's breasts. Pull yourself together, she tells herself. She must be professional. Warm and efficient. But most important, ethical. Her job is to relax Rita not to take her to nirvana.

She finishes by giving Rita a five-minute scalp massage. With Rita's head resting trustingly in her hands, she feels agitated, as if her innards are being plucked from her own body and sucked out into the cosmos.

She has repeated her affirmations first thing every morning for months now, 'reprogramming' her attitude from self-loathing to self-love, convincing herself that she deserves to be loved. OK. Now she's good and ready. Where is it?

Imagine going through your whole life and never experiencing the grand passion, she thinks. The waste.

She realizes just how mistaken she had been to project her dreams and hopes onto men like Sebastian and Roger. She still has so much love to give. Her accumulated and virtually untapped reservoirs of love and passion are waiting to be bestowed on that mysterious yet-to-be-discovered soulmate who must be out there somewhere, if only Athena could connect with him or her. A beloved companion who will share her beliefs, values and dreams for the future. A devoted partner who will appreciate all the mannerisms and idiosyncrasies that go to make up Athena's personality and, naturally, will generously overlook her flaws (or otherwise find them endearing). Someone who won't mind generous hips and thighs. A spiritual, mystical, intriguing person who is particularly attracted to red-headed women. Man or woman? Probably a woman, but you never know, thinks Athena.

Increasingly she is beginning to believe that Rita is indeed the someone special she has been yearning for. This awareness has crept up on her gradually, taking her by surprise, because Rita is such an unlikely match for her.

Athena continues to knead Rita's head, almost in a trance, certainly in a daydream. Currents of affection flow out through her busy fingers. But can Rita sense it, hear the secret music between them? Are her antennae as finely attuned as Athena's?

No, of course not, Athena, don't be gormless. Just because Rita doesn't currently have a male partner doesn't mean she isn't a het.

Or maybe she is keeping her options open? This is what Athena can't decide. She has tried probing Rita about her past. But she actually knows very little other than a few sparse details concerning her family. A large Italian Catholic family. Rita was the baby, indulged and spoilt. Now her parents are in their eighties. Her

231

mother, who has Alzheimer's, no longer recognizes her children. Even her husband is a puzzle to her. 'Who is that man?' she asks her daughters. 'What is that strange man doing in my house? Tell him to get out and stop bothering me.'

Tears spilled from Rita's closed eyes as she related this sad tale to Athena. She and her army of sisters take it in turns to cook and housekeep for her parents.

What other tidbits has Athena extracted from her new friend? Apparently she hasn't been in a relationship for a few years. This fact surprises Athena. Rita appears so confident and lively. Is she nursing a broken heart? Or is she like Athena, merely fed up with being let down by inadequate men who never came within a mile of satisfying her needs?

After Roger had run off her confidence had taken a battering. But through the hard times she had always believed deep down that one day she would find another man, someone kinder and more loving than either Roger or Sebastian, with whom she would form a happy and mutually satisfying relationship. A relationship in which she would not need to be constantly looking over her shoulder to catch the spectre of abandonment waving at her.

The years had rolled by. Jewel had grown into a monster. And disappointingly, Athena's fantasy of an ideal relationship had never materialized. How can this be, she has asked herself over and over. Is she so undeserving, so unlovable that no-one out there recognizes what riches she has to offer?

On and on goes Athena's inner dialogue. But finally the massage must come to an end. She has other clients booked in. In fact she is running so late because of her infatuation and foolish daydreams that her next client may well arrive before Rita has had a chance to put on her clothes.

Rita climbs off the massage table still in a daze.

She smiles at Athena. 'What a wonderwoman. Thank you.'

'A pleasure.'

Before Rita leaves they arrange to meet to catch a movie.

Athena has to know for sure. She makes an appointment with a clairvoyant to get another opinion. How should she proceed?

The clairvoyant is deadheading her roses in her front garden when Athena arrives. A sprightly old woman in a floral smock and purple capri pants, she points her pruning clippers at Athena and directs her towards the front entrance.

'Let yourself into the lounge. I'll be there in a minute.'

Athena can hear a dry cough then the sound of shoes being scraped on a doormat. Shortly afterwards the old woman totters in on incongruous high-heeled platform-soled red sandals and grins at her client. Her legs are like bent twigs and her freckled arms are criss-crossed with fresh scratches.

'Now then.'

She sweeps a pile of gardening magazines from the glass-topped coffee table, draws the curtains and tosses the protesting cat outside. She flops down on the sofa opposite Athena and kicks off her shoes.

'Give me a few minutes.' She closes her eyes and scrapes one crusty-heeled foot against the other. From where she is sitting, Athena catches a glimpse of chipped crimson-polished toenails and a whiff of perspiration.

She studies the room while she waits. Several framed petit-point needlework pictures of roses and kittens adorn the length of one wall. A bag of knitting is propped against a carved wooden chair. An embroidered satin cloth is draped over a television-shaped object. The lampshades and the tops of the sofas and chairs are covered in protective sheets of plastic and there is a scratchy sound as the clairvoyant leans back on the sofa and makes herself more comfortable.

One bright eye winks open and regards Athena.

'Have you come with a particular question today?'

'Well, yes, I have, actually. I've made a new friend and I want to know more about this friend, what her role might be in my life.'

There is a long silence during which Athena anxiously stares at the woman to check if she is still awake.

'This woman is a puzzle,' murmurs the clairvoyant after an interval spent with her eyes closed. 'She is eluding me. A strong woman. Knows her own mind.' One eye opens again to gauge Athena's response. Athena leans forward in her seat, lips softly parted.

Yes.

'She keeps her own counsel and is afraid to allow anyone close to her.'

Rita to a T. This woman is the goods all right, thinks Athena, relieved.

'She's not sure about you, though,' continues the clairvoyant. 'She thinks you're too intense, too needy. She believes that you want more from her than she is prepared to give. She has lost the ability to trust her feelings. And this is where you can help her and possibly reach her.'

'How?' asks Athena eagerly.

'Pull back,' the clairvoyant advises. 'Bide your time. Move slowly. She who hastens loses the prize.'

There is another long silence.

That's it? thinks Athena, disappointed. She is about

to pay eighty dollars to discover something she already knows?

'No cheques. Cash only,' says the woman, her eyes still closed. 'You can leave it on the coffee table, thanks. I hope the information was useful to you.'

About as useful as a poke in the eye with a sharp stick, thinks Athena, rummaging in her wallet for four twenties.

She still feels uncertain and confused. Perhaps the clairvoyant was right after all, she should bide her time. Allow the friendship to flower at its own pace, and then whatever happens will develop at exactly the time it is meant to.

But what if it doesn't?

Chapter Twenty

Bridget

'You're a lucky woman,' smiles the specialist.

Bridget stares up at him groggily. He's got to be kidding.

'You made the right decision over the double mastectomy,' he tells her. 'We found a tumour in the second breast which hadn't shown up in your mammograms. It was only a matter of time – as we suspected.'

Tears squirt from her eyes. She feels as weak and exhausted as if she has been mown down by a huge truck.

He pats her hand clumsily. 'You'll be pleased to know that the operation was a great success.'

'Thank you.' She gulps.

It's over. She doesn't have to do anything but lie here in her hospital bed and let her body heal itself.

Her new breasts, as far as she can tell so far, look OK. No bandages. There's packing. Taped and stitched cuts. A morphine pump.

It's not so bad. Better than she had imagined.

She begins to feel very pleased with herself.

It's over.

*   *   *

Two weeks after the operation she is out of hospital and back at home. Her friends rally around, but she quickly becomes exhausted by the steady stream of visitors and well-wishers. They're crawling out of the woodwork of her life. Women she hasn't seen in years, now reclaiming their relationship with her, however tenuous. Fear keeps others away. Clare gets on the phone and gives these ones a bollocking.

Bridget can see it gives Clare an outlet for her own fear.

There are even a few who come to gawk, the same people who are no doubt also drawn like vultures to the scenes of road accidents, or to watch some other poor bastard's house burn to the ground. Witnessing someone else's misfortune serves to highlight their own lucky escape. They may have cheated death themselves, but astonishingly on this occasion they still expect to have tea made for them and biscuits served.

Who is to bustle about boiling the kettle, rinsing the cups? Bridget? But she's lying limply on the bed or the couch, craving company yet at the same time wanting to be simply left alone to sleep and rest. She's able to walk around a little, but she's not able to do much because even standing upright is still painful and awkward.

She is very, very tired.

Athena steps in. She prepares vegetable juices for Bridget. Lends her relaxation tapes. She comforts her by gently massaging her hands and feet. Clare monitors the visitors. Agnes returns many of the phone calls. She encourages well-wishers to make a time, to phone before getting in the car, not to just drop in. The etiquette of illness: don't outstay your welcome. Bring something with you. Don't expect to be entertained. Don't come armed with tales of gloom, illness and death.

'I can't bear anyone who is negative,' insists Bridget.

'Agreed,' replies Clare.

'How *are* you, Bridget?' the women all ask, arms full of flowers, heads full of dietary advice.

What is she supposed to say in reply?

'You're looking *great*, you really are.' Considering you've just had half your chest hacked off.

She feels as if she has been excavated.

Five of the visitors have brought with them a book by a well-known American advocate of the power of positive thinking in overcoming illness. It contains a list of reasons why people may have caused their particular illness. Clare skims the contents and immediately tosses the books into the rubbish bin. Athena retrieves one of them and smuggles it into her bag.

Clare follows her out of the room.

'What do you see in books like that?'

'Logical explanations for why things happen.'

'Bridget did not cause her illness, Athena.'

Agnes arrives and joins in.

'Of course, Bridget has always been a very *controlled* person,' says Athena.

'Controlled?' Clare gives her a sharp look.

'Maybe if Bridget had been less tight, less restrained, not holding on to so much repressed anger, then she might not have got cancer in the first place.'

Clare reacts angrily. 'Oh, so it's all her fault, is it? Her tight-arsed manner, am I hearing you right? You silly woman.'

'I didn't mean . . .' Athena retreats a couple of steps.

Agnes quickly ushers her friends out of the house to prevent Bridget hearing the rest of the argument.

'Bridget has been bloody unlucky, that's all. There is no punitive God, no glib explanation. It just *is*. Her *attitude* did not bring on her disease. We have to accept it and hope to hell the surgeons have cut out every last cancer cell in her body. She hasn't got — I don't know — some kind of weird death wish. That would be ridiculous.' Clare glares at Athena and then turns to Agnes. 'You agree with me, don't you, Agnes?'

'We are never going to know for sure what caused Bridget's disease. Put it down to residual karma. Who knows?' Agnes shrugs.

Clare is breathing quickly and her face is pink with fury.

'Now I've heard everything. *Karma?* Pay-back time? I suppose you're going to try to convince me that Bridget is paying off some kind of karmic debt from a previous life and she's going to be somehow purified by her suffering. *Bullshit.*'

'Why do ghastly things happen to good people, Clare? How else do you explain it?'

'Not by swallowing unthinkingly a load of New Age mumbo-jumbo rhetoric and religious hocus-pocus, that's for damn sure. You can keep your judgements.' Clare strides down the driveway and in a few minutes they hear the sound of her car starting up.

'Clare is so blind. Why can't she see that assuming responsibility for your illness is *empowering*. There's a lesson here for Bridget. This is part of her journey — clearing her blocks, her negative energy,' says Athena.

Agnes doesn't trust herself to reply. She snatches up a broom and begins to sweep up the dead leaves in Bridget and Matthew's driveway with brisk, angry movements. She turns her back on Athena, who after a moment or two spent standing uncertainly in the middle of the driveway re-enters the house. Soon she comes back out the front door and walks quickly to her car without acknowledging Agnes, who is shovelling the leaves into a wheelbarrow.

*   *   *

'Would you mind shaving my legs?' asks Bridget. 'I look like the Hairy Woman of Borneo. Matthew does his best, but he misses bits.'

Agnes organizes towels and a bowl of warm water. She slots Cassandra Wilson into the CD player.

'Lovely,' smiles Bridget. 'I could listen to her all day.'

Agnes lays the towel under Bridget's legs and settles herself on the side of the bed, razor in hand.

The large bedroom has been transformed into a sickroom. The bed has been moved next to the window so Bridget can look out into the garden to watch the birds feed. She has a special three-sided curved pillow, a fluffy red shawl, a cordless phone within easy reach, a ghetto blaster and a pile of CDs, tissues, water jug and glass, a little bell to summon help, vases of flowers, two seats for visitors. She likes to keep the room scented with fragrant oils. It has become increasingly crowded with lush plants. The walls are crammed with her big canvases, a celebration of vibrant colour.

'I know. I'm still a real colour freak,' says Bridget, tracking Agnes's gaze across the walls. Alongside her is a recent stack of hand-made greetings cards from her students.

'Tell me what happened this morning. I could hear the three of you arguing.'

Agnes feels a strong urge to get stuck into Athena, but instead she tells Bridget the truth.

'You don't think I haven't asked myself the same questions a hundred times. I have *tried* to understand why this has happened to me, to find meaning, to not think of myself as a victim. I've driven myself crazy with the answers I've come up with. You don't know the half of it. In the beginning I asked myself, even though I haven't believed in a God in years, if perhaps I had been mistaken and the cancer was a punishment for my sins.'

'And have you come up with an answer?'

'No. I don't think there is any meaning. That's the hard part, accepting that an awful lot of the stuff we have to deal with is just random, part of the human condition. A flick of the dice.'

'Do you believe that you'll come back?'

'If I drop dead?'

Pause. 'Yeah, something like that.'

'Again, who can say for sure? The only thing I do know – I have to find my own path through this maze and it's not going to happen overnight. I've never liked being told what to do. People seem to believe that because I've had cancer I don't have my own opinions, that I'll accept every drop of advice on my bended knees.'

'Like, kiss my arse, why don't you?'

'Exactly. Thank you, Agnes. I still have to let off steam, you know, that hasn't changed. People have this unreal image of cancer recovery patients – a bit like nuns, or martyrs, don't you think?'

'Yeah. Pious, passive, obedient, offering up their suffering for the glory of God, or whatever. You know how it goes – not my will but *thine*.'

'Mmm. Something like that. Whereas my inherent nature is still the same. Having cancer is not like a conversion.'

'I would have thought it was.'

'Sure, it's a wake-up call. But I haven't experienced a Pauline vision, a Road to Damascus type thing. In a way I wish I had.'

'Shall I teach you to meditate?'

'I have been meditating,' admits Bridget. 'There is nothing I haven't tried. All the diets and treatments, the vitamins and visualizations, the affirmations, the pills and potions.'

'And . . . ?' The razor is poised in mid-air.

'Well. Something's working, God knows what though. I do think that my attitude is going to play a big part in my quality of life, so I've simply got to get on with it.'

Agnes focuses on her task, gently rubbing moisturizer into Bridget's legs.

'I think you're being very brave.'

'I wouldn't call it bravery. I certainly don't take anything for granted any more. But I don't have a choice, as I see it, other than to be positive. I can scarcely believe that a year ago I didn't think I could be happy unless I could have a baby.' She laughs ruefully. 'I can now appreciate every single minute of my life *just as it is* – even if it means exercising patience while recovering from surgery. I'm learning to live one day at a time.'

Bridget believes everyone is staring at her chest. Is she imagining it, or do the glances of both men and women slide quickly over her, not quite meeting her eyes but instead lingering on that part of her body that has been reconstructed, wondering what it looks like, yet feeling too shy or awkward to ask to see it.

Her sense of self has taken such a battering that she can't even begin to convey to her friends the huge shifts in perception fermenting inside her. Who is she now that she has had a double mastectomy and has two fake boobs? She is accustomed to reading the appreciation in the eyes of men when she enters a room. It is a new experience for her to elicit sympathy, morbid curiosity, or pity. Her beauty has been a weapon, a shield, a bonus or an obstacle (depending on the circumstances, or her state of mind), at the very least something she can count on as night follows day.

Now she is altered and it seems as if everybody knows it.

'They are staring at you not in pity but in admiration for your bravery,' insists Matthew.

Her close friends have made peace with each other and now demand to see the results of the reconstruction. They're pleasantly surprised.

'What did you imagine?' grins Bridget. 'A female Frankenstein?'

They study the recently created breasts, the cuts, the tape, the stitches.

'I love my new breasts already. I'm very proud of them.'

'When you stop and think what was actually *done* to your body and how normal it looks now, apart from the cuts – it's fucking amazing.' Clare pours everybody stiff gin and tonics. She raises her glass. 'Here's to the new wonder boobs.' Her smile is polished and bright. She is on the verge of tears.

Bridget tenses. There is a swift intake of breath before she laughs. But the others visibly relax. So, this is how they'll ride it through, she thinks, on an up beat. Humour.

'To the new boobs,' she agrees, only someone else has to raise the glass for her.

Encouraged, Bridget slaps on her make-up, puts on a pretty nightie. She asks Clare to paint her toenails. She has a powerful need to surround herself with feminine things. Beautiful bed linen, flowers, perfume.

To think she used to think of herself as a private, reserved person. In the past weeks she has had so many people – mainly men – prodding and poking, interfering with the breasts that formerly only Matthew saw. She has had to relinquish modesty and pride. Her body has become a railway station.

243

'Am I still attractive?' she asks Matthew. It seems hours rather than seconds before he replies.

'I love you more. Your spirit. Your bravery.'

She points to her chest. 'This here. My new boobs. Do you think you can love them – that's what I'm asking you.'

He hesitates. His eyes water.

'I still find you the most beautiful woman on earth.'

She dissolves and it's Niagara Falls time again. She's still an emotional yo-yo.

Make cancer your friend. That's what the survivors in the cancer manuals advise her – these first hand accounts from women who have spat in the face of the devil, who have peered over the edge of the abyss and returned to tell the tale. Before the mastectomy she had viewed her malignant growth as a trespasser, an enemy, an invader of the heart and spirit. A thief in the night who would rob her for ever of the way things were, imposing his own tyranny of response in pain and suffering. A companion who had selected her from among all the thousands of others from whom he (yes, it was a he) might have extracted his payment.

She is exhorted by Athena, as well as by others with similiar views, to grow from the experience. They don't expect her to come out of the illness unscathed, but at the very least she can, if she chooses, Athena tells her, become a better person – more spiritually aware, having gained insights denied others who remain blissfully, ignorantly healthy. The idea is that she will then become wiser, filled with more compassion for both herself and others.

It's up to you, Bridget. Become an active participant in your recovery.

'Hogwash,' says Clare and she creates another word on their Scrabble board.

Which puts everything in perspective, because some days Bridget is able to behave with saint-like restraint and acceptance. On others she is loaded up with self-pity and complaints, likely to burst into tears as soon as someone looks at her the wrong way. If she squanders her 'opportunity to grow' does that mean she is a failure? Unworthy?

'Spare me,' says Clare as she pours another cup of tea for her.

'But death is now part of my life in a way it never was before.'

'Oh, don't be so morbid.'

'You don't understand,' says Bridget in a patient voice. 'I've had to learn to accept the possibility of my death while at the same time not giving up on the idea of living. Make sense?'

Clare doesn't want to talk about death. She sees it as her mission to cheer up Bridget.

Her friends are sympathetic, encouraging. But . . . they don't understand.

Only those who have been there know. Survivors of her age, who are now volunteers, come to call on her. They listen with knowing smiles and grimaces. They come armed with their black humour. Their jokes about prostheses and plastic surgeons are so dark that no-one but a survivor could dare to find them funny. Miriam, one of the volunteers, exhorts Bridget to go on and live dangerously, to take risks and do all the things she has ever wanted to do and not got round to.

What has she got to lose?

Gradually Bridget recovers her strength. To her surprise she has in some ways coped with the ordeal better than her friends.

In the meantime her life and plans are on hold for six months while she recovers from her surgery. Six weeks

after her surgery she undergoes a course of radiotherapy.

Hands reach out to her: Matthew, Clare, Agnes,
Athena, her parents. Brothers, sisters, aunts. Strangers.
Professional caregivers and so-called health providers.
The volunteers. A chain gang. She is passed from hand
to hand like so many beads on a rosary.

But she has come through the fire. She will survive.

Chapter Twenty-One

Agnes

Agnes calls Daniel, as promised, on returning to her apartment from visiting Bridget. He is proving to be amazing in a crisis – she can absolutely count on him to do and say the right thing.

'How was it?' asks Daniel, warm and interested on the end of the line.

Agnes considers. Moving? Special? Astonishing? Replenishing? A privilege? All of these.

'The news is good, isn't it?' asks Daniel. 'The operation has been very successful. Bridget is going to survive.'

Agnes mutters a yes and bursts into tears. She can't even find the words to describe her relief that the ordeal of Bridget's operation is over. She and Clare had been very preoccupied with trying to support Athena, who had been on a crying jag lasting several hours while they waited with Matthew for the marathon surgery to be completed. On the day of the operation none of them had been able to contemplate the idea of going to work. They had camped at Matthew and Bridget's house and drunk huge quantities of coffee and tea. Matthew stoically made repeat orders of banana pancakes throughout the day to occupy himself.

'Would you like to be alone, or would you like some moral support?' asks Daniel in a loving voice.

'I'd like company. Yours in particular.'

'That can be easily arranged.'

Thank God for Daniel, thinks Agnes as she puts down the phone. She hasn't leaned on anybody in years. It's a great comfort to her now when she actually needs it. An unexpected gift.

'Tell you what,' says Daniel, when he arrives bearing Thai takeaways. 'Why don't we get out of Auckland? Go on an outing this coming weekend. We could go up north to a beach. Stay the night at a nearby motel. Would you like that?'

Why did I bother with a young kid like Simon, thinks Agnes for the umpteenth time.

They wander down the long golden sweep of the beach front at Pakiri, hand in hand. I'm happy, realizes Agnes, exulting in the sharp salt air, the light dancing on the water.

They stroll beside the water towards the bluff. Oystercatchers scurry at the waves' edge on graceful red legs. Large horse mussel shells dot the sand. To their right are sand dunes splattered with marram and pingao grass. On the hills and farmland beyond, gnarled old pohutukawa trees are braced against the prevailing northerly wind, their leaves tipped silver in the sunlight.

On their return along the beach in the late afternoon, the shadows reach with giant hands down the slopes, highlighting the long-established cattle tracks that ridge the hillside.

'We're lucky,' says Agnes, her senses heightened by

the recent crisis with Bridget. She clings to the thought of Daniel, her pleasure in the crashing surf, the sight of the fishermen with their rods, the bare-chested young man with his backpack and black dog, the children playing beach cricket, the couple entwined in the dunes. Anything that reflects stability in a world that seems to her increasingly impermanent. It's daunting to think that she will eventually lose everyone and everything she loves. With her mother, for instance, it will be sooner rather than later. Agnes makes a resolve to improve the relationship with her mother while she still has the opportunity.

How does her mother fill her days? It's long been a mystery to Agnes. Since her father died her mother has developed a new group of friends. Most are widows like herself. Nearly half of the women her mother's age are learning to fend for themselves.

Her mother wears a permanently disgruntled expression on her face. She still hasn't forgiven Neville for abandoning her.

'*Mum!*' Agnes becomes annoyed when her mother takes this line. 'Dad didn't abandon you – he died of a heart attack.'

'Same thing. We had all these plans. The caravan trip down the South Island. Driving around Australia. Exploring the outback. Why did we wait?' She gazes at Agnes with her mournful eyes. 'I never expected to end up living on my own. It's a terrible thing, Agnes. You're used to it. But I went straight from my parent's house to marrying Neville.'

She annihilates a colony of ants with her damp sponge as if they represent all her lost opportunities.

'You could still travel.' Agnes tries to be helpful. 'Why not go with your friend Betty? Or what about Lynn? Olive?'

Her mother sniffs. 'I'm not going around the coast with Betty. The burden. It'd be me doing all the thinking and planning. Lynn isn't well enough and Olive can't afford it.' She finishes wiping the bench. 'So. There we are.'

Excuses, excuses. Agnes wonders if her mother is actually clinically depressed.

'Tell me about this fellow, Daniel. When am I going to meet him?'

'Soon,' promises Agnes.

'So is Christmas.' Her mother begins wiping a glass-topped dining table that is, from what Agnes can see, already spotless, like everything else in her mother's house.

She hasn't yet got round to filling her in on Daniel's background. The responses can be so boringly predictable.

'Where did you meet him, Agnes?'

'At a Buddhist meditation class.'

Her mother pauses for a moment in her wiping. The silence is alive with accusation as yet unexpressed.

'I take it you've turned your back on the good Lord then?' The voice is pained.

'Mum, don't play games. You know very well I haven't been a Catholic in years.'

Nor are any of her siblings, a source of immense pain and regret to her mother. But is it their fault if their mother persists in viewing all her children as extensions of herself, setting the scene for endless conflict? Her mother imagines herself stabbed in the back, when all her children are doing, it seems to Agnes, is simply being true to themselves.

'Hmmmmph.'

Agnes watches as the wiping becomes more frenzied. The damp cloth skims over the mantelpiece, skirting board, the front of the cupboards, the little

radio her mother carts around the house on her house-
work trolley so she can surf the talkbacks.

Agnes decides the subject of Daniel's former career
can definitely wait until another visit.

'When are you going to settle down, Agnes? By the
time I was your age I had seven children.' She pecks
at a cluster of porcelain statues of saints with her
duster.

Agnes can sense her mother has come to an end of
her patience. Fed up with attending to her duties and
responsibilities all her life. What good has it done her?
Has it made her any happier? More fulfilled? A better
human being?

Noelene and Neville. What did they find to say to
each other? Agnes gauges the level of discontent from
the line of her mother's mouth. If Noelene was the type
who stamped her foot when she couldn't get what she
wanted, this is probably what she would have shouted
to an uncaring and indifferent world: 'WHERE IS MY
SLICE OF THE PIE, YOU BASTARDS?'

But she's not the type and never will be, reflects
Agnes. Her mother favours the indirect approach. A
litany of veiled complaints and innuendos follows her
progress through the house. *Not that anyone would
notice . . . Not that I want to be any bother to anyone,
Agnes.*

A knot of tension in her stomach swells. Her mother
will give her an ulcer before she's finished. Why is she
always made to feel as if she has to justify her so-called
selfish life? A life without babies, a life in which her
mother sees no viable role for herself.

'Mum, I *am* settled down. By myself. I have a career.
I'm a success, in case you hadn't noticed. I own my
own apartment. I have good friends — they're my
family. I care deeply about them and I'm very involved
in their lives. My life is busy and stimulating — the way

I like it. I'm happy. You don't have to worry about me. I can take care of myself.'

The disappointment lies quivering between them, a pulpy mass of tangled raw nerves and suppressed emotions. Agnes knows that the source of her mother's disgruntled manner, the true reason why she is threatened by Agnes's independence, is that until the past year she had mindlessly abdicated responsibility for her own life.

'You know me, I'm a duffer about money,' she had always claimed.

Not any longer. She can't afford to sit back now that Neville and his patient concern are for evermore absent from her life.

Her mother climbs on a chair to tease out a spider's web from the upper section of wall with a broom head. 'You'll miss out on having a baby if you don't look out. Thirty-nine, *my goodness*,' she chirps.

Any responses of empathy or concern Agnes might have felt fly out the window. She takes a deep breath. Counts to ten.

Finally the swirl of feverish activity ceases. Her mother perches on the end of her seat to drink her tepid tea, one foot thrust forward, poised for take-off. A scratching sound as the folds of her nylon petticoat are rearranged. Her mother is shrinking. Legs marbled with veins, arthritic knees, pain in her hip, but . . . 'mustn't complain', her feet in their cheap tartan slippers, fake fur trims worn to a blunt fuzz, hair rinsed and set once a month. A new set of false teeth due soon. Bills paid on time. Years of doing without. She doesn't even know how to enjoy herself any more.

Does her mother truly believe that her martyrish enduring of her pain and frustrations will guarantee her a place in heaven?

Agnes could weep.

'Stop *blaming* me,' mutters Agnes's telepathic mother once she has nibbled her shortbread until it is only a tiny wedge held between thumb and forefinger.

Agnes goes cold.

'Who said anything about blaming?' She hears the edge of irritation creep into her voice.

'I wanted you all to be happy. Was it too much to ask?' continues her mother in a dull voice. She begins to weep. Tears of defeat drip onto the recently wiped table top.

I can't bear this performance, thinks Agnes. She is winding me up again. How she longs to run out the door and return to the sanity of her apartment.

'I tried *so* hard to be a good mother.'

Our Lady of Self-Righteousness.

'You were.' Agnes corrects herself. 'You *are* a good mother.' The gauge against which all other achievements are weighed and measured, or instead found wanting.

'*You* don't think so.'

Our Lady of Self-Defence.

'Yes, I do.'

'I don't believe you.'

Our Lady of Denial.

I can't win, thinks Agnes, searching for a way to change tack.

What is this drama that she and her mother seem compelled to act out again and again with relentless predictability?

'*Why* do you feel blamed?' Agnes is determined to nail the source of her mother's perpetual complaints.

Her mother quickly backs off. 'I didn't mean it like that.'

It's all there in her mother's face: *What would Agnes know? Too busy making money. Out having a good time.*

253

'Well, how *did* you mean it?' Agnes watches mesmerized as her mother shreds the tissue she has just plucked from her apron pocket.

'Oh . . .' Sigh. Downward glance. 'It doesn't matter.'

Our Lady of Perpetual Sorrows.

'If it doesn't matter, then why did you raise it?' Agnes is exasperated.

But this is far too confrontational for her mother who commences a frenzied rewiping of the table.

It dawns on Agnes that what they are discussing has nothing remotely to do with what is actually bothering her mother. It is simply a diversion, a hook she has flung into the conversation pit to inform Agnes in an oblique fashion that she is peeved with her life.

'Why are you upset?'

'I'm *not* upset.'

No-one ever listens to me.

Agnes isn't surprised by her mother's denial of her feelings. She realizes she is expected to slowly tease out the truth from her mother's contradictory responses. But not today, she has neither the time, the inclination, nor the energy required.

Noelene the Martyr swallows the bile of her life. She says in a wistful voice: 'It would be nice to have a bit of fun. A laugh now and then.'

Lonely, lonely, lonely.

Agnes feels both guilty and responsible. She should take her mother on outings. Visit more often. Make more effort.

Duties and responsibilities, Agnes.

Agnes has often tried to put herself in her mother's shoes, but at the point where she might begin to feel compassion, her imagination fails her. The colossal load of disappointment, frustration and resignation appals her. Never resentment – this response would be deemed too passionate, too inappropriate for the careful restrained life her mother has constructed around her.

Lucky Athena. Where Agnes's mother is conservative, tentative and martyrish, Athena's mother is bold, determined and adventurous.

Once Agnes had suckled at this shrunken woman's tits, although she can scarcely believe it now.

All those children she has sacrificed her life for. How can it be that only Agnes remains in Auckland? Her siblings are scattered not only across New Zealand but across the globe. Tom in Vancouver. Maurice in Sydney. Helen in London. Babs and her tribe in Wellington.

'Gotta run, Mum. I have some calls to make to set up a shoot tomorrow. I need to check in with the props guy and the make-up artist.'

Her mother does some clever rearranging of the lines in her face, contriving to appear resigned, and at the same time mildly offended. Agnes is left with the impression that she has just dropped a turd in her mother's path. Her career, her whole life will always be a complete mystery to her.

'And how is Bridget?' asks her mother in a concerned voice, just as Agnes is about to trot off down the path, a container of home baking under her arm.

Great timing, Mum.

Agnes turns. She pauses. The sight of the stooped figure of her faithful little mother, her bandy legs in the sloppy tartan slippers, the ubiquitous duster in one hand, brings a lump to her throat. The white blob of candyfloss hair shines in the light like a worn halo. God's exhausted little servant.

'She's been through hell, Mum.'

There is a catch in her voice. Pain and grief churn in her guts.

The angle of her mother's body changes. 'The poor

wee soul,' she murmurs without taking her eyes off Agnes.

Agnes nods miserably.

But she doesn't move away.

'The poor wee mite,' adds Agnes's mother in a quiet soothing voice. The duster falls from her hand. It lies neglected on the ground.

Agnes swallows hard.

'Her parents must be hurting like the very devil over it.'

With a strangled wail Agnes flings herself, big lump though she is, into her little mother's arms.

'There, there,' croons Agnes's mother happily, as she would to any hurt child. 'There, there.'

Chapter Twenty-Two

Clare

Matthew has taken to dropping in on them once or twice a week but rarely for longer than an hour.

'Poor bastard feels guilty if he leaves the house to go to his job,' remarks Adrian after another of Matthew's fleeting visits.

'Wouldn't you? Can't be easy being the main caregiver. Bridget's cancer has consumed his life for the past few months.'

'Not so,' insists Matthew when he next visits and they broach the subject with him. 'It's Bridget's mother who has taken over my life.'

'That bad, eh?' says Adrian. To Clare's astonishment he is simply drooling empathy. He is being amazing. She is very impressed.

'*Mate*, you don't know the half of it.'

Clare has noticed the matiness exhibited even by professional men in each other's company. 'Fuck'n oath, mate,' Matthew will growl to Adrian and mock-punch him in the chest.

'I suppose you find this parody of the Kiwi bloke side-splittingly funny.'

'I do, as a matter of fact, Clare. We're talking *irony* here.'

Matthew and Adrian laugh uproariously at this.

Matthew may be under a tremendous strain, but he is still a very sexy man, thinks Clare, surprising herself.

He has a lovely taut high bum. He's not as tall as Adrian, who has a lean body, a slightly owlish expression and large hands and feet, but he is fit, firm and well proportioned.

Clare drags her attention away from Matthew's physical appeal to the subject of Bridget.

'Why don't you suggest to Eileen that you'd prefer the weekends alone, but that you'd welcome her support on weekdays. She'd probably be relieved, quite honestly, if you put it to her like that.'

Matthew groans and lifts his glass to Adrian for a top-up. 'Saint Eileen the virgin martyr – I'm telling you,' he says in a bogus Irish accent.

Clare types the contact details for the caregivers' list on her laptop. *Tappity-tap-tap.* Actually, she is really keying in the *revised* caregivers' list. People who were pissed off because they weren't on it and who insisted – no, demanded – that they be included. Extraordinary how many friends Bridgie has. And they all believe they have rights. Well, fuck them.

'Who the hell is Sylvia Adcock?' she grumbles, squinting at the tiny screen.

'Some teacher friend.' Athena, bearing a tray of tea and shortbread.

'I thought I knew Bridget.'

'You do.'

'No. It seems I don't.' Does Athena understand how disturbing and unexpected it is to be confronted with these utter strangers with their competing demands, their 'will you do afternoons, or do you prefer mornings'? Their opinions on the benefits of the various food and vitamin supplements. The two mothers and the aunts who drop in with casseroles and flowers from their gardens.

Even Matthew, the loyal and decent Matthew, has been reduced to a bit part in a play that someone else is directing in his own home, surrendering to the rosters, phone calls, the comings and goings of health professionals as well as visitors bringing their plates of food and sympathy. Although everyone feels sorry for him, the attention is focused exclusively on his wife.

Clare observes Matthew strive to do the right thing and be kindly but politely elbowed aside by others who believe they know better. She sees him attempt one caregiving role and then discard it for another. None fit. There is always someone who thinks he should do it differently, or else simply do more.

'Yeah, and at the end of the day someone has to still pay the mortgage,' she heard Matthew complain to Adrian.

It is not about the mortgage. Matthew *wants* to escape to his office and demanding clients, he has told Adrian. He cannot remain in the house day and night being ordered about, especially by Bridget's mother. 'It's — "Have you done this?" and "Don't forget to do that."' He mimics her voice. He can no longer have an occasional night in front of the telly, let alone read a book. There are often thirty phone and fax messages to return. Sometimes he's still going at midnight. And that's not counting the e-mails, the endless cards and flowers.

Clare scans her print-out. The women in Bridget's life have taken over — her mother, Matthew's mother, two aunts, Athena, Agnes and herself. Not forgetting

Bridget's art dealer, three artists, a librarian friend, the yoga teacher, the counsellor sent by the Cancer Society, the dietician, the GP, the pharmacist – all women.

And now this bloody Sylvia Adcock is muscling in on the act. Exactly how well *does* she know Bridgie anyway?

Clare shows the list to Athena to see if she has left out anyone important.

'I've never heard her mention half of these people.'

'You must have.'

Clare has always believed she knew almost everything about Bridget there was to know. It seems now she was mistaken. Has she ever known and understood the real Bridget and her world, or only the carefully edited and sanctioned version Bridget would allow her to access? She recalls the dozens of conversations conducted over the years, first in budget flats, student cafeterias, buses, on beaches, and later in cars, planes, cafés, exhibition openings, kitchens, over dinner tables. They have laughed and cried together, danced, walked, eaten, driven, played squash together in their twenties. For twenty-five years, since they were fifteen-year-old convent girls with a newly awakened interest in boys, Bridget has given her opinions and support over the various lovers she and Agnes have lusted over. She has stuck around to pick up the pieces when their relationships disintegrated.

'I don't know what to think any more.' Clare's head is bowed over her laptop. A tear plops onto the M key. She doesn't bother to wipe it away.

Athena is stricken. The Clare she knows rarely cries. 'What's the matter?'

Clare shakes her head. 'Everything is the matter.'

Clare develops a sore throat which escalates into a

severe head cold. Her sinuses throb. She feels miserable. Uncharacteristically she doesn't complain. After all, it is not as if it is *she* who has just survived a double mastectomy and a breast reconstruction.

She can't visit Bridget, because the risk of infecting her doesn't bear thinking about. Instead she writes affectionate and amusing little notes which Adrian leaves in the letterbox for Matthew to collect.

Alone in the house day after day, working her way through packs of tissues, coughing up phlegm, Clare is red-nosed, her hair greasy, eyes streaming, body aching, face pasty. Instead of relaxing, she finds herself reviewing the impermanence of everything for which she has worked and sacrificed herself. She has lived as if she would be around for ever, surrounded by the fruits not of her loins but of her labours, products of her clever mind and astute business sense. Yet what does any of it count for in the long run?

She has spent her life wanting and grabbing. For security. Love. Success. Money. Acknowledgement. Each satisfied longing has predictably been followed by fresh cravings and ambitions, succeeded inevitably by disappointment.

For several years it had seemed as if Adrian was a solution – the subtotal of happiness. Then a baby became her latest 'must have'. As if a baby could fill the void. Even a baby is only a creature on loan. A dependant who grows into a child and then a teenager hell-bent on rebelling and then leaving.

Loss seeps into her bones. It has always been there, but she has not recognized its presence – she was too busy denying it. She has viewed the constant changing nature of all things and people as just another challenge to be overcome. If she only worked harder and focused more sharply on the object of her desires perhaps she might create lasting happiness.

Previously Clare had not imagined there being a moment when she was not interested, curious, alive, passionate about someone, seeking answers to her many questions, or lusting over the beautiful and the exotic. She plans to die a very old woman wearing her Dior bra, clutching her Prada handbag in one hand, a strong gin in the other. Hair dyed and well cut. Lipstick on straight and bright. A survivor. A goer. Paying till the last moment for hired help, if she can still afford it, because there will be no beautiful daughters to see her out. Instead, a trail of long-dead lovers and mourned old friends.

What, after all, will all the fuss have been about?

Of course she is sick, stuck and in crisis mode, Athena tells her. Naturally no doctor can make her well. It's her body trying desperately to get a message to her.

'What kind of message?' asks Clare warily.

'To think about your lifestyle.'

'Oh *puh-lease*. You sound just like my mother.'

'There's no point in giving you antibiotics,' announces Joan, her doctor. 'You need warmth and rest. Keep up the fluid intake. Take lots of vitamin C.'

In the past Clare would have staggered into work, been inefficient, played the martyr, forced herself to put in a full day no matter how bad she felt. She had programmed herself to believe this was what you did if you were running your own company. And it goes without saying that she would have ignored advice from anyone who dared to suggest she would be wiser to take to her bed.

She remains at home resting. Right now she couldn't care less about work. Why should one task, one goal, matter more than any others?

What is the point of anything?

'Ever thought of acupuncture?' suggests Athena.

'No, never.'

Athena gives her a name on a scrap of paper. Norman Ng.

What has she got to lose? Clare calls him up and makes an appointment.

She is shown into a small room painted a duck-egg blue and lined with large anatomical charts of the human body. She sniffs the bitter smell of burning herbs. Norman Ng is a middle-aged Chinese man with a gentle manner, dressed in a white business shirt, grey wool trousers, Nike sports shoes and black-framed pebble-thick spectacles.

He takes a pulse reading on each of her wrists.

'What can you diagnose?'

'Lung weak,' he states. 'Liver and kidney weak. There are many toxins in your body. Now, please show me your tongue.'

'Will the needles hurt?' asks Clare.

'Needles will not hurt.' Catching her expression, he elaborates. 'Maybe at the beginning, but afterwards it is not a problem. Don't worry, please.'

Sure.

Clare closes her eyes. There are limits.

'New needles,' he informs her. 'Only use needles one time, then I throw away.'

The possibility of infected needles hadn't occurred to her. He dabs spots on her head, neck, hands and legs with what smells like meths. There's a sharp ping of pain as each needle is inserted. She would rather not know just how deeply they penetrate her skin. Needles pierce her skull, neck, hands, feet.

He abandons her for forty minutes. It seems like hours. She is worried about lifting her needle-infested

263

arm to check her watch in case she inadvertently pulls out the needles. Twice he comes over to check them as if he were holding a fishing line and feeling for a responsive tug on the other end.

She lies there thinking. She knows she has been consumed by this urgent drive to achieve, has clung to the world with its attachments and seductions as if they were an end in themselves.

How to be different?

'My mother has a picture of a deer above her bed,' says Clare.

Bridget nods.

Clare continues. 'A skinny deer. With huge eyes. A shaft of sunlight over her. Two cute Bambis frolicking around her in a sun-drenched lime meadow. Big pink blossomy flower heads in the foreground. Arcadian.'

'It *says* something about your mother,' murmurs Bridget.

Clare bends forward to catch an insight into her mother. 'What does it say?'

'I don't know. There's a naivety there beneath the brittleness, I suppose.'

'I'm determined to understand Mum before I die.'

Oops. The D word. Not to be spoken. Just like the C word. Funny how often the D word crops up in everyday conversation. People pretending they're never going to die yet *dying* to possess everything – knowledge, power, love – to be everything while there is still time, to make a statement, to be remembered.

'Mmmm.' Bridget sounds weary.

'I should go,' Clare says, standing up. 'Can I get you anything before I leave?'

Bridget drifts into a light doze. Clare pulls up the covers and tiptoes out of the room to make herself coffee.

Now that the worst is over, Clare is reacting to the emotional strain. She retreats to the kitchen and collapses over the sink. Like every other available flat surface the bench is overflowing with vases of flowers, drenching the room with a cloying scent. No sooner does Matthew dispose of one vase of drooping flowers than several more arrive to take its place. The freezer is stacked with gifts of food. Fish pies with crumbed toppings, easy-thaw and heat-in-a-minute pumpkin and kumara soups, chicken casseroles, apple pies, courgette and mushroom quiches, and beef lasagnes.

Clare takes her coffee into the lounge and flops on the couch.

Her eye is caught by Bridget's painting. One of her most successful and certainly the most dramatic in scale, it extends the length of one wall. Two erotically charged bodies – Bridget and Matthew? Intertwined in such a way that the viewer can barely discern where one finishes and the other begins.

'She cried when she finished painting it, because she thought it the best work she'd ever done,' says Matthew who has just arrived home from the supermarket.

'Here, let me help you.' Clare hugs him. 'You check on Bridget and I'll unpack this lot.'

Chapter Twenty-Three

Athena

They might have little in common but it hasn't stopped Athena thinking about Rita a great deal over the past weeks, despite her fears for Bridget. She wants to know Rita more intimately. And – something else she has never attempted before – she is prepared to take the initiative.

Where does she start? It's like being sixteen again and still a virgin. Green as. Scared stiff of getting it wrong and making a fool of herself.

Her fantasy life blossoms as she begins to do something she hasn't done for years – to think about sex.

But how can she discover whether or not Rita favours women, so that she doesn't make a complete idiot of herself?

'I'll put out a few discreet feelers,' offers Clare, with her numerous contacts in the magazine world.

'Would you?'

Clare returns to her in a few days.

'The news is good.'

Athena is happy and optimistic one moment, the next full of doubts and despair. Why should Rita be attracted to her? Clare says she has it on good authority that Rita is gay — but what if she has been misinformed?

But imagine if it *is* true, *and* Rita is not involved with anyone else?

'What's eating you?' asks Jewel suspiciously. Her mother is uncharacteristically preoccupied, and oblivious to Jewel's comings and goings. She doesn't react when Jewel is rude, doesn't even seem to hear. In the absence of any reaction Jewel becomes less abusive. But she can't resist pointing out to her mother that she is going about the house with a silly expression on her face, and does she realize she looks like a psych patient?

'Do I?' Athena laughs at herself.

Jewel shakes her head. Her wacko mother.

Athena examines the detritus of her life. She views her house with fresh eyes. Change is in the air. She begins with the chests of drawers and wardrobes, systematically emptying out each drawer, sorting through every garment until she has a pile for the City Mission, another to give away to family members, and an ever-expanding heap for a garage sale. Next she repeats the process with all the cupboards, cabinets and shelves in the house. Day by day. Room by room. How has she come to own such an assortment of useless junk? Why has she hoarded so many trinkets, cards, letters, shabby clothes she no longer wears, threadbare towels? Gadgets and utensils that she had believed might come in handy, but instead lie buried, unrepaired and uncared for, in the bottom of cupboards, or else abandoned in cartons in her basement. The weight of her possessions has suddenly become an intolerable burden.

She pores over old theatre programmes, greetings cards, postcards and photocopied articles. She rediscovers the letters and poems written to her by Sebastian, and later Roger, so many years before. Old emotions flutter from the long-forgotten words and phrases, sentiments that now fill her with astonishment. Had Roger really referred to her as a foxy chick? And Sebastian's words reveal him not as the cavalier arrogant young man who over the years her memories have shaped him to be but instead as an idealistic, witty and charming person very smitten by the sweet young Lizzie. The words 'sweet' and 'tender' appear frequently dotted through his love notes to her.

So accustomed has she become to believing herself unattractive and unlovable that she now has great difficulty believing the evidence to the contrary. But here it is, tangible proof that on two occasions in her life, at least in the initial stages of the relationships, two human beings have fallen passionately in love with her. Can she really have inspired such intense feelings and responses?

Determined to divest herself of the static energy clinging to the ghosts of Sebastian and Roger, she burns most of the old letters and diaries. By eradicating the past she hopes to free herself finally to become someone completely different in her forties.

Someone who might prove attractive to Rita.

She loads up cartons of magazines for the local hospital and stores piles of books ready for the garage sale.

In spite of herself Jewel becomes interested in what her mother is doing. She begins to make suggestions, to offer advice. She holds up a set of carved elephants and brass trinkets purchased by Athena in her twenties and begs her to get rid of her hippy kitsch.

Did Athena really drag the child Jewel through India and Nepal?

'*Yes, Mum.* When will you realize that you have *never* been a normal mother?'

Jewel hauls out her own possessions and assesses them with a critical eye. She makes her own contributions to the piles to be sold or given away.

When she has evaluated each possession Athena hires an enormous bin. Into it they heave all the rubbish that no-one else could ever possibly want. Numerous garbage bags, mouldy curtains, warped planks of wood, rusting shelf brackets, paint cans, a broken barbecue kit, an ancient stove, chipped plates and mugs, mildewed bedding.

After the purge Athena quickly realizes that it won't do to limit herself only to reducing her possessions. Now she embarks on the house itself. For the first time she forces herself to view dispassionately the dull and uninspiring colours and shabby furniture surrounding her. What do they say about her?

Nothing. They have absolutely nothing to do with her. She is living, with increasing discomfort, in someone else's life, speaking another person's script. Take control, she urges herself repeatedly.

Attracted by the flurry of activity, Athena's mother has her own opinions and objectives. She volunteers to help with repainting the interior. They study colour charts. No consensus is reached until Athena with a resigned sigh surrenders to Jewel's wish to live in a white house. They store most of their possessions in two rooms and take themselves off to stay with Athena's mother while a floor sander comes to strip the wooden boards and then lightly stains them. When the smell has disappeared they lay down huge drop cloths and either paint or sand most evenings and weekends. They begin with Jewel's room and progress to Athena's bedroom, her workspace, the lounge, the bathroom, the kitchen. After three weeks Athena's mother's own commitments reclaim her. Predictably, Jewel's initial enthusiasm falls off. Undaunted, Athena hires two students to assist her to finish the job. A carpenter arrives to make small repairs – to loosen jammed sash windows, to replace wobbly door handles and install shelves.

Athena has always lived frugally, struggling to make ends meet. But over the years she has slowly whittled away at her mortgage until she is now in a position to borrow a little against it.

Windows are measured for new wooden blinds. The City Mission arrives to collect the old sofas and Athena and Jewel go shopping for replacement furniture and new bed linen and lighting. Since Athena began to instigate the changes in their environment Jewel's behaviour has become a little less objectionable. The day Athena gave her the money to choose her own brand new bed linen and duvet cover she actually smiled and squeezed her mother's arm with excitement.

Athena has continued to visit Bridget most days in the gaps between client bookings. Jewel has sometimes accompanied her in the late afternoons. Jewel reads to Bridget while Athena massages her face, hands and feet. It's good for Jewel to have to think about someone other than herself for once, thinks Athena, pleased.

Her busy schedule begins to take its toll. When Athena has exhausted her financial and physical limits and can see that Bridget is much improved, she takes to her bed for two days to recover and reflect. She feels as if she has climbed a mountain.

All that remains is to seduce Rita.

Now that Jewel is apparently no longer ashamed of her home, to Athena's surprise she invites the legendary Wing, whom she first met at a nightclub in Karangahape Road, home for dinner.

He is a slim, handsome Chinese boy of eighteen. His long black hair is tied back into a sleek ponytail and he arrives at her house wearing a beanie, dark glasses, a leather jacket, basketball boots and baggy trousers.

One glance is all it takes for Athena to understand what it is about Wing that appeals to her daughter. He is very cool. He has street cred. Every label on his back is one that Jewel/Sarah has vetted and approved. He is scrupulously clean. He is tidy, organized, ambitious and acquisitive. Jewel is obviously charmed by his accent, although Athena is quick to observe that she doesn't hesitate to correct him if she thinks he has made any errors in grammar or pronunciation.

His parents live in Hong Kong and they run a computer software company. Wing is currently staying with an aunt in a five-bedroom porticoed mansion in Howick.

'Does your aunt like living here?'

'She and my uncle came here for the good life. They worked hard all their lives – this country is their reward. My uncle is also in the computer business. Before they emigrated my uncle was working maybe ninety hours a week, so much pressure. My aunt didn't see him much. They believed that here it would be less stressful than in Hong Kong where it is rush-rush all the time. But here my aunt is lonely and sometimes depressed. She doesn't speak good English, so I am teaching her.'

'Has she met many locals?'

Wing shrugs. 'They mix with other Chinese, but most of the time they keep to themselves.'

'They're *mega* wealthy,' confides Jewel after Wing has departed. 'We're talking swimming pool, three-car garage, security systems – you name it. They live in a huge mansion. Unreal. So over the top. Wing is given an allowance of five hundred a week. His parents bought him the sports car. They pay his cellphone bills. He is *so* lucky.'

Athena is not so sure. He has the wired energy of a caged tiger.

'Does he feel resentful that his parents have abandoned him in a foreign country?'

'He says they had no choice.'

'What do you see in him?' Athena has no real sense of just who this quietly spoken man is. Will he be good to Jewel?

'He *worships* me.'

Athena makes certain that Jewel will be out until late before she invites Rita to dinner one Friday night. Her bedroom is now a lover's boudoir of gauzy layers of muslin curtains, new white damask bedspread and crisp white cotton sheets. Even the shrine to her namesake has a new embroidered cloth. She places a vase of white roses on the bedside table, lights the oil burner and fills the bowl with drops of ylang ylang and clary sage. She meditates beforehand to calm her anxious thoughts. How can she appear sexy and at the same time disguise as much of her body as possible? After trying on and discarding most of the contents of her wardrobe she settles on a white linen shirt and long skirt.

Rita admires the changes in the house. She praises the dinner, Italian fish stew. They talk for a couple of hours at the table and then Athena moves them along into the lounge where she puts on a k. d. lang tape.

They sit opposite each other on the two new couches softly illuminated by the new standard lamp. Will it be Rita who makes the first move? Or should it be her as it is, after all, her house?

'Well.' Rita smiles brightly. 'Here we are.'

'I don't know how to do this.' Athena smiles nervously. Unfortunately, she hasn't rehearsed what she

272

is about to say. She had imagined that when the time was right words would flow from her lips – persuasive, eloquent – and that Rita would reciprocate with delighted surprise. *Oh, so you feel this too* . . . or something along these lines.

Instead, what is this?

An awkward pause. Then . . .

'Do what?'

Rita seems genuinely puzzled.

'Ah . . . You know . . . It seems . . . Anyway.'

Athena flounders. Gives up. Stares wretchedly at Rita who is cannily giving nothing away. No little straw of hope there for Athena to grasp and nurture.

'Look, what I'm trying to say is . . . Oh shit, I'm no good at this . . . I *really* like you,' Athena blurts out. 'Well, more than like, actually.'

But Rita is wriggling uncomfortably on her sofa.

'Is it me? Have I given the wrong impression?' asks Rita carefully.

'Wrong impression?' Athena's stomach does a dive.

'I'm not a dyke, if that's where this tortuous conversation is leading.'

'I . . .' Words fail her.

What happens now? Athena wishes there was somewhere she could hide, wishes she could fast forward the minutes until Rita leaves and she can bury her head and her humiliation under the bedcovers.

'I'm sorry, I've got it wrong. Never mind. Please forget what I said.' Athena can feel herself blushing in embarrassment. She stumbles on, unable to stop herself even though she knows she's making an intolerable situation even worse by gabbling on like a complete maniac. What must Rita think of her?

Has she really misunderstood the situation so badly? What about the light touches on her arm to illustrate a point, or to establish a connection during an animated conversation? Athena reflects on the meaningful glances, the lingering gaze. The hugs that seemed to her to be more heartfelt than the ordinary run-of-the-mill embraces between friends.

Rita's voice breaks into her thoughts. 'I think it's time I was heading off. Got an interview to crack in the morning.' Her tone is cool and impersonal.

On a Saturday? *Give me a break*, thinks Athena, getting to her feet.

All right. She is going to hold herself together. There's no way she is going to allow Rita to see how totally gutted she is.

After Rita has departed, the farewell at the front door being excruciatingly polite, Athena rings Clare, who, miracle of miracles, is home on a Friday night and still awake.

'She's in denial.'

'Not from where I'm standing.' Athena sniffs. Her voice, even to her ears, sounds pitiful.

'She's playing cruel games with you.'

'I don't think so. She's made it abundantly clear that she's definitely a het, Clare.'

'Maybe the woman I know at her magazine got it wrong. She seemed pretty convinced that Rita was into women.'

'You mean she was just speculating? And now I've humiliated myself, all for nothing? I feel devastated.'

'So, now what?'

'I'm stumped.'

'You're smitten bad, girl.'

More like obsessed and besotted, thinks Athena. She can't get Rita out of her mind. This latest debacle only confirms her fears about the risks of entering into relationships. Why had she expected it to be different this time?

'Give it a few days, make a friendly call. Check out

the lie of the land. Keep it light. Casual,' suggests Clare, trying to be encouraging.

'Oh, *very* casual. Absolutely.' As she puts the phone down Athena is engulfed by self-pity and regret. Who did she think she was, to attract someone like Rita?

Athena is restless in her bed, unable to sleep. She's out of her depth. Rusty at intimate relationships. Sex hasn't exactly been top of her mind in the last ten years. When the subject of her own sexuality has come up in conversation with her close friends Athena has confessed that she hasn't masturbated in years. The idea that she might pleasure herself had seemed not only unnecessary but also irrelevant. She had got by for years without even the vaguest acquaintance with her genitals, she said. Why disturb something that probably didn't even work any more? For all she knew the entrance to her vagina might have sealed up to the point where even an object the thickness of a pencil wouldn't have squeezed itself in.

'Masturbation,' Agnes always declared, 'is *fundamental*.'

'Fundamental to what?' asked Athena whenever Agnes raised the subject. 'A healthy life? A well-oiled libido? If I do have a G-spot neither I, nor for that matter any man of my acquaintance, has ever located it.'

Until recently.

A month previously, for the first time in her life, Athena had purchased a vibrator. She had soon got used to the sound – a low drone not unlike that of a distant lawnmower – and became adept at bringing herself to orgasm.

Clare had asked her when she first realized that she was attracted to Rita. Thinking back Athena was sure it must have been the day when Rita first visited her house and put Jewel in her place. Or maybe when she had first massaged Rita's smooth body?

She is still astonished that she, usually the least confident of women, had been so sure that her feelings would be reciprocated. But like a guided missile with a faulty radar it appears that she has all this time been picking up nonexistent signals. She tries to convince herself that all is not lost, because she just isn't ready yet to relinquish her fantasy of becoming intimate with Rita.

At midnight Athena is still awake agonizing over the disastrous evening when the phone rings. She hesitates only for a few seconds before leaping out of bed and running for the phone, on the slim chance that it's Jewel on the other end.

'What is it? Where are you?' Athena can hear Jewel is spooked by something and on the verge of tears.

'I'm at the hospital – at the emergency department.' Jewel's voice cracks.

Athena is alarmed and instantly wide awake.

The information emerges in fits and starts. She and Wing were entering a club on Karangahape Road, the one where they had first met. An Asian man leaning out of a moving car with a gun – too dark to see exactly who it was. A drive-by shooting, it happened so quickly. She and Wing, in the wrong place, the wrong time. Wing had flung himself across her and caught the blast.

'He saved my life, Mum. I could be dead now.'

'How is he?'

'They're going to operate on him straight away, but they think he'll pull through.'

'I'll come and get you.'

'I think I should stay here.'

'Have you contacted his aunt and uncle?'

'Yes, they're on their way.'

'There's nothing more you can do then once you've seen them. It'll be hours until he comes around from the op. He'll most likely be put in intensive care afterwards.'

Athena quickly flings on a pair of leggings and a sweatshirt and reaches for her car keys and a jacket.

As she speeds to the hospital to comfort Jewel, she forgets in an instant the hundreds of times her daughter has heaped abuse and ingratitude on her. She remembers only the panic and fear in Jewel's voice on the end of Wing's cellphone. What matters is that her daughter has finally asked her for help. She is needed. Next of kin. The one who can be relied on in an emergency. She is propelled towards the accident and emergency ward as if a cord of blood still connected her to Jewel.

The lights are against her all the way up Karangahape Road. Alongside her, young men gun their engines at the intersections. She drives past seedy strip joints, dance clubs, the ubiquitous kebab takeouts, the happening cafés pumping out music for their customers who are having late night suppers on the pavement, past the drunks, the addicts, the clubbers, and the hookers and trannies who work the area.

Neon lights flicker in her eyes. Faces and cars are briefly illuminated by slashes of red and orange light.

'I'm the only mother you've got, girl,' she mutters as she finally pulls into the half-empty car park.

Two ambulances are backed up against the doors. An elderly man with a bemused expression on his face is being lifted out of one of the vehicles on a stretcher. Athena hurries in through the self-opening doors, past an empty wheelchair which has been abandoned in front of one of the doors, and joins the queue being processed at the reception desk. Welcome to the Department of Emergency Medicine reads the sign above reception and beneath it: *Nau Mai ki te tari Rongo a Ohorere.*

Ahead of her is an Asian family who have brought in a frail elderly woman to be examined and a huge Polynesian extended family who have arrived to enquire about an injured relative. The woman behind the desk checks each name on her computer screen and after processing each family presses the button to release the security door which opens to allow visitors through to the waiting area.

Athena gives Wing's name and is buzzed through the door.

She would cheerfully have paid over a thousand dollars just to see the smile of recognition and relief that appears on her daughter's face when she catches sight of her.

Jewel tells her that Wing is shortly to be operated on to remove the bullet and seal up the wound.

'He lost so much blood. I can't believe that much blood can be inside one person's body,' cries Jewel. Her face and clothing are smeared with dark stains. She is pale and shivering from exhaustion and shock.

Athena places her jacket round Jewel's shoulders.

'Come home with me and change out of these clothes.'

'No,' wails Jewel. 'I can't leave him. I have to *be here* when he wakes up.'

'But that won't be for many hours yet. There is nothing you can do in the meantime. If you get some sleep you'll cope much better tomorrow.'

'Sleep? You must be joking if you think I could sleep, not knowing whether he's alive or dead.'

Wing's aunt and uncle arrive and Jewel confirms what they have already been told at the entry desk.

Wing is about to undergo emergency surgery. The uncle speaks to a nurse. It will be several hours before Wing is able to speak to them and that's only if everything goes well. Athena watches and listens as the nurse attempts to reassure him. He swiftly relays to his wife, in Cantonese, the information he has just received.

The aunt looks bewildered. Her shoulders droop.

Athena introduces herself and guides the dazed woman to a seat.

Jewel is ignored by the aunt and uncle, who stare straight ahead. The silence becomes uncomfortable.

Athena attempts conversation and is rebuffed. Who knows what the couple are thinking, the kind of anxiety they must feel knowing they are responsible for someone else's son.

Jewel tugs at her sleeve. 'I've changed my mind,' she mouths.

They say goodbye to Wing's aunt and uncle, promising to return early in the morning. The uncle nods and asks the whereabouts of his nephew's car. Jewel hands over the keys.

The aunt gives Athena a timid little smile, her mouth quivering.

Athena is awake for most of the remainder of the night going over and over in her mind the events of the previous evening. First the debacle with Rita, then the shock of hearing about Wing being shot. Her poor devastated daughter. Her mind keeps returning to the knowledge that it could so easily have been Jewel who took the impact of the shot. If Wing hadn't stepped in front of her . . . Athena sucks in her breath. It doesn't bear thinking about. But then nor does the prospect of Wing not pulling through the operation.

*   *   *

Athena and Jewel are both up at six the following morning. After a hasty breakfast of tea and toast they return to the hospital.

The operation has been successful and Wing is now in an intensive care ward. He is very weak and Jewel won't be able to speak to him for another few hours. There is no sign of the aunt and uncle. The nurse explains that after hearing that the operation was successful and that their nephew was still unconscious the couple decided to return home for a shower, a meal and a change of clothes. They will be back at the hospital at Wing's bedside in a couple of hours.

Athena turns to Jewel with a smile. 'He is going to be fine.'

'Yeah, it looks like it.' Jewel agrees dully. She bursts into tears.

'It's OK, love. You've had a big shock.' Athena realizes how much she has missed being able to actually mother and cuddle Jewel. She expects at any minute that Jewel will slap her hand away and tell her to piss off.

But instead Jewel leans her head on Athena's shoulder. 'Thanks for being so sympathetic and kind, Mum. It really helps.'

Athena wonders for a moment if she has heard correctly. She stares at her daughter. Has she grown up at last?

She leaves Jewel patiently waiting at the hospital and drives to the supermarket determined to keep herself occupied until she can gain further news of Wing.

She returns from grocery shopping late Saturday morning and is astonished to find Rita waiting in her car outside the house.

'What are *you* doing here?'

Rita gives her a sheepish grin.

'I wanted to apologize. You really took me by surprise last night and I ran for cover. I've never been with a woman. The prospect of it terrifies the hell out of me.'

'I've never been with a woman either. You think I'm not nervous about the whole idea of it?'

Athena turns her back on Rita and begins to unload the plastic carrier bags from the boot of her car, hoping that Rita won't notice her shaking hands. She moves towards the house.

'Here, let me help.'

'I don't want your help,' says Athena curtly.

Rita runs after her and blocks her way. 'Give me a chance to make amends,' she pleads.

Athena turns to face her.

'I should have explained when you first turned up here. I've got other more important things on my mind right now. Last night my daughter's boyfriend accidentally got himself mixed up in an Asian gang revenge shoot-out. It seems that he was mistaken for someone else and shot. Jewel is half out of her mind with worry.'

'Poor kid. That's shocking. Is he alive?'

'He's been successfully operated on overnight. Looks like he might pull through OK, but he's still in intensive care. I'll be heading back to the hospital soon with some supplies for Jewel.'

'I've obviously come at the wrong time. Call me when you're free.'

'Stay for a bit. Why don't you finish unloading the shopping while I call Jewel for an update.'

She phones Jewel on Wing's cellphone number. She is still at the hospital keeping vigil but has been allowed to see Wing for a few minutes before his aunt and uncle had returned.

'Until I saw him for myself, I didn't actually believe he was alive.'

'How was he?'

'So weak, Mum. He could hardly keep his eyes open. He has tubes everywhere and big bandages. I got a shock.'

'I'm sure you did. I assume that you want to stay on at the hospital. So, can I do anything for you?'

'Well . . . the food in the canteen is crap. It's cold in the waiting room and I've run out of decent magazines to read.'

'I'll be there in about an hour. OK?'

She feels torn. If Rita weren't here she would go to the hospital straight away with provisions.

Rita assists her with unpacking the vegetables, fruit, barley, miso and tofu into the fridge.

Athena pours them lemon and ginger tea and waits.

Rita stirs honey into her tea. 'I want to apologize again for what happened last night.'

'Don't give it a thought,' replies Athena gruffly.

'But I've given it a *huge* amount of thought. In fact I stuffed up the interview I did earlier this morning because I was feeling so bad. And I've decided that I haven't been fair to you, or strictly honest. I've been a coward. I'm not a dyke. That part was true.'

'Uh huh.' Athena sips her tea.

Now it is Rita who is uncharacteristically tongue-tied, Rita who struggles to find the words to express her confused emotions. Apparently she too likes Athena a lot. Well, more than *like* actually, she ventures, not realizing that she is repeating almost word for word Athena's own declaration.

'Mmm.' Athena is non-committal outwardly, but inside she feels the first flutters of hope. She listens intently to Rita's stumbling words.

What she is trying to say, only she knows she's not making a very good job of it, is that although she has never thought of herself as a dyke, she is, if she is perfectly truthful, attracted to Athena – and at the same time, shit scared of her feelings. The way she sees it, she just *happens* to be drawn to Athena, who just *happens* to be a woman . . . but that doesn't make her a lesbian . . . does it?

What is Athena's opinion on the subject?

Athena's head snaps up. Her heart is in her eyes. She takes an instinctive step forward.

Rita takes a step back. She is breathing heavily as if she has run a marathon. Her face is flushed. Her fists are clenched. She doesn't realize it, but she is baring her teeth in a grimace.

Athena too retreats. It's all uncharted territory. Rita might very well bolt out the door at any moment if she puts a foot wrong.

'Love is where you find it,' she says. 'Does the sex of the person matter? Really? Love is love, after all.'

'I suppose it is.' Rita doesn't sound convinced. She grips the benchtop, white-knuckled.

'Oh Rita,' sighs Athena, her voice full of aching longing.

'*Athena.*'

Neither of them is clear what, if anything, should happen next.

Athena feels a sense of urgency. Take control of the situation, a little voice inside her head directs her. Seize the moment before it slips out of reach for ever.

Impulsively she reaches out and wraps her arms round Rita.

Rita's hand grazes her bare arm. The touch is scorching.

'I've never done this before either,' confesses Athena in a shaky voice.

'Well, as I said, that makes two of us.'

Chapter Twenty-Four

Clare

Clare begins to anticipate with pleasure her sparring encounters with Bulldozer. He has begun to offer her rare glimpses of another self, revealing the existence of a softer man than she had expected. At the same time he possesses that palpable air of authority characteristic of someone who is accustomed to being listened to and taken very, very seriously. He wears his authority easily, as if it were a divinely bestowed mantle.

'How can you defend a man whom you know to be guilty of murder, or multiple rapes, beyond a shadow of a doubt?'

Bulldozer adjusts his position in the leather armchair. 'Because every individual has a right to expect a fair trial. And what's more, who am I to anticipate what twelve ordinary people will decide on one day, in one court, on one specific charge, involving one particular defendant? The prosecution has to prove the case. I'll wait until they do. Or try to.'

'Off the record, you don't really believe that justice and right prevail, do you? That what goes on in our courts actually results in fairness for anybody?'

'Yes,' he replies. 'In most instances I do.'

He grins and gives her a long steady look.

Unaccountably she blushes under his scrutiny.

Generally he's in a hurry to move her on because his meetings are stacked up. But today he is in an expansive mood. It's almost as if he's timetabled ten minutes for idle chat at the conclusion of their meeting.

He catches her staring at a framed photo on his desk. 'My four daughters. Little beauties, aren't they?'

Should she pretend interest? How does he feel about having so many daughters? Had he longed for a son?

'Got any kids yourself?'

'No.'

Clare has learned to brush off the question. The curiosity and the judgements. The words left unsaid being just as potent as the polite and surprised: 'Oh, *haven't* you?'

And there she is – shrinkwrapped. Career woman. End of story.

Apparently.

'So what are you planning to do with the rest of your life then, Clare?'

'You mean professionally? More of the same, I guess.'

'Woman like you,' says Bulldozer. 'World's your oyster.'

It already is. Or seemed to be until recently.

He gives her a speculative glance. She holds his gaze steadily until he breaks into a smile, his deep-set blue eyes twinkling at her. He may not possess Adrian's creative flair – the only traits he shares with Adrian are his cleverness and sharp wit. He may not be the world's most handsome man, but he is too sophisticated and smart for her to dismiss as an insensitive bully. He makes her feel alive.

Clare gives herself a mental shake. What is she doing comparing the two men?

Bulldozer goes on to talk at length about himself. His recollections of his time spent at university. His published work. His friends and his detractors. It dawns on Clare that he isn't really interested in hearing about her life, her ambitions, hopes and fears. What he mainly wants is to talk about himself.

Why had she expected otherwise? Regardless of his egotism he usually manages to leave her feeling agitated at the close of their meetings. Not knowing where to put herself. Feeling that no matter how confident and stroppy she might appear to him, inside she is nothing less than a blancmange.

She knows for certain that he admires her in a professional capacity, but as to what he thinks of her as a person, she has no idea. He's not a man who flirts or comes on to her. Dermott Maloney has his boundaries set very firmly in place.

Weeks later.

'Of course you can borrow my apartment on Tuesday,' agrees Agnes. She scans Clare's flushed face, recognizing the telltale signs.

'Sure you know what you're getting yourself into?'

Clare nods. But she can't afford to listen to any advice, to heed any warnings. She has butterflies in her stomach. Her cunt has turned into Mount Vesuvius. She is about to go off with a bang.

He made the first move to her surprise.

'Put me in my place if I'm imagining things,' he had said. And: 'Think about it.'

She thought about it. His wife. The four lovely girls. *Light of my life, they are.*

Thinking about it wasn't going to get her anywhere. Thinking about it meant she wouldn't do it.

She wasn't going to think about it any more.

She was going to do it.

'We shouldn't be doing this,' he says in a hoarse voice so unlike his usual peremptory issuing of instructions and questions.

'No. I know.'

But they do it anyway.

She unbuttons his sky-blue shirt. She has a moment of pure disbelief. Dermott Maloney is touching her breast. Not just touching either – more like swooning.

Will he confess their liaison later? . . . When it's over. Do they still use those dark little confession boxes with the grilles?

For Clare understands only too well that what they are doing cannot possibly last.

He takes his time over her and this is a surprise. He plays with her breasts, strokes her belly with exquisite slow circular movements that send shivers through her.

'I'm hungry for you.'

Again, she feels disbelief. She and Bulldozer?

Get out of here.

What about his wife and family? His faith? His reputation?

She can't stop now, she's gone too far. And she is very, very turned on. She loves his intensity. Any moment and he'll be quoting poetry at her.

She welcomes him into her body with a deep sigh of pleasure.

'Bad news, I'm afraid,' announces Fran when she returns to the office.

Clare is incredulous.

Harmony Heaven. The client whom she developed from nothing. The client who, although now the least profitable, is the one to whom she feels the most personal loyalty. The client for whom she has slashed fees, written off time, slaved on numerous weekends over the years, has just jumped ship and gone over to the opposition.

'But why?'

'No reason apparently, and they're not taking calls.'

'I'll drive round there,' says Clare. 'That's what I'll do.' She is hurt, furious, humiliated.

Fran sits her down. Pours her a gin. 'And what will that achieve?' she asks.

'They owe us,' argues Clare.

'Business is business,' says Fran. 'Someone made them a better offer. We're no longer flavour of the month.' She pats Clare on the back. 'Don't worry,' she says, 'we'll always find a way to make a buck.'

Agnes greets her at the door after work. It's the second time Clare has been at Agnes's apartment in one day.

'So. How was your power fuck?'

Clare frowns. 'That's not how it is.'

'No? Aren't you flattered that one of Auckland's leading barristers is taking such a personal interest in you?'

She pulls the gin bottle out of the cupboard, the ice tray from her tiny fridge freezer and selects a small lemon from the fruit bowl.

Clare is taken aback at Agnes's confrontational greeting. She watches her brisk angry movements as she prepares their drinks and feels uneasy.

'Is this a meaningful relationship? Or an ultimately sordid little affair no different from the half-dozen or so you've previously launched yourself into in the past?' Agnes pauses and looks suspiciously at Clare. 'You're not looking for a potential father for a baby, after all . . . Are you?'

'Are you kidding?'

'Then get that smile off your face, Clare – you're not living in a Mills and Boon romance.'

'I wouldn't want a baby that'd turn into a tubby female version of Bulldozer. Although judging by Bulldozer's blooming health and boundless energy he's the product of a robust gene pool.'

'That's not what I asked. Is there nothing you wouldn't stoop to, Clare, to get what you want?'

Silence.

'Of course I'm not trying to get pregnant with Bulldozer. I haven't lost my marbles – although you're treating me as if I have.'

'Are you bored with the predictability of your life? Was it plain curiosity?'

Clare is furious. 'What *right* do you of all people have to climb on the moral high horse with me? You push me too far. Just because you're an old friend – it doesn't entitle you to question my actions.'

'Are you savouring one last fling before middle age? You've always sworn that you'll age disgracefully, that you'll go in the end not with a whimper but with a last shout of rage. Where does the rage come from, Clare? *Tell me what you're angry about?*'

Clare jumps to her feet and paces the room, her fists clenching and unclenching at her sides. She breathes quickly. There is a hard lump of pain in her gut.

'I'm angry at fucking everything. My oldest client has just dumped us. Adrian won't let me have a god-damned baby. His kids won't give me the time of day. I'm tired of the fucking grind of my life. I've lost the plot. I'm questioning the way I work, just as you seem to be. I want a change but I don't know what kind of change, let alone how to go about it. I may end up leaving Adrian. My body is ageing no matter how much I exercise, or how carefully I monitor my diet. I have all this shit whirling around in my head at all hours. I wake up in the middle of the night and my heart is pounding . . . with terror.'

She sits down abruptly. Where have all those words come from?

'Your Dermott Maloney is merely a distraction then from the real issues that you're not addressing.'

'I am addressing them. I think about the problems in my life every bloody day.' Her voice rises. 'I just haven't come up with any practical solutions yet. All right?'

Veins pulse in Clare's neck. Her face is flushed. She is on the verge of tears.

Agnes is not about to let her off the hook. She slams down her gin, grabs Clare and gives her a good hard shake. Clare is so shocked that she can't immediately think how to respond. She gazes at Agnes with her eyes popping, her mouth opening and shutting without making a sound. Tears of rage and humiliation squeeze between her lashes and drip unchecked down her cheeks.

'*Wake up, Clare!* The man is married. You say he has kids. Christ, think of the carnage if it gets out of hand.'

'It won't get out of hand,' replies Clare stiffly. 'I have the situation under control.'

'You'd be a first then. From what you tell me of the man, this is out of character for him. You may not have lost your head, but he has. The guy is thinking with his dick. Take pity on him. Send him home to his wife. Do yourself and his family a big favour. Think about it.'

'I told you, read my lips, it is under control,' snaps Clare. 'No harm done.'

'So far.'

'As far as *I* am concerned. But from now on I'll be very careful.'

Agnes pours Clare another gin. 'The sex must be incredible, that's all I can say. Swinging off the chandeliers stuff.'

Clare's tears dry. She gives Agnes a sheepish grin.

'Fucking amazing. I had forgotten that it was possible to experience that kind of ferocious intensity. I can't give it up yet . . . Soon. I'll end it cleanly and compassionately.'

Agnes snorts in disbelief. 'I've heard it all before. Clare, listen to me. I've been there myself. Believe me, the few over-the-top thrills in the beginning do not make up for the agony and shit fights at the end when the wife cottons on and your man finally wakes up to what is at stake. Not only that, have you forgotten that you're still in a relationship? What about Adrian? Or do his feelings not even count?'

Clare slumps over her drink. She feels as if all the stuffing has been knocked out of her.

'I know you're right,' she agrees wearily. 'I'll give Bulldozer his marching orders.'

She looks across at Agnes who is gazing at her not unsympathetically.

'Sort out the situation at home first before you go leaping into bed with someone else, OK?'

One week later:

'My beautiful girl.'

It's true he does make her feel like a girl, a not unpleasant feeling, even though there is only a six-year gap in age between them. She will give him up as she has promised Agnes, but not just yet. Tomorrow. Next week. Next year.

He is awash in emotion. Tears trickle down his face as he shudders to a climax.

Who would have thought, marvels Clare, that tough old Bulldozer could be so sentimental and emotional – without his suit, without a courtroom, without a crowd hanging on to his every expensive word.

'I suppose you think I do this all the time,' he mutters, wiping his face.

'I don't have any opinions on the matter, but I'm curious, yes.'

'I'm an old-fashioned man, Clare. I've been true to my wife.'

Don't go all guilty and weepy on me. Please.

'Uh huh.'

'You don't believe me? It's true. I've broken the rules for you.'

What is she expected to do? Get down on her bended knees and thank him?

'Mmmm.'

'She's been a good wife to me.'

'Why the past tense? She is alive, isn't she?'

'Twenty-five years we've been together,' he continues as if she hasn't spoken.

Clare doesn't want to know. Now he's breaking her rules. Keep the family right out of it. Separate out that part of your life and leave it where it belongs – at home. Not in the bedroom. Not after such terrific sex.

Tears glisten in his eyes. 'I couldn't run out on her, Clare.'

Clare blinks. Has she missed a chapter somewhere?

'Dermott, give me some credit. I'm not asking or expecting you to leave your wife and family. Heaven forbid. Let's just enjoy this for what it is – a pleasurable interlude – with no expectations on either side that it be anything other than what it is.'

'So this doesn't mean anything to you?'

'Yes, of course it does. But it doesn't necessarily follow that it's going to cause me to turn my life upside down.'

'You're a hard woman. Get up to this all the time, do you – fucking your clients?'

Clare is startled at the change of mood. She dislikes the way he can suddenly turn on a person. Although it's a trait that probably makes him very good in court.

'Don't provoke me. I'm not one of your bloody witnesses. And I'm not hard. I'm realistic. My sex life is none of your business, and no, I don't make a practice of fucking clients. I've got more sense. You're the first on that score, if it makes you any happier.'

Later when he has put on his suit and along with it his customary air of authority, she curses herself for being such a fool as to believe that she could compartmentalize this part of her life when dealing with a man like Dermott Maloney.

Shortly after his return to his office, he leaves a message of apology on her voice mail.

She returns his call but he is in court, so she leaves a message asking him to call her. At the end of the day when she still hasn't received a reply she leaves another message. She plans to see him one last time and tell him it's over between them and she'll deal with the repercussions for their business association another time.

The following morning she retrieves the messages on her cellphone. True to form Bulldozer was at his desk early. There is a reply from him timed at seven-thirty suggesting a meeting later in the day. She wonders if he has any clue. Perhaps he has arrived at a similar conclusion.

She calls his office at nine-thirty to agree to the time. There's a pause on the other end before his secretary says in a strange high voice, 'Oh, this is terribly awkward. Has no-one rung you, Clare?'

'About what?' Clare's mind scrolls through the possible scenarios. She's wrong on all counts.

'I'm sorry. I don't know how to put this – other than bluntly. Dermott died at his desk this morning from a heart attack. We're all in a state of shock and disbelief.' Her voice disintegrates. Clare can hear muffled crying.

Clare expresses her shock and sympathy before carefully putting the phone down. She is stunned.

Fran saunters into her office humming. She frowns. 'What is it?'

Clare gulps, reaches for another tissue, mops her eyes and adds it to the sodden bundle in her bin.

'Dermott Maloney has just keeled over from a heart attack. I had been attempting to set up a meeting with him. He left a message on my cellphone only minutes before he died. Apparently I was the last person Bulldozer called before he died. Sobering, isn't it? All that vigour. That powerful presence.' Clare snaps her fingers. 'Like that. Gone.'

'I need a drink,' says Fran. 'A good stiff one.' She marches over to the booze cabinet and pulls out the whisky.

Clare can't get the words out to tell Fran the truth.

Bulldozer's funeral is huge. Nuns, priests, the works. A huge choir. The full Catholic send-off. Clare and Fran squeeze into a back row. The large old church is packed to capacity. Moving eulogies and tributes flow from two fellow members of the legal profession, from a brother and from his old friends. Clare studies the stricken wife as she emerges from the church after the ceremony, two young girls clinging to her. She is an attractive woman in her mid-forties who has been steamrollered by shock and pain. Her stooped body has collapsed in on itself with grief. Two teenage girls hover close by. Although he had mentioned his family, she had never until this moment been able to picture him as a father, as someone who actually had a life out-side his driven work habits. Poor dear Bulldozer. He was barely recognizable in his coffin. The carefully manicured hands lay peacefully on the mound of his stomach.

On her return to the office she finally erases with the press of a button the last words of Dermott Maloney from the saved messages on her cellphone.

'Are you happy, Adrian?' asks Clare one evening. The question plops with a tiny but not insignificant splash into the conversational vacuum.

Alerted by the tone of voice Adrian sighs, lowers the novel he is reading, removes his spectacles and rubs his tired eyes.

He seems (or is it only Clare's imagination?) to have aged since she last studied him closely. How can she not have noticed the new lines around his eyes? Has she been unobservant, or simply too preoccupied with Bridget's surgery and her own problems? If she stares too hard he takes on the aspect of a stranger.

The interloper occupying the most comfortable seating in their lounge is sprawled out full-length on it. His long thin legs, crossed at the ankles and clad in black fine wool socks, are propped up on a wing of the sofa he has converted into a mini think tank. He is surrounded by a stack of magazines and books with markers flagging articles and chapters he had planned to read (before he got sidetracked onto his new novel), a sketch pad and pencil and a tray of snacks – brain food. Until Clare had asked her question he had indeed looked extremely happy, but this is not the kind of 'happy' to which she is referring and they both know it.

'Happy?' replies the stranger in Adrian's familiar reedy voice. 'I can't answer that.' He yawns, stretches and slumps even deeper into the sofa, almost as if, thinks Clare, he is trying to hide under a wall of creative stimuli. 'I'll have to think about it.'

She is annoyed. 'Can't you do better than that?'

There is a whinnying sound. She can't tell if it is a

laugh or a groan. He deserves a good shake-up.

Adrian sits up and looks her in the eye. 'Whatever I say is bound to be the wrong answer, I can tell by your mood. If I agree to being happy then you'll say how *can* I be, when obviously we have so many problems. But if I confess I'm unhappy or dissatisfied, you'll burst into tears and imagine our relationship has irretrievably disintegrated, demanding to know why I've hidden these feelings from you. Am I right?'

'Yes. I suppose so.'

'Can I return to my book now?' he pleads.

'It's *impossible* to conduct a serious conversation with you.'

Adrian recognizes the tone of voice. Sensibly he does not react, or make eye contact. He keeps his head down, like a good chappie. Eyes his Ian McEwan novel with longing. In an act of reckless daring he even opens it, but after hearing Clare's breathing increase in volume he prudently closes it again.

Clare gets to her feet. She stands over him, hands on hips.

He cautiously raises his head. Her hair is alive with static electricity. The bones in her cheeks stand out in sharp relief. There is no mercy in her eyes. She is in pain, full of bitterness and anger. At the root of it all there is bound to be something he has said or done, failed to do, failed to intuit. She is going to let him have it. Days of stored-up crimes, real or imagined, there is no way of knowing.

He stifles a groan.

Under pressure, Adrian has, after much procrastination (all documented by a disgruntled Clare), recently read two best-selling personal growth books by American relationship gurus. He trawls his mind to recall any vaguely useful snippets from his reading. Inspiration strikes – the mirroring technique. He sits up straighter. First rule of the game: never confront an adversary while prone.

'It's difficult to conduct serious conversations with me,' he repeats in a carefully neutral voice.

Clare's eyes narrow. She should rip his damned book off him.

'It's always me who initiates any discussions about our relationship.'

'That's true,' he agrees mildly. 'You always seem to initiate the discussions.'

His compliance is too much for Clare. She lunges forward and snatches his book. 'What exactly are you playing at?'

'What am I playing at?' repeats Adrian in an injured voice.

'Yes. *You.*' She prods him and still he refuses to react. 'Stop agreeing with me. Don't you have any ideas of your own?'

'No,' responds Adrian with alacrity. If he can carry this off he might get back to his book soon.

In the face of such apparent goodwill Clare relinquishes her grievances. She bursts into laughter. Soon they are both laughing helplessly, rolling about on the couch.

Adrian considers it is now safe to tickle Clare.

She protests. Squeals. Ineffectually fends him off.

'You bastard! Don't. No. Oh! Wahhh! Owww!' She reaches down and grabs his balls.

'Hey! That's below the belt.'

'What is?' She puts on an innocent face.

'This!' Adrian quickly unzips his jeans and pulls out his erect member.

Clare lowers her head down onto him. She can no longer remember the original question. Neither can Adrian.

My beautiful girl.

'What's the matter?' asks Adrian, sounding concerned. 'Why the tears?'

'It's nothing. Truly.' Clare closes her eyes. She nurses her private grief over Dermott Maloney like a true stoic, except at the times (usually after sex with Adrian) when her self-control disintegrates and she experiences a degree of anguish and regret that almost does her head in.

The previous night she had a dream in which she came upon a tiny baby lying on the ground, dehydrated, suffering from malnutrition and almost dead. She had rescued the baby, of course, and over time revived it with patient love and care.

What did the dream signify? she wonders now. What new thing had blossomed into life and then been almost killed off? Was the little half-dead baby a symbol of an aspect of herself, or did it represent the relationship she had embarked on, so heedless of the consequences, with Bulldozer? A relationship that had brought her alive again to her senses, allowed a little flame to flicker into life, that had been abruptly snuffed out.

In the privacy of the bathroom in the middle of the night Clare weeps for her life. She mourns the fact that she is no longer young and will lose her looks. She mourns Bulldozer and the way he made her feel. She misses their sparring, the intellectual challenge of the man, as well as their sex. She misses her intimacy with Agnes, who is less available to her now that she is spending more of her leisure with Daniel. She aches over Bridget's lost breasts. She grieves over the knowledge that she will now most likely never bear a child. She mourns the fact that she no longer loves Adrian as much as she did, or even as much as he still appears to love her. And she weeps too for all the other things in her life that make her sad, but that she can't remember right now, because it's three in the morning. A time when every little thing seems a hundred times worse than it actually is in the daylight hours, when, mysteriously, she still experiences moments of feeling herself to be invincible.

Clare may have nagged Adrian to read a few personal growth books, but she is nevertheless surprised when she discovers he has put his new knowledge to good use elsewhere. He is actually attempting with men the kind of friendships she takes for granted with her women friends. For she has finally realized that Adrian's recent uncharacteristically long phone calls, made at odd hours, have been conducted not, as she had suspected, with a lover, but instead to a group of prospective candidates for a men's group he is proposing to set up.

'A men's group?' Clare wonders if she has heard right, especially considering the teasing and mocking she has been subjected to about her own associations with women. He's only ten years out of date in the male bonding department. However, better late than never. 'Are you doing this to get back at me?'

'Why do you persist in viewing everything solely in reference to yourself?'

'Am I to be amateurishly dissected, like a frog in a science experiment? My thoughts, words and actions exposed to the unsympathetic scrutiny of your boys' club? What if they decide I'm an unsuitable mate for you?'

Adrian bursts out laughing. He wipes his eyes and shakes his head. 'You're too much. We haven't even had our first meeting and you're already so threatened by it that in your mind we're already separated. It's not like you to be quite so paranoid, darling.' He ruffles her hair.

'Sorry.'

*   *   *

Their relationship is not without its fleeting moments of genuine intimacy and pleasure. She can't deny it. But despite this, her instincts tell her that Adrian is drifting away from her, just as she is from him.

Adrian puts his arms round her. 'Believe me, you have no reason to feel insecure.'

Clare is more confused than reassured. 'Are you telling me the truth?'

Adrian regards her solemnly. 'I could ask the same thing of you.'

If she had been truly happy she would not have entertained for a moment the thought of climbing into bed with Dermott Maloney, let alone acted so recklessly. For during this time, although Adrian may have agreed to read a couple of books to please her, he has still steadfastly refused to accompany her to counselling, insisting that the baby issue is her problem, not his.

'You tell me that you desperately want a baby. But if Adrian continues to view the baby issue as one with which he need not concern himself, is your relationship a true partnership?' asks Fiona.

'I ought to leave him soon, before it's too late for me to conceive with someone else.'

'Even if you leave Adrian do you realize there are no guarantees you'll find a man whom you can love, who is unattached – and also enthusiastic about having kids?'

'One child. That's all I'm asking. But you're right. It's not as if I can drag some poor unsuspecting fellow in off the street, demand he hand over his sperm and then stick around to change the nappies and dish out child support. Maybe it's already too late for me to find a father for my child. Should I be seriously considering conceiving through a sperm bank and settling for being a single parent?'

'Clare, being a parent is challenging enough even when there are two of you involved – you'd have to be very sure it was what you wanted before you made the decision to go it alone.'

'What it comes down to – do I want a baby more than I want my relationship? Shit, what a choice. And if I make the wrong decision I could end up alone and childless, having in the meantime given up my relationship with Adrian for nothing.'

'It's a risk. But who knows if your relationship will survive. Your resentment at not being able to have a child may possibly turn out to be greater than the sum of your love for him . . . or not. On the other hand, you may experience a grieving process, then put the whole business behind you and simply get on with your life. A different life to be sure . . .'

'That's the problem. Because I always imagined that one day—'

'One day in the far distant future . . .'

'Yes. One day I would have a baby and that would define a different kind of life. It would force me to take a step back from my work, maybe even take some time out.'

'And if you don't have a baby does this mean you don't believe you have an excuse, a reason to step off the treadmill?'

'Something like that. If I don't change the status quo, then I'll have to make a new plan.'

'Why not? Is that so terrifying an idea?'

'My future seems blank. I'm in a fog, this weird kind of limbo. I can't see a metre in front of me, let alone next week, next year.'

Two weeks later Adrian announces over breakfast that he and his group are going away together soon for a men's weekend.

301

'Blokes only,' he jokes. 'No sheilas allowed.'

'Why didn't you tell me you were planning this?' Clare's eyes flash, but Adrian ignores the warning.

'I'm telling you now,' he replies in a calm voice without removing his concentration from his newspaper. A true news junkie, he continues to mechanically spoon muesli into his mouth while his eyes rake the columns for his daily fix of wars and famines, rapes and robberies, or fresh outbreaks of scandal, disaster and disease. Clare observes his mouth curve into a pleased smile as once again his worst fears are confirmed.

Clare's own breakfast of wholegrain toast and lemon honey lies neglected on her plate as she contemplates Adrian's hunger for information. For one more day he can breathe a sigh of relief that his own home and hearth have once again escaped the ravages of other people's politics, other countries' greed and mistakes.

Adrian licks his lips and picks up his coffee cup, holding it out optimistically for more.

She gives him a top-up. Adrian's morning rituals are sacred. On the occasional weekday mornings when his peaceful routine is shattered by the presence of his sulky and argumentative teenagers, and he is thus unable to pay homage to the daily harbinger of bad tidings, he is transformed into a grumpy, unreasonable referee. On these mornings Clare invents client breakfast meetings or changes her gym schedule and disappears with a clear conscience before all hell erupts.

Chapter Twenty-Five

Bridget

Several months have passed and everyone around her, reassured the crisis is now over, has returned to her or his busy life. Matthew has now caught up with the backlog of work at his office. People have assumed that she too will gradually pick up where she left off.

Except that both she and they had not taken into account a fundamental fact.

She is now a completely different person.

And not just physically.

She has worked her way through all the videos she has meant to watch, caught up on recent gossip, read the latest novels – the stack beside the bed is diminishing. She is even up to date on the soaps. She has become addicted to Oprah and Ricki Lake.

But you're also a painter, Bridget. Remember?

She works on a smaller scale because it is easier on her arms and begins with a self-portrait. Nude.

Matthew shakes his head. 'You don't take the easy road, do you?'

She gives him a lascivious grin.

That's progress.

*   *   *

'How is your mother's novel?' Bridget asks Clare when she next calls to collect her and take her out for coffee.

'As predicted,' answers Clare.

'Tell me, I *really* want to know. I'm not having proper conversations. They're all one-sided. People seem to feel that their own problems don't bear comparison with a double mastectomy. Pain is relative, isn't it? But if my friends can't be themselves with me then I've got a problem.'

'That's the thing about cancer. It does rather put our pathetic little worries into perspective.'

'God, Clare, don't be so bloody pious. Make me laugh. Please.'

Clare relaxes. 'She's . . .'

'Yes, I know — a cow of the first order. So tell me quickly, have you read it yet?'

'Well, yes and no.'

Bridget raises an eyebrow.

'I rang Dad. He sounded a bit flat.'

'The dragon woman making his life hell as usual.'

'You got it. So I went over one evening when Mum was out. We had a couple of drinks. And before you know it, we've snuck a look at the manuscript.'

'And?'

'We were disappointed.'

'She can't write for toffee?'

'Actually it wasn't that bad. Overwritten as you'd expect, but no, it was the content. About a woman with a tiresome husband whom she ends up murdering.'

'How did this go down with your dad?'

'As you would expect. He's looking for himself in the novel of course.'

'Did he find himself?'

'The jury is still out on that one. Anyway, we're safe. It'll never be published.'

'How did her group respond?'

'She's been told to add more sex.'

'That'll be a challenge.'

'Won't it?'

Bridget takes a nap after Clare has departed. She lies perfectly still and listens to the sound of her breathing. She places a hand over her heart and feels oddly reassured by its steady rhythm. She visits sites of buried memories and excavates them. A time of reckoning. Will the scales of happiness versus unhappiness, justice and injustice, success and failure, balance in her favour? She embarks on her personal journey, the archaeologist of her own life. Room after room of her past reveals itself to her, she enters through one open door after another. What does she discover in her search? Answers to questions that have always puzzled her? The meaning of life itself? Or instead, a meaningless void where there is perhaps no reason for her illness, no purpose in her having lived at all.

How happy she and Matthew had been together, the happiness that is part of innocence. They had carried the lightest of emotional baggage.

She has possessed twenty years of joy. It is more than most people achieve over a long lifetime. It is not the big events of her life which now flood into her mind but the simple pleasures so long taken for granted. Her red rhododendron bursting into flower and reliably heralding spring every year. The warmth and comfort of Matthew's groin nestled against her buttocks spoon fashion.

The miracle is, she has not lost any of the things that really matter.

She also realizes as she recovers just how much Matthew loves her. Their relationship has not only survived the crisis, it has become stronger than ever. How would she have managed without his love and support? She knows this is not always the case. She has heard of several women in her exact circumstances whose partners and spouses couldn't last the distance.

Matthew tells her how acutely aware he has become of his own mortality through coming to terms with her cancer. It's a fact further emphasized by their childlessness. Bridget's gifts and talents will not be inherited by anyone.

Bridget is aware that no-one ever asks Matthew how *he* is feeling. The focus continues to remain on her. She suspects that beneath his determinedly cheerful demeanour he still feels scared and powerless.

'No matter how much effort he makes he cannot guarantee to protect me and keep me alive.'

'You know, you're bloody lucky to have Matthew,' Agnes reminds her.

Chapter Twenty-Six

Agnes

Agnes and Daniel are enjoying a lie-in. Daniel is relishing the fact that he doesn't have to attend Mass. 'Each Sunday it's still there as a little nagging reminder,' he admits. 'Even after all this time.'

'Do you ever have doubts about your decision?' asks Agnes, pulling the duvet up to her chin.

'No. I've finished with the Church. I couldn't go back. Not now.'

'You mean us? Fucking and all that. Mortal sin and hellfire.'

'Don't play the ingenue. You know it's more complex than that.'

She doesn't want to begin her day with an argument, although there have been a few of those recently, especially now that the first flush of attraction has dimmed and they are no longer on their best behaviour.

Reminding herself just how fond she has grown of Daniel, Man of Paradoxes, Agnes rolls over to be nearer to him, breathes in his scent with delight, strokes a sinewy thigh, smooths the soft down on his belly with her right hand.

'Wouldn't it be wonderful to make a baby?' he murmurs, snuggling into her body, kissing her nipples.

She freezes. Pushes his head away from her.

How did they get on to the subject of babies? An image of her mother comes immediately to mind, holding in her arms the latest gift from God who is only six months old. She is still breast-feeding and already pregnant again. Every fifteen months another baby, depending on the rate of miscarriages. How did her mother survive it? Is it any wonder, thinks Agnes, feeling fully justified, that she has turned her back on Catholicism and motherhood, determined to create a life as opposite to her mother's as is humanly possible?

Agnes has a long memory. It was penance for breakfast, punishment for lunch and purgatory for dinner. Saint Noelene the Martyr. Our Lady of Self-Sacrifice and Denial. The woman who had no opinions, who never acted on instinct, never lost control. Even now she continues to pray for her daughter Agnes the Slothful. Agnes the Sinner. Agnes the Selfish.

'I have no buried desire to have children.'

Foolish Daniel. He's not listening, not reading the signs. He treads the path from which previous fearful angels have fled in droves.

Agnes views motherhood as a swamp she will sink into right up to her neck until she becomes invisible. Brain-dead. Trapped. The only sign of life a pair of resentful eyes and a frantic mouth cheeping 'What about *me*? I deserve a life, don't I?' No-one ever truly believes that Agnes can possibly mean what she says. When someone is insensitive enough to rope her into the Let's Play Happy Families routine, invisible buttons all over her body are sounding off like sirens shrieking *No! No! No!*

A quizzical look is directed her way. 'Are you sure you are being utterly truthful here?'

How boringly predictable. A little spurt of anger flares and is squashed. She doesn't want to fight, but she has to give him the message loud and clear.

'You don't give up, do you? What is this? The confessional? You want to play priests, is that it? *Spare me.*'

He stares up at the ceiling with a grim expression.

Remember, Agnes, this man was once a conduit for exorcizing demons, forgiving sins, for transforming wine into blood, bread into flesh. And he's in *your* bed.

'I *like* my life.'

'Do you ever experience feelings of loss because of your decision?'

'My lost motherhood, you mean? Yeah, like a hole in the head.' She can see she has spoken too harshly and modifies her tone of voice. 'Occasionally I do. But the doubts don't last, believe me.'

They are lying on their sides studying each other carefully. Agnes is wary of the intensity of feeling that has developed between them. In relinquishing some of her independence she has something to gain, but she is also aware of how much she has to lose.

He too is obviously unhappy at the turn the conversation has taken. His hair is rumpled. There is a small scratch on his chin. Men and their shaving wounds, she thinks.

'Back off.'

She can't bear his reproachful glance and averts her face.

He doesn't give up. He rises on his haunches and peers over to observe her. He says nothing. Waits.

Her eyes glisten with unshed tears. He has succeeded in getting under her skin, as she had feared he might.

'There's so much I want to do that doesn't involve having children. I've made a conscious decision. A *decision*, not just something I've just drifted into. I've created a viable life. It's what I want. Besides, we're still getting to know each other. What's the hurry?'

'At our age we don't have the luxury of time. You've just turned forty. I'm in my mid-forties.'

'*So?* Am I missing the point here?'

'I feel the pressure of time marching on.'

'But *I'm* not trying to make up for lost time, at least not the way you seem to be. I've already got out there and *lived*. Had all kinds of adventures. Backpacked to remote places. Witnessed amazing sights, become acquainted with some weird and wonderful people of all nationalities. I've climbed mountains, taken risks, been down the political activist path, forged a business. You name it – I've been there. Seen it, read it, discussed it or photographed it. Eaten, drunk, smoked or inhaled it. And there's so much more that I long to experience and couldn't do if I was hampered by a child.'

'*Fine*. OK.'

But Agnes knows it is not fine for him at all. She struggles to hang on to her own sense of what is right for *her*.

She hauls herself out of bed, puts on a warm robe and makes coffee, sticks on Tori Amos.

Good friends, food, books, a decent stereo and car, a place of her own, work that satisfies her about two-thirds of the time, the prospect of an exhibition, regular travel, her indulgent scented baths, her meditation practice. She knows she has achievable ambitions.

It's more than enough, dammit, Daniel.

He steals up behind her, winds his disconcertingly long arms round her waist, kisses and nuzzles into the nape of her neck.

Agnes melts as he intends her to.

'You're a strong, gorgeous, capable and talented woman. It's enough. I'm sorry I pushed you so hard.'

He's sorry right now, she thinks, but what about tomorrow and the day after and so on, when he'll be unable to resist having yet another attempt to persuade her.

'Do you ever think about whether your life has meaning?' Agnes asks Clare at their weekly lunch.

'Constantly.'

'And . . .' prompts Agnes.

'And most of the time, yes,' replies Clare. 'The rest of the time I feel as if I have to justify why I'm *only* in public relations. Why public relations? Why not journalism? Why not a novel, for Christ's sake.'

'Because PR pays better, as you well know.'

'True.'

But Clare is only listening with half an ear. She scans the café to see if there is anyone she knows.

'Have you recovered from your little episode with Dermott Maloney?'

'We live our lives forwards and understand them backwards? Who said that?'

'I don't know.'

'Anyway, in answer to your question – I'm understanding Dermott backwards. I'm still puzzled by my own reckless behaviour. And . . . I haven't reached any earth-shattering conclusions yet.'

'It may take five years. Ten.'

'For ever. A blip on the time line.'

Clare enquires after Daniel. Agnes confides that he is placing pressure on her to seriously consider having a child with him.

'He's barking up the wrong tree on that one, isn't he?'

'You got it right there, sister.'

'Want to trade partners? How would Daniel like to be a sperm donor?'

Clare laughs at Agnes's startled expression.

'Whoa! Joke!'

'How did we end up so out of sync with the men in our lives?'

'If I were Athena I'd say better luck next time.'

'Once around is enough for me. I've no desire to be reincarnated, thanks.'

'Do you ever lie to yourself?' she asks Clare after they have received their coffee.

'I can't answer that. I hope not. I try not to, but who knows. Maybe my whole life is one big self-delusion. What do you think?' She sips her long black in a reflective mood.

'I think we lie to ourselves all the time. It's why you're in public relations and I'm still doing work for advertising agencies.'

'We have a choice? What about mortgages?'

'We could live more simply. Not eat out. Not ever travel. Not buy any luxuries.'

'Not live, you mean. Get real. We're not twenty any more. We're not ten either, believing we'll be rewarded in an afterlife that's populated mainly by dead Catholics.'

'Is there a connection with Catholicism, our upbringing? This obsession with making our lives count? The need to impose meaning or seek justification where patently there is none? Bridget and Athena's desire to believe the best of everyone they meet? My fear of failing, of commitment? Your fixation with success? Can you stand back from Catholicism and see it for what it is?'

'And what would that be? Something that can be tightly defined? I don't think so. You know what they say. You can take the girl out of the convent . . .'

Their food arrives. Agnes picks at her wild mushroom risotto. Clare slices into her panini with enthusiasm.

'So much we had to accept with blind faith. It *was* blind.'

Agnes lifts her head. They grin with delight at this further evidence of the other's defiant apostasy.

'We are all blind. The world is full of bewildered uncomprehending people who *know* their lives are totally out of their control. What makes us any different? The older I get the less I understand, the more questions are unanswerable. I will die, I swear to you, with only one word on my lips: why?'

'Agnes, you're so fucking intense.'

'Fuck off, Clare.'

'Fuck off yourself,' replies Clare with easy good humour. 'I love you too, Agnes. But we can't sit here all day. I wish we didn't have to return to work. We have supported ourselves unremittingly for the past twenty years and no doubt we'll do so for the next twenty, no matter how much we bitch and moan and rave about the so-called bloody meaning of life, this is fucking *it* – as good as it gets. There is no reprieve. No "something better round the corner".'

'It's not good enough.' Agnes is stubborn, mouth set in a line. If only she could see herself, her expression at this moment is a repeat of her mother's and probably her mother's before her and world without end, amen. 'We're halfway through our lives – if we're lucky. The time remaining to us has to count.'

'Has it occurred to you, Agnes, that maybe our lives might never actually contain meaning? Neither of us, in the final analysis, making a real difference. We may have to settle, God forbid, for being ordinary, simply filling in the allotted three score and ten as pleasantly as we can, and trying not to hurt others in the process—'

'But what constitutes an ordinary life?'

'Sheer survival? Paying the bills on time? Struggling to conduct a decent relationship? Searching out and succeeding in attracting meaningful work? Doing no harm? Feeling entitled to extract a modicum of pleasure from this mortal coil? You tell me.'

'Living in the here and now and not worrying about all the pain and shit that may never happen anyway.'

'Not living in fear,' adds Clare.

'That's right.' Agnes feels more determined than ever not to succumb to Daniel's pressure to have a baby.

She has a definite bottom line. He has crossed it. So it's pretty obvious to her that fairly soon he's going to have to make a choice.

She hopes he chooses her. But if he doesn't, she'll get over it.

She always has in the past.

Chapter Twenty-Seven

Clare

'Adrian is going away to do some male bonding,' Clare announces to her friends. 'Whoopee!' She has decided she has no option but to be a good sport about it.

Two days of pleasing herself. No compromises required.

'Make the most of it.'

'I plan to. I'm having a girls' night.'

It's quickly arranged. Agnes and Athena will both stay over at Clare's house on the Saturday night. Unfortunately Bridget has not yet recovered sufficiently to have the stamina for a night out or she too would have been included. Life must go on, Clare reminds herself. Fears for Bridget are never far from her mind, but for tonight she will try to push them into the background.

Adrian displays no curiosity as to how she will occupy herself in his absence. To punish him, even though she is extremely curious about his activities, Clare likewise does not enquire about his plans. He gives her a perfunctory kiss before departing. She reflects on how five years previously this degree of detachment would have been unthinkable. Not only would they both have assiduously discussed the details of each other's weekends in advance, they would also have expected pleasurable and lengthy post-mortems once reunited. They would also have given each other heartfelt hugs and long passionate kisses before going their separate ways. They would have missed each other, eagerly anticipated seeing each other again.

'*Piss off then, go and have your mid-life crisis,*' yells Clare to Adrian's departing back. Afterwards she was annoyed with herself for not keeping her mouth firmly shut.

Why oh why can't passion be sustained? Despite all evidence to the contrary, she has expected her own life and loves to be the exception to the statistics. Even when aspects of living with Adrian have driven her crazy with irritation she has persisted in the hope that things will improve if only she makes sufficient effort. She has tolerated Adrian's habit of leaving dirty clothes on the floor and steeled herself not to pick them up. She has endured the passion for cricket and rugby, his habit of whistling. Where is the harm in whistling? It could have been a mania for collecting keys. Or speaking when his mouth was full. Farting and belching in bed. Both of her former partners had been guilty of the two latter habits.

Clare wanders the house in the wake of Adrian's departure feeling like an amputee. She knows it's pathetic. Think of all the lovely time she is about to have alone.

The rooms are all tidy. Nothing is out of place. There is no pressing task to claim her attention. Nothing in fact that cannot wait. Now that she is attempting to work less, to create a life outside work, the time she does spend on her own sometimes weighs heavily.

None of her siblings or nephews and nieces live in the same city. She sees her parents once a fortnight. Until very recently there has been little time to indulge either in hobbies or in additional study. Should she take up a craft, learn a language? Take on board her mother's challenge that she is too wrapped up in herself and should do good deeds – as the nuns also had advised. Visit the sick and the dying?

Clare shudders. It's been bad enough dealing with Bridget's cancer.

Too wrapped up in herself? Clare reflects on the bevy of women about the city who assist her to maintain her body, her business, or her environment: her psychotherapist, personal fitness trainer, hairdresser, leg waxer, masseuse, dentist, doctor, physio, acupuncturist, cranial osteopath, not forgetting her personal assistant, house cleaner, office cleaner, lawyer, accountant, insurance broker and business mentor.

'What interests you?' Agnes had asked her.

Clare had not been able to give her a glib answer. Everything. Yet nothing in particular. Books. Theatre. Films, art, politics. Food – as long as she doesn't have to cook too often.

Clare prepares the house for her friends. Already she is slipping into her own rhythm in Adrian's absence. She's eating when she feels like it, cold snacks in front of a book. Listening to music – her choice – as the mood takes her.

She places a tall blue glass vase of fresh flowers in the lounge, pours a few drops of ylang ylang oil onto the water inside a little clay burner and leaves it on the coffee table.

She checks the level of the single malt whisky. Agnes is very partial to it. Personally she prefers brandy, while Athena is fond of Bailey's. For dinner she will prepare an artichoke frittata accompanied by roasted pear and blue cheese salad. For dessert: tiramisu – and to hell with the calories. Just the thought of all that gorgeous mascarpone cheese makes her mouth water. Breakfast the following morning: freshly roasted coffee, croissants, Brie and a pot of her mother's homemade raspberry jam.

Athena arrives first. She sniffs appreciatively.

'Mmm, what a heavenly scent. Is it ylang ylang?'

She dumps her jacket and overnight bag on Clare's bed, fluffs out her hair, smooths out the crinkles in her mauve linen shirt. She enters the lounge beaming. 'I've been looking forward to this all day. You've no idea.'

Carole King is on the stereo.

'For old time's sake.'

'Next you'll be dragging out Phoebe Snow and Leonard Cohen.'

Clare grins mischievously. 'However did you guess?'

Athena whoops. 'Yes!'

Clare cannot remember having seen Athena so animated in a long time.

Agnes arrives. Clare smiles a welcome. She knows she is happy again, joy billowing against her chest as she surrenders to it.

'What's it like having the house to yourself?'

'Sheer bliss.'

No-one for her to have to make allowances for. No-one reacting to every statement she makes.

They sit on a couch while Clare continues with her food preparation, making croutons, roasting pears, slicing artichokes into quarters, peeling half a dozen cloves of garlic.

Athena sips her white wine. 'Tell us about your new man, Agnes, we're dying to know.'

Clare stops squeezing her lemon to catch the answer.

'He's a caring and thoughtful man. But he's also nervy, inexperienced, lonely, floundering. Oh, and he has a bad haircut and no dress sense.'

'Just what you need,' observes Clare with a wry smile.

'Put like that I know he doesn't seem a likely proposition. But then I'm not your average punter either.'

'True,' smiles Athena.

'So. Have you been to bed with him?' Clare pulls open the oven to inspect her pears then turns to look at Agnes.

Agnes gives a broad grin. 'Yeah, I have.'

Clare closes the oven door and wipes her hands. 'What was he like?'

Agnes's eyes sparkle at them over the rim of her glass. 'That's my business.'

Athena puts her feet up.

Sebastian is hung out to air.

'So . . . is he still running around in designer dresses?' asks Athena.

'I think I saw a man in a kilt a week ago who looked very like Sebastian,' recalls Clare with glee.

'The last of the big fuckers of the seventies and eighties,' gasps Agnes.

The others howl in response. Tears spurt from their eyes.

'You can always tell the *big* fuckers.'

'I can spot the *genuine* ones a mile off,' shrieks Agnes.

'Do you prefer big dicks or little ones?' Clare asks them.

'Actually . . . I prefer women,' announces Athena. 'Agnes is not the only one with a new love in her life.'

Clare knows all about it but Agnes demands to be brought up to date.

'Who? Tell me.'

'Her name is Rita. She comes from an Italian background.'

'So. When are we going to meet this woman?'

'You're invited for dinner next week.'

Adrian is for the high jump next.

'You know,' muses Athena. 'I feel I barely know Adrian. After five years in and out of your house. Despite being your closest friends. It's as if he barely acknowledges us. We're kept on the periphery of your life.'

Agnes: 'Clare is a collaborator in this. She agrees to it. So it's not only Adrian's doing.'

Athena: 'Are you ashamed of us, Clare? I get the feeling that he neither likes nor respects us. It's different with Matthew and Bridget. There I always feel welcome. Included.'

Clare shakes her head vigorously. 'You've got it all wrong,' she protests.

'Men come and go in your life. Women are the true constant. We're what you have when everything turns to shit.'

'Who said it's turning to shit?' exclaims Clare with indignation. 'I have my life under control.'

'Do you?' challenges Agnes. 'Not from where I'm standing.'

'You judgemental bitches.'

'Your friends.'

'Some friends, I don't think.' Clare sighs. 'You don't see what I see. If you did, could—'

Agnes: 'He becomes a different person when he's with you. Is that it?'

Athena (gently): 'Does he have your best interests at heart, Clare?'

Clare: 'He has his own interests at heart. Why shouldn't he?'

Athena: 'You may as well be flatmates. People who share the mortgage, a few meals together, and otherwise have separate finances. Where is the working together for the common good?'

Clare: 'You sound like my mother.'

'If you are serious about having a baby,' Athena says bluntly, 'you should leave Adrian.'

It is not as if Clare hasn't already come to the same conclusion. She envies Adrian his life, his uncomplicated future plans. There is no clock whirring away inside him. He is not, as she seems to be, driven by something bigger than her own puny will.

'Do you have any regrets at not having children?' Clare asks Agnes as they make another pot of coffee. It's shaping up to be an all-nighter.

'I have absolutely no regrets,' replies Agnes adamantly. 'None whatsoever. I value my independence too much.'

'Yes, but what have you done with your independence?'

'Meaning that the only justification for not succumbing to the myth of motherhood and the nuclear family is to produce great works of art, or something for the public good?'

'You don't have to do the same thing all your life, Clare,' remarks Agnes, half asleep on Clare's black leather sofa. Athena is already asleep. 'You can change direction. Who wants to do the same thing they decided to do when they were twenty?'

Clare can't seem to stop thinking about whether or not she should have a baby – especially since it's seeming increasingly likely that if she wants one she is going to have to do it on her own.

*   *   *

'Everyone expects me to reproduce,' complains Clare to Fiona. 'I feel a huge pressure. I have to justify my selfish life.'

'Everyone? Selfish? Who is placing this amount of pressure on you?'

'My mother.'

'And you believe her?'

'What's my excuse if I don't have a child?'

'You need an excuse? Isn't your work meaningful?'

'It's satisfying. I work too hard. But it's my business – my choice. I haven't discovered a cure for AIDS, or taught a kid with special needs how to read, if that's what you mean.'

'Perhaps you expect too much of yourself?'

'I could arrange to fall pregnant by accident. Plenty of women do that. Conveniently forget or choose to forget to take their little pill and they go ahead and have unprotected sex. But at some deep level they—'

'They do know what they're doing. But is that how you want to have a baby, by practising deception rather than contraception?' asks Fiona.

'No, of course not. But that's not to say that the thought hasn't crossed my mind.'

It's lonely being the only one she knows in her wider peer group who doesn't have a child, apart from Bridget and Agnes. And Bridget would have had a baby by now if it had only been possible. Clare clings to the idea of Agnes. She can depend on Agnes not to have a child.

Most galling of all, Mark her ex has impregnated his young 'babe' Sandra. Clare has been obliged to endure the nauseating spectacle of her gloating face and fat stomach as she does her pregnancy workout at the gym.

'I wish I were a man. Then I wouldn't have to

322

choose. I could continue to focus on my work. If I were a man I could have a wife, someone who would bear my kids for me. You see, I like the *idea* of kids but at the same time I don't actually want to do the staying at home bit. Who wants to be the primary caregiver?'

Not her.

Chapter Twenty-Eight

Athena

Now that Wing is back on his feet again he has begun to stop over the occasional night.

'I'm seventeen now, Mum, you can't stop me,' says Jewel.

Once Athena has realized that there is no way she can prevent her daughter from having sex with Wing she buys huge quantities of condoms and crams them into Jewel's undies drawer. If Jewel is going to be sexually active then it may as well be under her roof so she can keep an eye on the situation. Better that than in the back of Wing's car.

'God, Mum, there's no *way* I'm going to get pregnant. I'm never going to have children. What a drag that would be.' Jewel has decided she wants to be a doctor. She now studies for long hours on school nights without being prompted. She must achieve a top A-grade bursary or she'll be forced to radically rethink her career options. Jewel has an ambition to become very, very rich, to create a life for herself that is as opposite to her mother's as possible.

Mother and daughter eventually come to an arrangement. Jewel tolerates Rita staying over two or three nights a week and Athena does likewise with Wing, but only on weekends. A cosy routine develops. Jewel studies for three hours each day in the late afternoons. Rita prepares hash browns and grilled mushrooms for Sunday brunch. Sunday evenings, before he heads off back to his aunt's, Wing cooks for the four of them.

Food is very important to Wing. The manner in which vegetables are diced and presented, the length of cooking time, the heat of the wok. He carefully balances the various tastes of sweet and salty, acid, bitter and hot in his food combinations. He has presented the household with a new wok which he has instructed them how to clean and maintain.

'Never use detergents or pot scrubs.'

He shows them the traditional method of rubbing the wok with sliced ginger, strips of chive and, when it has been washed and dried, rubbing a little oil into it.

'The chives prevent rust and the ginger takes away the smell.'

Wing also presents Athena with a solid mortar and pestle. He is scathing of her kitchen equipment and never fails to arrive at her house without some small gift. One week it is a sharp knife.

'Your knives . . .' He rolls his eyes to show his disapproval. He shows her the Chinese way to cook rice, how to steam a fish.

Another weekend he arrives with salted duck eggs. Athena makes a space on one of her kitchen shelves for the growing collection of Chinese supplies: five-spice powder, clumps of root ginger, jars of shrimp paste, dried chillies, salted kale, cashew nuts, a packet of dried mushrooms, a can of bamboo shoots, water chestnuts, oyster sauce, sesame oil, rice flour, egg noodles and lemon grass.

'I am showing you my respect with my cooking,' he tells Athena.

He is growing on her, no doubt of it. When was the last time she had been shown respect with a capital R?

He speaks with nostalgia of Hong Kong's *dai pai dongs* – noisy, crowded street stalls that sell cheap and tasty snacks – dumplings, seafood, noodles, pancakes and congee. His listeners can almost hear the scrape of spatulas clattering against steel woks, the spitting of hot oil and the tantalizing smell of fried garlic and ginger. He describes too with mouth-watering relish the Sundays when he and his extended family would visit a *dim sum* restaurant and enjoy steamed glutinous rice stuffed with meat and elegantly wrapped in lotus leaves and the succession of delicacies wheeled out on trolleys: rolls, cakes, dumplings, puffs, balls and croquettes containing water chestnut, turnip, chicken feet, stuffed beancurd, shark's fin, squid, crab-meat, pork and chicken.

'It is my personal tragedy,' he announces solemnly, 'to enter a household of vegetable eaters.'

'No chickens' feet and blood in this household, thank you. We'll convert you to being an animal conservationist before too long, see if we don't.'

Wing makes Athena a little bow.

'I was born in the year of the dog, this means I am generous and patient. I will charm your entrails with my vegetable delicacies.'

Athena gives him an impulsive hug. He ducks his head, embarrassed by her affection. Everyone can tell he is very pleased.

Everything now appears to be going so smoothly in her life that Athena has trouble believing it. From past experience she has learned not to trust that the goddess of happiness will pay her more than a fleeting visit.

Even the long-awaited dinner at which Clare, Agnes and Bridget had been officially introduced to Rita had gone off brilliantly. Rita looked fantastic in a new white dress that nicely set off her dark tan. She had assisted Athena in the preparation of the meal – endive salad with goat's cheese and spaghetti puttanesca. This in itself was the first time since the era of Sebastian and, later, Roger that she had entertained with a partner. Athena had discovered that Rita was not a confident cook, although she could produce a few basic stand-bys she could cook blindfolded, for instance, hash browns, lasagne, fish pie and cauliflower cheese. She had a distinctive personal style which she summed up as 'white everything' and an unexpected talent for interior decoration. With a slight rearranging of Athena's possessions and careful placement of prized objects and flowers she had transformed the dining room and lounge.

Athena was uncertain. 'It's beautiful, but I don't know if it's me.'

'Mum, it's fab. Whatever you do – don't change it back to how it was,' said Jewel, running out the door to go to a movie with Wing.

Clare, Agnes and Bridget had arrived in a flurry of curiosity, exclaiming favourably on the changes in Athena's environment.

'I enjoyed the "behind-the-scenes" piece you wrote on the PM, couple of months back,' commented Clare.

'Thanks.' Rita glanced over to Athena and exchanged a secret smile. 'The story took months to set up, as you can imagine. You know how reserved she normally is about her private life.'

'With good reason, I would have thought,' Bridget chipped in. 'Losing one's privacy, always being on show, newshounds waiting like vultures for her to trip up – it must be one of the less appealing aspects of taking on public life.'

'I wouldn't lose any sleep over it,' grinned Rita. 'I'd

say she is more than adequately compensated for the inconvenience, wouldn't you?'

Athena could tell immediately that her old friends approved. But then how could anyone not admire Rita, she thought with pride. Within minutes of her arrival, Agnes was discussing with Rita the various merits and flaws of the work done by the freelance photographers featured in her magazine. Clare and Bridget went on to add their own opinions about the magazine's idiosyncratic style.

'I'm about to be made editor, it's going to be announced in the next issue,' announced Rita.

Athena led the toast and everyone noticed how very much more outgoing she had become since Rita and she had developed into a couple.

'Tell me, Athena, what is it exactly that you and Rita do together?' asks Agnes a few weeks later.

Athena does not immediately respond. Agnes and her salacious desire for nitty-gritty details. She has no desire to demean the perfect and astonishing sex she enjoys with Rita on an almost daily basis by giving a blow-by-blow account to Agnes. It would be tantamount to betraying her intimacy with Rita. Until now she has only played at sex, bypassing erotic love. She is afraid that her miraculously reciprocated emotion will be snatched from her, that talking about it will somehow attract bad luck, reduce it to mere mechanics. I do this, then she does that; the sum total is bliss.

Agnes will not be so easily fobbed off, however. 'Go on, don't be a prude, tell Aunty Agnes.'

'No.'

'Oh, go on,' urges Agnes. She puts on a puppy act, beseeching. 'Come on, pretty please.'

Despite herself, Athena is disarmed. She gives a wicked grin. 'Use your imagination.'

Agnes leans closer. 'Do you . . . you know . . . use toys?'

'Toys?'

'Stuff you strap on and stick in. Leather gizmos. Jelly rubber dildos.'

Athena blushes and shakes her head.

Agnes raises an eyebrow. 'No?'

Athena has always believed that men had scrutinized her body as if it were no more than a juicy piece of steak – a good feed if the fat was trimmed off. It's still a pleasant surprise that Rita views her as something curvaceous, soft, sweet and ripe she longs to savour.

'Is your eyesight defective?'

'If I tell you first thing every morning and last thing at night how beautiful I find you, will you believe me?'

Rita: thin, eager, sharp-tongued. Spirited and vivacious. Critical. Only not where Athena is concerned.

'But why do you love me?' Athena is genuinely puzzled. Too many years of viewing herself as unlovable and unappealing have left their scars.

'Let me count the ways,' smiles Rita. She holds up the fingers of her hand and ticks off Athena's qualities.

'You're nurturing.'

'Like a mother?' Athena groans.

'No. A lover. You're so easy to please. Tender-hearted, loving. Sympathetic. Kind and generous to everyone. Relaxing to be around. It's chemistry, babe.'

But intellectually challenging?

'I do like a rigorous debate,' laughs Rita. 'I also like to take the piss. It's the way I am.'

Athena envies Rita her ease with words. Finding the right explanations or descriptions is never a problem. She erects towers of theory and opinions. Athena scurries behind her lover trying valiantly to keep to the path but inevitably becoming lost. Rita's logic competes with Athena's intuition. Cynicism versus gullibility. The cogs of Athena's mind, rusty from lack of use, sharpen up as Rita patiently schools her in logic. She is lovingly encouraged to become more assertive. Memories of lengthy discussions over dinner tables with Sebastian and their friends surface, bringing to mind people she hasn't seen or thought of in years.

But even Rita's love and attention cannot protect Athena from the stress of her precarious financial situation.

There has been a downturn in Athena's massage business. The situation has not crept up on her. On the contrary it has been a sudden, and therefore completely unexpected, reversal of her fortunes. A slow December. Only two clients in January. Few bookings ahead for February. Christmas had been a squeeze, but at least the lack of bookings had made it possible to spend more time caring for Bridget.

'What are you doing about it?' asks Rita, concerned.

'I'm doing loads of affirmations to manifest more clients – prosperity thinking. Releasing my poverty mentality – on a *cellular* level.'

'*Manifest?* Could we apply a little logic to the problem, Athena? Let's get practical.'

Athena frowns, shrugs. 'OK. I admit I don't know what to do. It's scary. I thought I had a business.'

'I could write an article about you. Raise your profile.'

Athena is wary. 'What would you say about me?'

'Hype and bullshit. No, seriously. I'm sure I could place it with my magazine as long as it isn't too New Age in tone.'

'I don't think you're the right person to decide that,' says Athena defensively.

'Don't be such a hippy.' It's Rita's most derogatory term for use on her lover. *Hippy*. Away with the fairies. Not living in the real world.

'You don't want publicity? I give up. Why don't you ask Clare for advice?'

'I hate asking for help.'

'Don't be an ostrich,' snaps Rita, exasperated. 'If you won't call her, I will.'

'It's none of your business.'

'*You* start dealing with the problem, then.'

'It's not my fault, you know.' What would Rita know? She's always had good jobs on newspapers, money coming in regular as clockwork every week, no teenager to support. She has it made. Athena begins to feel sorry for herself. The more Rita becomes exasperated with her procrastinating and lack of action, the more she retreats into her shell.

'What I need is help, not criticism,' she says huffily.

Rita and Jewel give her hard looks. In this matter of Athena's financial crisis they are united in their views. She sees the judgement in their eyes. Jewel picks up the phone and dials Clare. She passes the phone to her mother. 'Get advice from the Oracle, why don't you, mother goddess.'

'You need a database,' states Clare. 'Follow up everyone you've massaged over the past year.'

Athena squirms. How Clare loves dishing out advice.

'Don't get technical on me,' she warns.

'Don't you be so prickly. Are you keeping a record of your clients?' persists Clare. 'They walk in the door, you take down their contact details, enter them in your system, spit them out as address labels, follow up each person every ninety days with a phone call, a note,

331

a flier containing a special discount for multiple bookings. Do you offer gift vouchers? Advertise? Remember to distribute your business cards? Let's work out a promotional and marketing plan that'll see you through the next year. Maybe you could give a few talks, write some articles, raise your profile.'

Athena refuses to catch Rita's eye.

'I don't want to *bother* people.'

'C'mon. Aren't you proud of the service you offer?'

'Databases and marketing plans are too *commercial* for me,' objects Athena. 'I feel exhausted just thinking about it. Besides, I don't have a computer.'

'But *I* have,' Jewel reminds her, bringing coffee for herself, Rita and Clare and a herbal tea for her mother.

'There you are,' says Clare with a smile. 'Problem solved.'

Sure, thinks Athena. And pigs might fly. The day when my daughter lifts a finger for me. Always demanding clothes, gadgets, shoes, school outings. It never ends. Next it will be university fees, textbooks.

'Try it, Mum,' pleads Jewel. 'I promise I'll help.'

'We'll do a swap,' suggests Clare. 'I'll help you market yourself and you can give me massages. Deal?'

'Deal.'

'Using technology, being businesslike *and* following a New Age path – they don't have to be mutually exclusive, you know.'

'I don't want computers in my life.'

Clare gives her a pitying look. 'Why don't you give my way a try. The "universe will provide" theory you seem to operate by isn't working – it's too passive.'

'Insisting on having control over every aspect of your life isn't necessarily the answer either,' retorts Athena, stung by Clare's criticism. She bangs a mug down on the table and the tea splashes over the rim.

Neither woman bothers to wipe it up. 'Ever heard of the word surrender?'

Clare throws back her head and gives a mocking laugh. '*Surrender?* Go bury your head in the sand if that's what you want. Slide deeper into debt, why don't you?'

They glare at each other across the table. Athena stands up. She hides her hands behind the chair so that Clare won't see that they're shaking. She wants to yell. She is about to cry. She could strike Clare.

She does none of these things because Clare in her impulsive manner comes over to her and places an arm round her. '*Please* let me help you. I can't bear to watch you struggle when it's so unnecessary.'

Athena catches a waft of Clare's *Tendre Poison*.

'All right, we'll try it your way,' she agrees.

Outside in her little courtyard the leaves of the potted gardenia stir gently in the breeze. Cicadas chirrup joyously in the background. The ceramic wind chimes clank together as the wind lifts and dies away. Her tamarillo tree is top heavy with its cargo of green fruit. Now that she has unburdened herself and Clare, Jewel and Rita have all promised to help her to make her little business more efficient, Athena feels happy and excited. She gazes across at the lawn, yellow in patches, legacy of a particularly hot summer. She could cheerfully fling herself head first into the spongy grass to savour the damp mossy earthy smell.

She doesn't, of course, but this is what love does to you, she realizes, makes you spontaneous, crazy, reckless, unheeding of consequences.

And alive to all her senses.

'How would you feel if Rita moved in?' Athena asks Jewel.

Jewel considers. Life in the household has improved since Rita came on the scene. For one thing her mother doesn't hassle her so much now that she has someone to take her mind off her daughter's bad attitudes.

Not only that but Rita has been putting mega effort into helping Wing perfect his English.

Wing wants to be a journalist. Like Rita. He thinks she is majorly cool.

So does Jewel. Rita knows how to dress too without looking naff. She's even bought Athena some OK clothes. Plus she brings over heaps of free magazines from the company she works for.

There's no question really.

'OK,' says Jewel.

Chapter Twenty-Nine

Clare

Clare hadn't planned to leave Adrian. Not seriously. It just happened. A window of opportunity, you might say. A tenant moved out of one of their apartments. It had been an apartment Clare had always liked. Not too small. Not too large. If you stood on tiptoe in one corner of the lounge you could actually see the sea.

The apartment was white, empty and inviting. Without giving it much thought she packed a few things and set up camp.

To see how it felt.

She had their spare queen-sized bed moved over by a removal van. A ghetto blaster. A few CDs. Heather Novo. Sara McLachlan. Some Brahms and Elgar. Nothing that Adrian would miss or fret over.

She ate takeaways and watched a lot of bad television.

She saw Adrian every day for an hour or so and they talked without resolving anything. At night they each slept alone and each felt their aloneness and the peculiar yet interesting states of mind this brought about. Clare had no desire to see anyone much. She couldn't cope with going to the office. Her friends kept phoning but she didn't return the messages. Later.

Clare spent most of her time sleeping. She wondered if she would ever stop sleeping. Sometimes she cried for hours at a time and she worried that she might not be able to stop that either. But she always did. Being alone didn't kill her as she had once feared it might.

'OK,' says Adrian when they next meet. 'I give in. Have a baby. If that's what you want.'

Clare gives him a long calculating look. She recalls in minute detail just how worn down she had become from their battles over the issue. She doesn't know what she wants any more.

'I need time,' she says.

She has scarcely stopped to draw breath for the last twenty years. All she has done is work. And work. And work. She feels as if she has run a marathon race only there isn't a winner. The only thing she is sure about right now is that she has to stop everything for a couple of months until she figures out exactly what it is that she wants to do next.

She has lost her way, can no longer remember what to prioritize, or even if she should prioritize. She has never succeeded in getting on top of her 'to do' list. As soon as one raft of tasks is completed another set pops up to take its place.

Late at night curled up under her duvet she tries to see the point of anything she has ever done. The thousands of meetings she has attended blur together in her mind. The images that stay with her, unsurprisingly, are those of a more personal nature – sharing a joke with Agnes, gripping Bridget's hand at her bedside, making love to Adrian, throwing a cushion at him when he pissed her off, having a drink with Fran on Fridays in the late afternoon, being fondly massaged by Athena.

What has her life amounted to? Why does it now seem to matter so much whether or not her life can be said to contain an atom of meaning? It is not as if it is she who has had cancer and a brush with death. Not her who has had her beautiful breasts chopped off.

But it may as well have been. The degree of empathy she has experienced with Bridget has split her open. If she is to live her own life from now on as if every day was her last, how will she do it? Where should she start?

She picks up the phone. It is three in the morning but she knows that the person at the other end won't give a damm, she'll be so relieved to hear her voice after her period of reclusion.

The phone rings and rings.

Agnes's voice when she finally answers is thick with sleep.

'I need someone to tell me I'm not crazy.'

'You're not crazy.'

'Thanks.'

'Was there anything else, you cot case? Because it's frigging three in the morning.'

Clare laughs.

'So, got any decent coffee in that new swank apartment of yours?'

'Is the pope Catholic?'

'I'll be over to drink it at eight,' promises Agnes.

Clare climbs happily back into bed.

The phone rings.

'And while you're at it, make it double strength.'

Clare settles into her new life as a single woman. Agnes's visit is followed almost immediately by one from Fran, who launches herself through Clare's door like a galleon in full sail. The room opens up to accommodate her unspoken questions, demands, accusations. Clare has a feeling of dread in the pit of her stomach not unlike when she was a child and had done something naughty for which she was about to be punished. Inside her, apparently still alive and kicking, there lives a bad girl – defiant, irresponsible and unrepentant.

Fran will give it to her straight. And what will Clare reply?

Her mind is right now a complete blank.

Demonstrating an impressive self-control Fran saves her questions until later. She hugs Clare and gifts her with a large bunch of flowers and a basket of feijoas, kiwi fruit, tamarillos and oranges. How like Fran to be so generous, thinks Clare with a pang. She had forgotten recently that her business partner not only needs her, but also cares about her.

She accepts Clare's offer of a cup of tea and plants herself down. In her dark red suit and with her large breasts and solid thighs, she is a ripe exotic flower blooming on Clare's squashy white couch.

Clare sits uncharacteristically mute before her. She can sense the anger seething inside Fran. Her mouth is dry. She tries to control her trembling hands, daren't give herself away by picking up a cup and saucer.

'*Do you realize*—' Fran stops abruptly. 'No, obviously you don't. I've had to lie. You wouldn't believe the gossip going around . . . But you're obviously still in no state . . .'

She pauses to replace the air in her lungs before setting off again.

'Oh, what the fuck! I'm your business partner. Or have you forgotten, while you've been playing ostrich? Fill me in, Clare. I'm not a mind reader. I need to know what you've got planned. Clients are demanding to speak to you. I can only put them off so long.'

Clare puts her head in her hands. She wishes Fran

and the world she represents would take themselves off somewhere else.

'*Well?*' persists Fran. She frowns.

'I've left Adrian.'

'Thanks for putting me in the picture, but I'd guessed as much. I know you've not been happy for a while.'

'I'm sorry I've been elusive, not returned your calls.'

Fran brushes her apology aside. 'What else is going on? You may as well confess the whole goddamn stinking mess to Aunty Fran. If we need to make tough decisions then I need to know what I'm up against.'

Clare feels guilty and responsible, as Fran intends. What sort of partner has she been over the past couple of months as her life slowly unravelled? Fran's face clearly mirrors the strain of carrying the weight of the business by herself. She always sounds so tough, but Clare knows that inside she'll be a bundle of anxieties. She is entitled to the truth.

'I was having a relationship with Bulldozer – Dermott Maloney – before he died.'

'How long did that go on?'

'Couple of months.'

'I can't believe I didn't see what was under my nose. Who else knew?'

'Only my friend Agnes.'

'She encourage you, did she?'

Clare gives a hollow laugh. 'Hardly.'

'Tell me the rest.'

'I felt completely betrayed by Harmony Heaven. They got right under my skin.'

'Yep, but that's business, hon. You know that, I know that – the whole goddamn world knows that. Nothing lasts for ever. Keep a little of yourself in reserve, is my advice, darl.'

'I think I really want to have a baby even if I have to do it on my own.'

'You'll have to convince me on that score. Next.'

'That's it.'

'Nothing else?'

'That's the important stuff.'

'Whew!' Fran pulls out her diary and pen. 'Let's sort out some interim measures to keep clients happy.'

Agnes prowls around Clare's new apartment.

'You remember how you joked about Daniel being a sperm donor for your baby?'

'Yeah,' replies Clare.

'Well, I just happened to mention it to Daniel.'

'You did what?'

'Why not? Ever since you mentioned it, the idea has sort of taken root in my mind. I've thought a lot about it. So has Daniel. In fact, he's hardly talked of anything else. He wants to come and talk to you himself. But I said I'd talk to you first.'

'But you hate babies. You've always made that clear.'

'Not exactly. I just don't want one that I'm totally responsible for. And I know what you'd be like – Adrian is right. You'd have a nanny installed so fast . . .'

'Well . . .'

'Don't kid yourself on that score. Once you'd stopped breast-feeding, I'm sure Bridget would love to take care of the baby. And then there's Athena and Rita who would want to be involved. Daniel is praying for a boy so he can take him to the footy.'

'You're acting as if it's already a *fait accompli*. How do I know you and Daniel will stay together?'

Clare is crying so hard she can hardly see. Even Agnes has a good weep. Then she admits that actually Daniel is right now waiting outside Clare's door.

Clare visits Bridget in her studio in the back garden. She's working on a new painting – another self-portrait. Her face and hands are smeared with paint. The radio chatters in the background. She looks up, surprised to see Clare.

'It's great to see you're back into it again,' says Clare.

Bridget smiles across at her. 'I'm enjoying painting more than I have in a long time. I still become easily exhausted. But every day I can feel my strength gradually returning.'

Clare sits on a stool alongside Bridget's easel. 'There's something important I need to discuss with you. Do you mind?'

Bridget shakes her head. 'Course not.'

'Daniel has offered to be the sperm donor for my baby.'

'Uh huh.' Bridget squeezes a dollop of yellow ochre onto her palette.

'I'm giving his offer serious consideration.'

'Mmm.'

'You don't sound surprised.'

'Agnes mentioned it to me.' Bridget wipes her wet brush on a rag and dips it into a splurge of Naples yellow.

'Did she?' Clare is annoyed.

'Please don't be offended. Agnes, Athena and I are closer to you than your own family. Naturally, we're extremely interested and want to be involved.'

'Athena knows about this too? God, I may as well have published my talk with Agnes and Daniel in the newspapers.'

'Calm down. I was hoping you'd talk through the idea with me.'

Bridget lays down her brush on the lip of the easel.

She swings round on her revolving stool and gives Clare a beaming smile. 'I'd just love it if you had a baby.'

'I haven't decided definitely yet. I don't want to be swept away by Daniel's enthusiasm and yet . . . it's hard not to be.'

'How do you feel about him playing a fairly active role in your child's life, as opposed to the hands-off role of most sperm donors?'

'I'm spending a lot of my free time with Agnes and Daniel at the moment. The more I get to know the guy, the more I like him. He grows on you, as Agnes discovered. He's someone I could count on. I want my child to have a regular relationship with a father figure. I believe that Daniel could more than fill that role.'

'Agnes has no problem with that?'

Clare shifts position on her stool and laughs. 'Agnes? She's just so relieved that Daniel has stopped hassling her about having a baby. A lost cause there, as he now realizes. That's difficult for him. She had to work hard to convince him that she has genuinely never felt a strong biological urge to become a mother. But I can see that he really is very serious about Agnes. You know what she's like – so generous and accommodating, but at the same time a free spirit.'

'Do you think that she has fully thought it through?' asks Bridget.

'As much as anyone can in the circumstances, I think.'

'Don't delude yourself about how difficult it will be at times, how isolated you'll feel, even with our support.'

'The middle of the night jags with a crying baby?'

'That's the one.'

'I'm scared about how well I'll manage, I admit it. That's why I change my mind every five minutes. I've

342

had tough decisions to make in business over the years and I've left relationships. But all of these agonizing decisions pale into insignificance in comparison with deciding at the age of forty to attempt to have a baby on my own.

'I'm a talker, a writer. Words are my tools of trade, but do you think I can explain to myself, let alone to anyone else, exactly why I'm about to turn my life upside down for ever? Bridget, have you ever had a compelling desire to do something for which you had no logical explanation?'

Bridget grins. 'You're asking *me* that question? Me of all people.'

'I want to give motherhood my best shot, but having to use a sperm donor, not actually having sex with the father, somehow it makes it all seem so calculating. I never thought I'd ever say this, but there are certain advantages in being able to fall pregnant by accident. Having a choice means you can literally delay the decision for ever.'

'Have you thought about how you'll combine your work with motherhood?'

'If I do succeed in becoming pregnant we'd probably take on another staff person until I was available to be full time again. I would take the first three months off completely and live on my savings. I've agreed with Fran that in the fourth month I'd resume work with one of our key clients. I can't afford to be without an income for more than a few months. And to be perfectly truthful, I've realized that I'd probably go nuts if I was to give up work completely.'

'You don't have to. Clare, I would love to be involved.'

'Agnes and Daniel would also be part-time parents, remember.'

'So would Athena and Rita, most likely.'

'Can I really count on you?' Clare stares seriously at Bridget.

Bridget reaches over to hug Clare. 'Have I ever let you down?' she asks fiercely.

'No.'

'What about Adrian?'

'What about him? He made it only too clear to me over the past year that he wasn't interested in fathering a child with me. Of course, now that I've walked out on him, he's prepared to agree to anything to get me back, but it's too late now, can you see that?' Her voice cracks.

'Yes, I can.'

'He would be having a baby for the wrong reasons. So, as far as I'm concerned, he's lost the right to a vote on this issue. With Daniel it would be more clear-cut. We would draw up a legal contract together with a lawyer, sorting out reasonable access for him and terms for both of us.'

'You'd give him a voice?'

'Bridget, when you get to know Daniel, you'll see what I mean. I trust him.'

'You don't want to wait for a bit in case you form a new relationship with a man who actually wants to have a child with you?'

Clare walks over to the window and looks out into the garden. 'I can't rely on that. I simply can't afford to wait any longer. It really is now or never.'

'I'd like to put my vote in the ring, if it helps,' says Bridget firmly. 'I'm prepared to look after your baby for two or three days a week and fit my painting around it. I know Matthew will happily go along with that. Daniel and Agnes would help out at weekends. Athena could do the odd half-day.'

'Is this too much to ask of friendship?' asks Clare.

Chapter Thirty

Agnes

Agnes and Daniel have sex three times in the one night. A record for Daniel, but not of course for Agnes, but hey, who's counting?

Puffed up with pride, Daniel teases her.

'And now for your penance . . .' he says in a very, very, very serious voice.

'What?' she asks, immediately alert to the tone of his voice.

'You can put up with me until one of us shall die.'

His face is bright with happy expectation.

How can she disappoint him? It's true, she does love him, probably more than with her bad track record she has ever loved anyone.

But still. Does she really want to turn her life upside down? Lose her apartment? Her independence?

His smile wavers.

'I'm asking you to marry me, isn't that obvious?'

He doesn't get it.

'I'm just not the marrying kind.'

'You've been stringing me along?'

'No, are you kidding. I'm *very* committed to this

relationship, even more now that Clare has finally succeeded in getting pregnant.'

'Then what . . .'

'We have to negotiate the terms. I don't want a goddamned ring. I don't want to move in with you. I *love* things *just* the way they are. Time together. Time apart.'

'How can I be sure of you?'

'You can be sure of me one day at a time.'

'But . . .'

She kisses him with great tenderness.

Chapter Thirty-One

Bridget

Friends are astonished at Bridget's newfound joy in life.

'If I hadn't had cancer to cope with, I think I might have developed into a very bitter person,' she confesses.

Agnes stares with admiration at this luminous being, her friend, and for once in her life has nothing to say. Tears prick her eyes.

'Isn't it wonderful news about Clare?' asks Bridget.

'I still can't get used to the idea of her being pregnant,' replies Agnes.

'Me neither. But I haven't seen her look so happy in a long while.'

'When she's not throwing up, that is.' Agnes grimaces.

They recall Clare's anguish as the months ticked by while she tried to conceive. The way she fussed over her diet, cut out alcohol completely, began taking folic acid, reduced her training sessions at the gym to give her a more moderate exercise regime. The jokes about Daniel making the sperm run. The way they all became obsessed with Clare's ovulation dates.

* * *

Bridget is no longer simply coping with the day-to-day challenges of recovering from illness and experiencing the tiredness at the end of each week of radiotherapy. She has never had so much time and opportunity to reflect on the course her life had taken prior to the first diagnosis of cancer.

The anxiety that previously had spread like a stain over her days has miraculously disappeared. In its place is a new calmness and contentment, a refusal to be upset by the petty irritations of life that had previously occupied her and gradually worn her down. She is adding to the collection of baby clothes she snatched back from the City Mission and is building a lovely supply for Clare.

Once her course of radiotherapy has been completed she banishes any further talk of cancer and begins to put into action some of the plans she has mulled over during the long months of convalescence. Why live for tomorrow, when there is today to be appreciated?

She knows for certain that she does not wish to continue teaching art at a secondary school and is working on her painting again with a renewed interest. She'll combine that with helping Clare to care for her baby. Life will be full and satisfying. She also hopes to be accepted as a volunteer for the Breast Cancer Support Service, although they say it's too soon yet for her to be involved.

She has discussed with Matthew the idea of making changes in their lives. The notion of him working less has been mooted. There are fundamental differences in their future plans and objectives that have not been evident prior to this. Matthew has made it obvious he is relieved to be free to submerge himself in the frenetic activity of his law practice again. His cases and appointments lend structure and purpose to his life and without them he has floundered.

Six months after Bridget's operation Matthew arrives home early from the office quietly complaining of a headache and an upset stomach. Concerned, Bridget despatches him immediately to bed. When she enters the bedroom to check on him shortly afterwards she is disturbed to find him in floods of tears.

She can count on the fingers of one hand the number of times she has witnessed him break down with emotion during their twenty-one-year relationship. She sits down alongside him on the bed taking his warm hands in hers.

'What is it?'

She herself cries so easily and frequently that both of them are inclined to shrug off her tears as just another passing rain shower – quickly started and generally just as quickly ended. This is different. His tears frighten her. A rock crumbling to dust.

He shakes his head, wordless, in answer to her questions.

'When you're ready.' She sits patiently.

He cries for some minutes more before he is able to speak coherently about what is bothering him.

Collapso, he tells her. At the end of his tether, sorry.

There was the shock of her cancer recurring of course. But now that she has made such a spectacular recovery he is puzzled to be experiencing enormous amounts of despair and hopelessness.

He can't explain it. But there it is. He knows he should feel relieved and happy, but instead he now feels like shit. He doesn't know what to do about it, where to put himself. He can't even convince himself that he has played a major role in her recovery. A combination of medicos, luck and Bridget's new positive attitude have all contributed – plus the determined interference, help and advice from her friends, her parents, aunts, and female neighbours, the cancer volunteer visitors. Really, he needn't have been there. Everyone else has coped, visited, helped with cooking, shopping.

She lets him talk.

He keeps apologizing over and over while she repeatedly assures him that there is nothing he need feel he has to apologize for – on the contrary. She insists that she is extremely relieved that *finally* he is expressing his bottled-up grief, frustration and anger.

She asks herself if she could have been as strong had their positions been reversed. She thinks not. But that's men, isn't it? Poor creatures, conditioned to be strong, fearless, in control. Always believing they knew best. Any wonder they dropped dead of heart attacks long before their women.

Even Matthew has slipped into the predictable role. She questions whether she has expected too much of him, whether she has placed too heavy a burden on him.

This is when she realizes with a start that she no longer requires a rock, because she now has indisputable proof of her own strength. Now it is her turn to be bold – the risk-taker. She is required to have regular medical check-ups, but this does not mean she cannot consider travelling overseas for a short period.

In the face of Matthew's lack of enthusiasm she begins to consider the prospect of travelling alone, something she has never seriously considered previously. She would be home well before Clare gives birth.

'You're mad,' says her mother. 'Don't you want to be near your doctors, the hospital? It's far too soon, in my opinion.'

'I don't have cancer any more, remember.'

There is no excuse any longer to delay transforming her life into a great adventure now that she has miraculously been given a second chance. To celebrate all there is to be celebrated. Minute by minute, hour by hour. She has never before taken any real risks in her life.

'When will you be back to your old self?' Matthew blurts out. Their household has been turned upside down for months and here is Bridget needing more changes.

'You should be pleased I'm excited about something, that I'm actually planning for the future.'

Matthew is silenced.

Bridget takes stock. She is never going to be exactly like her old self and she is still discovering who the newly reconstructed Bridget is – someone who is more accepting of herself, more at peace. Living for the day.

Matthew holds her tightly, then releases her. She can read the anxiety in his eyes, just as six months ago he recognized hers. She stares at him with great sympathy. Despite his appearance of coping he has not fully accepted that her illness and suffering have changed her irrevocably and that her responses to it will continue to exert an influence on her future. He has tried to take her suffering into himself and absorb it as proof of his love for her. Suffering has liberated her yet it seems to be paralysing him.

'Come with me,' she urges. 'I'll probably only be gone five weeks. We could have such fun, you and I.'

He shrugs helplessly. 'I can't just . . . leave everything. I have responsibilities, even if you don't. One of us has to earn a living.'

'Why work so hard?' asks Bridget. 'What for? I don't mind if we live simply.'

This is now possible for they have recently cleared

the mortgage on their house. There are no children to put through university, no huge commitments other than Matthew's obligations to his partners.

'I'm scared to love you too much, Bridget, in case you die. You're my entire life, my everything,' he weeps, forgetting for a minute his preoccupation with his cases, his work. 'I couldn't live without you.'

She has known and loved him just over half her life and during that time, until she had gone to hospital, they had rarely spent a night apart.

'I'm not planning to die for years, but then nor am I running away from death. I need to get away for a while. I wish you would come, but if you can't, I'm still intending to go. I'll be back before you've even noticed I've gone.' She smiles reassuringly.

In the end what can she say that will comfort him? Already she is moving on – not away from him, not really – always keeping him in sight, in mind, but he cannot own her any more than she can capture a fleeting sliver of moonlight dancing on the lawn.

THE END